Y0-AST-681

THE DOORMAKER

THE DOORMAKER

*Journeys in the
Fairworld
Volume I*

JACK TWOHEY

fairworldfantasy.com

Copyright © 2022 by Jack Twohey

All rights reserved. No part of this book may be reproduced in any manner whatsoever without written permission except in the case of brief quotations embodied in critical articles and reviews.

The characters, places, and events depicted in this volume are entirely fictitious, any resemblance to real persons (living or dead) is coincidental.

First Printing, 2022

TO COLONEL T, USMC

Vietnam

Korea

World War Two

Contents

Prologue		1
1	"The Golden Bird"	3
2	"Things of Another World"	15
3	"Hae-jin"	27
4	"Conference at the House of Wog"	44
5	"Harin's Vault"	55
6	"A Rite of Atonement"	64
7	"The Drixi"	72
8	"The Man in the Suit"	81
9	"Breakfast after a Long Night"	92
10	"The House of Dackery"	102
11	"A Long March"	117
12	"The Fortress of the Drixi"	130
13	"Of Birds and Foxes"	144
14	"A Locked Door"	163
15	"Residence at 26 Bodgerstreet"	173
16	"Falknir"	188
17	"The Kingdom of Linster"	202

18	"Of Millers and Yeomen"	216
19	"Robin Goodfellow"	226
20	"The Battle of Mortimer's Mill"	239
21	"Gurth the Witch"	254
22	"The Occupation of Elmstead"	261
23	"Three Earls and an Outlaw"	272
24	"There's Always Politics"	283
25	"The Bishop of Larchester"	300
26	"The Moment of Truth"	313
27	"On Hostile Roads"	322
28	"Manhunt"	338
29	"The Lady Edith"	353
30	"A New Name"	367
31	"The Battle of Beckby"	378
32	"The Storming of Ardgar"	391
33	"A Late Return"	408
Epilogue		419
About The Author		423

Prologue

The sun was setting in the west, casting its last rays upon the face of an enchanted alien world. The rolling fields of the Kingdom of Linster radiated like a rippling sea of pale gold, and the woodlands were silhouetted darkly against the amber sky. In the little village of Tresham the whitewashed cottages of the peasants were bathed in a warm red light, while farther away in the mighty city of Larchester the stained glass windows of the great cathedral gleamed like bright fires in the reflected light of the sun.

Not far from the village of Tresham, a lone woman was running through a field of barley. All around her the darkness of the night was closing in fast like an army of black clad soldiers armed with chains and traps with which to snare her. The sun had at last forsaken the sky and fled beyond the horizon, and as the woman ran her blonde hair streamed behind her like yellow grass whipping in the gale of a typhoon. At length, the woman at last stumbled breathlessly to a halt before the fringes of a small wood. Her chest heaved and her knees fairly shook as her eyes searched frantically in the gloom beneath the dark trees which brooded menacingly above her.

"Sykes!", the woman cried softly. "Sykes! Where are you?"

At first, there was no reply. Then, somewhere amidst the shadows, something stirred. The woman caught her breath for a moment, and then released it with a momentary sigh of relief as a man's voice called softly back to her. "Joan! Joan is that you?"

A moment later, a man stepped out of the woods. He was dressed in yeoman's clothes, soiled and bedraggled with many days of wandering, and in one hand he carried a great quarterstaff. As he sped to her side, the woman Joan reached out and grasped the man's hand. As his fingers closed tightly around hers they quivered slightly with barely contained agitation, and in his eye there was a wild gleam of excitement.

"They've come!", the man Sykes said with a hoarse whisper. "They've come at last!"

Joan drew a sharp breath as her heart began to race. After all this time, it couldn't be true. It just couldn't. "Where, Skyes!", she whispered back, "Where are they?"

"Come, I will show you!."

Joan followed as Sykes turned swiftly back to the woods, still holding her hand. Sykes pushed his way aggressively through the trees, as though the pair of them were being pursued by some unseen peril with the might of kings at its command. In a few minutes, Sykes at last stopped, and shaking slightly with excitement he pointed out into the gloom beneath the trees. "There Joan, just over there!"

A faint light was now visible a little ways into the woods ahead. As the pair began to approach, Joan was soon able to make out several orbs of green, yellow, and red light hovering in the air like little floating lanterns. And standing in their midst, only just visible in the faint light, was a small group of robed people. Tears were now streaming down Joan's face. It had been so long. So many years of suffering and heartbreak. So many long years of searching, waiting, and hurting. Now, at long last the search was over. At long last, all her frantic hopes had a chance to become reality. As Sykes led her slowly into the light, Joan began to cry with joy. For now at last, the fairy folk were listening.

I

"The Golden Bird"

Lindsey Fluger was only slightly past eighteen. What there was of her was barely over five-foot-five, with plain grey eyes haphazardly bordered with an excess of eyeliner, hair a dull sheenless black as can only be produced by cheap dye, a chest as flat as a twelve year old's and stomach that refused to ever be flat enough no matter how little she ate. And little did she eat indeed. Her jeans rode high on her legs and low on her hips, for they might have as well have been made for a child, not a young woman. "Anorexia" was an ugly word indeed, yet it was one that had been associated with Lindsey in hushed tones since she'd started high school, at about the same time at which her disposition had shifted to one of a general melancholy and discontent.

It was hoped that life in college would bring about a change for the better in Lindsey. But hope had been disappointed. The few friendships she'd made in high school faded quickly, and in five months at university had so far not been replaced. She scored only just well enough in the uninspired assortment of classes she had undertaken thus far, but among those few individuals who sustained any degree of concern for her it was generally regarded that Lindsey was faring ill in all but the most marginal and superficial of respects.

It was one afternoon after a pedantic exposure to the dubious rigours of PHYS 1001 *"The Physical Sciences and How they Ruin Your Life"* (or something to that effect) that Lindsey sat curled up moodily in a corner of the open lounge in the Anthropology Building Annex No. 2 (Weathermen Hall). She had no appetite for the wilted looking salad she'd acquired from the cafeteria at a ludicrously inflated price (like everything else which was sold to the students on campus). Nor had she any appetite for the sight of those perfect looking girls in panty-length shorts across from her, texting their friends or else entangled around their boyfriends. Nor had she any appetite for the billboard bearing adverts on a general variety of topics such as Salsa Night at the Union next Thursday, the weekly meetings of Students for the Ultimate Society (free pizza provided by The Youth Socialist Front), and queries for roommates fond of animals and not allergic to cats. Nor had she any appetite for the thought of the homework lurking wickedly inside her backpack, her empty expectations for spring break, or even the golden sun shining through the brilliant green trees outside. Lindsey sat with her back to the corner and her stick-like legs drawn up to her speckled and picked chin, and her thoughts lying in a pool of despair.

Lindsey sighed wearily to herself.

"There really isn't anything for you here, is there?", a voice seemed to say in her head.

Lindsey shook her head to herself.

"No. I don't even know why I try anymore. I just want it all to end."

"Would anyone miss you?"

"I don't think so."

"What about your family?"

"Well....I guess they would...maybe...kind of."

"For how long?"

"Huh?"

"For how long would you be missed, and how soon would you need to be back?"

"Huh?"

"Stop dithering in disbelief and answer the question, I don't have much time."

"What the..?"

"Fine", the voice cut her off. "I'll let you think it over. We shall speak again before long. Tah!"

Lindsey started. Everything about her seemed normal. Had she been asleep? She must have been. Weird. Maybe the new dosage of antidepressants was doing weird stuff to her brain, making her drowsy and giving her screwed up dreams.

Her next class was at one o'clock: CHEM 1115 (*Social Issues in Organic Chemistry*), followed immediately by ENG 1002 (*Introductory Electrical Engineering: Race and Privilege in the Sciences*). She hated every moment of them. At three forty-five, she was back in her dorm room, flung on the bed. Her roommate had moved to the sorority house earlier in the semester. That was fine. Lindsey would rather be alone anyway. She pulled her pillow out from behind her head and hugged it to her chest as she stared blankly at the ceiling.

"Well, what about it? Have you made up your mind?"

Lindsey continued to stare blankly.

"I don't have much time. I need to know now."

Lindsey thought for a moment. Was she starting to have hallucinations or something? She sat up and looked around. What on earth was going on?

"I'll tell you all about what's going on, but first I need an answer. Are you coming or not?"

The voice was real. It was a real sound, not just a hint in her head like before. Lindsey uttered a squeak, and spun around wide-eyed towards the window, half hiding behind the pillow. The window screen had been pulled straight out of its fixture. And there, sitting on the sill and flicking the displaced screen about casually in one claw, was a huge bird. The creature was of a golden, almost metallic color with highlights of red. It was very nearly three feet tall, and on it's head it bore a great scarlet crest like a cockatoo. It's beak was sharp like an eagle's and had an iridescent sheen to it, while it's claws were black like coal. And likewise were it's eyes, one of which was cocked like a polished bead, staring critically in Lindsey's direction. Lindsey stared for a moment in a hush of disbelief. The Bird returned her gaze with an air of restrained patience as it continued to idly twirl the window screen. After a few moments, the Bird casually tossed the screen aside, scratched itself for a moment, and then brought its gaze back to bear on Lindsey as it spoke.

"Well, now that you've had a good look, I hope you're sufficiently satisfied that I am not an illusion that we can talk."

Lindsey could still barely get her words unstuck. "I....."

"Don't feel embarrassed", the Bird said. "I often have this effect when I appear unannounced, particularly to persons of this world such as yourself, unacquainted with what lies beyond."

"What lies beyond?"

"Quite."

"Lies beyond what?"

"Beyond the horizon. At the other end of the rainbow. Around the corner, on the other side of the door, over the fence, on the far side of the water, and across the field beyond the edge of the trees."

"What.....what are you talking about?"

"Why the Fairworld, of course. Or whatever name you wish to give it. Fairyland, the elf world, the realm of faerie, I'll leave the choice of nomenclature up to you. But hurry, we haven't much time, I need you to make a decision."

"....what decision?"

"Are you coming, or are you not?"

"...coming?"

"To the Fairworld."

"I don't believe this."

"I'm not asking you to believe, I'm asking you to decide. Belief will attend to itself, according to your decision."

"What do you want from me?"

"A decision!"

"No, I mean....why do you want me?"

"That's a different question entirely."

The Bird scratched himself again whileLindsey watched, still largely dumbstruck with the whole situation. A moment later and the Bird again cocked a beady eye at Lindsey and spoke. "You have noticed, I am sure, that I am not an ordinary sort of bird. I have certain capacities which distinguish me, such as keen intelligence and witty conversation, as you may also have noticed. But another of my gifts is that I have a certain ability to read a heart at a distance. Very often, I can merely observe a person from a long way off and be able see what sort of a person she is, which is how I have come across you. You see, I spotted you particularly as I was flying over this world in search of someone like you. You have character and potential, you see. I read these things in your heart. And I read also that your heart is rather heavy laden, and it occurred to me that you could really do with an opportunity to do something especially good and out of the ordinary. Do you follow me thus far?"

Lindsey stammered. "I......I guess......kinda."

"Good enough. 'I guess kinda' is well enough to be expected under the circumstances, and we can improve from there. If, that is, you decide to come with me to the Fairworld. You must give me your answer quickly, for if you won't come then I must find someone else as soon as possible."

Lindsey didn't know what to say. Silence hung for a while, until at length the Bird spoke again. "Well, if you won't ask questions I can't give you answers. I can't stay any longer, but I can give you until nightfall to make up your mind." The great bird hopped off the sill and into the middle of the room, a sudden motion which instinctively sent Lindsey hiding further behind her pillow, if such were possible. The Bird looked at the floor, cocked his head first this way, and then that. Then, seeming to abruptly make up his mind, he drove his beak through the thin dormitory carpet, and then proceeded to drag it backward, cutting out a crude square of carpet about two or three feet across. In all the shock and astonishment of the moment, Lindsey nonetheless found herself wondering how on earth she was going to explain the condition of the floor to the Resident Hall Director. When he was finished, the Bird clucked to himself in a self satisfied way, and spoke. "If you decide to come, just peel off the carpet here and step in. If not, don't, and it should seal up again by tomorrow. Goodbye." And with that, the Bird hopped out through the window and disappeared into the sky.

How long Lindsey remained fixated on the spot which the Bird had vacated she couldn't be sure. At such times, bewilderment has a tendency to hold sway above most everything else. At length the numbness subsided a bit, and Lindsey was very nearly convinced that she had been asleep and dreaming. Except for that torn up bit of carpet. Ah, of course, the carpet must have been torn already, and she had merely fallen asleep while staring at it, and dreamed the rest. Of course that's what happened, and she could prove it to herself. Lindsey rolled lightly off the bed. Then she remembered that the window was still open with the screen popped out. Vacantly she walked to the window, shut it and drew the curtains with a shiver. Then she crouched down to where the line of tattered fringe protruded above the carpet's weave. With a firm, self assured grasp, she seized a bit of the torn filaments, and pulled. With a bit of a pop and a tear, the section of carpet came away cleanly in her hand.

Thereupon, Lindsey abruptly fell backward with a half-scream on her lips as a blinding light burst forth from the floor beneath her fingertips. Lindsey retreated to one corner of the room, still clutching a square of carpeting in her hand, while from a matching hole in her dormitory floor a soothing yet painfully bright ray of daylight radiated from beneath. A cool breeze wafted from the hole, along with the smell of fresh air and faint sounds of wind rippling through vegetation. All was still. Save for Lindsey's panting breath and racing heartbeat, at any rate. Lindsey stared at the outrageous reality before her in a mental whirlwind of both utter disbelief and absolute certainty. *"I'm not asking you to believe, I'm asking you to decide. Belief will attend to itself, according to your decision."* The recollection of the Bird's words echoed through Lindsey's mind as she faced an inescapable quandary. There was a hole in her floor. A confounding invitation to another world, an impossible reality just sitting there brazenly in the middle of her bedroom. And there she was, just standing there. What in the world was she supposed to do with a thing like this?

Gradually, her mind began to adjust to her situation as her thoughts flew about frantically to set themselves to order. Alright, be calm now. You have no idea really what's going on around you. You're probably hallucinating. Just stay calm, and think. Try touching it, see if it really is a hole. It will probably disappear the moment you reach for it. Maybe you'll just wake up and find out it's all just a dream. Try pinching yourself. Ouch! Okay, just stay calm. That still doesn't prove anything. Just take a look at that hole. Lindsey took a deep breath, and in that moment she made a decision: She was in control. She still didn't understand what was happening, but she was certain she was sane and more or less thinking clearly. With a casual strength that would have been impossible a moment ago, she walked forward and knelt beside the opening in the floor, and cautiously looked in over the edge of the carpet.

Inside the hole, she could see grass mingled with an assortment of weeds and wildflowers such as you might find in any ordinary field on our own world. It was daylight, and somewhere the sun was shining. The ground looked to be about three or four feet or so below the hole, an easy enough drop if she were careful about it. It was only a matter of choosing. And there it was. A truly unimaginable opportunity before her. It was simply up to her to choose. And in that moment, Lindsey did the most reckless thing of her entire life. With a cautious, almost giddy sort of feeling, like the moment before one slips into a cold swimming pool, Lindsey sat down and swung her legs into the gap. The cool wind below tickled at her bare ankles and sent a shiver up her spine. She hesitated for just a moment. And then she jumped.

The drop was a bit further than she had thought. In a terrifying second, she fell to the earth and landed hard and stunned on the springy turf. For a moment she lay dazed on her back, unmoving save for the heaving of her breast in the wake of the alarming fall. She was staring up at a dark square hovering above her in a clear sky of glorious blue. The smell of wild flowers surrounded her, and the breeze carried the quiet buzz of insects and a distant bay of sheep, along with the occasional hollow clatter of animal bells.

Lindsey's mind was still trying to catch up with everything that was happening. In a moment she realized that the dark square hovering above her was actually the hole in her dorm room floor, appearing dim and faded against the luminous blue of the sky. How far she had fallen she couldn't really guess, but she was sure that it was too far for her to reach the hole in the sky above her and escape whatever consequences might follow from her decision. She was just wondering where she might find a ladder in this place (wherever she was) when she realized that the hole was disappearing as the dark square opening faded away into the sky above. Suddenly panicked, Lindsey scrambled frantically to her feet, but it was too late. The hole, the doorway to the only world she had ever known, had closed. And Lindsey was alone in the Fairworld.

The Fairworld, or whatever it was that bird had called it, was to all appearances not all that much different than the world Lindsey was accustomed to. Not hereabouts, at any rate. It was a mountainous land, with rocky crags and wooded hills obscuring her view of the horizon on all sides. Small patches of meadowland undulated through the sharp dips and rises of the earth, pierced at all places with islands of bare rock, while trees and shrubs made scattered intrusions upon the grasses here and there. The patch of grass on which Lindsey had landed was itself nearly enveloped by an assortment of boulders, and having had a look at her surroundings she was rather grateful she hadn't landed a few feet further away in any direction.

Voices. Yes, voices alright, just barely carried on the breeze. Coming from somewhere over that way-ish. Lindsey could only assume that the Bird had meant to meet up with her here (wherever "here" was). And, even if it were not the Bird she were hearing, she would certainly need to connect herself with humanity in some way (assuming of course that 'humanity' was what inhabited this place). Having taken quick stock of herself she had promptly concluded that with only her clothes to her possession, her worldly resources at present were distinctly limited, and it wasn't as though she were a girl scout or something, who knew which roots and berries were healthy and nutritious and which ones would instead leave you with spasms and a brief future. Whatever was about to happen, she would certainly need to find help in short order if she expected to survive all of this. Following the voices wasn't particularly easy. The wind was irregular, whistling randomly through the rocks and throwing sounds around like dry leaves on a windy autumn day. And if that weren't enough, there were plenty of other noises to confuse the navigational ear. The rush of the wind itself, the buzz of insects, and the sound of sheep.

It didn't take Lindsey long to find the sheep. They seemed to be everywhere, clumping their way to and fro in shifting schools like fluffy fish with legs, pausing to nibble here and there at grass and weeds only to suddenly drop everything and trot off again with the herd the moment one of them fancied a bit of random motion. They were not feral, that was for certain. The bells were evidence of that. So many bells! Every move was accompanied by a sonorous clank, and the air was filled with a soft chorus of bells and bleats. It seemed impossible to isolate any other noises. However, where there are domestic animals, there is usually to be found a domesticator. If Lindsey couldn't find the the Bird, her next best chance for survival would be to find the proprietor of this livestock. While observing the ebb and flow of the bleating wool producers, Lindsey noticed another queer characteristic of her surroundings. Many of the stones were unusually regular in shape. In point of fact, they were cut. Though broken, scattered, and weathered, it quickly became obvious that a large number of these stones had been worked by the hands men (or at least creatures like men). Moreover, some were still stacked. Blended into the rocky terrain and obscured by vegetation and centuries of decay, there were ruins; square stone in stacks and rows hinting at what were once walls, floors, and foundations.

Yet these ruins were not the only thing nearby which bore the mark of intelligent builders...intelligent of a sort, at any rate. For amidst the crags and slopes, only partially visible from Lindsey's vantage, there was a great stone mound. There was no mistaking that the thing was built that way on purpose. As Lindsey teetered on a rock for a better view, she could see clearly that it was a great heap of stones; some plucked raw from the earth, some chiseled and broken, and all heaped together in a haphazard mess whose only guiding principle appeared to be to make the most massive rock pile imaginable. Lindsey couldn't be sure of it's size, but from what she could see she thought that it must be something like a hundred feet high at the very least. That such a monstrous thing could have been the work of mindless geology seemed to her impossible.

The wind carried forth again the sound of voices. This time, Lindsey thought she could clearly make out a direction: The voices came from somewhere near the great mound of stone. Another moment found Lindsey picking her way across the rocky maze towards the mound. The mound was further away than it had at first appeared, and further still given the meandering route which Lindsey was obliged to take in order to reach it. Indeed, it was well nigh an hour before Lindsey at last found herself at the foot of the edifice.

It was truly immense. Less tall perhaps than Lindsey had at first thought (for it was perched on a hill), but no less impressive by girth. And as crude as it had appeared at a distance, closer inspection revealed a greater measure of architectural consideration (so to speak). While there appeared to be no particular regularity to the overall shape, the mound was partially encircled by rings of massive pillars of varying sizes; some of made of stacked stones, others composed of single upright rocks. There were perhaps twenty such pillars in all, set in two or three uneven rows at differing heights on the mound. It seemed as though the idea was to ultimately ring the whole mound with the things in several tiers like a great lumpy wedding cake, for it was clear to her that the structure was unfinished. Grass, weeds, and small shrubs sprung from between the worn stones at lower levels, which became thinner higher up as the stones appeared less settled, stacked with gaps and colored unevenly where one part had lately been buried and another exposed. The pillars too showed signs of labor both old and recent, some of them fresh and others weathered and grown with moss. And looking closer still at the nearest of them, Lindsey could see that some were engraved with freshly cut inscriptions; crude pictograms and disjointed lettering. If nothing else, Lindsey was impressed that whoever was building this monstrous thing was not the most sophisticated of craftsmen.

It was at this moment that a shadow passed fleetingly over Lindsey's head, and a large boulder made an abrupt landing about halfway up the mound with a resounding crash, only to begin rolling back down part way again with a shower of pebbles and shards. Lindsey darted out of the way even as the bulk of the avalanche rumbled to a stop some feet away. And then an awesome thing appeared.

2

"Things of Another World"

The thing was about twelve feet tall, or near enough that the effect was equally impressive. It was a sort of grayish color, shaped very much like a man save that it's proportions appeared off, being particularly oversized in the shoulders, arms, and head. It was attired in a sort of sarong made of smartly sewn sheepskin which started about halfway between the armpits and the waist and ended just above the knee in a neatly finished hemline. Its garment was held up by a belt which carried a couple pouches and a colossal knife-like implement (which was, in fact, a massive two handed sword which had been repurposed as a tool, with its quillons broken off and it's rear edge blunted). Its feet were shod in reinforced hide in a manner midway between a boot and a sock. The thing prodded the recently disturbed rock with its foot, releasing yet another minor avalanche of gravel as it did so. Looking about with an air of satisfaction, the thing snorted to itself and turned around to look down, directly at Lindsey.

"Noice, ain't it?"

Lindsey gasped with a sudden sense of panic at the realization that the thing was aware of her. Its manner was hardly aggressive though, and to be sure its comment was purely conversational. Lindsey relaxed. And for the first time, she got a good look at the thing's face. And that gave her another shock. It might have been better if the thing had possessed only one eye in the middle of its head, or had fangs like a wild boar, or something else equally monstrous. But the real dreadfulness of it all was that the thing's face was really rather ordinary, if a bit craggy and goggle eyed, with a nose that might have given a vulture a touch of envy. Overall, it's face reminded Lindsey of a particular algebra professor she had been obliged to endure during highschool. Yet these reasonable features seemed exaggerated and oversized even for a creature of such height, and were likewise set upon so extraordinary a frame as to render even the most ordinary of faces a sight terrible. The owner of this dreadful countenance appeared to be expecting some sort of intelligent reply from her, and as she cringed under its baleful gaze Lindsey felt like she were living in a nightmare (in fact, a part of her still couldn't say for certain that she wasn't). With no reply forthcoming, the giant seemed to conclude that his companion was perhaps a trifle slow witted, and that further exposition was required. He waved a massive hand in the direction of the great rock pile behind him as though he were displaying a great and sophisticated work to a small child who cannot be expected to properly understand such things. "Been building it for years", he said. "It's a marvel, it is. That's wot I builds it for, to be marvelous."

Lindsey managed to find her voice. "It's very nice", she said with a slight tremor.

"Noice is exactly wot it is! Marvelous and noice. That's exactly wot I builds it to be. It's wotcha call Art. It's a monument, it is."

"A monument?"

"It is."

"A monument to what?"

"Ah, well, that'll be a longish story, it will. Lemme have a sitdown and I'll tell ye." The creature seated himself with a grunt, upsetting quite a bit more gravel as he did so. Lindsey retreated quickly and climbed atop a moderately sized boulder. Whatever else this creature was, he was clearly a hazard to all and sundry, even with his most innocuous movements. The creature looked Lindsey square in the eye and spoke. "So. Have ye heard of me grandfather?"

"Huh?"

"Me grandfather. Have ye heard of him?"

"Uh, no....I don't think so, anyway."

"Exactly. Of course ye ain't heard of him! Big feller he was, though, a full head taller than meself. He could lift twice his weight twenty times a day and then some. Fought in the king's army, he did. Smashed plenty o' men and horses in his day. Did good service he did, and was given his choice o' pillage in compensation. Brought back bags and bags o' sheep, and the family have been shepherds ever since. But have ye heard of him? Nope! 'Course not! So!" The giant scrutinized Linsey closer. "Who's the king's great great great great great great great grandfather? Wot was his name? Betcha don't know!"

"I......I don't know. I guess I'm kind of a foreigner. I don't even know who the king is."

"Foreigner, eh? Should'a known by the way ye dress. Most girlies don't go around in nuthin' but their stockin's, beggin yer pardon. I take one look at ye and says to meself 'that's an odd lookin' sorta girly. Dress all funny, and underfed too.' Fancy some mutton? Got plenty hereabouts.."

"Uh...no thanks...I'm a vegetarian."

"Never heard o' the place. Must be pretty far away. How'd ye get here?"

"Uh.....well.....this will probably sound crazy, but you see, I talked to this bird...."

"Ha!"

The giant threw his head backward and unleashed a torrent of barking laughter, upsetting more gravel as he rocked himself back and forth. "Ha! I should'a known it! That bird just won't give up, will he?"

"Uh.....I guess."

"Ha! Just wastin' his time he is. Well, that's no matter. So!"

The giant waved his arms all about him. "Ye see these rocks? Lots of 'em broken houses they are. Old, old, old houses. Built a long time ago. All old and broken now. Ye know who built 'em?"

"No."

"Neither do I. Nobody does. Nobody remembers nuthin' about 'em. Folks who built 'em are dead a long long long time ago, and nobody remembers. They had themselves kings, had themselves wars, did themselves great deeds and stored themselves treasure, and who remembers? And who cares?"

"Maybe archaeologists?"

"Never heard of him either. But if he does care, that's because of what?"

"Well, the ruins I guess."

"Exactly! That's the secret, ye see. Nobody remembers ye for who ye are or what ye done, or what ye have. Not in the end. They'll only remember ye if ye leave somethin' behind. Somethin' so big they can't help but notice it. That's why I'm building it, see?"

"The rock pile?"

"The monument. Exactly! It's not half done yet, it's gonna be so much bigger when it is. And after I'm long gone, my monument will still be here. And folks will see it, and wonder about who built it. And I've been puttin' stories on it, carvin' it into some o' the rocks, so as folks can know about me more."

"What kind of stories?"

"Oh, stuff I done, stuff I do. I got three hundred sheep round these parts...I think...so I put in that. I moved a really big boulder last week and put it on the top o' me monument, so I put in that too."

"Have you ever done anything really big...heroic I guess....that you could write about on your monument?"

"Nope. Ain't gonna either. Don't need to. See, most folks think they're gonna be remembered if they do heroic stuff, but they ain't. Not unless they got themselves a monument. But who needs to do heroic stuff when all ye need is to build yerself a monument, like I done already? Me, I'm gonna be remembered no matter what I do, 'cause I'm building meself a monument, see?"

"Uh....I guess. You work on your monument every day then?"

"Yup. Everyday for the last sixty years, one rock on top o' the other. It's gratifying, it is."

"Yeah....I guess it would be."

"Aha! *There* you are!", a voice suddenly interjected.

The interruption was followed with a tremendous beating of wings and the Bird descended upon them from somewhere out of sight. He alighted on one of the stone pillars, and after preening himself for a moment, addressed Lindsey. "So here you are! I am pleased you decided to come." The Bird then turned his attention to the giant. "So, have you reconsidered my offer, Barri?"

"Nope. Still ain't gonna do it. Told ye already."

"But think! Reflect! Reconsider! Surely you want to do something more with your life than tending sheep and piling rocks?"

"No I don't."

"But you are capable of so much!"

"So?"

"A fellow of your potential could be doing so many great things!"

"Ain't gonna, though. I got me sheep to tend and a monument to build, and that's enough for me."

"But think of how noble it would be! Think of the service you would be rendering!"

"Don't need to. I already thought about it, and I thought it was a rotten idea. Won't do it and that's that."

"Oh really! Lindsey, do talk some sense into this thick witted behemoth!"

"Hey, I don't even know why *I'm* here", Lindsey said. "What do you want with either him *or* me?"

"Got himself a hare-brained scheme, he does", the giant said, tapping the side of his nose sagely. "He's always got himself a hare-brained scheme. Bothers me about 'em all the time."

"I beg your pardon, this is only the second time I've come to you with a proposition!", the Bird objected.

"Too many already."

"And here I thought I read your heart well! You mean to say that you absolutely refuse to render aid in this noble and charitable venture?"

"Yup. I'm wotcha call stubborn."

"One last time, I implore you!"

The giant rose, unleashing another cascade of gravel down the side of the rock pile as he did so. He bent low and looked the Bird squarely in the eye, and spoke. "No.", he said. "Now go away." The giant straightened himself and lumbered off down the hillside through the maze of rocks. His strides were wide and he covered the distance quickly, pausing only for a moment to call back with a parting remark: "Tell the girlie to eat some mutton and put a little fat on her.", the giant said. "She'll need every bit of it if she's thick headed enough to go with you!" And, with that, the giant was gone, and Lindsey and the Bird were left in silence. After a few moments, the Bird spoke.

"Well, I suppose that's that. Strange, though, I was so sure that I understood him." The Bird cocked an eye at Lindsey. "Well, I suppose we should be getting a move on."

"Yeah, about that...."

"We have a few more stops to make now, I'm afraid. I had high hopes for Barri, but as he is unwilling...."

"....Hey now look, I'm not so sure...."

"...but I think though that we can manage without him. Now what was I....."

"...Excuse me, mister, I think you owe me an explanation..."

"Goodness!", the Bird suddenly shouted, fluttering his great wings.

"The time! We haven't a moment to lose! Quickly, follow me!" Here the Bird vaulted into the air and began flying speedily down the slope. About to lose sight of the only being who likely had the power to return her to her own world, Lindsey practically threw herself from the boulder she was sitting on and scrambled madly after him, half muttering an assortment of curses and personal criticisms directed at certain annoying avians.

The Bird stopped short and landed to examine a small patch of loose gravel. Cocking his head thoughtfully first one way and then the other, he drove his beak between the pebbles and drew a crude square, much as he had done in Lindsey's dorm room carpet earlier. As he finished the shape, the pebbles within the rude outline gave way as if there were suddenly nothing beneath them, and fell downwards with a noise like a bag of marbles poured out on the ground. With a cry of "This way, follow me!", the Bird dove down the hole, and as Lindsey came running and panting behind she all but collapsed beside the hole, swung in her legs and dropped herself through as well. Lindsey hit the ground with a shock. All around her, the world had suddenly become much darker. Lindsey scrambled upright and looked around. She was surrounded by trees, and had landed in a mass of ferns in the midst of a clearing of some kind. The Bird was nowhere in sight. Where on earth was she now?

It wasn't quite a clearing. Rather, upon looking about herself Lindsey realized that she had in fact been deposited beside a dirt road. It was twilight, and a dim glow of golden sunlight was hugging the horizon. A moment ago at the giant's monument it had been full daylight, but here it was nearly dusk (or dawn, Lindsey couldn't be sure). They must have come quite far from where they were before. Looking upwards Lindsey caught a glimpse of a patch of bright light fading away in the air above the place she had landed. There was no going back that way. There was a sudden whoosh and the Bird appeared, flying in from somewhere behind her. He swooped about her again and cried in a hush: "Quick now, keep quiet! This way!", and glided off down the road in the direction of the sun. Lindsey jogged in pursuit. The road came to an abrupt turn, and here the Bird alighted. Lindsey stopped just behind, and stared out at the vista before her. The road dipped sharply away into a rolling valley of vibrant green trees dipped in tinges of warm gold from the sun, looking lush, soft and spongy from Lindsey's vantage. There was a stillness in the air, undisturbed even by the faint calls of assorted birds in the distance. Lindsey breathed heavily in the peace of the moment as her eyes drank in the richness of the world all around her.

"Duck!!!"

Lindsey was jolted out of her reverie. Without warning, there came a series of sharp swishes and thwacks as several arrows embedded themselves in the ground around her.

"Fly! Back to the woods!"

Lindsey was dragged to her feet as the Bird snatched her arm in one claw and beat the air in retreat, with Lindsey running frantically alongside. More arrows shot through their air behind them, and Lindsey felt a searing sting as one of them grazed her leg. Yet with adrenaline raging through her body Lindsey ran without breaking, ran as she had never done in her life while the Bird led the way back towards the trees. They had covered a couple dozen yards before the Bird veered suddenly off the road and into the trees. Lindsey followed, tramping and stumbling through the underbrush, until suddenly the Bird shot upward to the tree tops, crying back "Hide in the brush. I will lead them off!" Lindsey collapsed amidst the ferns and pressed herself as flat to the earth as she could. There was silence now, which went on for what seemed like an eon. Then gradually the sound of voices filtered bit by bit through the trees.

"Where'd it go?"

"Hanged if I know. Could've gone anywhere."

"Nothing up ahead, must of gone off the path. It can't have been going that fast."

"It can fly, though."

"Not with that boy in it's claws."

Lindsey chafed silently. A *boy*?

The voices were speaking again.

"We should split up, fan out into the woods. First one to see the bird gives a shout and the rest of us come running."

"Forget the bird, we've got a job to do."

"But think of the reward!"

"Think of the irons the High Commissioner will have ready for us if we let Hae-jin slip away again."

"Look, there it is!"

"There it goes!" The voices devolved into confused shouting as they were joined with sporadic thwacking noises which Lindsey guessed was the sound of arrows being shot. The noise faded quickly as the archers ran off again somewhere in the woods, and in a few moments there was silence.

Lindsey remained huddled among the ferns wondering what on earth she should be doing next, cursing herself for having been so foolish as to have followed the Bird. I mean really, she thought to herself, what sane person jumps through a hole in their floor into another dimension or something without bringing a platoon of Navy Seals with them, or a least a little bit of food and some camping gear? It was being borne upon Lindsey that she hadn't eaten more than a wilted salad in the last several hours, and after having been ignored all afternoon her stomach was beginning to address her with stern reproach. On top of that, her thigh was bleeding where one of the arrows had grazed her. Suddenly, from behind her there came a soft cough.

It seemed as though Lindsey had been doing a lot spinning around in surprise that day, as she again made a rapid shift in her attention and turned around. Towering over her a few feet away was a large man, tall and of massive proportions in every dimension. He was in no way an unnatural giant, but rather one of those men of above average size who are neither particularly obese nor especially fit. His appearance was not what Lindsey would have expected to encounter in "fairyland", or wherever this was, for he was dressed in an old fashioned double breasted suit of dark blue pinstripe and wore a grey homburg hat. His countenance was a bit swarthy, his hair a greasy black and peering from beneath bushy black brows his dark eyes were simultaneously soft and inscrutable, yet razor sharp like hard obsidian. In all, he gave Lindsey the distinct impression of a high class gangster from the age of Prohibition. With one hand, he tipped his hat politely, while in the other he held a silver handled walking stick of vaguely oriental flavor. The man in the suit stood there for a moment, regarding her silently. Then with a measured action he took a large silk handkerchief from his breast pocket, in a single movement flicking it outward with two fingers, allowing it to unfold itself as it fell away freely, and proffered it to Lindsey.

"To staunch the blood."

Lindsey took the handkerchief. The man in the suit then produced and opened a small dark colored bottle.

"Iodine. You don't want to get an infection; medicine in The Fairworld is often unequal to our modern standards." Then, the man handed Lindsey a small folding knife. "For utility. You may keep these articles."

The man in the suit then tipped his hat cordially again, and began to walk in the direction of the road. Seemingly on an afterthought, the man stopped and turned to face Lindsey once more. "A parting word of advice, Miss. Do not trust the Bird." And the man went on his way.

Lindsey scrambled to her feet. "Hey! Hold on, wait a sec...ouch!" Lindsey was distracted for a moment by a sudden sting from her injured leg. When she looked again an instant later, the man in the suit was gone.

3

"Hae-jin"

One shock after another was starting to give Lindsey a vague feeling of annoyance. There were far too many people going around disappearing and reappearing here and there for any sensible girl's liking. It would, Lindsey reflected, be mildly useful if these folks would just stay in the same place for a few minutes at a time. Still, she was grateful for the iodine. Not anxious to be pantless for any amount of time in this distinctly unpredictable place, she instead used the pocket knife to cut her jeans open a bit wider, dabbed the wound with some of the iodine bound it up snugly with the handkerchief. Pocketing the bottle of iodine and the knife, she then began to creep cautiously back towards the road. There was a beating of wings, and abruptly Lindsey was rejoined by the Bird. "Well, that was more or less satisfactory", the Bird said. "They should be sufficiently lost by now that we will be undisturbed for the remainder of the time we are here."

"Who were they and what did they want?", Lindsey replied. "We could have been killed!"

"A slight hiccough, yes. I hadn't been watching the time. But it's all well enough, we're out of it unscathed."

"*You're* out of it unscathed. They got me pretty well."

"Eh? Bless me! Let me attend to it!"

"Forget it, I put iodine on it. Let's just get out of here first."

"Quite, yes. Getting out. We've got to fetch Hae-jin first though."

"Who is Hae-jin?"

"I'll let him tell you himself. Follow me!"

They were soon back on the road, and turned again in the direction they were headed before they were attacked. There were now a few arrows embedded here and there in the ground along their way, or else stuck deep in various tree trunks along the road. Lindsey shivered. They came again to the edge of the valley. This time no hail of archery was there to await them, although far in the distance behind them Lindsey thought she could hear faint shouts now and then. Apparently the Archers were still fairly closeby. Hopefully they wouldn't be coming back this way any time soon. Lindsey picked up her pace a bit as she followed in the wake of the Bird.

The road wound to and fro down the hillside. They did not travel along it very far before the Bird led the way off the road and into the trees. For some distance they picked their way meticulously through the brush and bramble (or rather Lindsey did, for the Bird simply flew over it all). Eventually they came upon an unremarkable rocky outcropping which was overgrown and largely obscured by the foliage. Here the Bird stopped, and whistled. There was silence for a moment. Then, some of the boughs overhanging the rock face stirred and then fell away, revealing a small cave opening, wherein stood a man, with a sheathed sword in his hand.

He was not very tall. Wiry and athletic, he appeared to be in his late thirties or early forties, with bronzed skin, distinctly Asiatic features, and a regal, commanding bearing. He was dressed in rugged silks and wore a red headband with a bronze badge in its center, and his hair was bound in a topknot. He carried his sword in its sheath rather than wearing it at his side, holding it at the ready with the stout wooden scabbard poised to act as a sort of shield in the event he was attacked before he could draw his weapon. He regarded Lindsey and the Bird warily for a moment, then relaxed his posture, bowed slightly and spoke. "I am pleased to see you, Bird. Whom have you brought with you?"

The Bird gestured towards Lindsey. "This is Lindsey Ann Fluger. She will be participating in our little venture. Lindsey, may I introduce you to General Moon Hae-jin. It's only a little thing, but I do think I should mention that you will depend on one another for your lives over the next day or so. Shall we go inside?"

Hae-jin led the way into the cave. It was small, hardly big enough for more than a couple people. It was devoid of any signs of habitation save for a single leather bag resting in one corner. The man Hae-jin was definitely traveling light. Hae-jin squatted down near the entrance where he could see fairly well through the concealing foliage, and looked Lindsey over with a mix of wariness and curiosity. "You are foreign, Lindsey Ann Fluger", Hae-jin said. "I take it that the Bird has brought you from a land which is at least as far away as his own (wherever that may be)."

"Further, in point of fact", the Bird said cheerfully. "Lindsey is not of this world, but from the other world of which I told you."

"The one you say my ancestors came from?"

"Precisely."

Lindsey was not enjoying being spoken of in the third person. Moreover, she had some serious questions at this stage. "Okay, look", she said brusquely. "You said that Hae-jin and me were going to depend on each other for our lives. What's that supposed to mean? I've jumped through worlds, faced giants and been shot at, and you still haven't given me an explanation. I think you owe me one."

"You speak Han remarkably well, Lindsey Ann Fluger", Hae-jin remarked with curiosity.

"Call me Lindsey", Lindsey said, "And what do you mean, 'speak Han'? What's Han?"

"Ah, yes, I should have mentioned that", the Bird suddenly interjected. "You probably didn't notice (people usually don't), but you haven't been speaking English since you got here. Just before I spoke to you today, you see, I breathed the Gift of Tongues in your ear. It's one of my little talents. I find it quite indispensable in such situations. One's associates need to be able to understand one another."

"Gift of Tongues?"

"Quite. It's an extremely complex and potent enchantment (though simple to deliver once prepared), the net effect of which is that one can understand most forms of speech, and likewise speak them in turn, usually quite instinctually. I've known people to go for months chatting away in languages otherwise alien to them without even realizing it. I also gave the gift of tongues to Hae-jin, as you will both be needing it where you're going."

"Which is where?"

"West of here by a few thousand miles, a place called the Hinterlands, which lies in Northern Eptomar."

"That's far away indeed", Hae-jin remarked. "You weren't exaggerating when you told me I would be going into exile."

"Under the circumstances I thought you'd find it a welcome opportunity", the Bird replied.

"I do. I worry about my people though."

"With you out of the way I don't think the Li will bother with your family."

"Can somebody explain to me what's going on here?", Lindsey interjected.

"Eh? Oh, right, yes" the Bird said. "Hae-jin, you see, has been having some difficulty with the Li government of late, and suffice to say things have become rather awkward for him, which is why I thought he could well do with an opportunity for change...sooner than later."

"I can imagine. Those guys were hunting him with bows."

"I'm afraid my life would in all probability be quite short and painful were I to remain in my homeland any longer.", Hae-jin observed ruefully.

"Why would anyone want to hurt you?", Lindsey asked.

"This is what happens to all who run afoul of the Li."

"Who are the Li?"

Hae-jin regarded Lindsey for a moment, perhaps trying to decide for himself just how much explaining would be necessary. He then leaned forward a bit and traced a crude outline in the dirt. "This is the land of Zhongyang, which lies on the far eastern side of the continent of Eptomar. We are out here, in the northeastern part of Zhongyang. There are many nations here in Zhongyang, but the most powerful of all is the empire of the Li. My people are called the Hancheon, and most of our kingdoms and cities are tributaries of the Li. The Li rule us by the appointment of High Commissioners, who dictate the will of The Lotus Throne to our kings and princes, who must obey."

"Why don't your people kick the Li out?"

"We have tried. The cost to our people was too great, for the rage of the Li is a terrible thing."

"Were you a rebel? Is that why the Li are hunting you?"

"I have lived my life in the service of my people and prince, and in doing so I have achieved great fame and reward. But the demands of the Li are severe and often unjust. Likewise there are many in the court of my prince who serve their own ends and seek to destroy their rivals, often through currying the favors of the Li. It is one of the ways the Li have always been able to dominate us. They exploit the rivalries within their tribute nations and turn our officers and captains into willing pawns. But I will not be a pawn, and I will not be an instrument of injustice. And for that, I have paid dearly. I have gone from holding the highest rank in our armies to being a fugitive in my own country. A week ago I commanded twenty thousand soldiers. I had a thousand acres of fertile land, a great house, and a hundred servants. Today, I have nothing but a single sword and a price on my head. My wife is long dead, and none of my children ever survived infancy. I have nothing left to live for here. But I am not yet ready to die." Hae-jin fell silent. Lindsey felt a compulsion to say something, anything, but found herself at a loss. Unsurprisingly, somehow, the Bird was not.

"Well my good fellow, this is precisely why I approached you in the first place to be a partner to this little venture of ours. I take it you've made your final decision then?"

"I don't see that I have much else to choose from."

"On the contrary! If you decline to assist us I will of course do everything in my power to help you escape your current predicament (after which you will be on your own). But I think the proposition I have for you, while risky, is much more interesting (and, I daresay, more meaningful) than simply removing you from the clutches of the Li and their henchmen. You need only decide."

Hae-jin mused in silence. After a few moments he looked up, first at the Bird, and then at Lindsey. And then he replied. "Why not?"

"Splendid! ", the Bird said, flapping his wings with satisfaction. "Utterly splendid! I knew I was right about him, didn't I tell you Lindsey?"

"No, I don't think you did.", Lindsey remarked.

"Eh? Well, no matter. Come, collect your things Hae-jin, and we will all be off!"

"Now hold on just one second!", Lindsey insisted.

"You had something to say, my dear?", the Bird asked.

"Yeah, I sure as hell do. You haven't told *me* yet what this venture is, or asked me whether I'm still going to come along or just punch you until you take me home."

Hae-jin chuckled. "You picked a hot ember there, Bird! Be careful you don't burn yourself!"

"Have I really not explained everything to you, my dear?", the Bird said. "Goodness, but I'm in such a flutter today! It all comes from having to manage appointments across multiple worlds and continents, I defy anyone to keep their pebbles in order with such a schedule. Let's see, where shall I start?"

"Somewhere other than here, if you don't mind", Hae-jin said insistently. "The High Commissioner's men aren't too far away."

"Steady notion, Hae-jin. Let me put a hole in the floor." Just as he had done previously, the Bird cut a rough square in the detritus of the cave floor with his shiny black beak. The dried leaves and twigs sagged and clung together, and the Bird had to give them a little shove before they fell away in a bundle. The Bird then went through himself.

Hae-jin then grabbed his bag and swung his legs into the hole. Before dropping through, he took a last look towards the outside the cave. He then turned to Lindsey. "Somehow, I feel this is the last I shall ever see of my homeland."

"You don't know that for certain", Linsey said, trying to sound reassuring.

"I don't. But I feel it for certain." Hae-jin then dropped himself through the hole, and after calling up to say he was out of the way, Lindsey followed. Lindsey landed with a now-familiar sort of shock in a patch of vibrant green grass awash with wildflowers. All around her was a pleasant woodland, though clearly removed from the one she had just quitted, and she lay beside another road....or to be more precise a narrow path, hardly more than a couple feet wide, which was paved with smooth cobbles. And on it were two rather extraordinary rabbits.

They were large rabbits, but that was not what made them extraordinary. No, rather it was the way in which they sat on their back haunches and held small baskets in their forepaws, and the slack-jawed way in which they were staring at her. Their fluffy white chins drooped limply in a paralysis of bewilderment, while each ear was pricked erect in a shocked rigor mortis, and their black eyes blinked wide in utter astonishment. Lindsey looked back at the rabbits and smiled nervously. The rabbits looked at one another.

"And now there's a third one!", said one rabbitt.

"Shocking!", said the other.

"Fell out of the sky, just like that!"

"I've never heard of such a thing!"

"Nor I!"

"Nor anyone!"

"Hardly credible!"

"Hardly respectable!"

"Uh, hi?", Lindesy interjected, propped herself up on an elbow.

"It talks!", said the first rabbitt.

"The other ones didn't talk!", rejoined the second.

"Uh, yeah. I talk.", Lindsey said, "Do you know where the "other ones" went?"

"Shall we talk back to it?", said the first rabbitt.

"I don't think so", said the second. "Not proper without a proper introduction anyway. Best ignore it do you suppose?"

"I don't know, we might want to ask it if there mightn't be more of them. Are they going to start falling out of the sky very often do you suppose? And landing on top of us, our houses and our gardens?"

"This seems to be the last one. Let's just ignore it."

"Hey, listen." Lindsey said as she began to get up.

"Scatter!", the two rabbits cried in unison.

The two rabbits dropped their baskets and dashed off on all fours into the woods. Lindsey stood up and cursed silently to herself. Talking rabbits now, huh? More like a bunch of rude scaredy-cat talking rabbits.

A shadow fell across the ground before her, and Lindsey turned to see Hae-jin approaching.

"Where are those Rabbits off to?", he asked.

"They just ran away", Lindsey said. Did you hear them talk!"

"They talked?", Hae-jin asked, frowning slightly.

"Is that normal in this world of yours?"

"I don't know actually. I've heard tales, but I have certainly never witnessed such a thing before myself. We must be quite far from Zhongyang indeed, or perhaps in yet another world entirely."

"Where's the Bird?"

"He told me to come back here for you, and that we'd meet him at a signpost just up the road. Come."

They followed the path for some distance before reaching the signpost the Bird had spoken of. It was a tidy object, smartly crafted with two elegantly carved signs, one pointing to the left and the other right, for here the path had come to a fork. The signs bore the first examples of writing which Lindsey had seen in this peculiar world. She recalled the words of the Bird regarding the "gift of tongues" she and Hae-jin had supposedly been given. The whole thing was a bit weird, but whatever it was it somehow worked, and apparently it even applied to writing. She could plainly see that the words were neither written in modern English nor with any alphabet she had ever seen. Yet, she could read it all quite clearly.

The signs gave very little to go on, however. Each was shaped like an arrow, and bore only a list of names (or a least what Lindsey thought might be names):

> *RABBITS*-LEAFLEAPER
> *RABBITS*-REDCARROT
> *RABBITS*-ROUNDHOLE
> *RABBITS*-TUFFLETUFT
> *FOX*-GOODBURROW
> *RABBITS*-LONGEAR
> *RABBITS*-GOODDIGGER
> *WOGS*

Lindsey felt a gentle tap on the shoulder. She turned to meet Hae-jin's eye, and he pointed at the ground by the base of the sign, where Lindsey saw four feathers of an unmistakable golden hue lying on the road, arranged in an arrow towards the left hand route. Lindsey turned again to Hae-jin. "I guess we're supposed to follow the arrow, then?

Hae-jin merely shrugged, and began to walk in that direction. Lindsey followed. Just visible through the trees ahead, Lindsey saw what appeared to be a small structure. Hardly big enough for a house, it seemed more in the way of a large shed. Yet a house it proved to be as Lindsey and Hae-jin reached it. And up ahead, there appeared to be another, and still another. The structures were definitely complete dwellings, ordinary looking cottages, well built and painted in bright colors, each surrounded by a small yard containing a garden plot or two and a few tiny outbuildings. They were mainly distinguished by their size, having apparently been built for the comfort of very diminutive tenants, which Lindsey could only assume were Rabbits. Indeed, painted above the door of each house there was written a name, corresponding to those which had been on the signpost back at the fork. Rabbits-Leafleaper, Rabbits-Redcarrot, Fox-Goodburrow....and Wogs.

The eighth house along the road was a bit unlike the others. Taller, larger, and a bit more sprawling, dilapidated and drooping in every direction, with overgrown grounds and not an inch of fresh paint in sight, save for the lettering above the door which bore but one word: "Wog". And at Lindsey's feet along the path, there were four golden feathers arranged in an arrow, pointing directly at the house. Lindsey and Hae-jin exchanged a look. Then together they approached the door, and Lindsey knocked. There was silence. Lindsey knocked again. This time, muffled voices, then silence again. Lindsey knocked for a third time.

Muffled voices again, followed by a scrabbling noise, and in a moment the door opened with an unpleasant sort of creak. If sounds could be seen, the creaking of the door would likely have looked very much like the creature who had done the opening. Already becoming rapidly accustomed to strange sights, Lindsey was nonetheless taken aback by the individual who was now glaring petulantly at her. It was just under five feet tall or so, and shaped more or less like a human in most respects. Scrawny, boney, with skin like a mouldy tangerine, its face was angular and its nose a full four or five inches long. It had ears of equally outrageous size, shaped very much like those of a donkey, and were full of bristly black hairs. It was dressed in vaguely medieval looking attire in faded colors, and on its head was a bright yellow cap. The creature gazed up at Lindsey and Hae-jin, blinking back and forth between them for a moment with a look of bewilderment, then recognition, followed by a dark scowl.

"Oh hell. Humans!" And the creature slammed the door shut.

Lindsey and Hae-jin looked at one another, speechless for a moment. Hae-jin opened his mouth to say something, but was interrupted when the door was opened again and the creature reappeared. The creature looked sternly at them for a moment, and then spoke. "You do realize that this is impossible? At least it's supposed to be, at any rate. It's not allowed. I never agreed to see anyone impossible. You can tell that Bird that I won't have anything to do with flagrant impossibilities."

Hae-jin remained speechless, but Lindsey did not. "In my world, little orange monsters with bad attitudes are considered impossible, so that makes us even. The Bird told us to come here, so here we are. If you don't want to talk to us, fine. We'll wait here for the Bird."

"Now now now missy, don't be getting all hoity toity at me."

"Hey, I don't have to take any garbage from 'impossibilities', mister monster."

"Well of all the cheek!"

And the creature slammed the door again. Hae-jin coughed. "You didn't have to insult the.....the...the whatever it was."

Lindsey threw up her hands. "Look, I've just about had it up to here. Earlier today I jumped through a hole in my floor without any idea why or where it led and I still don't even know what I'm supposed to be doing here and I'm still not even sure whether I've just done the stupidest thing in my life or if I'm just plain crazy and hallucinating it all. If that's not enough to give a girl something to bitch about, then I don't know what is."

"I understand, Lindsey Ann Fluger....."

"And you can call me Lindsey."

"I understand, Lindsey. This is new to me as well. Let's wait for the Bird. When he comes back...." Again Hae-jin was interrupted as the door opened and the creature emerged for the third time. It stood there glaring for a moment, and Lindsey glared back at it. Lindsey raised an eyebrow. "Well?"

The creature shuffled. "Fine. You can come inside. But don't say I didn't warn you, because I'm going to right now. Dire consequences will come of this ill fated encounter, you can take my word for it."

"And what is your word worth?"

"Fifty-one silver marks."

"Oh great. And how are we supposed to trust you then?"

"By paying me fifty-one silver marks. That's my price and I'm sticking to it. The Bird can pay up or do without me. Come inside, and I'll dig up some cold ham and beer. Don't thank me, the Bird will have to pay for that too." With that the creature swung his door wide, and beckoned inward.

The interior of the house was dim, cramped and cluttered. The walls and ceiling were decked with hooks and knobs of all sorts, from which hung every manner of object, from pots, tools, and bundles of herbs to old clothes, armor, and rusty weapons. Battered furniture was stacked high with an equally mixed assortment of articles, and the floor was strewn with nut shells, wood shavings, the odd bone or two, and other sorts of careless refuse. A chicken was rummaging about the floor, and fluttered off to perch on the mantelpiece as Lindsey and Hae-jin entered the room. Beneath the mantle there was a table set with a half eaten meal at which two more creatures sat, eyeing the newcomers warily. Their host waved grandly about the room. "Welcome to the house of Wog. I am Alwog. These are my brothers...." Alwog indicated to the two creatures at the table. ".....that is Berwog, and that is Gerthwog."

To Lindsey all three appeared wholly indistinguishable, save for the color of their caps. Their host Alwog wore a yellow cap, while Berwog's cap was red and Gerthwog's was green. The one called Gerthwog addressed Alwog while jerking a rude thumb in Lindsey's direction.

"Humans? You know they're illegal, Al."

Alwog shrugged. "Sure I do. I'm thinking we should charge more, seeing as they're humans, properly impossible and all. I'm thinking sixty silver marks would be more like it."

The one called Berwog piped up. "You mean sixty-one! You can't divide sixty by three, not evenly."

Gerthwog rolled a disgruntled eye over to his other brother. "Yes, you *can* divide sixty evenly by three."

"No you can't!"

"Yes you can. Use 'rithmetic!"

Berwog squinted and began to count on his fingers. "...Nope, still don't come out even. Sixty-one I say!"

"No, sixty. Here, lunkhead, I'll prove it to you." Gerthwog seized a fork and began carving sums into the table, muttering the results to his brother.

At this point, Hae-jin addressed Alwog. "What do you mean, humans are illegal? And impossible?"

"They're against the law. Against the law and against the magic. Therefore, they are impossible. Humans aren't allowed here, that's the law of the Drixi."

"Who are the Drixi?"

"The law-givers 'round these parts."

"Ah? And what do these Drixi have against humans?"

"Most everything, so it seems. Don't want them around no-how."

"And yet you are willing to defy them?"

"The Bird got you here, didn't he? Got you here right past all that Drixi magic. I'm thinking the Bird's magic must be better. I'm always happy to offer my services to the party with the better magic....for the proper fee, of course."

"Of course."

"Of course. Sit down, make yourselves comfortable. Don't know when that bird will be back."

Alwog slouched over to the table and flung himself into one of the chairs, propping his feet up next to the cold ham and between the faces of his two brothers, who were now in the heat of an argument. Hae-jin squatted down in a relatively clear part of the floor. Lindsey took one look at the floor, then another at the filthy furniture about her, and decided to remain standing. The brothers Berwog and Gerthwog continued to argue. Alwog leaned back, humming and whistling and muttering snatches of lyrics from ribald sounding songs. Hae-jin remained silent, and Lindsey began to wander around what little there was of the confined room. Her eyes lighted upon the mantelpiece, which was remarkably clean compared to any other surface in the room, containing only a peculiar wooden structure not unlike the sort used to display bottles of fine wine, on which there were three objects which appeared to be the substantive remains of three large eggs, one of a vaguely yellowish hue, one of red, and the other green. As she took a step closer for another look, Alwog spoke up with a nod in that direction. "Those are ours, of course. Family heirlooms."

"Yours? Are they eggs?"

"Of course they are."

"Are you telling me you and your brothers hatched from eggs?"

"What do you take us for, freaks?"

"Um...."

"I forgot, you're a human. You breed like the Rabbits and Drixi. Why any creature should be born outside of a proper egg is beyond me, but I suppose your hereditary defects are your own business."

It may have been Alwog's intention to further elucidate on the specific shortcomings of live birth, but he never had a chance to speak, as from the door there came a pair of dull thuds which reverberated throughout the house and shook it's creaking timbers, leaving a bewildered hush in its wake. Berwog and Gerthog had stopped arguing, and all three Wogs were staring in the direction of the door. Lindsey and Hae-jin exchanged a concerned look. Alwog arose, and tiptoed over to the door. He opened his mouth to speak, but before he could a throaty voice came from outside.

"I was told by the Bird to come here. Open up."

4

"Conference at the House of Wog"

The voice spoke with a certain authority which caught everyone off guard. Hardly hesitating, Alwog shot back the bolt and opened the door a crack to peek outside. He was nearly bowled over when the door was shoved open the rest of the way from outside, revealing a tremendous golden brown Bear. The Bear looked calmly over the room's occupants, and then proceeded to pad nonchalantly inside. For a moment she drank in her surroundings with a regal, disdainful air before at last speaking. "What a disreputable den", she said in a sonorous, condescending tone. "If I had known what sort of company the Bird was letting me in for, I would have thought twice about coming, make no mistake." Alwog bristled visibly, collecting his hitherto misplaced confidence. "Well then, Mrs. Holier-than-art-else-Bear, just who do you think you are? I don't recognize you, you're no local Bear."

"Thankfully not, if the local Bears are in any way comparable in breeding to yourself. My name is Ursilda, and I've come a very long way indeed. Just precisely what does the Bird want in bringing me all the way to the land of the Drixi?"

"I haven't the foggiest. The Bird made no mention of working with any bears. If he had, I'd surely have charged sixty-six silver marks."

"Sixty-seven!"

"Shut up, Berwog!"

The Bear sniffed. "Mercenaries. How vulgar. Well, can anyone tell me where that dratted Bird has got to? I've got two cubs at home, and I have no desire to leave them any longer than necessary. The Bird promised this venture would take but a single night, and that's all I'm willing to spare him."

"First talking Rabbits, and now a talking Bear", Hae-jin remarked under his breath. "What sort of conjurer's circus do you suppose we have gotten ourselves into, Lindsey?" The Bear's ears pricked, and she turned with menacing deliberation to face Hae-jin, eyeing him levelly. "You, sir, are a rude human. Rude and foolish, to provoke a Bear."

"I have slain more than one bear in my life", Hae-jin replied, holding the Bear's gaze.

"As have I slain more than one man."

"Then I should say that we are perhaps peers, in our own way."

"I doubt very much that you would find yourself the equal of my society. Am I to endure the society of uncouth men as well as ugly hobgoblins in this quest?"

"Well, there's also me", Lindsey cut in. For the first time the Bear seemed to have taken notice of Lindsey. "And a scrawny little Evecub too? What *does* that dratted Bird have in mind?"

"Watch who you call scrawny. And rude. You're pretty darn free with your criticisms yourself, you know", Linsdey retorted. Ursilda licked her jowls pensively. "Well, you're a stout one, Evecub, as little as you are. You impress me. Perhaps the Bird is not quite so mad, to have chosen such as you and I."

"You think pretty highly of yourself, don't you?"

"I am Ursilda. I have borne a hundred cubs in a hundred years. I have slept under the stars of ten thousand winter nights, and have dreamed ten thousand winter dreams. I have traveled from the Falls of Lora Inerion to foothills of the Peaks of Luda. I have slain a hundred hunters and a hundred panthers and have scattered a thousand wolves, and all Wights in my realm fear my wrath and covet my favor. I am Ursilda, and there is none other like me."

"Yeah….I kinda guess there wouldn't be."

"Quite right, Evecub. You are wise. Your mother raised you well, for a human."

"Hullo, hullo! I see that everyone is here!" The door had been left open in the wake of Ursilda's remarkable entrance, and all eyes now turned in that direction to see that they had been at last joined by the Bird. Beside him stood a tallish sort of woman with a large satchel, wearing a long cloak with the hood thrown back, revealing fine locks of pale dun. Her face was smooth with little signs of age, suggesting to Lindsey that she might be in her mid thirties or so. Her eyes were of striking steel-grey which met Lindsey's gaze with a measured keenness that seemed to carefully take note of every detail. The woman held Lindsey's gaze for a moment before the conversation of the Bird caught their attention.
"…..and so things took a bit longer than I expected" ,the Bird was saying, "but everyone is here now, and we might as well all meet here under the kind hospitality of the good Wogs."

"Our hospitality starts at a copper a head, Birdie", Alwog said coldly.

"Eh? Oh right, of course. I shall of course cover all expenses. Do be so kind as to keep up a running tally, my good Wog, as these matters tend to slip my mind."

"No worries on that score. Such things *never* slip my mind."

"Well, then, shall we begin?" The whole party made themselves as comfortable as possible in the cramped front room. The cloaked woman who was accompanying the Bird now stepped forward and spoke. "My name is Joan Greyflower. I come from the of Kingdom of Linster, which lies in the Hinterlands far away from here. It is on the behalf of my nation that the Bird has gathered you all here. For many years now, my people have labored under a great misfortune. A terrible curse which has withered our crops, sickened our beasts and taken our children. Our only relief comes when we succumb to the demands of the one who laid this dark enchantment on our land: Gurth the Witch, a sorcerer of terrible power. Only then do the rains come and the diseases abate. But the demands of Gurth are terrible. In payment for relieving us of the miseries which he himself has inflicted on us, we must surrender to him a portion of our brothers and sisters, to be carried to faraway courts in the southern deserts to become the slaves of witches, a valuable service for which Gurth is rewarded handsomely by his masters. For the witches are ever in need of more human chattel, and their appetite has been increasing of late. We are weak from years of plague and famine, and we cannot resist him. Those who reject his demands starve, sicken and slowly die. The king and the nobility have long since surrendered to our oppressors, and demand that all people shall collect the Due of Gurth.

I have no doubt that by now all of you have guessed the purpose to which you have been gathered: To put an end to the Curse of Gurth.

It is not simply a matter of killing Gurth. Many have tried, and all have failed, and the vengeance of Gurth is so hideous that the king has forbidden that any further attempts should be made. But even were we successful it wouldn't be enough, for the curse itself would still remain. For you see, ours is a wicked land. Petty witchcraft has long been practiced among the common people, and so long as the peasants were content our rulers would look away. And Gurth exploited this venality. He came offering us spells and incantations with wondrous effects of every sort, and the people bought his remedies without regard to the darkness of the magic which produced them. I am a midwife. I know the remedies of nature, and I know at least to discern between the remedies of magic, both black and white. I and others warned the people that Gurth purveyed naught but black magic, but few would heed us. The rest debased themselves in his diabolical incantations with abandon, for the rites were intoxicating and their effects marvelous, seducing the mind and numbing the heart. And when Gurth was at last ready and laid his curse upon the land, he bound with it all the wickedness of the people. Though my people may now repent their folly, the stain of their crimes remain. The spell can never be broken without also expiating the onus wrought by the sin of the people."

Lindsey now spoke. "Excuse me?", she said, raising a hand as she did so, "Excuse me, but how do we do all this? How are we going to break the spell?"

Joan turned to the Bird and spoke with some surprise. "You mean you haven't spoken with her?"

"Er, no, actually. Not yet. I thought it would be better, you see....."

"Well, I suppose you know your own business....."

"I do."

"...but I would have told her sooner."

"Thorns, brambles, and beesting!", the Bear interjected, "Enough dithering! Why bring all of us into all this, if you just need to break some spell or other?"

"Hear hear!", concurred Alwog, "I hate to agree with the Bear, but we Wogs are professionals. We don't sign any contract until we know what it's all about, an advance estimate of the number of heads we'll need to break, and how much extra charge we need to apply for added risk."

"Permit me to continue, then", replied Joan, "and I shall explain our request to the rest of you. I have long sought a remedy for this abomination upon our land, and at length I found counsel with the Good Folk, who took up my cause...."

"Good lord! You don't mean to say you brought *fairies* into this? First humans, now fairies, this is wholly unacceptable! That'll be a hundred silver marks!"

"A hundred and one!"

"No, a hundred...no wait, you're actually right this time, almost...make it a hundred two."

"A hundred three!"

"Shut up! A hundred two will do enough..for now."

"Yes yes yes", replied the Bird, "you have my word that all will be paid in full. Now, can we permit the good lady to continue?"

"Thank you", replied Joan, "As I was saying, my cause was taken up by the Good Folk, who studied the curse, and uncovered a way to break it. They instructed me on what to do, and they likewise sent the Bird to assist me. We will soon be traveling to a place not far from here. It is a mountain called Vorn, with which some of you, I understand, are already acquainted."

"Sure we are", said Alwog, "My brothers and I spent three years working in the mines 'round those parts, we know that mountain like the backs of our hands."

"Excellent. Again, the Bird has chosen wisely. You and your brothers will be invaluable for our task."

"Which is? You still haven't gotten to that bit, though I'll wager I already know what it is. You want to get inside Harin's Vault, don't you? Well it won't work, it's impossible. It's sealed by magic inside solid rock, and nobody's ever been able to dig through."

"We shan't need to dig inside."

"So you're going to break the seal, eh? Ha! You're Bird is good, but I'll wager he's not that good. The vault was sealed shut long ago by the ancestors of the Drixi, and no one has been able to open it since, not even the Drixi themselves."

Here the Bird bristled slightly. "You forget, my good Wog, that I am an associate of the Good Folk."

"But you're not actually one of them, are you?"

"Er, well, no..."

"...Exactly. I'll still wager you can't do it."

"Ha! I'll wager you a hundred silver marks that I can!"

"Ha!, yourself. You won't get out of our bill that easy. It'll still be a hundred and two silver marks, plus our choice of loot from the vault."

"You may not have an opportunity to access the vault. We will only be able to open it once, and even if we succeed it will only remain open for a short time before closing again, and you and your brothers may be otherwise occupied when that happens."

"How so? You are expecting trouble, I take it?"

"In point of fact, yes. Gurth has informants scattered throughout the Kingdom of Linster. But likewise, so too have the eyes and ears of the Good Folk been turned to that land of late. The Good Folk believe that Gurth is already aware of our intent to break the curse. They also believe that Gurth already knows (or suspects) that our efforts in that regard are taking place here in the lands of the Drixi. Obviously, if this is true then our enterprise may be in grave peril, which is why I have been directed to assemble so formidable a party as ourselves."

"In the name of the Mother Bear!", Ursilda interjected, "Why must you drivel over everything you say? I take it then that we are to deal with this man called Gurth and keep him occupied until you've opened the vault and gotten what you want from it?"

"Er, yes. Quite. Couldn't have put it better myself."

"Of course not. I am Ursilda, nobody puts things better than me. That makes for one man, the Evecub, three hobgoblins, and myself in all. This should not be difficult, I myself am more than enough to handle one puny human sorcerer."

"I do not think that Gurth himself would come. The witches have spread their influence far and wide, and in times of need they can communicate quickly over great distances. There are any number of means by which an important sorcerer like Gurth could have gotten word to the nearest coven. The witches value their supply of slaves quite highly."

"That's all well and good, but what if......."

The conversation dragged on for quite a while, as the party debated this and that. Through it all, Lindsey still felt she still didn't have a clear idea about what her role in all of this was, and whenever she spoke up to ask a question either Joan or the Bird would quickly steer the conversation in another direction. At last, when the Wogs had gone off into other parts of the house to assemble their gear for the expedition and Joan, Hae-jin, and Ursilda at last had an opportunity to step outside the now insufferably stuffy front room, Lindsey addressed the Bird directly.
"Look Mr. Bird", Lindsey said assertively. "You still haven't told me what my role in all of this is. I'm not a fighter, I don't have any special skills or talents. Why am I even here?"

"You're here because you were the right person at the right time, my dear. Pure and simple."

"And what's that supposed to mean?"

"Well, when my associates make the decision to intervene somewhere, they choose their allies based on the particular qualifications and circumstances of the specific parties involved. Birds like me, chaps like Hae-jin, and sometimes even people from your own world."

"Your associates? You mean the Good Folk?"

"Quite."

"And just who are these 'Good Folk', anyway?"

"Why, only the greatest and most ancient of all the elves and fairies!

This entire world was built by them. It is their legacy and their domain, and all the inhabitants of this world are in their charge."

"If that's true, then why the heck do they allow stuff like this to happen in the first place? From what I've seen so far it looks like a lot of bad stuff happens in this world of yours."

"Well, while this world does technically belong to them, my associates are far from being omnipotent. They are neither gods nor demigods. But even if they were gods it wouldn't make much more of a difference. You see, the Good Folk believe that people must be permitted to govern themselves, and that the world must follow the course charted by the sum of its inhabitants, for good or for ill. It is an inevitable consequence of having a proper reality, don't you know. If my associates actually did manage absolutely everything that happened in the world there wouldn't be any reality at all, not in any meaningful sense. The world would merely be a sort of theater, and the people in it merely shadows to be manipulated like puppets for the amusement of the gods. The Good Folk have no desire for such a world. But likewise, neither are the Good Folk content to stand by idly where evil and suffering abound. They therefore try to strike a suitable balance in these matters, which is where birds like me come in."

"Huh", Lindsey said skeptically. "I feel like that would be a pretty darn difficult thing to get right. It all must get really complicated really fast."

"Dreadfully complicated, my dear Lindsey, dreadfully complicated. It's all quite beyond me really, and I'm glad none of it is my decision to make. I merely do what I am bidden, and that's quite enough for me."

"So you just leave it all up to the Good Folk, huh? Frankly, I would want to ask them more questions than that. Do people like me ever get the chance to talk to your 'associates'?"

"Quite possibly, my dear Lindsey", the Bird said. "Quite possibly."

5

"Harin's Vault"

The party was gathered outside the house of the Wogs, who had at last assembled their accoutrements for the adventure ahead. They made for a wickedly eccentric appearance, tightly girded in studded coats of plate topped with helmets like broad brimmed steel hats (one painted yellow, one green, and the other red) beneath which the Wogs' mule-like ears drooped comically. Each wore a bulging pack on his back and an assortment of tools and weapons dangling from his belt. And each carried a stout looking staff tipped with a nasty blade consisting of an ugly array of prongs, hooks and curved edges. Overall, they presented a comfortably ferocious impression which (under the circumstances) was some consolation to Lindsey in light of the unknown threats ahead of them.

The Bird began his usual procedure of tracing an outline into the ground, though the verdant grass clung together annoyingly well and it took a disgruntled shove from Ursilda to get the ragged square of sod to fall through the portal in the ground. One by one the adventurers dropped through. Ursilda was first, since nobody wanted to be on the other side when *she* came tumbling out of the sky. Which was just as well, given the great She-Bear had some difficulty navigating the hole and became stuck halfway through, and it took the collective efforts of everyone else to shove her through the rest of the way. Lindsey was the last to go. She sat down on the grass, swinging her legs into the hole, and prepared to jump. A movement to one side caught her eye, and Lindsey twisted her head to look over in that direction. It was nearing sunset by now. The deep, subdued green of the trees was turning to bright limes and cool olives as the leaves bathed in the fading golden rays, and the tiny road was turning into a river of brass amidst the final glory of the day. And upon the road, standing at a bend not far away, was a large man in a homburg hat, silhouetted against the brilliant light, watching her.

From the hole below her, Ursilda's sonorous voice filtered upwards, still berating the Bird for not having made the hole big enough. Lindsey was debating whether to get up and confront the stranger in the homburg, or tell the others first, when Ursilda called up to her to stop dithering and dallying, and Lindsey was promptly yanked down the hole by an impatient, iron paw. Upon landing Lindsey scrambled to her feet. "Hey!", she snapped. "Before you pulled me down I saw someone up the road. He was watching us."

"Pah!", said Alwog. "Neighbors. Those Rabbits are always being nosey."

"It wasn't a Rabbit, it was a man."

"Impossible."

"Yeah, and so am I. It looked like a man, anyway."

The Bird clicked thoughtfully. "Might have been one of Gurth's agents. Better close up right away." The Bird began fanning his wings at the fading hole above them, which then began to disappear a bit faster. "If he is one of Gurth's men, he'll be warning the others that we've arrived at Mount Vorn. There is little time to lose. Come, the vault is just ahead."

The landscape around Mount Vorn was freakish and marvelous. It couldn't have been very far from the home of the Wogs, no more a few tens of miles perhaps, for the sun was still only just above the horizon. It's leisurely descent spread rays of brilliant gold across a landscape of wild stone pillars of variegated red, bursting forth in every direction from a maze of meandering ruts and gullies, some clogged with mud and slag, others grown over with rich grasses. Above all was the great peak of the mountain itself, a visage of brooding serenity awash in the molten gold of sunset. The Bird flew ahead and perched on a rock pillar, calling the others to follow him. And so they made their way.

The terrain was rough and tortuous, filled with jagged obstacles and dangerous slides and all manner of impediment. Here and there were the remains of mining implements; bits of wagons, scaffolding, and other flotsam sunk and settled with age, the iron rusted and wood bleached and splintered. The Wogs explained that this face of the mountain had not been actively mined for some time, the operation having mostly shifted to the opposite face many years ago. The wild landscape was the result of the mining techniques used there, which involved artificially eroding the mountainside by cutting sluices into the earth and flooding them with fast moving water, or else drilling narrow, lateral wells through the hillside and filling them with water until the mounting pressure at last shattered the surrounding rock. Though the mountain was less bountiful these days, at its height the Wogs said that the operation produced over ten thousand Drixi pounds of lucrative tin every year.

The party was moving roughly laterally across the mountainside, climbing just slightly. Here and there a young tree could be found where the mining had been abandoned for longer than it had elsewhere. The sun had at last passed beyond the horizon, only a few embers remaining at the rim of the sky, and the world was drifting into twilight. The trees were becoming more common and dense now as the followers of the Bird reached a place where no mining had been undertaken in many years. They had entered a rather dense copse when abruptly the way opened before them into a narrow passage of rock which plunged quickly below the level of the surrounding ground. It was a dry creek, cut by years of runoff through a long abandoned workman's path. As they followed it Lindsey observed that it was descending downward into what appeared to be a large open area ahead. This proved to be a wide pit, sunk perhaps twenty feet or more below the surface of the ground and open to the sky, where a few stars could just now be seen. In its center there was a tremendous rock, as large as a small castle keep, standing by itself as if on display. All around it the earth had been cleared away, and it's surface was scarred and cratered, evidence of the vain efforts of generations of disappointed treasure hunters. The rock towered forbiddingly above the ground, it's surface darkly mottled in a way very unlike the reddish rock everywhere else. And the sight of it filled Lindsey with dread. The Bird settled on the ground before the great stone, and signaled the others to gather about him. "Right, here we are! Behold Harin's Vault!"

"It looks like a big rock to me.", Lindsey commented.

"That's what it is. The vault is inside the rock."

"And how are we to get inside?"

"Leave that to me. Joan, myself and Lindsey are to remain here to open the vault. Wogs, you know the area well and should conduct a patrol above the pit. Keep to the trees, lest you be seen. Ursilda will form a second patrol, her sense of smell will match..."

"...exceed...", the Bear cut in.

"Er, quite, match or exceed any effort by our adversaries to advance in stealth. Hae-jin, I want you to conceal yourself in the woods near the entrance to the dry creek we just came down and stand watch to alert Ursilda and the Wogs of any intruders coming by that route and to guard it with your life if needed. You do know how to make a nightjar's call?"

"No", Hae-jin replied dubiously.

"Screech owl?"

"No."

"Whippoorwill?"

"No."

"Oh dear. Well, I suppose you can just shout 'Hoy!' instead. Right, now, everyone off!"

The Wogs muttered some crude observations about taking orders from ridiculous, babbling birds, but clattered off nonetheless, their armor and equipment making a bit more noise than Lindsey felt especially comfortable with. Ursilda merely grunted and heaved off on her own into the darkness.

Hae-jin met Lindsey's eye for a moment. He then made a shallow bow and made his way back up the creek bed. The Wogs may have known the terrain and Ursilda may have been convinced of her own invincibility, but it was Hae-jin who inspired Lindsey with the most confidence. Somehow, she felt sure that he would give his life for another if such a thing proved necessary. Why she should think so she couldn't rightly say at the moment, she just knew for herself that he was that kind of man. It was a small bit of comfort against the chilling darkness which she could feel beginning to creep up all around her. She turned to confront the Bird. "Well, now that we're here and everyone else is gone, are you finally going to tell me what this is all about?"

"Oh yes, quite right! Down to business. Now, inside the vault there is quite a stupendous number of *enormously* valuable artifacts, but that's not really all that important. Once you get it open you need only grab whatever you find handy. You see.....”

"Wait a minute! Once *I* open the vault?”

"Oh yes! Didn't I explain that part already?”

"No, you did not.”

"Ah, yes, I suppose I didn't. Er, well, perhaps Joan should explain.”

Lindsey turned a frustrated eye towards Joan, who met her gaze unflinchingly. Joan held Lindsey's gaze for a moment, and then spoke. "Do you recall what I said about the curse which rests on my land?”, the woman said. "How it's power is tied to the crimes of my people, and only through the atonement of those crimes can it ever be lifted?”

"Yeah, sort of.”

"Well, this object, Harin's Vault, is sealed by a very powerful and primal sort of magic, and it can only be opened through a series of mystical rites which entail an offering of tremendous power: A human sacrifice.”

"What!”

"There's no need for alarm!”, the Bird cut in. "We have not brought you here to harm you.”

"Oh yeah? And just who do you think you're going to sacrifice?”

"The Bird and I will not be participating in the sacrifice. Only you will.”

"Uh huh, that's kind of what I figured. You've got just two seconds to tell me why I shouldn't start running right now.”

"This is a bit difficult to explain”, the Bird said. "But let me start by assuring you that the sacrifice in question is not at all what you might think it is. It will entail a certain amount of discomfort, but in the end you shall come through it unharmed."

"So I *am* going to be the sacrifice, huh? That's what I figured. Goodbye!"

"Give us one more moment, Lindsey", Joan interjected. "This is precisely why I said the Bird should have explained things in advance."

"You better explain things right now then, and do it real fast."

"Alright, alright. Please be calm, and let me proceed. What we are asking is that you make a sacrifice of yourself on our behalf, by way of making an offering of your own life experiences. Your hardships, your sorrows, the dark feelings and evil memories you carry in your heart. The Bird read your heart the moment he saw you, and he perceived the burdens you carry inside you."

"I'm not really all that burdened."

"You may be more so than you think. The Bird saw it for himself, and he was convinced that you are greatly distressed. And for my own part, I am inclined to agree with him. I see in you a person whose heart is overwhelmed with an unbidden darkness. For a long while life has been unkind to you, and in many ways unjust. It is tempting to say that life owes you a debt for such years of undeserved suffering, but the reality is that life is by nature incapable of making good on the debts that it owes to the innocent. But you have the power within you to take control of these things for yourself, to transcend your own grief and direct it to a higher purpose. We need you to forsake the debt that life owes you, and offer it in exchange for the debts incurred by my people."

"What Joan is trying to say", interjected the Bird, "Is that what we need is a sort of proxy sacrifice. When the Good Folk sought a remedy for the plight of Joan's people they carefully examined the black magic of the Curse of Gurth to uncover its secrets and discover a means for its undoing. In this way they were able to discern the various weaknesses of the spell, and with this knowledge they devised a formula by which the spell could be broken. You see, the practice of black magic has a sort of cumulative effect. The more of it there is, the more potent it becomes and the more dire its effects. When Gurth proffered his dark arts to the people of Linster he did so with a purpose, drenching the land with evil magic so that when he at last laid his curse upon the kingdom he bound with it all the darkness which the people themselves had wrought for him.

"To undo this sinister artifice, something is needed to purify the land of the black magic which now impregnates it. In pondering this conundrum, The Good Folk concluded that the simplest means by which this could be done would be to disassociate the people of Linster from the deeds which they themselves had wrought. This could be achieved through the agency of a disinterested third party. This person could assume the burden of the people's responsibility, and then redress these deeds by virtue of her own personal tribulations. This could be manifested in a ritual of atonement, the completion of which would serve as a magical catalyst with which to strike the curse at its weakest point. Harin's Vault is not in itself of any particular importance to us. However, it requires a human sacrifice in order to be opened, which serves as a suitable vehicle by which the ritual of atonement may be performed. What we need from you now, Lindsey, is for you to volunteer yourself to succumb for a brief moment to what you might call a spiritual death: To momentarily relive every instance of sorrow and hardship in your life from the most trivial to the most tortuous as a substitute offering in reparation for deeds wrought by others. I'm afraid I can offer you no recompense for this service, for in order to work the sacrifice must be as pure as possible. This is why an alien from another world (such as yourself) is ideally suited for the task. The magic would not work if Joan or any of her people were to do such a thing for themselves, for they would directly benefit from it. In contrast, in your case once you return home to your own world you will have left all this behind, and will be as far removed from the fruits of your labor as possible. Indeed, save for ourselves, no one else may even be permitted to know the full extent of your role in this, if we are to have our best chance of success. The act of opening the vault will constitute the physical manifestation of the ritual itself. Once this is done, all that is required is to retrieve a sample of its contents (anything will do) and bring it back to Linster to serve as a tangible sign that the ritual took place and a physical manifestation of its completion. This will be sufficient to break the Curse of Gurth and deprive him of his hold on the people of Linster. There are a few other details regarding the specifics of the ritual itself which Joan shall explain to you (the proper recitations, motions, and so forth). But what I have just described is the essence of the matter. It is your choice whether we proceed further."

With that, the Bird fell silent. Lindsey was silent for a moment, frozen in a sudden tangle of emotion deep within her heart. And then, she gave her answer.

6

"A Rite of Atonement"

The sky above Harin's Vault was full of pale stars glimmering distantly in the cold darkness of the universe, as a half moon gradually made its descent into the horizon. At the feet of the vault, an array of flickering candles were scattered about among an occult web of stones set at various points within an intricate pattern of interlocking circles and polygons which had been traced into the ground. In the center of it all was a ring of pebbles containing two small clay vessels which held burning incense. For some time now Lindsey had been sitting by herself at the periphery, reciting in her mind the sequence of incantations which Joan had taught her. The Bird had gone to keep watch from the air, and Joan had just finished putting the finishing touches on a central pentagram which she was tracing in the ground inside the ring of pebbles between the two incense burners. Now she approached Lindsey and gently touched her shoulder. It was time.

Lindsey felt nervous. Very nervous, rather like she was about to take a flying leap into a frozen lake and be graded on how big a splash she made. Nevertheless she rose to her feet and followed Joan to the central pentagram. Next she changed clothes, first removing shoes and socks, and then everything else, until for a brief moment she stood before the universe in only her skin, though hardly as nature would have intended her. For the moon shone painfully on what little flesh she had, stretched as if to breaking across so many bones that one could almost count each of them. Joan now produced a flimsy shift of rough sackcloth, thinly woven and open at the back, offering no protection against the cut of the night breeze. Lindsey donned the penitential garment, and then knelt in the center of the pentagram, her bare knees digging uncomfortably into the earth. She now bent forward with her hands over her face in deep concentration, every rib and vertebrae she had projecting out through the fleshless skin of her pallid spine. And then she began.

The incantations were more than just the language of magic. Woven amidst the strange words and weird idioms, there was a thread of thought, each sentence constructed to help guide Lindsey's concentration along a path of dark self reflection. Bit by bit the phrases and imagery began to conjure memories in Lindsey's mind, memories she would much rather leave buried.

Joan had remained crouched at Lindsey's side for a moment, supporting her gently. Now, she drew the incense burners closer, and added a touch of some powder to each. As the two burners suddenly began to gutter with thick plumes of dark smoke Joan at last stepped aside and retreated to the distant perimeter of the clearing. For from now on Lindsey had to be on her own.

Lindsey shivered as the heavy scent of the smoky incense wafted up to her. For a moment her thoughts became clouded, until abruptly her mind broke through the haze into a state of painful clarity, fixated in a terrible place where reason was absent and bleak emotion reigned supreme. With each inhalation her imagination seemed to expand in leaps and bounds, while with each exhalation a new memory came to mind, each one more vivid and more agonizing than the last. She was breathing quickly now, and trying desperately not to cry. The scenes drifted before her mind one by one, all magnified and distorted to terrible proportions. Each memory brought a wave of associated emotions with it, of the kind which had haunted her existance for many long years. Feelings of worthlessness and self loathing, helplessness and bereavement, followed by guilt and humiliation for having succumbed to it all in the first place, which began the cycle of anguish all over again. The pain grew as each successive wave of emotion mounted on the other, and Lindsey felt a terrible sense of exposure as a frigid breeze swept into the clearing and gripped her skin like icy claws. The pain in her heart was so great now that she was beginning to feel it in her body, starting at her fingertips and spreading across her limbs in pulsating throbs. Lindsey was beginning to feel light headed. She felt her face contorting into a grimace that stretched and stretched but could never break into a sob. She felt that in another moment, she would surely explode.

"It's time to leave."

She had not heard the words. Rather, they had manifested themselves in her mind.

"It's time to leave, Lindsey. It's time to let go."

Lindsey began to feel more in control.

"Let go."

Still no words. Just thoughts in her mind. She began to take control of her breathing. She took deep breaths at first, easy, measured, and serene. As she did so her state of consciousness began to shift again. She felt herself drifting into a dreamlike state as a distorted version of the world around her was beginning to take form. She saw herself sitting in the midst of a warped and bleak landscape at the foot of a great shadowy caricature of the rock of Harin's Vault, while far in the distance black mountains were silhouetted against a flaming horizon. As she gazed at the imaginary vista around her, she realized that this was exactly the sort of place she had been living in for so many years. Dark, hopeless, and twisted beyond recognition, a place where reality itself had long since disappeared into a void of numb mindlessness where only sorrow existed. And there was no reason to stick around. Far in the distance, she could just hear the faint refrain of a lone flute echoing defiantly through darkness, while from somewhere outside this chimerical vision Lindsey felt a cool breeze against her skin as a current of fresh air from the real world wafted into her lungs. For years she had been living in a private hell all her own. And she wasn't going to live in that place any longer. With one last look at the spectral hellscape around her, Lindsey got up and walked away. And then in a flash, it all disappeared.

Lindsey's eyes snapped open. The imaginary world was gone, and she was back in reality. She was still kneeling in the exact spot where she had begun the ritual. The incense had burned itself out, the gravel below her was thrust painfully into the thin flesh of her knees, and her freezing skin was drenched with a cold sweat. Suddenly exhausted, Lindsey collapsed to the ground and began to cry.

Joan was by her side in a moment, undoing the clasp of her cloak and wrapping the cloak snugly around Lindsey's chilled body, hugging her tightly while murmuring soft words of encouragement. Lindsey rested her tear stained face against Joan's breast, still breathing heavily from crying as Joan held her. A proper, thorough cry had relieved Lindsey enough that she could at last bring her mind back into focus. The nightmare was over, and Lindsey now breathed in the cool, refreshing air of reality all around her. "Well done Lindsey, you did it! Look, the vault is open!"

Lindsey turned her eyes toward the great black rock, somehow looking not quite so large and black as it had before. In its side there was now an opening, a domed arch above a tall doorway from which streamed a warm light. A broken shale of rock was poured out before it, creating a sort of ramp which was the only approach. Joan helped Lindsey to her feet. "It will seal up again in a moment. Go inside now, there's not much time." Lindsey paused to pull her shoes on nonetheless. She was not about to be going over all that sharp rock in her bare feet. Wrapping Joan's cloak about her, she clamored up the rockfall, and slipped through the door.

The door led to a stepped passageway no wider than was the door itself, spiraling upward into the heart of the great stone. The interior was perfectly smooth, bored out of the living rock without any sign of brick or mortar, and was illuminated by a golden glow which seemed to come from nowhere. The passage must have curled nearly all the way around the inner circumference of the rock before it opened into a great vaulted chamber which was taller than it was wide, rather like the interior of an egg, and filled with warm light which seemed to emanate from the very walls. And it looked to Lindsey like some sort of Tut's Tomb.

In the center was a great golden statue of some being which looked half man, half dragon with six eyes on its face, each composed of different colored gemstones. The perimeter was completely lined with a dazzling array of precious objects. Statues, urns, goblets, crowns, swords, shields, mirrors, books, talismans, scrolls, and heaven only knew what else. Everywhere there was gold and silver and a rainbow of brilliant gems. Lindsey stood dumbfounded by it all, distantly wondering to herself who had gathered such a hoard and why it had all been locked away so many ages ago.

But that was speculation, unimportant at present. Lindsey had a job to do. She began to wander the room, looking for something small she could carry out with her easily. Suddenly, she had a sense that she wasn't alone anymore. She turned quickly, wrapping her cloak more closely about her. Through the door there loomed a massive figure, a towering man in a double breasted suit and grey homburg hat.

There was no mistaking him. He was definitely the same man who had given Lindsey his handkerchief and iodine in Zhongyang, and had apparently been following her ever since. The man met Lindsey's eye and tipped his hat cordially, as Lindsey backed a bit further in the room, wrapping her cloak about her more tightly. What did the man want? Was he an enemy? Lindsey glanced about her for anything which she might use to protect herself, and reached for a rather fearsome looking battle axe. As she did so, the man raised one finger. "I shouldn't bother with the axe, miss. It would be troublesome to carry. A small trinket perhaps would be more suited to your purposes." The man stepped over to a small gilded cabinet, and perused its contents briefly. "Aha, I thought as much. Something such as this will do." He extracted a small piece of jewelry, a medallion of some sort on a silver chain, and tossed it to Lindsey. "Now if you will excuse me." The man stepped over to a pile of books and scrolls, and began rummaging intently. Suddenly, he snatched up one of the books, opened it, turned a few leaves, snapped it shut again and then thrust it into his coat with the savage swiftness of a tiger. He turned to Lindsey, and tipped his hat again. "Thank you miss. You have been most helpful. Good afternoon." And then the man stepped out through the door from whence he had come and disappeared down the passage.

Lindsey stood still for a moment, wondering what the hell had just happened. A vague feeling of having been used in some way was starting to creep over her her. Suddenly, it occurred to her that wherever the man had come from, he must have come past Joan and the others. Why hadn't they……

A jolt of panic shot through Lindsey. Had something happened to the others? Still clutching the medallion, she ran out of the treasure room and down the stairs. Outside, the candles had been extinguished. Joan was gone. The man in the suit was gone. Instead, before her stood six tall beings in grey robes with hoods pulled low, obscuring their faces. And each now began approaching her while reaching into their robes and drawing short, wickedly curved swords which glittered in the moonlight.

Lindsey thought quickly. She didn't think she could run down the shale fast enough to get away, not without falling. If she went back in the vault, she'd be trapped. The robed things were starting cautiously up the shale now. Lindsey knew she had only a few seconds. What to do? The loose shale. Lindsey bent and snatched up a sharp rock from the slide and threw it at the leading figure. The rock missed as the thing ducked, but all six suddenly hesitated, and Lindsey began frantically throwing rocks at the whole group.

"Joan! Hae-jin! Anybody!" Lindsey's voice all but screeched as she grabbed for more rocks, barely able to keep up the barrage, much less aim. The robed things were part way up the slide now, halting and ducking as they tried to anticipate each projectile. One of them began to charge straight up the rockslide, and Lindsey turned and ran back inside the vault.

She made it breathlessly into the chamber, her pursuer perhaps only a few seconds behind her. Frantically casting about, Lindsey grabbed the large axe she had picked up earlier from the piles of treasure, and swung it straight at the door just as the robed thing came charging through. The thing fell with a hideous sort of gurgle. Lindsey didn't even stop to see if she'd hurt it, she leaped over its collapsed form and headed back down the passage. She wasn't even thinking no;, all she could do was run.

She nearly ran straight into the rest of the group, who were just now pressed at the door. With a shriek Lindsey swung her axe at the lead one, who careened backward against the unexpected attack, stumbling into his comrades as he did so. All five seemed to lose their footing on the shale simultaneously, and they rolled backward down the rock slide into a heap on the ground.

As her assailants struggled momentarily to untangle themselves, Lindsey started to make her way down the shale, but backed off right away as she nearly lost her own footing on the loose shale, which was still moving. The robed things were now hauling themselves to the feet even as the last of the shale was tumbling into them. Lindsey slung the medallion around her neck, and brandished the axe. She had a sickening feeling she probably wasn't going to make it this time.

Then, down on the ground to one side of the robed figures, the man in the suit suddenly returned, appearing out of nowhere in the midst of the pit. In one hand he clutched a silver knobbed cane, in the other a small, nickel plated pistol. And as he approached the group of robed figures, he began firing.

The robed things scattered in pandemonium ahead of the unexpected attack, some of them apparently hit. Eleven shots rang out, and the man in the suit then coolly changed magazines, and continued to shoot. Lindsey knew this was her chance. She scrambled down the shale as the robed figures screamed in some horrible sounding language to one another in confusion. She made it to the bottom and ran behind the man in the suit.

The man in the suit reloaded again, and continued to fire at the robed figures. Two of them were writhing on the ground and one was still, while the remaining two were running towards the perimeter of the pit.

The man turned to Lindsey.

"Now's our chance. Come with me."

With that, he slashed at the air with his cane, tracing an arc which left in its wake a thin trail of fire. Jamming his pistol into a pocket he grabbed Lindsey's wrist in an iron grip and dragged her through the ring of fire. And both disappeared into the night air.

7

"The Drixi"

It was a beautiful night, really. The moon shone brightly amidst a chorus of scintillating stars, the air was clear and cool and the breeze courted the trees with a soothing rush of reverberating leaves. Hae-jin felt a remarkable sense of peace, utterly ruined of course by the fact that he was quite busy trying to keep watch for an unknown foe in a foreign land for the protection of persons Hae-jin had only met a few short hours ago, all this after having been turned out from his home and branded an outlaw in his own land just a few days before.....Really, it was all a bit much. Thoroughly mad, in point of fact. Hae-jin had been in wild and unpredictable situations before, but nothing remotely like this. In joining the Bird's enterprise, Hae-jin had been given a chance at finding a new life for himself, and thus far it had certainly gotten off to an extraordinary start. Where indeed it would all lead in the end Hae-jin couldn't imagine.

It was quiet. Distractingly quiet. One could nearly be drawn into a trance by the beauty of it all. But Hae-jin had to focus. Right now, there were people whose lives depended on his vigilance. Though lost in a whirlwind of weird experiences, this was something he knew. Hae-jin was an old veteran. He had long known the weight of such responsibilities. Such was his way of life. This was something he understood, and this was something he could meet with certitude. Alien though the world now was to him, there are some things which never change. Honor, duty, and loyalty to one's friends. And one's instinct for battle.

Something was wrong. Was it a sound? The movement of large groups of well armed men is a difficult thing to conceal. Perhaps it had been the clatter of armor, or perhaps an errant footfall. Whatever it was, Hae-jin had heard it, and somehow he already knew what he would see as he peered out past the forest edge. Yes, just out there. Just a couple of them, careless perhaps, or overconfident. Tall figures in grey robes, armed with spear and shield. At least they were well enough trained to keep their spear tips pointed to the ground, where there was less chance of someone seeing the glint of moonlight reflected in the steel. But the damage was done, they'd let themselves be seen. Hae-jin could count only two, maybe three. But his instincts told him there were more. Many, many more.

Suddenly, Hae-jin froze, his ears pricked, listening intently. From somewhere behind him, there was a voice, desperate and terrified. It was Lindsey, calling frantically to Hae-jin and the others. There was no time to lose. Hae-jin was about to head for the pit when the men in the distance began to move. And there were more, dozens more, moving in swift order from concealment among the rocks and gullies. One appeared on a brilliant white horse which shone majestically in the moonlight, who beckoned to the men to follow as he spurred his animal towards the woods. Hae-jin knew he couldn't help Lindsey now by returning. He could only hope Ursilda or the Wogs had heard the call also. Taking a breath and mentally preparing for combat, he stepped out into the creek bed, and drew his sword. The robed warriors stopped their approach just out of reach, leveling scores of spears at Hae-jin's chest. From all around, commands and cries could be heard as more unseen soldiers converged on the place. Hae-jin surmised that there must have been several hundred soldiers surrounding the area of the vault. The warrior on the white horse spurred his animal closer, and spoke. "In the name of Lords of the Drixi, I command you to surrender immediately. You are under arrest as an illegal impossibility in violation of the sacred edicts."

Hae-jin raised his sword and aimed the point at the warrior's face. "I am General Moon Hae-jin. I shall kill any man who advances upon me."

"Drixi advance upon you, not men. You are completely surrounded, Moon Hae-jin. Surrender, and you may yet be permitted to live."

"Heaven alone will permit me to live or die. I am resigned to either. Are you equally prepared to die?"

"I have no need to be. I have already won." From far behind him, there now came a peculiar popping noise that sounded to Hae-jin like New Year's firecrackers. The man on the horse had heard it also, and appeared disturbed. "You will surrender now, Moon Hae-jin, or I will order my warriors to slay you where you stand."

"Then give the order."

"As you wish, human." The mounted Drixi raised a gloved fist. With a shout, the warriors attacked. Hae-jin had only a moment to act before the warriors were upon him. Catching his scabbard up like a spear, he hurled it at the face of the leading warrior, who, with well drilled instincts, immediately ducked behind his shield. But the distraction had upset his rhythm just enough, and for a fleeting moment the wave of soldiers was bottlenecked, and Hae-jin ran pell mell back down the narrow creek bed to a point so tight that hardly two could stand abreast. There he halted, and turned to make his next stand.

The soldiers crammed their way through the gully, their large shields pinned to their sides. The sudden vulnerability of the formation was not lost on the Drixi, and the soldiers slowed their pace slightly and approached with caution, closing steadily. It was a hard contest now. The first soldiers were now within spear's reach, and though only a few in the narrow confines could wield their weapons with any measure of dexterity, Hae-jin was still pressed hard to beat aside their points with his sword. A cry went up, and Hae-jin took a quick look behind him.

More soldiers, coming up the gully from the rear. The Drixi must have already taken the vault below! There was no point in holding out any longer. Hae-jin broke and leapt for the treeline, skipping through the brush as best he could. From behind, he could hear the shouts and clamour of the Drixi as they gave pursuit. They had broken ranks and were now climbing out of the creek bed. Some of them were now free enough to throw their spears, which fell heavily about Hae-jin as he ran. One of them nearly clipped his ankle, and Hae-jin tripped and fell. He clamoured to his feet momentarily, and then stumbled again in the brush as more spears fell hard about him. In a moment, he was surrounded by Drixi warriors leveling a forest of spearheads at him, and the contest was over.

Hae-jin was hauled roughly to his feet, his arms seized and pinned behind his back. He was all but dragged out of the woods and back to the gully, and was then marched the rest of the way to the base of the vault. The clearing about the vault was a picture of military order. Torches had been driven into the ground as soldiers made their way to and fro. In the center, the Drixi commander had dismounted, and stood now beside his white horse, conversing with his lieutenants. Hae-jin saw a fresh pile of black shale against the side of the great stone of Harin's Vault, which created a sort of ramp. But there was no opening to be seen. Three bodies in grey robes were lined neatly in a row upon the ground, apparently dead. Nearby stood two other figures in identical robes with the hoods pulled low over their eyes, keeping out of the action. And in the center of the clearing sat Joan and the three Wogs, disarmed and under heavy guard. There was no sign of the Bird, Ursilda, or Lindsey. The warriors stopped before their commander, exchanging a brief word before proceeding and shoving Hae-jin roughly to the ground among his companions. He met Joan's eye, and her gaze was steady, but she remained silent. The Wogs merely stared off into the woods, ignoring Hae-jin completely. Silence appeared to be the order of the moment, and Hae-jin sat down wearily without speaking a word.

For the first time, Hae-jin had an opportunity to get a clear look at the Drixi. They were tall beings, thin and willowy of build, so much so as to appear slightly unnatural, or at least not entirely human. They were armored in glittering steel scales sewn atop padded coats which reached just above their knees, with jackchains wrought in various designs running the length of the arms. Their heads were protected by short conical helms with mantles of mail, their faces obscured by steel visors faced with linen, which was painted like colorful masks. Likewise, their tall, hexagonal shields were painted with dazzling patterns and fantastic animals, and everywhere they bore images of eyes, either as central devices or worked into the intricate patterns.

There was movement now where the Drixi officers had been in council. The commander was approaching the prisoners, accompanied by two of his lieutenants. Hae-jin watched as they approached and came to a stop just out of reach, towering over their captives with a nebulous menace. The Drixi commander regarded Hae-jin and the others for a moment, his own eyes invisible in the shadow of his mask, while the eyes engraved all around the circumference of his helmet seemed to do all the staring required; eerie inanimate sculptures keeping an unseeing watch in every direction. The Drixi then raised a pair of gauntleted hands bearing six fingers each, and removed his helmet. The Drixi had pale skin dotted with many freckles, luxurious platinum colored hair and wickedly pointed ears like that of a demon. His face was of a fairly ordinary shape, though tending a bit towards the angular, and his lips were pale and his eyes a bright violet. A third eye was painted in the middle of his forehead in a deep purple dye. The Drixi was exotically beautiful, simultaneously magnetic and repellent in a way which struck Hae-Jin as more like that of an uncaged tiger than anything else. Intractable, wary, unpredictable, and consummately dangerous. The Drixi commander met Hae-jin's eye without speaking. Then, he addressed the Wogs. "Well, Alwog of Wog. Do you have anything to say to your lords? I expect you already have a plethora of lies prepared for me."

"Not in the least", the Wog said evenly. "I have no idea why you have arrested me and my brothers. We were merely out for a walk."

"This far from your home? And in full armor?"

"Dangerous out here. I heard a rumor there were humans about. Gotta take precautions. And when it comes to that, why are you forcing me and my brothers to sit so close to two of them? Dangerous, I call it. A hazard to public safety. I'll protest this before the Arbiters!"

"So you swear you know nothing about these humans?"

"Positively nothing."

"You're a liar, Alwog."

"Never seen the like of them before! How could I? They're *supposed* to be impossible, you know. The Drixi are *supposed* to have fixed it so. Have your bosses bungled again?"

"Mind your tongue, Wog, if you want to keep it." The Drixi then turned to Hae-jin. "Where's the bear, human?", he demanded.

Hae-jin decided that it might be best to go along with the theme outlined by Alwog, and perhaps improve upon it. He bit out each word carefully, as if he were an ordinary foreigner with no gift of tongues to grant him mastery of the local language. "I...do not....understand....I do not know your language much."

"You were speaking quite fluently earlier in the creekbed."

"I speak only so-so, some good, some bad. What did you say?"

"Where is the bear?"

"What is bear?"

"Don't lie to me! We were informed that the Wogs were seen with three humans, a bear, and a golden bird. The bear attacked my warriors and gravely wounded two of them before fleeing into the woods. I want that animal, human."

"I do not know about bears. Why not ask bird you speak of?"

The Drixi held his temper. He turned a glaring eye upon Joan. "Well? I assume *you* can't speak Drixi either."

Joan stared dumbly back at the Drixi, opening her mouth and gurgling while pointing to the back of her throat. The Drixi snorted derisively. "A mute, and a feigned one, I'll warrant", he said. "We'll loosen your human tongues soon enough." The Drixi turned to his lieutenants. "Continue to search the area. We'll hold this lot."

"Shall I direct some of the men to interrogate the prisoners, sir?"

"We'll leave that up to the Arbiters. Leave the prisoners unharmed unless they attempt to escape. Kill them immediately if they should attempt to do so."

And that was that. Hae-jin and the others sat for what seemed like hours, hardly moving and without speaking. The Drixi went to and fro, passing orders and reports. It was remarkable to Hae-jin that they should be going to so much trouble. Based on the snippets he could overhear, he estimated that there must have been at least three hundred Drixi in the area. So many troops to apprehend just a handful of alien intruders....the Drixi must be very fearful of foreigners indeed, or at least fearful of humans. That, or there was more going on than first met the eye.....

Hae-jin found himself examining the two robed beings standing beside the row of dead bodies. They were not dressed like the warriors, though their robes were of a similar cut and color. Nor were they participating in the search. They remained aloof and interacted with no one save the Drixi commander, who spoke to them briefly only once. The Drixi likewise kept their distance, hardly even approaching them. In all the bustle of the operation, the area about the robed figures remained clear.

Dawn was beginning to break. The Wogs had fallen asleep in a pile. Joan's head was sagging on her breast, and Hae-jin kept catching himself nodding off. It had been a thoroughly miserable night. A horn now sounded from somewhere outside the clearing. The prisoners all snapped awake as a minor commotion spread through the ad-hoc encampment. In another moment there was a second horn blast, and then a third. Three horsemen now entered the clearing. Two of them were clearly Drixi, armored as were the others, with their helms surmounted with brilliant plumes, and their cloaks held with great jeweled brooches. The third was swathed entirely in grey robes, hooded and unarmored, and Hae-jin noted the three mysterious robed figures at last abandoned their vigil by the bodies and approached the newcomers along with the Drixi officers, who saluted the mounted Drixi by touching their temples with an open palm (which appeared to represent the act of covering their eyes for a moment, without actually doing so). The Drixi officers spoke to one another, while the robed figures remained silent. They gestured towards the prisoners on a number of occasions, and Hae-jin was hardly surprised when at length a group of soldiers was dispatched in their direction, and Hae-jin, Joan and the Wogs were hauled roughly to their feet and marched over to the group of officers. The two mounted Drixi sat on their horses with their helmets resting on their saddles, their violet eyes tracking the prisoners and their faces inscrutable. As they approached, Hae-jin was marched past one of the grey robed figures, and he took that moment to take a quick look at them up close for the first time. Just beneath the rim of the hood, Hae-jin saw something dreadful. A long, reptilian sort of snout, covered in dark scales, and just the hint of a pair of yellow, serpentine eyes. From beside him he heard a suppressed gasp from Joan, she too must have seen that face. Whatever the creature was, it was like nothing Hae-jin had ever seen before. The Drixi officers interviewed them. Again, the Wogs foreswore any knowledge of Joan, Hae-jin, and the others. Joan continued to play the mute, and Hae-jin continued his pretense of not understanding the language. The Drixi were not in the least bit convinced by any of their performances, but did not press them further. The robed creatures said nothing.

It was apparently decided that the prisoners were to be taken away by the newcomers while the original troop remained behind to continue searching the area around the mountain. Before they departed, Hae-jin observed the robed creatures conversing with their newly arrived counterpart. Meanwhile, the dead bodies were laid on carts, along with the captured possessions of the prisoners, and horses were provided for each of the robed creatures. Apparently they would be accompanying the prisoners also. Hae-jin shivered. Hae-jin, Joan and the Wogs had their hands bound in front of them now, and they were strung together like fish on a line. At last, they were marched out of the dreary pit surrounding Harin's vault, exhausted and stumbling into the light of day. There were perhaps a couple hundred more troops now all around the area of Harin's Vault, freshly arrived reinforcements to help bolster the search, while another substantial company of soldiers were to escort the prisoners to wherever they were going. The Drixi certainly took no chances. And then the march began. To where, Hae-jin could not even guess.

8

"The Man in the Suit"

Lindsey halted, breathless and disoriented. A moment ago she had been fighting for her life at Harin's Vault, and now here she stood with her erstwhile rescuer. The gravel had turned to floorboard, the empty pit to papered walls, the sky to a plastered ceiling, the chill air to a comfortable sort of must, and the screams and cries of her assailants into silence. Now, she found herself inside an old house. How old she couldn't be sure, but it was certainly not new construction. Through the heavy wood-framed window the last vestiges of moonlight shone through, illuminating the room in a grey twilight. The paper on the walls was faded (and peeling in places), the floor scratched and worn, and the woodwork cracked and split here and there. The room was all but empty, save for cobwebs, an end table, and a chair.

The man in the suit said nothing. He stepped to the window and looked out, with the air of a master inspecting his domain after a brief absence. He then pulled down an old fashioned wind-up curtain, and motioned Lindsey to follow him out of the room. The hall was pitch dark, but only for a moment, for the instant they were inside with the door shut behind them the man in the suit flicked on a lightswitch. Immediately the hall was bathed in the warmth of old incandescent bulbs. The man in the suit turned to Lindsey, and removed his hat. "My apologies for the necessary abruptness. The circumstances afforded no capacity for gentility."

"Who are you?", Lindsey demanded guardedly.

"I suppose that I am your rescuer", the man said. "Yeah, thanks", Linsdey replied. "But who are you? What are you doing here? I mean not here, but at the vault......you've been following us all this time haven't you? Who are you, and what do you want?

"I shall answer your questions in due course. But first, perhaps I should show you to my drawing room. If you would come this way, miss..." The man led the way down the hall into a darkened room. The moon must have been on the other side of the house, for the interior of the room was swathed in darkness, while outside Lindsey could see a hint of rolling parkland. The man crossed the room to the windows and began to close the curtains. "Where are we, anyway?", Lindsey asked.

"New England", the man replied. "Connecticut, to be precise."

"And this house?"

"Mine."

"And you are?"

The man had finished closing the curtains. He reached now to a table lamp, and flicked it on. The room was heavily paneled and lined with bookshelves. Thick velvet curtains now covered the windows. A fireplace with a colonial looking mantle filled one side of the room, over which was mounted an assortment of exotic looking weapons. Everywhere there were odd curios of some sort. African masks, old flintlock pistols, animal heads, Chinese jade and blue ceramics, assorted seashells and coral. In one corner there was an old radio, in another a victrola.

The furniture was an eclectic mix of styles ranging from victorian to asiatic, colonial, and art deco, all very old.

The man had turned on a second light, and was now looking Lindsey up and down. Lindsey was keenly reminded that she was still wearing basically nothing but a scant piece of sackcloth and a borrowed cloak, which she now drew about herself a bit more tightly. The man clicked his tongue disapprovingly. "You will be needing a change of clothes, of course. If you would follow me again, I should have something which you can use. You can leave *that* in here, for now." Up to now, Lindsey had forgotten that she was still clutching the axe which she had taken from Harin's vault. Gingerly, she leaned it against a chair, unsure whether it was a good idea to let herself be parted from a weapon (under the circumstances). However, whoever this man was he had already gone out of his way once to protect her, and if he'd had any idea of assaulting her now he'd already had plenty of opportunity to disarm her. She set the axe down.

The man led the way back through the hall and into a spare bedroom filled with as equally an eclectic mix of antique furniture as the drawing room. The man turned on a lamp and opened a large wardrobe, from which hung an assortment of old, neatly pressed clothes intermixed with bags of mothballs. "Please select anything which suits you", he said. "I have no use for any of these clothes, whatever you take you may keep."

"Thanks", Linsdey replied uncertainly.

"You're quite welcome", the man replied cordially. "When you're finished I will be in the drawing room." With that, the man left the room and shut to door behind him, which Lindsey promptly locked. The wardrobe contained a fair mix of clothes; all of them in good shape, but old. Very old, many decades at least. After a brief inspection Lindsey selected a off-white, vintage looking drop waisted dress trimmed in green, buttoning at the front, with a pleated skirt and deep pockets. It hung quite loosely over Lindsey's withered frame, but it was a good enough fit. As she closed the buttons her hands brushed the medallion which still hung from her neck. She paused, and turned now to look in a mirror which hung on an antique vanity beside the wardrobe.

The medallion was composed of golden strands woven into a swirling interlace pattern, with four lobes at even intervals and a small rose colored crystal at its center, all glittering brightly against the ripples of Lindsey's emaciated chest. Supposedly this thing would break the curse on Joan's kingdom, if Lindsey could ever manage to get it there. Lindsey finished buttoning her dress, concealing the medallion between the fabric and her skin. She discarded the rough sackcloth shift, leaving it folded on the bed, but she took Joan's cloak. She didn't want to owe the strange man for anything more than necessary, and she had a feeling she might wind up needing the extra warmth. Besides, she may someday be able to return it to Joan. What had happened to Joan, anyway? And the Bird and the others? Where were they when she called? Had something bad happened? Were they alright? Why did they leave her? At any rate, apparently she was now back in her own world. Though in this house full of antiques and collectibles, she wondered whether she hadn't been transported back in time eighty or ninety years.

She had no difficulty finding her way back to the drawing room. The door was left open, and there were more lights on. She returned to find the man seated comfortably in an easy chair, wearing an old smoking jacket and examining the axe which she had left behind. The man looked up. "Ah, very nice", he said. "That dress belonged to one of my nieces. I always thought it was quite fine, it suits your complexion very well."

"Thanks", Lindsey said neutrally. "Won't your niece want it later though?"

"All of my nieces are now deceased, I'm afraid."

"That's awful! I'm so sorry!"

"Thank you, but it is not so bad as it might sound. They all lived long lives by the measure of men."

"What do you mean by that?"

The man did not reply. He looked back down at the axe. "Quite a remarkable specimen", he said. "Vorpal, and good quality vorpal at that, possibly of ancient Sauvlandic origin."

"Vorpal?"

"Yes. You can tell by the violet hue of the steel. The color varies in intensity, depending on where the steel was forged, the quality and so forth. The shaft of course is Black Narwhal, quite rare indeed. Have a look at it." The man handed Lindsey the axe. Before her attention had been focused entirely on staying alive, and it was only now as she held the weapon in her hands again that she really took a good look at it. It seemed relatively light weight for its size. It's shaft was a grey-black bone about four and half feet long, which was weirdly springy for bone and helically spiraled to a sharp steel shod point. The head was very wide but also very thin, with a long sweeping edge which was canted slightly forward. It was made of a brightly polished steel with a faint violet hue which became more intense further away from the sharpened edge.

The man was still speaking. "..Vorpal of course is an Elven alloy. It is not particularly extraordinary as steel goes, quite average and even a little on the soft side. It often has to be laminated at the edge with ordinary high carbon steel in order to hold a proper edge. What makes it special is the ease with which it can be enchanted. A weapon made of vorpal is typically used with spoken or otherwise triggered enchantments, which (in the hands of a skilled user) can enhance the weapon's performance beyond that which is possible with ordinary steel. Things like splitting hardened steel armor or intercepting large numbers of fast moving projectiles. But in unskilled hands it's really just an exotic looking weapon, nothing more. Some vorpal weapons can impart the skills and experience of their previous users onto their present owner, but that does not appear to be the case with this one. Vorpal weapons have been produced by the Elven smiths for millennia, and continue to be made to this day. But this particular weapon is quite ancient, and I daresay extremely valuable (even though it is not one of the weapon's which teach). It would likely be worth a king's ransom in the Fairworld."

"Speaking of", Lindsey cut in, anxious to get answers. "We're not in the Fairworld anymore, are we? You said we were in Connecticut."

"Correct."

"New England."

"Yes. New England, just as it has been for generations."

"So you're from my world...our world...you're not from the Fairworld at all?"

"Not originally, no. Like yourself, I am one of the many few who have crossed between. By that I mean that while there are many like us who have crossed, our numbers are really quite few as a proportion of the human race as a whole. You see, there is a sort of constant leakage between the Fairworld and our own. Has been since the dawn of history. The fairy folk have always tried to conceal their existence from the world at large, but their influence is nonetheless unmistakable. Once you've seen enough of both you can clearly observe the cultural continuities across both worlds. The exact degree of their influence has varied in different places and in different periods. There have been times when the fairy folk were more kindly disposed towards the people of our world, and actively encouraged humans to migrate to theirs. On occasion they have spirited away entire populations, absorbing whole tribes and fiefdoms into their world and erasing them from human history. The last large-scale interaction that I am aware of seems to have occured in western Europe sometime during the mid 14th to late 15th centuries, with a brief resurgence towards the end of the Renaissance and the dawn of the Industrial Revolution. Since then, the fair folk have engaged with us less and less, and in more recent times they have gone to great lengths to discourage any large-scale interaction with our world."

"But how did you learn to cross between worlds?", Lindsey asked. "That thing you did with your cane earlier...."

"Yes, the technique is a secret which the fair folk guard very closely, for *they* certainly don't want us all to come and go from their little world at will (as they themselves do). But they couldn't keep it from me, not forever. It took years, but I eventually wrested the secret from them and learned the ways of Doormaking. Speaking of doormakers, I noticed that the Bird wasn't there when you needed him: I had to return for you."

"Where was he?"

The man shrugged. "I warned you back in Zhongyang not to trust the Bird. I see I was right."

"Yeah, I guess you were, maybe. Thanks for coming back for me, by the way. Why did you do it?"

The man shrugged again. "It was the decent thing to do. Would you care for something to eat?" The man gestured towards a tray which was newly set on one of the tables, containing coffee, plates of cheese, crackers, and what looked like salami. Lindsey declined politely. The man regarded her critically for a moment, but said nothing, and Lindsey instead sat down in one of the chairs.

"How old is this house?", she asked.

"It was originally built in 1681."

"How long have you lived here?"

"I was born here."

"Oh. I guess it must be nice to live in the same house you were born in."

"I suppose so."

"And this is still the twenty-first century?"

"Yes it is."

"Good. For a while I wasn't sure, this house feels like something straight out of the old days. It could be a museum. Where did you get all this stuff? Sorry, I guess I shouldn't be asking so many personal questions. I still don't even know your name."

"Yes, I suppose I have been most remiss. Allow me to introduce myself." The man stood up and towered over Lindsey, his visage somewhat terrifying as his frame faded into the darkness above the light of the table lamps. "My name is Horatio Dackery. I am, shall we say, a longtime student of the arcane and supernatural."

Lindsey stood up and extended her hand. "Pleased to meet you Mr. Dackery. My name is Lindsey Fluger. It's nice to meet you."

They shook hands and sat down again. "How did you end up at Harin's vault right when I'd gotten it open?", Lindsey asked. "I guess that was because you were following the Bird and me."

"Correct", the man said. "I was indeed following you."

"Why?"

"I have been searching for a way to get inside Harin's Vault for many years. When I learned that the Bird was going to make an attempt, I thought it was the best chance I was ever likely to get. I was right."

"Huh. The Bird sure isn't very good at keeping a secret, is he? You got what you wanted, I assume?"

"Yes."

"What was it?"

"Oh, just a book. Like I said, I am a student of sorts. I study magic."

"Yeah, I kind of guessed that. How did you get involved with the Fairworld?"

Dackery was pouring himself a cup of coffee. He cocked an eye now at Lindsey. "How old do I look to you, Ms. Fluger?"

"Huh? Oh, I dunno. Um...forty maybe?"

"Would you be surprised then to know that I was born in the year 1889?"

"What!", Lindsey exclaimed. "You've got to be kidding....though I guess with all the stuff I've seen today....but that would make you..."

"One hundred twenty-eight."

"Well, you sure as heck don't look it."

"I really haven't aged much over the last eighty years. But I am getting older nonetheless. I feel it every day."

"How did you manage to extend your life so long?"

"I've studied the magics of longevity quite extensively. It is, shall we say, one of my pet interests. Some have even called it an obsession (rather rudely, I think)."

"But how did you get started?"

Dackery leaned back in his chair, and sipped at his coffee. "The study of spiritualism and the occult were quite fashionable when I was a young man. I acquired a keen interest in it, and began drifting among the various esoteric societies that were cropping up everywhere back in the early nineteen hundreds. I quickly found the occult world to be populated by an assortment of charlatans and self deluded megalomaniacs. Though I confess to have participated at first, I gradually became disgusted with their grotesque rites and amoral excesses, and I turned to studying on my own. I learned to discount the various forgeries and fantasies which were being circulated in those days, and began instead to travel among the great libraries of Europe and America to study the secrets of the past. There too I found all manner of delusional nonsense, written in books by (purportedly) sober and knowledgeable men (with degrees from some of the most exalted institutions). But then, at long last, I discovered something real. Hidden amidst millennia of gibberish from strained human minds, I began to find references to another world. Just hints at first, enough that I had an idea of where to look further. And the more I looked, the more I found. And eventually, I found a Door.

I was amazed, of course. And overjoyed. I began to explore the Fairworld, and sought out the fairy folk everywhere I could. And I found them, and offered them my worship. But they rebuked me, and condemned me for treating them as gods, which is perhaps the truest thing they had ever done. For I learned quickly that they are not gods in the least. No, no gods could be so capricious as they. They have their rules, you see. And they use them to hoard their magic for themselves. They do not care about the suffering of the human race, not here in this world and not even in their own, really. They entice people to their world only to leave them to stagnate in whatever backward social state they originally came from. Wars, plagues, famine, crime, hate, heartbreak. All of these things plague the human race of both worlds. And what have the fairy folk ever done about it?"

"I think they try to help. I mean, that's what they brought me to do."

"Yes, they brought *you* to do it, didn't they? Why couldn't they have done it themselves? Why do they have these little games where people have to do this or that, running errands for the fairies and getting themselves hurt or killed in the process. And for what? To do that which the fairies themselves should have done in the first place."

Dackery set down his coffee. "Ah well, that's neither here nor there I suppose. You're in the middle of all this, and that's what counts. It's quite late now, and we both could use some sleep, I think. I have no great love for the fairies, but they at least are not as bad as the beings who tried to kill you tonight at the vault. We should be safe here for now, but they are a resourceful lot. Though the fairy folk do their utmost to prevent it, sometimes witches and the like manage to open doors to our own world nonetheless, and if they are really irritated they may try to pursue us. You may have use of the guest room I showed you earlier. Be sure to keep the door locked and the window securely bolted. My own room is in another part of the house, but I shall sleep in here tonight to ensure you are not disturbed."

9

"Breakfast after a Long Night"

Lindsey did not sleep well. Sequestered in Dackery's guest room with the door and window bolted and barricaded with as much furniture as she could readily move, she spent the night in a swirl of semi-consciousness, filled with cries, shrieks, and dark shadows as her thoughts drifted numbly among questions and fears, in between moments of wakefulness, all the while begging vainly to herself for anything like true sleep.

She awoke suddenly, the half thoughts and half dreams vanishing in an instant as her mind burst into consciousness. Something had happened. Lindsey looked about herself. Yes, something had happened alright. She'd gone to sleep in a bedroom of a strange house somewhere on the East Coast. And now here she was awake, in a completely different place. She wasn't lying amidst the sweaty tangle of sheets she'd gone to sleep in, but on a bed of dry moss. The dingy room was gone, and all about her the morning sun pierced through the tops of great trees towering above a forest of giant ferns. What had happened? How had she come to this place? Apparently, she had been transported from her room sometime during the night. Was this Dackery's doing? Or had the Bird returned and dragged her through one of his holes while she slept? Or was this the work of something else entirely......

Lindsey pulled herself to her feet and began to walk about. Wherever she was, it was by far the most alien place she'd experienced yet. She pinched herself a couple of times to rule out whether she were dreaming, but it really wasn't necessary. Once you're fully conscious, there's never any mistaking reality over a dream, and this was most certainly real. The landscape was a strange mixture of the exotic and ordinary. Everything seemed quite normal at once, yet at the same time wholly unfamiliar. Great plants like ferns, or perhaps palms, grew about her on all sides, and Lindsey found herself staring at them, trying to place where she'd seen such things before, even as she could swear to herself that she'd never seen their like. Then, the truth hit her. They weren't ferns at all. They were grasses. Yes, now that she realized it she recognized all the plants about her. The perfectly ordinary, just of enormous size. Here there was a dandelion stalk nearly fifteen feet high with a flower the size of a boulder. Over there were clovers the size of dinner plates. Either she was walking in a land of giants, or Lindsey herself had shrunk to only a couple inches tall.

The whole place was aglow with a sea of lustrous green as the morning sunlight washed the dim recesses of the verdant floor. Beyond the towering heights of the giant grass Lindsey could just make out the brilliant green of leafy trees, which in a bizarre twist of perspective still appeared strangely normal in proportion, just oddly distant, very close yet far away. She appeared to be in the midst of a lightly wooded area, for the ground was not so dense with grass as it might be, with patches of bare dirt here and there mingled with bright clover and fuzzy moss, and small columns of dun colored mushroom caps. Even so, visibility was poor in this miniature jungle, and Lindsey could hardly see more than twenty feet or so in front of her (or perhaps twenty inches....being so small made things rather confusing in that regard) after which the world became obscured with a menagerie of tiny plants.

The ground crunched beneath her feet, and Lindsey looked down and realized that she was standing in the middle of a patch of brightly colored pebbles, poured out on the ground around her like gravel. It filled a roughly circular area immediately where she stood, then formed into a narrow but thickly laid trail which meandered away from her and gradually disappeared into the grass. It was unquestionably a path. It seemed to Lindsey that nothing natural could have created such a thing, and given that the path began conveniently near the precise spot at which she had awoken, it seemed also to her that whoever had brought her here meant for her to follow it. Whoever it was, if they'd had any intent of doing her harm they'd already had more than enough opportunity to do so, and Lindsey decided that at this point there was nothing to be lost in playing along and following the path to wherever it went. The path meandered to and fro through the grass and among the clovers and mushrooms. Up ahead, Lindsey could faintly make out some brilliant splashes of bright red objects, which were too large to be wholly obscured the grass. What were they, giant flowers? Or were they mushrooms? Yes, they were definitely mushrooms, enormous red and white speckled toadstools in fact. There seemed to be a lot, and the path was leading Lindsey in their general direction. In a short while the groundcover opened up a bit, and Lindsey found herself at last among the toadstools. There was a veritable grove of them, their stems wide like stately oaks, with pure white gills and stalks drooping with ruffs, and brilliant red mantles speckled with white nodules. It was a magnificent spectacle, and Lindsey paused to gaze at it for a moment before continuing again down the path.

"Where are you going?"

Lindsey halted. A voice?

The voice had come from the grove of mushrooms. It was real, definitely not something in her mind. Turning back, Lindsey's eyes searched among the scarlet fruits, to light almost immediately upon a small red mushroom only a few feet away. There, sitting beneath the shade of the mushroom's wide hood, was a small being. Its body was short and just a little bit rotund, and its limbs were long and willowy. It sat cross-legged with its hands resting in its lap, its long fingers intertwined and its thumbs twiddling together idly. It was dressed in vaguely medieval attire, with pointed buff colored shoes and tight hose of deep green. It wore an embroidered tunic of cheerful lincoln green, with wide scalloped sleeves each hung with a tiny silver bell, with its waist girded by a long buff belt set with a simple wooden fipple flute thrust casually into it. Its shoulders were draped with a long cowl of deep saffron with scalloped dags, and on its head was a stocking cap of matching hue with a very long tail terminating with another silver bell. Its head was peculiarly elongated, wider than it was tall, with large, drooping ears protruding almost comically to either side. Its features were flat and smooth save for slight crows feet about its deep set eyes, which were large, narrow and catlike, twinkling with cryptic merriment. The creature sat there, motionless, eyeing her keenly with a wide, inscrutable smile fixed across its oblong face. And then it winked.

"Good morning, Lindsey", the creature said in a light tenor voice. "Where are you going?"

Lindsey hesitated a moment. "Uh....I don't know, I guess. I was following this trail."

"To where?"

"To wherever it led, I guess."

"Which is here, if I'm not mistaken", the creature said. "Would you care to pause and have something to eat?" The creature opened his palms as he spoke, and before him now was a large loaf of brown bread, round like a Bundt cake, sitting atop a raised platter of brass elaborately pierced with a pattern of stars. Lindsey realized that she was hungry. And it would take a pretty sorry sort of idiot to have brought her all the way here just to poison her, so she sat down across from the creature and began to eat with him. The food was delicious, whatever it was. Somewhere between cake and bread, it was dense and moist, and mildly sweet with a slightly nutty flavor. Up to now Lindsey hadn't realized just how hungry she was, and she ate well. Indeed, it felt as though she had not eaten quite so well in years. At length the creature spoke.

"Food is good, but what is food without pleasant conversation?", it said. "What shall we talk about?" Lindsey snorted to herself, almost choking as she did so (she had just taken a particularly large bite of bread). She swallowed quickly, and wiped her mouth. It was about time for some answers. "Maybe you could tell me where I am, and give me an explanation as to why you brought me here", she said tersely. "It was you who brought me here, wasn't it?"

"Yes", the creature said affably. "I thought it was time we had a proper interview. As to where, you and I are in a transient place at present. For the moment you are here, but soon enough you shall be returned to where you were, if that is your wish."

"And who are you?", Lindsey asked insistently.

"My name is Elred", the other said. "My people of old have called ourselves the Alva, but nowadays most everyone refers to us as simply 'The Good Folk'. Rather kind of them to thus describe us, I must say."

"Uh huh. So you're the ones responsible for all of this?"

"All of what? The bread you mean? Do have another slice!"

"Thanks, I think I will. No, I mean you're the ones responsible for this whole scheme, getting me and Hae-jin and Joan together to open the vault and all. The Bird works for you, doesn't he?"

"Ah yes, I see what you mean. Yes, the Bird is indeed one of our servants."

"He abandoned me", Lindsey said pointedly. "I went into that vault and got what he wanted, and when I came out he was gone, and Mr. Dackery had to save me. What do you say to that?"

Elred continued to smile pleasantly, but there was a flicker of emotion in his eyes and he briefly pursed his lips before speaking again. "Yes, indeed. That did happen, didn't it? Most unfortunate. Things have not gone quite as planned."

"Are you telling me you've screwed up?"

"In a word, yes. Slightly. I like to think that we have experienced only a minor hiccup in our choreography."

"Oh yeah? And you expect me to believe that? You run this whole world, don't you? That's what the Bird says. Now I'm supposed to believe that people as powerful as you screwed up anyway, just like that?"

"We *built* this world, Lindsey", the other said gravely. "And likewise we do our best to keep it in good order. This world is our realm, and our responsibility."

"You don't do a very good job", Lindsey said bluntly. "There is a lot of ugliness in the world; wars, famines, plagues..."

"In *your* world", the other corrected. "The wellbeing of your world is your own business, not ours. We have far less power in your world than we do in our own, and most of our efforts in that regard are, by necessity, dedicated to protecting your world from the things which lurk in ours. Not to say that we don't have wars and diseases and things here in the Fairworld. We do. But here, we have more power to manage them so as to minimize their offensiveness. We do not compel people to do our will. We are not inclined to rule as brutes and tyrants. But we do try to do our best behind the scenes to keep things as tidy and pleasant for everyone as possible, while keeping out of mortal affairs for the most part. Which is where people like you come into the picture. Have some more bread?"

For a moment they ate in silence. At length Elred spoke again. "What happened at the vault, Lindsey?"

"We opened it. I went in, found something to take back, and then came back out and found out that everybody else was gone and only those *things* which attacked me were there, and then I got away with Mr. Dackery's help."

"This much we have already learned", the elf said dismissively. "But what happened to *you*, Lindsey. How have you fared through all this? This is what concerns me at the moment."

"Why are you concerned about me?", Lindsey asked guardedly.

"I am inclined to be concerned about everybody", the elf replied. "But at the moment I happen to be concerned specifically about you."

"I get it", Lindsey scoffed. "You just want me to finish the mission."

"Of course I do", the elf said evenly. "But that is entirely up to you, Lindsey. If you would prefer, I can take you home right now and that will be the end of the matter. But that is not what I'm asking right now. What happened to you at the vault? How do you feel about it?"

"I don't know. I'll have to think about whether or not I want to go through with this. What happened to the Bird? Why did he leave me?"

Elred made no reply. Lindsey waited, casting as accusative a gaze at him as she could muster, even as her own feelings of hurt and confusion dug at her spirit. This creature owed her an answer, and he wasn't giving one. "Well?", the girl demanded. "Are you going to give me an answer? Or are you going to string me along too, just like the Bird?"

For the first time, Elred's smile broke, and he appeared distressed. "I'm afraid I don't have an answer for you. Not a proper one, at least. The fact is, we don't yet know what happened to the Bird. We've rather lost track of him for the moment."

"Ha! That's rich."

"Entirely true though, I'm afraid. I must confess, I can offer no explanation for his conduct. He has not contacted us, and we have not yet located him ourselves. It is my hope that he is merely a bit discombobulated at the moment. Who knows, he may be quite preoccupied trying to track everybody down. If not...."

Elred fell silent again.

"What about Hae-jin and Joan?", Lindsey insisted. "And the Wogs and Ursilda?"

"Ah, that's a bit of a sticky problem. It would appear that the Drixi were alerted to their presence at the vault, and they dispatched a substantial number of soldiers to arrest them."

"What!"

"I'm terribly sorry, I do seem to have naught but bad news for you."

"You've got to do something!"

"We will. My brethren are already making the necessary arrangements."

"Damn that Bird. He really has messed up, hasn't he?"

"So it would seem."

"What are you going to do about it?"

"That depends. What are *you* going to do about it?"

"Huh?"

"You still have a mission to complete. If you don't wish to, we will of course honor your choice and take you home. But if you wish to continue that will of course change things. How we proceed at this juncture depends on your decision."

"You want me to decide now?"

"It would be helpful."

"I don't know how I feel about this."

"I quite understand. Here, take this."

Elred opened his hand and produced a small gold coin as if from thin air, and handed it to Lindsey.

"When we are finished here you will be returned to Dackery's house. Take time to think things over, and when you have made your decision use the coin."

Lindsey looked at the coin. It was gold, or at least of gold colored metal, perhaps slightly larger than a penny. On one side, stamped in high relief was an image of a crescent moon with a face on it, and on the other there was an image of a mountain with a smaller crescent moon to one side above it. "What do I do with it?"

"When you are ready to speak with me again, turn it over twice in your hands, and recite the phrase which is written on it."

"Thanks. I'll think it over. I promise."

"Thank you. But you still haven't answered my first question. How are you faring through all of this? Personally, I mean."

Lindsey reflected for a moment. Elred's question was unexpected to be sure, and in the whirlwind of experiences over the last few hours she'd really not had a moment to think about how she felt about anything really. "I guess I don't know, really. I mean, I haven't really had time to think about things. I guess I'll have the rest of my life to do that (assuming I don't get myself killed doing all this). But I guess I feel....I don't know....I guess I feel kind of better."

"Better about what?"

"I dunno, about everything I guess. I feel like I'm more free, like I've finally had a chance to let go and move on."

"Good!", the elf said, clapping his long hands together. "I am glad you are feeling better. Keep thinking things over, and we shall meet again one day and speak of this again. In the meanwhile, I realize that clean forgot to provide any butter, and I think a bit of tea might also be in order, unless you would prefer coffee?"

"I think I'll have tea. And some butter, thank you. I guess I have an appetite."

"Of course you do. It's Breakfast after all. Breakfast after a very long night indeed."

10

"The House of Dackery"

Lindsey awoke. She found herself lying in a sweaty tangle of a bed in a strange room, staring up at the ceiling. She sat upright with a jerk and looked around. Yes, this was definitely the same room she had gone to sleep in the night before. A room in an old house somewhere in the heart of the New England, belonging to one Mr. Horatio Dackery.

Had she gone somewhere during the night? She could remember every detail perfectly. The grass, the mushrooms, and the creature sitting under said mushrooms. Had it all been a dream? Or had Elred indeed brought her back to Dackery's house, just as he had promised? She swung her legs over the side of the bed, sending a shower of breadcrumbs onto the floor. Apparently she'd brought back a few souvenirs from her dreaming, and made a mess of Dackery's bedroom with them to boot. A sudden thought struck her, and she glanced around the room. There, on the nightstand, was a small gold coin. Apparently the breadcrumbs weren't the only souvenir she'd brought back from her nocturnal adventure. She picked up the coin and examined it again. There, written on one side, was the inscription Elred had spoken of. The words which were supposed to reunite her with the creature, who would then presumably whisk her off to wherever she wished. It was merely up to her to decide where she would go.

From outside, she thought she heard a noise. A comfortable sort of clinking and clanking, accompanied by the faint odor of bacon. Her stomach grumbled greedily. She wasn't particularly hungry, but still had an appetite for some reason. Decisions could wait. She pocketed the coin and then began to pull furniture away from the door. It was time to see what the hospitable Mr. Dackery was up to. Lindsey made her way to the sitting room. The drapes were still closed, and the lights were off. There was no sign of Dackery. Lindsey began to explore.

At the end of the hallway she came upon a stairwell leading down to the first floor. Presumably the kitchen would be down there. Going down, she came to a second hallway, which she followed past a number of lonely looking rooms, most of which appeared wholly disused, with the furniture draped with dusty holland covers. The passage ended in a modestly spacious kitchen. The ceiling was rather low, and the floorboards creaked beneath her as Lindsey stepped in. On one side there was an exterior door and a pair of tall, heavily built windows looking out into a small vegetable garden. On the other side was a great stone fireplace, although the word hardly seemed sufficient to describe it, for it was as nearly wide as was the whole room and was tall enough for a man to stand upright inside it. The fireplace was set so deeply into the wall that it formed almost another room unto itself, with a shallow ledge at the rear containing two or three small ovens set deep into the stone. But it was clearly no longer used for its original purpose, for much of it was now occupied by two modern contrivances; a steel double stove and refrigerator. Though 'modern' was a relative term, for even these were old and looked to have been in their prime sometime in the early 1950s, their teal paint contrasting weirdly with the stone around them, which was blackened by three centuries of soot and smoke. In another part of the room there was a free standing steel sink, bolted to the floor, with the plumbing passing awkwardly into the floorboards. The walls were papered with a decades old floral pattern that was still comfortable and cheerful even as it was faded, discolored and peeling in places.

And in the center of the room there was a large table, where stood Mr. Dackery in shirtsleeves, slicing some fresh bread. Dackery looked up and gave a smile which was probably intended to be pleasant, but against his naturally brooding features it still looked more like a scowl.

"Good morning, Ms. Fluger. I trust you slept well."

Lindsey opened her mouth to speak, but in an instant thought the better of it. She was not sure that she really trusted Dackery, and she decided to keep the evening's additional adventures to herself.

"Sure. How about you?"

"Well enough. Breakfast will be ready in a moment. Please, pull up a chair."

Lindsey did so. Dackery finished slicing the bread, and then went over to the stove and brought back a luxurious platter of pancakes, hashbrowns, scrambled eggs, sausages, and of course bacon. If nothing else, Dackery was a gernous host. As they ate, Dackery talked. He spoke of the building, its history, when it was built, how many times it had been remodeled by its various tenants, and his own recent efforts to keep it from being eventually noticed by the National Historic Register. He spoke of the kitchen garden, the plants he cultivated and the fresh vegetables he acquired from it. He spoke of wallpaper which needed cleaning, old timbers which creaked, ancient trees which had become overgrown, and a nearby creek which had problems with flooding. All in all, he talked a great deal without actually saying much of anything at all. Nothing significant anyway. Finally, a full three quarters of the way through the pitcher of maple syrup, the conversation came around to more important matters.

"Of course, we will need to arrange transportation to get you home", Dackery said. "Plane tickets are out of the question, since I doubt the Bird brought you to the Fairworld with proper identification, but we may be able to arrange something by train."

"Why don't you just take me there yourself?" Lindsey said. "That portal (or whatever it was) you used yesterday to get here, why don't you just do that?"

Dackery shook his head. "It may seem a bit counterintuitive, but doormaking is really not a very discreet way to travel. To be sure, it is instantaneous, but it invokes very powerful magic indeed, and for those already on the lookout for such things it can be very easy to see."

"Um...aren't we alone?", Lindsey asked, looking around a little sarcastically. "How's anybody going to see us?"

"By scrying. There are any number of methods, which (no doubt) our enemies are employing at this very moment in search of us. Were I to make a door as I did last night it could expose us to them like a flare. Better to avoid such methods unless absolutely necessary."

"But the Bird does it all the time", Lindsey protested.

"And his enemies caught up with him, didn't they?", Dackery said pointedly

"But you were making doors, too."

"It was necessary in order for me to follow the Bird. That, and I was confident the Bird wasn't on the watch for me. Nor would it have been a disaster had he eventually discovered me. We are acquainted."

"I'd kind of gathered that much. How long have you known the Bird?"

"Long enough."

"Are you enemies?"

"Not precisely. In fact, the Bird has taken consultation with me from time to time. It was I who suggested the utilization of Harin's Vault as a means to complete his quest."

"What!"

"Indeed. Some months ago the Bird approached me with one of his schemes. He was discreet in what he told me, or tried to be anyway, however I was nonetheless able to deduce much of the rest for myself (specifically, that he needed a bloodless sacrifice of some kind, and a very powerful one at that). Although I declined to participate, I suggested that he try opening Harin's Vault as a means to his ends. For many long years I had sought a way to enter the vault, to no avail. The Bird's quest was a unique opportunity."

"So the Bird tried to recruit you too, huh? Why did you say no?"

Dackery shrugged. "I do not trust the Bird."

"Why?"

"Do you really need to ask? Look at your own situation. Where is the Bird?"

Lindsey fell silent. Dackery's words were unsettling, to be sure. Somehow she felt like changing the subject. "So what's the deal with Harin's Vault anyway? Why lock the place up like that?"

Dackery leaned back in his chair and cradled his fingers together in a way that made him look like a professor about to expound on some esoteric topic. "Harin's Vault was built almost two thousand years ago by the ancestors of the Drixi", Dackery said. "At that time the witches of the Middle Wastes were at the very height of their power, and their empire had expanded outward, from the marches of Ursiland in the north to the heart of Meridiana in the south. So much so that they were on the verge of bringing down the entire Reman Empire itself (which of course they ultimately did). Suffice to say, it was a period of extreme instability. Even the Good Folk were getting involved. In those days, the lands of the Drixi were ruled by one Harin the Golden, who as you might guess by the sobriquet was rather affluent. He built the vault as a royal treasury which would be secure against the tumult of that age, a magical receptacle which was locked in such a way that it required a human sacrifice (or rather Drixi sacrifice) in order to be opened. Yes, I concur it's a nasty idea, but in those days the Drixi were even nastier than they are now (which is no small insult). The trick though was that the sacrifice had to be both voluntary and pure. To their dismay, the Drixi soon discovered that anything that could be done to induce a person to submit to death (either by way of coercion, devotion to the monarch, promise of riches for their heirs, or what have you) would detract from the conditions of the sacrifice. They could never find a voluntary victim who did not have a strong personal motivation of some kind, and thus the Drixi could not open their own vault once it was closed. Harin the Golden was now Harin the Broke. I hate to think of how many poor souls the Drixi must have gone through before they realized the matter was hopeless, or what must have happened afterwards to the magicians who had put the thing together in the first place. Anyway, as the years went by the vault was gradually forgotten, only to be eventually rediscovered when the Drixi began mining the area for tin. Then all the old scrolls and manuscripts were pulled out and read again, and as word got out people started trying to get inside the thing to retrieve all the fabulous wealth that the ancient records said were in there, for the vault had been meticulously catalogued before being closed. But no one succeeded, and there the place remained to be locked up forever...until last night that is."

"Yeah, about that", Lindsey said thoughtfully. "To be honest, I still don't feel like I understand what the heck I was doing last night. I did what Joan and the Bird asked me to do, and I don't mind having done it. It wasn't that hard, in the end. But I still don't get why I did it. I mean, why would making a sacrifice break the curse on Joan's country?"

"It has to do with the nature of the black magic involved with the curse", Dackery said. "Broadly speaking, 'black magic' is usually defined as magic which is either evil in purpose, or evil in nature. For example, if a person were to perform an otherwise harmless spell with the idea of using it to do harm (such as murdering somebody), that would be considered black magic. On the other hand, if a person were trying to use magic for a worthy purpose, but in doing so utilized a harmful act (such murdering someone, to use the same example), then that also would be considered black magic. This may seem simple on the surface, but in reality the issue of black magic is a complicated tangle of conflicting ethics, since everybody has different ideas of what constitutes morally good behavior.

"But the problem becomes even more complicated when you factor in the nature of magic itself. You see, magic exists largely outside the realm of physics as we understand it. As such, we have no real way to perceive it, at least not without the aid of magic itself (which puts the cart before the horse, as it were). You can't observe magic unless you already have magic. I strongly suspect that the Good Folk and possibly certain other beings have some innate ability to perceive it. But for ordinary mortals like you and I, we are faced with the difficulty of trying to manipulate something which cannot be seen or touched. In general, the only thing which can be directly observed are the outcomes. Much of the practice of magic therefore revolves around doing things which can subtly shift the magical currents around you, sort of like making ripples in water. Thus, performing a spell involves a sequence of actions which are calculated to shift the currents in a certain way for a desired result. This could be anything, from a string of words, to a sequence of movements or a combination of chemical ingredients. In general, I have found that the profundity of the deed tends to affect the power of the resultant magic, but in theory any kind of deed might do. It is merely a matter of finding out which actions will generate the desired result. All of this comes together in ways which are highly subjective, and deeply linked to the psyche of the spellcaster and the metaphysical circumstances of the world around him.

"A key aspect of the subjective nature of magic is that the mechanics of the magic itself are not only dependent on physical words and actions, but also on the mind of the magician. Thoughts, conceptions, and emotions can all be wrapped up in the mechanics of spellcraft. When this happens, what was previously a purely abstract phenomenon suddenly becomes integral to the operation of the magic itself, just like the wheels of a clock. Obviously, this kind of thing can be very difficult to grapple with. Therefore, good, functional spellcraft is based purely on factors which are controllable and reproducible, with as little dependence as possible on internal biases or fleeting psychological states.

"However, the reverse is true when the design of the spellcrafter is to deliberately create something which is difficult to reproduce or undo. In this case, a spell may be intentionally crafted in order to exploit certain emotional states and internalized ideas. This is usually a very difficult thing to sort out, which can be very useful to those who engage in predatory magic.

"Because of this, cultural context becomes a critical factor in the practical application of magic. Every society has its own systems of normative morality. Scruples and taboos are prevalent wherever you go. It could be anything from blaspheming the gods to using plastic bags while shopping; if an individual or society holds these things as prohibited it can become a taboo. When a person engages in magic which involves violating their own taboos, these ideas may become integrated into the fabric of the magic itself. I believe this is what Gurth did in

Linster. He convinced the people to engage in various acts of spellcraft which systematically violated their own cultural mores. It doesn't matter how trivial or superstitious those taboos may or may not have been, the fact is that their beliefs became incorporated into the system of magic wrought by Gurth. Any attempt at breaking Gurth's enchantment would necessitate directly addressing these culture-bound beliefs in some way. This is what you did at Harin's Vault. You successfully neutralized the factor of belief by assuming the role of the savior figure and performing an act of personal atonement on behalf of others. In a word, you were a sort of magic scapegoat. It was a straightforward and effective method to untangle the problem, and to their credit the Good Folk worked out a way to pull it off neatly with as little harm as possible."

Lindsey was silent for a moment as she digested this information. It seemed to fit together, in a weird sort of way. Assuming of course Dackery knew what he was talking about. Or that he was being truthful with her. After all, he did seem to have his own personal agenda of some kind.

"So what did you really want from the vault, Mr. Dackery?", Lindsey at length asked, "Was it just that book you took? It must be pretty valuable, otherwise you wouldn't have gone to all the trouble of tricking the Bird into having me open the vault for you."

"I did not trick the Bird, I merely offered a suggestion, one which seems to have worked out exactly as was required...except that it hasn't. You're here after all."

"We'll get back to that, but right now I want to know what you're up to. All you took from the vault last night was just the one book, so I guess that was all you were after. What was that book?"

"As I said, the vault was thoroughly cataloged before it was closed. Years ago I uncovered references to a certain valuable manuscript, of which only a few copies ever existed, all of which are either lost or thoroughly inaccessible (even to a man of my own substantial resources). One of them was recorded to have been inside Harin's vault, and so indeed it was….but not anymore."

"Well, what is the book about? Why do you want it?"

"I think I may be permitted to keep my own confidences. That book is my affair, not yours."

"You only got hold of it because of me."

"And I have already told you more of it than I would have otherwise. But perhaps we shall yet speak again on the subject. In the meanwhile, I need to place a call with Amtrak to see about arranging tickets to get you home. Worst case scenario I may have to pose as your guardian. Forgive me, but may I know your age?"

"Eighteen."

"That should do. We'll tell them you're sixteen and under my care. I think I may also concoct something or other to further dim the curiosity of the good officers of our national railroad, just in case. Security requirements are of little value if you're too befuddled by burnt Arigrocia to properly apply them."

"Thanks. I really appreciate what you're doing. But I haven't decided yet where I am going."

Dackery cocked an inquisitive eye at Lindsey. "By that do you mean you are considering carrying on with the Bird's little adventure?"

"I think I may be permitted to keep my own confidences, thanks", Lindsey replied evenly. "I need some time to think about it."

Dackery eyed Lindsey keenly for a moment, his expression suggesting a strange mix of dissonant emotions, disappointment and disdain mingled with admiration and regard. For a moment it seemed as if Dackery had no response for Lindsey's reply. Dackery held Lindsey's gaze for another moment, and then shrugged. "Very well. Please take as much time as you need. I shall need to clean up here; no don't get up, please allow me to be a proper host and clean up myself. Perhaps you would care to take a walk? Last night I was concerned that we might have been followed, but it has been several hours now and there has been no sign of the witches. If they've not acted by now then they must have lost our scent. At this point they probably have no idea where we are, so it should be safe enough to go outside. The grounds are quite spacious, and I find nature to be conducive to thought. The kitchen garden is just outside that door, and there is a path from there leading to the creek." Dackery began clearing the dishes away, and Lindsey stepped outside into the garden.

The kitchen garden was arranged in rectangular beds framed with faded grey timbers and planted with fragrant herbs and leafy vegetables. There were several such plots laid out in grid, like a blocky maze, the gravel paths of which eventually passed through a rickety picket fence on the far end and rolled downhill from there towards a meandering line of bushy trees which betrayed the presence of the creek. Dackery's house was located on a low hill, and the surrounding countryside consisted of rolling farmland. Green fields bound with hedgerows heaved and shifted like an earthen sea, dotted here and there by a white farmhouse or red barn bobbing upon the ocean of grass like upright buoys, while a little further beyond the grass gradually broke upon a tide of lush green woodland heaving in great swells of hills which faded off into the grey distance.

The morning air was cool, and even had a slight chill as the wind whipped about Lindsey's bare legs as she approached the creek, the silent waters of which could hardly be seen between the thick foliage of the trees which enveloped it. As she reached the treeline Lindsey turned to walk parallel to the creek, and tried her best to concentrate. She had a great deal of thinking to do. It was perhaps her first real moment of introspection since yesterday when she left the world she knew, and to be sure it was a gross understatement to say that a lot had happened in that time. She had met a talking bird, stepped through a hole in her bedroom floor and landed in another dimension of some sort, met all sorts of queer beings and finally landed up back in her own world, on the run and in fear of her life. All in all, Lindsey was finding it rather difficult to wrap her mind around it all, and she felt a bit like her head was about to cave in on itself under the pressure. Not even Calculus had been this bewildering. Yet somehow she had to piece all this together for herself, and soon, for she needed to make a decision.

Lindsey reached into her pocket and retrieved the gold coin Elred had given her. The metal shone brilliantly in the morning sun, and Lindsey found herself gazing vacantly at it. What on earth was she supposed to do? For some time Lindsey walked along the edge of the creek, absorbed in her own thoughts while anxiously turning the gold coin over and over in her hand and hardly noticing anything else. She could always just go home. She hadn't asked for this adventure, and she certainly hadn't asked for it all to have gone wrong the way it had. She would be perfectly within her rights just to call the whole thing off. The Bird, wherever he was, had made a hash of things. He could just go ahead and sort out the mess he'd made, and leave Lindsey out of it. Lindsey found herself recalling the giant, Barri. He'd had that bird pegged, alright, and so did Dackery. Lindsey was just a foolish little twerp for having ever trusted the creature.

But then again, the Bird wasn't the only one involved. As angry as she was at the Bird, there was still Hae-jin, Joan and the others. None of this was their fault, and wherever they were they were probably still up to their eyeballs in this mess, maybe even worse off than she was. All Lindsey really knew of their mission was what Joan and the Bird had told her, but it seemed pretty apparent to her that, in all probability, this man Gurth wouldn't be any nicer to them than he would be to her. The others could be in terrible danger right now, for all she knew. And presumably she herself held the key to solving the whole problem. She still had the medallion around her neck, and taking it to Linster would supposedly break the curse and put an end to the whole thing. Afterward, Hae-jin, Joan and the others wouldn't be in any danger and everybody could just go home in peace, and the people of Linster wouldn't have to suffer anymore. There were an awful lot of people who were depending on the success of the Bird's mission. And right now, it seemed that such success now wholly depended on Lindsey. Maybe she didn't care about the Bird. But she cared about Hae-jin. She cared about Joan. She cared about Ursilda, and she even cared about the Wogs. And she had made a promise. The Bird might break his promises, but Lindsey was determined that she would never do so.

Lindsey's mind was made up. She didn't like it, really, but she was going to do it anyway. She'd have to go find Dackery and thank him for everything, and tell him that she'd decided to try her best to finish what she'd started. She'd given her word, and she intended to keep it whatever happened. With a sigh, she tossed the glittering gold coin lightly in the air and caught it again, turning around to return to the house as she did so. And then, Lindsey froze in her tracks.

Just above her, hardly a few feet away, there was a large bird perched in one of the nearby trees. It was definitely not *the* Bird. No, this was a different creature entirely. Smaller, shabbier, and colored like soot. It stared in Lindsey's direction over a long drooping beak with a pair of sharp black, intensely focused eyes, fixated on something in Lindsey's hand: The gold coin given to her by Elred.

Instinctively, Lindsey knew she was in danger. She clutched the coin more tightly in her hand, and had begun to back away when the dark bird uttered a hoarse cry, and spreading its great wings hurled itself towards Lindsey, its wicked talons clawing at her hand. Lindsey screamed and began to beat the bird back as hard as she could, but it was no use. In a moment the claw transformed into an iron fist crushing her wrist, and suddenly the bird was gone and was replaced by a man in dark shabby clothes. The man twisted Lindsey's arm and would have broken it had not Lindsey released her grip and dropped the precious coin. The man softened his grip a bit as he reached down to pick up the coin, a significant mistake, for at this juncture Lindsey bit him. With a surprised howl the man released his hold on Lindsey completely, and Lindsey broke and ran. No time to worry about Elred's coin, she was a dead girl for sure if that man caught up with her. Frantically Lindsey ran back towards the house, while behind her the man began to shout indistinctly. Lindsey ran faster than she ever had before, unable to even glance backwards to see if the man was in pursuit. All she could do was run. In the distance, she thought she heard a series of pops like firecrackers going off. She made it as far as the kitchen garden, and halfway to the door she at last caught her foot on the edge of one of the vegetable beds, and fell down scraped and bloodied onto the gravel. The man was right behind her, and as she turned she saw him towering over her. He was of medium complexion but his clothes and hair were as dark as that of the bird from which he had transformed, and there was a wild, determined gleam in his eye as he stood poised above her.

Suddenly, the kitchen door was flung open, and Dackery heaved his huge frame through, pistol in hand. He stretched out his arm and unloaded several bullets straight into the man's face, and the man collapsed onto the gravel. Dackery stepped into the garden and hauled Lindsey roughly to her feet.

"Quick, get inside. Now." Dackery bundled Lindsey inside of the kitchen and then bolted the door shut behind them. "Come on. We've got to leave."

"I thought you said they couldn't find us?"

"I was wrong. Quickly, we must go now."

Dackery led the way out of the kitchen and into the hall. There, in the middle of the floor was a dark, huddled form. It was still, unnaturally so, and as Dackery ushered her along Lindsey realized it was the dead body of a human being, dressed in dark clothes much like those of her previous attacker. Lindsey felt sick. Dackery led her down the hall a short ways before he came to a bathroom. The window was tiny and locked shut, and Dackery thrust Lindsey inside and handed her his pistol. "Lock the door, I'll be back momentarily. I will knock three times, like this. If anything else tries to get in, shoot it." And with that Dackery closed the door, and Lindsey was alone.

It seemed like an eon before he returned. In the meanwhile, all was quiet. There were no cries, no shouts, and no more gunshots. Either their adversaries were all dead, or they had withdrawn temporarily. Lindsey paced the tiny space feverishly, turning the pistol over in her hands and vacantly wishing she knew how to use it properly.

Suddenly, there were three knocks at the door. Lindsey tried peering through the keyhole to make sure it was Dackery, but she couldn't see anything. Steeling herself, she opened the door. Dackery stood there, hat on his head, a vintage suitcase in one hand and his walking stick and Lindsey's Vorpal axe in the other. Draped over one arm were a couple of coats, and buckled at his waist was a curved, oriental looking sword. Dackery collected his pistol, and handed Lindsey her axe. Then he dragged his walking stick across the wall and an opening appeared, wreathed in thin flame. And then, Lindsey Fluger and Horatio Dackery stepped through and disappeared, and the opening faded away, leaving behind an old and empty house somewhere in the heart of New England.

11

"A Long March"

Under different circumstances, it would have been a lovely day. The sun processed in its serene, perfunctory way through a bright and cloudless sky. The breeze was cool and gently caressed the flowering vegetation both great and small which coated the rocky countryside. Unfortunately, the countryside in question happened to comprise the dominion of Drixi, a land not known for its unqualified hospitality.

The Drixi army had been on the march since early morning after departing Mount Vorn, and it was now close to noon. They had been following a well paved road, which at this point intersected with a narrow, fast moving river. Here a halt had been called. The Drixi were fastidious creatures, and they busied themselves taking turns lathing their pale limbs religiously with water. Those not so occupied were refilling their water skins and distributing bread and ale among their company. The prisoners too were allowed to refresh themselves. For the moment their bonds were removed, and they were given food and drink and likewise permitted the use of the river....all under a close watch, of course. Throughout the entire morning the Wogs, Joan and Hae-jin had remained silent, not daring to speak (save for the Wogs, who grumbled a bit to one another), and that was not about to change.

Hae-jin had nonetheless managed to occupy his time with some measure of productivity. He silently observed the land, committing as much of its features and geography to mind as he could. He observed his captors, taking careful note of the distribution of their troops, their order of march, the disposition of their supplies, and all manner of things which only a professional soldier would notice. Not that any of it would necessarily prove useful, but it helped forestall boredom and the looming dread of hopelessness. In particular, Hae-jin took advantage of the imposed silence to listen carefully to that which passed among the Drixi. To be sure, the Drixi were cautious in what they said around the prisoners, but lips are ever prone to looseness and Hae-jin was nonetheless able to learn quite a bit from the inevitable chatter which flowed irrepressibly about him. The Drixi were nervous. That much he was able to glean. The fact that a group of humans had managed to circumvent whatever enchantments were in place to keep them out appeared to be a cause for considerable disquiet. Why the Drixi should be so afraid of humans in the first place Hae-jin couldn't guess, but it seemed to him that it was very significant to the Drixi that their defenses had been thus compromised. The potential implications of such a breach appeared to be a grave cause for concern, far more so than the actual nature of the incursion itself. The common soldiers seemed worried, and Hae-jin overheard several remarks questioning the ability of the Drixi leaders to properly protect their own people. It seemed that there was some kind of worrisome political situation at present, something going on outside the Drixi lands which the Drixi themselves were anxious to stay out of. There was a definite fear that something...or someone...would soon be going to war, and that the Drixi would be caught up in it and would inevitably fall under the oppressive influence of a certain, unnamed foreign power. A very specific, much feared foreign power it seemed, but one of which the Drixi dared not speak in plain language, and Hae-jin could gather but little else on the matter from what he managed to overhear.

However, it seemed that the mysterious, grey robed interlopers had something to do with it. Hae-jin overheard many a hushed and rueful remark about them, largely to the effect that the common soldiers considered them aliens and meddlers who were causing trouble, possibly holding undue influence over the Drixi leadership, and that the soldiers very much wished the lot of them gone from their midst as soon as possible. Only once during the course of the morning did Hae-jin have an opportunity to observe these beings again for himself. It was only for a moment, just as the army was coming to a halt at noontide. Hae-jin and his companions were being led from a position in the center of the column to the edge of the river when they passed closely by the creatures. They were sitting in a circle on the ground, their postures relaxed yet weirdly distorted in a way which suggested their anatomy was not entirely human, despite the fact that they walked on two legs as men did. Hardly a surprise, given the hideous reptilian countenances which Hae-jin had glimpsed previously. In their midst they had set down a clay bowl of some sort filled with water, and Hae-jin observed one of them placing within it a small sliver of what looked like obsidian. Nothing more could Hae-jin see, for by then he and his fellows had been shoved onward by the guards. However, after they were out of sight among the crowd of soldiers, Hae-jin still managed to learn one more thing about the creatures. Just one word: Zard.

Apparently that's what the things were called. At least that's what the Drixi called them, for as they moved away Hae-jin overheard the guards refer to them specifically by that name, bitterly speculating that the Zard must be taking counsel with their masters (from which nothing good could be expected).

The noontide respite proved uncomfortably short (made all the worse by the lack of sleep the night before and the grueling march of the morning). The Drixi seemed to be in a hurry. As the order was given to fall in, Hae-jin observed the Drixi officers gathered together, their masked helmets tilted back on their heads, out of the way. In their midst, perched on the saddle of one of their horses, was a small, brightly colored hawk, with which the Drixi officers were speaking. Apparently rabbits weren't the only talking animals in the lands of the Drixi, and in a short while the hawk took off and flew away past the head of the column. Throughout the rest of the day, Hae-jin observed the arrival and departure of several more brilliantly colored hawks (so brightly colored indeed that Hae-jin suspected their feathers had been dyed, perhaps as a sort of livery). It seems that the hawks were being employed as scouts, or maybe couriers. It would seem that wherever the Drixi army was headed, their arrival would be expected in advance.

The afternoon was thoroughly morbid. The day was warming up to become oppressively humid. Throughout the long, weary afternoon, Hae-jin marched shackled to his companions, becoming ever more sweaty and thirsty as the day wore on. As the sun sank low on the horizon the Drixi began preparations for encampment. Their hawks had been scouting ahead all day, and had identified a suitable location along the Drixi's route. Upon reaching the site, the commanders gave the order to make camp, and with the sound of a trumpet blast from a great ox horn the soldiers broke formation and began to work with well drilled efficiency, each man attending to his appointed task with no need of instruction. Copper-shod stakes were collected from carts pulled by oxen, and these were arranged about the encampment to form a menacing palisade. Once this was complete some of them began erecting circular tents in rows, like little blocks of houses, while others began erecting raised platforms along the perimeter of the palisade to serve as temporary watchtowers, using modular components carried on the ox carts. In a matter of a few short hours the Drixi had assembled a camp which was in essence a small fortified village in its own right. The spacious tent of the commanders was placed in the center of the encampment. To one side of this was a smaller tent, where the prisoners were deposited. A large stake shod with an iron ring had been driven into the ground in its center, and to this the prisoners were shackled with sturdy chains.

Hae-jin sat cross legged and weary on the hard ground, an iron cuff on one ankle. The chain had enough length to allow him to sit, stand, or lie down, but that was all. He was tired. At least he was accustomed to long marches. Joan appeared utterly exhausted, already lying on the ground and nearly asleep. The Wogs were bickering openly now, chiding and insulting the Drixi with every other remark. It was, frankly, a credit to their professionalism that the Drixi soldiers hadn't already cut out their tongues. Indeed, Hae-jin had watched as the Drixi built their camp, and he was impressed. Had he not become so recently unemployed, he would have introduced some of their practices to his own command. But likewise, there were also some things about the Drixi which disturbed his professional instincts. The Drixi were well drilled and organized to be sure, but there was still something lacking. The men knew their jobs perfectly, but they went about them in a casual sort of way, talking and loitering here and there just a bit more than was to Hae-jin's own liking. There was a certain sloppiness in the way they erected the palisade, and the design of the watchtowers suggested a greater emphasis on ease of construction than strength. All in all, it seemed as though the Drixi troops were fundamentally capable and well trained, yet at the same time suffering from a certain measure of complacency.

Hae-jin wasn't the only one to notice this. On more than one occasion Hae-jin observed the senior officers chiding the troops here and there. At one point Hae-jin witnessed an officer rebuking his men quite severely. The sense of urgency among the officers seemed at odds with the relative apathy of the troops. It was almost as if the officers knew something which the common soldiers did not. Hae-jin recalled the rumors he heard among the men during the day. Perhaps the threat of war was even greater than was suspected within the rank and file. At length soldiers came by the prisoners' tent, bringing water and hard cakes of barley. It was hardly an indulgent repast, but Hae-jin and Joan ate gladly. The Wogs complained loudly.

The evening was tedious. The Wogs bickered and griped, and Hae-jin was left to his own dark thoughts. At long last the Wogs ran out of things to bicker about and gradually fell asleep, scratching and sniffing in a great heap like a pile of old farm dogs, while opposite them Joan slept curled up on the hard ground as comfortably as could be managed. Hae-jin lay awake longer, gazing idly at the slivers of light which peeped through the gaps of the tent, and listening as the songs of the Drixi drifted on the wind from other parts of the camp. A full day had come and gone. Through it all, he, Joan and the Wogs had remained the captives of the Drixi. It would have been much more convenient if the Bird had turned up through one of his doors and extracted his allies from their predicament, but such was not the case. In all probability, the Bird was with Lindsey, probably close to completing their quest. Perhaps when it was all over the Bird would come back to find his missing compatriots, but a lot could happen before then. All in all, it was a sticky situation, to be sure. In choosing to follow the Bird, it seemed that Hae-jin had merely gotten himself from one hopeless situation to another. At least back in Hancheon he was in his own country, with knowledge of the land and the people, and perhaps one or two friends left who just might be trusted. But here he was a complete alien, marked by a foreign countenance, with no familiarity with the territory at all nor any connections whatsoever within it.

Still, there were certain advantages. At least here he was alone. Surrounded by enemies, he had only himself to look after, and needn't fear for the safety of anyone save himself. But no, as he thought further about it he realized that wasn't true. Looking across the tent he could faintly see where Joan slept, her form only just visible in the scant light. No, he was definitely not alone, there were indeed others whose welfare he should be responsible for. Lindsey was likely thousands of leagues away by now, but Joan remained in the same predicament as his own. As the moon shifted position in the sky a bit more of its light made it inside the tent, highlighting the graceful shape of the woman who lay in furtive repose nearby. She was beautiful, in a weird, foreign sort of way. There was no denying that. But Hae-jin had only recently lost his own wife, and the pain of that loss was still fresh and bleeding. He did not dare let anyone else into his heart, not now. The pain was far too great. But he had to protect Joan. He may have been unable to preserve the life of his wife, but he would make sure that he would safeguard this woman, even if it meant his own life. What else did he have to live for, anyway? A harsh fart from elsewhere in the tent reminded him that Joan wasn't the only one sharing his predicament. He was still well stocked with Wogs. With a mournful sigh, Hae-jin turned onto his side and did his best to make himself a bit more comfortable as he lay on the callous earth.

Sleep was elusive. Hae-jin instead found his mind drifting to and fro, his thoughts becoming slowly hazier bit by bit, but never quite approaching anything like true sleep. At long last he found himself in a distorted sort of reality, reliving the events of the day in semi-conscious dreaming. Then, through the dream, someone shouted. Hae-jin opened his eyes. Had the shout come from the dream, or had it awakened him from somewhere outside? Hae-jin listened. All was quiet. The entire camp seemed to be asleep by now. What was that? Another shout? Yes, it certainly was. There, just now there was another. In point of fact, there seemed to be a bit of a commotion erupting somewhere in the camp. A horn sounded, followed swiftly by others. In a few moments the entire camp was alive with shouts and cries. Hae-jin sat up. Beside him he could see Joan bolt upright as well. They exchanged glances, but said nothing. Meanwhile, one of the Wogs began to snore.

Hae-jin crawled towards the opening of the tent, going as far as the chain on his ankle would permit. With his shackled leg stretched as far as it could, he could just reach the flap of the tent and turn it aside to peer out into the darkness. The moonlight illuminated a scene of pandemonium. Everywhere Drixi were running about, some half dressed, others wearing bits of clothing and armor. Some were lighting torches, while others were forming up in groups. Suddenly, a group of Drixi scattered like startled doves as a huge shadow barrelled through their ranks. The shape lunged about at the Drixi, sending them running and stumbling in all directions. With a mighty sweep of its paw it tore a tent straight to the ground, and silhouette for a moment against the moonlight Hae-jin could see the outline of a great bear, and over the din he heard its mighty roar.

A group of Drixi had managed to collect themselves and were now making for the bear with spears lowered. With another roar the bear swept aside half of the spears and bowled over their wielders. Then the beast went rampaging off into another part of the camp, with the Drixi in hot pursuit. Hae-jin felt a touch at his side. Turning to look he saw that Joan had crawled up beside him. Their eyes met and Joan uttered one word: "Ursilda?"

Hae-jin nodded. He had thought the same. Hae-jin crawled back to the center of the tent and heaved his weight against the post to which the five prisoners were shackled. But it was driven deeply into the ground, and he could not budge it. Outside, the tumult seemed to be shifting further away. Hae-jin and Joan continued to waste their strength against the post as bit by bit the clamor died down. Now and again a horn sounded as patrols could be heard moving through the camp. Whatever opportunity for escape the bear's intrusion might have offered, it seemed to be rapidly slipping away now. At last, Hae-jin and Joan ceased their efforts against the post and leaned wearily against one another. Outside things seemed to have come under control, and for a moment there was silence. If it was indeed Ursilda that was out there and if she were indeed trying effect their escape, she had failed. Still, Hae-jin felt a warm sort of glow. If nothing else, it seemed that he and his companions had not quite been forgotten after all. Perhaps there was some hope yet.

Morning found the encampment slightly the worse for wear. The Drixi were in the process of disassembling the whole thing in preparation for the day's march, and as the prisoners were led out of their tent Hae-jin took some satisfaction in observing that a fair bit of the disassembly had already been done for them. There were torn down tents, overturned carts, spilled cauldrons, and sacks ripped open with their contents strewn across the ground. One of the watchtowers had been completely knocked over. On two sides of the camp the palisade had been broken through, marking where the bear had entered and subsequently exited. It seemed that the bear had made a clean escape.

For their part, the Drixi themselves showed the marks of the previous night's altercation. Many of them bore obvious bruises, and all of them seemed a bit rattled and out of sorts. It appeared that the only people in the camp who had any sort of a restful night were the Wogs, who had slept through the whole business. Upon observing the desolation about them and learning its source, the Wogs became rather merry, and mocked the Drixi mercilessly (until they started getting kicked).

Soon enough the army was again on the march. The Drixi seemed much more wary though, and progress was slower than on the first day. When they again pitched camp they did so with much more consideration, and this time they dug a trench around portions of the palisade. There was no singing or merriment, and the night went by drearily. The prisoners were shackled again as before, and their bonds were doubled. The Drixi were caught off guard once; they were not to be so embarrassed again. At one point during the night there was a cry raised among the guards. Hae-jin could not get over to the tent opening as before, but from the sound of it it seemed that something had been sighted along the perimeter of the camp. Soldiers were dispatched to drive off the intruder, and soon enough the commotion died down. Twice again this happened before dawn at last rose, and in the morning the general mood was grim and choleric as the Drixi broke camp. The pattern was repeated for the next two days. By day the Drixi were shadowed by some mysterious beast, which would harass their encampment camp by night. Never again did the bear manage to break past the perimeter into the camp itself, but with each passing night the Drixi grew ever more exasperated each time they were obliged to see the creature off.

On the fourth day of the march the Drixi called an unusually early halt. At first, Hae-jin thought it was the midday rest, but the column remained in formation and stood still. They were stopped on a low hill, and from Hae-jin's elevated position he could see the head of the column below, where the Drixi officers sat on their horses. They appeared to be watching the sky, and as Hae-jin attempted to follow their gaze he observed a large bird far in the distance. A messenger, perhaps? If so it was certainly not one of the hawks the Drixi had been dispatching regularly through the entire trip, for as the bird came closer it became clear to Hae-jin that it was not a bird at all. It was staggeringly large, and to his astonishment Hae-jin also observed that it was carrying a rider. The flying creature was approaching quickly now, and in a few moments it landed a short distance away from the head of the column.

It was a tremendous creature, nearly the height of a giraffe with clawed, leathery wings a full thirty feet wide, with a long bill and thick neck like that of some monstrous heron. Its skin was a yellow ochre color, banded with pale green, with a pebbly texture like a lizard's. When it landed it stood tall on both its hind legs and the claws of its folded wings, walking on all fours like a proud bat. Hae-jin himself had never seen it's like and had no name for the creature, but it was in fact a type of pterosaur, albeit a breed removed from those known to science through thousands of years of domestication. Upon the shoulder of its wings there sat a rider on a suitably shaped saddle. It was a Drixi of splendid appearance, girded in brightly enameled armor and brilliant silk robes of warm saffron trimmed and heavily embroidered with scarlet. The Drixi officers approached him on horseback, looking pale and drab by comparison. The dazzling pterosaur rider saluted deferentially to them nonetheless, suggesting to Hae-jin that he was perhaps a common trooper in an otherwise elite regiment. The Drixi officers conversed with the pterosaur rider for some time. At long last the rider saluted the officers once more, and with a tremendous thudding noise the flying reptile beat its vast wings and lifted itself skyward, soaring into the distance. The officers issued their commands, and the column began to move forward again.

As the column proceeded down the gentle slope, Hae-jin caught sight of the Zard again, swathed in robes as usual with hoods pulled low over their hideous visages as they gripped their horse's reigns with scaly claws. Their inhuman anatomy gave them a weird sort of posture when sitting on a horse, such that they always appeared hunched and stooped over in a way which was decidedly sinister. Hae-jin shivered.

Noon came and went, but the Drixi made no stop. It seemed as though they were in a hurry to reach their destination, and Hae-jin found himself hopeful that their long dreary march was at last approaching an end. The territory had become progressively more hilly and wooded over the last couple days, and by late afternoon the column had come upon a great valley. As the road took a bend and began to slope downwards into the valley, Hae-jin had a brief moment to behold the vista before him. The valley was divided into two forks by a line of craggy hills, and at its basin there was a wide, hearty river of deep blue which took a sharp bend in the crook of the terrain. All around, the rolling hills were covered with lush, green vegetation, and looking straight down the nearer fork of the valley Hae-jin could just discern the snow speckled ridges of low lying mountains in the remote distance. The line of hills which divided the valley at its fork were jagged with rocky outcroppings. At the top of this there was a great prominence, a narrow line of bare rock breaking above the treetops like a thin blade. And upon this, there was a castle.

The castle was tall, narrow, and long, snaking, sloping and zigzagging like some great stone highway in the sky as its foundations conformed to the slender wedge of rock below. It was covered with a great sloping roof of dark shingles atop a layer of plain wooden hoardings, which were relieved by only a single brooding turret with a short, slate colored spire. Nearby, Hae-jin spotted two pterosaur riders patrolling the sky around the edifice. As the column of Drixi soldiers descended into the valley the view of the castle was gradually obscured by the trees, save for the highest windows, which peered downward at all that went on beneath them like dark, ever wakeful eyes.

The road rambled sinuously into the valley, now moving parallel with the river and the line of hills on which the great fortress was built. Over the course of an hour the army marched thus, until at length they came upon a fork in the road, one branch of which took a sharp turn towards a wide stone bridge which crossed the river. This the Drixi took, and up ahead Hae-jin saw a number of buildings on the lower ridges of the hill, which sloped gradually downwards from the heights on which the castle rested. It was a small town. It was clear to Hae-jin now that the Drixi were headed for the castle above them, and as the army marched through the town's streets they passed by ambling rows of low log houses with gablet roofs. Most of them were covered with white plaster on one or more of the facades, and painted with swirling designs in bright colors depicting various flowers, animals, and many, many eyes. The villagers did not appear to be wealthy, but they were well dressed and clean. Wherever the procession of soldiers passed the people stared and whispered to one another in deep disquiet, and many of them abandoned whatever they were doing and went speedily to a large clapboard temple with a great pyramidal roof which reached nearly to the ground where it stood amidst a sloping and irregularly shaped plaza which served as the village square.

By now the army was well through the village, and was approaching the castle from the side opposite that which Hae-jin had first seen upon entering the valley. From this vantage, Hae-jin could see that the castle was in fact much larger than it had at first appeared, for the elongated portion which ran along the narrow peak comprised only the great keep. The rest of the castle sprawled down the hillside in descending levels of walled terraces dotted with multiple turrets and several large, thick towers.

They were approaching the main gate now, marching uphill along flat cobbles towards a ponderous, blocky structure projecting from one side of the lowest level walls. The structure was pierced with arrow slits within its thick walls, and covered by wooden hoardings, beneath the shadows of which Hae-jin could just discern the presence of grim Drixi guards cradling recurved bows. Two great banners we draped over the side of the parapet, one of teal and grey and the other of saffron and scarlet. As the army approached a deep, throaty horn sounded, and the great iron shod doors were swung wide.

And Hae-jin, Joan and the Wogs passed into the fortress of the Drixi.

12

"The Fortress of the Drixi"

The main gate led into a long tunnel overlooked by fortified galleries where the Drixi guards maintained their post beneath the shadow of the wooden hoardings. Here any invader who managed to break through the first door would have immediately found themselves deluged with all manner of horrid missiles with nowhere to hide. Just beyond these defenses was the lowest level courtyard. The yard was a densely packed affair, with much of the available space taken up by large, thick walled buildings which were themselves integrated into the castle walls. From his place amidst the crowd of soldiers Hae-jin could see very little of the yard itself, but higher up he could see the many tiers of turrets and parapets piled on top of each other as they crept upward towards the great keep.

Over the heads of the soldiers Hae-jin could just see the officers sitting on their horses, and they appeared to be deep in conversation. Then the crowd gave way to a group of saffron clad warriors who approached the prisoners. They were unarmored, but each wore a dagger and a large, straight, single edged sword at his side. They released the prisoners from the rope which had previously strung them together, but their hands remained shackled individually. They were then led out of the courtyard and up into the next level of the castle, where they came to another, much smaller yard. From there, the guards led them into a side building, and as they did so Hae-jin espied the Drixi officers who had accompanied them on their journey. The officers were ascending a covered wooden stairway leading to an elevated door in one of the buildings in the next tier up. And trailing behind the officers were the three Zard.

The prisoners were brought into a small room which was more or less empty save for a desk and several bare wooden benches. It appeared to be a waiting room of some sort, perhaps a place for the townsfolk to come and present their grievances to a castle scribe, to be subsequently brought to the attention of their magistrate. The guards directed the prisoners to sit on the benches, and once again they were left to wait. It was dark outside by the time anyone came to retrieve them. At long last there was a knock at the door and a teal clad officer was admitted. The prisoners were ushered outside where a grey robed guard detachment bearing lanterns was waiting for them. They were then marched through as series of twisted stairways and passages, snaking their way through the many terraces, on their way at last to the great keep. The courtyards along the way were largely empty. Here and there a few lamplighters were finishing their first rounds of the evening, while high above stars were beginning to glisten against the sky.

At length they reached the keep, and leaving the lantern bearers behind the prisoners were conducted through another series of winding passages and corridors to the great hall. The great hall was wide and long, with a high ceiling of vaulted timbers lined with narrow windows of greenish-yellow glass segmented in geometric shapes. On the far end was a raised dais on which the high table was placed, while elsewhere the room was filled with elaborately carved tables and benches, regularly spaced from one another to allow minstrels and other entertainers to wander the floor unimpeded. The walls were covered in an off-white stucco and painted with elaborate designs and scenes, and (as always with the Drixi) eyes were prominently figured everywhere. Hae-jin found himself wondering what on earth all those eyes were there for. Perhaps they were there to ward off malevolent forces of some kind. Or perhaps they served as manifestations of the eyes of protective spirits, forever keeping watch over the Drixi and their land. Either way, Hae-jin was of the mind that the Drixi appeared a little superstitious in the way they used them, even slightly paranoid, and at this point the ubiquitous motif had become in equal measure tiresome and unsettling.

The prisoners were now led to the high table now, where a small crowd had gathered. The table itself was a crescent shaped affair, lined on one side with high backed chairs facing the rest of the hall. Painted on the wall behind them was the silhouette of a colossal, six fingered hand, made up of densely woven floral patterns painted in many bright colors. The fingers of the hand were splayed, and above each one there was a single large eye, each of a slightly different design, with the pupil containing a distinctive sigil in gold leaf. Above each eye there was a label bearing the name of what seemed to be either a deity or a virtue (or perhaps both). As Hae-jin glanced again around him he realized there was some sort of theme to the murals which lined the great hall. The whole thing seemed to tell a narrative of some kind, beginning at the great six fingered hand and progressing clear around the perimeter of the hall to end up again at the same place at which it had started. It was composed mostly pictures, with only sparse text which was difficult to understand out of context (even for one blessed with a gift of tongues), but it seemed to tell a story of both creation and destruction, of the beginnings of gods, beasts, and Drixi, of great wars and deeds of the past and of things great and terrible yet to come, all beginning and ending at the great six fingered hand, which seemed to represent some sort of supreme power or primal creative force.

There was an open space on the floor before the dais, where under normal circumstances the principal entertainment would likely take place. Here the prisoners were ordered to halt, and it was grimly apparent to Hae-jin that today it was he and his companions who would be providing the entertainment. Metaphorically speaking, that is. There was nothing frivolous in the mood of the Drixi around them. The hall was filled with an air of seriousness. The officers muttered a few grave words to one another as the prisoners were brought into their midst, but otherwise the assembly remained silent.

Several officers were seated at the high table, dressed in teal or grey, their clothes finely wrought and embroidered but otherwise unremarkable. One chair was left empty, however. It was in the very center of the table, taller and grander than the others, and draped with a silken cloth of saffron and scarlet. To one side of the dais there was a large door, and issuing now from it was a procession of guards and servants dazzlingly attired in the distinctive blend of saffron and scarlet. These were followed by a small group of Drixi wearing simple robes of a deep sea green. The door was closed behind them as the last of the party filed into the hall, while three of the saffron robed Drixi ascended the dais and approached the high table, the officers at the table rising to their feet with respect as they did so.

The lead Drixi took the vacant seat at the center of the table, while one of his attendants took up position standing behind him and the other (presumably a scribe) took a seat on the far end of the table and began laying out writing materials. Once seated the lead Drixi motioned for the other officers to sit down as well. For a moment the air was filled with the dull scraping and creaking of chairs as the officers assumed their seats, and Hae-jin took that time to look over the Drixi who (apparently) was to be his judge.

The Drixi was by far the most sumptuously attired individual Hae-jin had seen yet. Every thread of his clothes was covered in elaborate embroidery, every buckle and aglet was made of either gold or silver, finely wrought and richly enameled with bright colors. A sizable dagger set with small jewels hugged his belt, and about his shoulders was hung a great chain of office consisting of golden plates shaped like eyes (as to be expected) fitted with multicolored crystals. His hair, like that of all Drixi, was of a pale platinum, while his eyes were of a particularly dark violet, which gazed penetratingly at Hae-jin past his stern, chiseled features. The Drixi leaned forward now, placing his elbows on the table and resting his chin and lips slightly upon his cradled fingers (which bore many jeweled rings). For a moment he gazed silently at the prisoners before him. Then he spoke.

"Alwog, Berwog, and Gurthwog", the chief Drixi said. "You have been arrested on charges of violating the Sacred Edicts through abetting an illegal and impossible infiltration of our hallowed lands. What have you to say in your defense?"

Alwog stepped forward, wringing his hands slightly while bowing and groveling in a most servile way. "So it please Your Worship", the Wog said, "it's a right honor to be sure to be addressed by one of the Arbiters. A right honor indeed! So it please Your Worship, my brothers and I are innocent!"

"Is that so?"

"So it is, Your Worship, so it is! We none of us have ever seen these humans before! Not ever!"

The Arbiter pursed his lips in a thin smile. "So you say, Alwog of Wog, so you say. Yet you were found in the company of these very humans upon your arrest at Mount Vorn."

"Not true, Your Worship!", the Wog protested. "I don't deny that my brothers and I were at the mountain (all perfectly legally), but never with humans! When we were arrested we were alone. No humans about, none at all! It was only later, Your Worship, after we were arrested that the army put us in chains alongside these humans (putting us at grave risk indeed). Until then we'd never laid eyes on these humans before, not ever, so please Your Worship."

"That's not what your neighbors say", the Arbiter replied. "I have eye-witness testimony to the effect that you were seen departing your home in the company of no less than three humans, a bear, and a large exotic bird, and that you then departed the vicinity by illicit and unnatural means."

"Surely you don't accept the word of Rabbits, Your Worship!"

"Thankfully I do not have to rely solely on the testimony of mere rodents, however wight-ish they may be." Here the Arbiter motioned to a guard near the door. "Bring in the Fox."

The Guard saluted and opened the door. A brief word was exchanged with someone inside, and in a moment another soldier entered escorting a small red Fox, which padded over to the dais. The creature made a peculiar bow with his forelegs, not unlike that of a trained show horse. The Arbiter then addressed him. "Your name?"

"Bartholomew Fox-Goodburrow, Your Worship", the Fox replied.

"Bartholomew Fox-Goodburrow, do you acknowledge your previous testimony that you saw the Wogs depart from their home in the company of three humans?"

The Fox made a sideways glance at the prisoners and fidgeted slightly. "Yes, Your Worship. In a way. But if I might clarify…"

"Yes or no will do, Fox."

"But Your Worship, I cannot swear to the fact that I saw them go freely and willingly."

The Arbiter scowled. It seemed to Hae-jin that he would rather not have been reminded of this detail. He looked again to Alwog. "It would be far better for you, Wog, if you answered me truthfully now. Or would you prefer that I order my men to fetch the presses?"

Alwog appeared shaken, but defiant. "You can't do that", he said stoutly. "You don't have enough evidence. The testimony of a wight-beast doesn't carry near enough weight as that."

"If this were a matter of petty thievery you would be correct, but it's not. This is a question of treason. I have more latitude than you might imagine, Wog."

The Arbiter then looked to Hae-jin and Joan. "As for you, I need no further evidence. Your presence here is a crime in itself. However, it also demonstrates that our defenses have been gravely compromised, and I require further information immediately. Your cooperation at this time is very much in your best interest....very much so indeed."

The Arbiter let the significance of his words sink in for a moment before proceeding further. "I will give you an opportunity to answer my questions now, of your own volition. I demand to know where you have come from, for what purpose you have entered our lands, and by what means you have nullified our defenses in so doing. Be forewarned that I have many and varied means of ascertaining this information for myself. This is your opportunity to surrender these facts freely, and to thus perhaps save yourselves unnecessary....discomfort. What is your answer?"

The Arbiter waited menacingly for a reply. But none was forthcoming. Hae-jin's mind was racing, trying to come up with something to say without exposing his friends to grave risk. Would Lindsey and her mission really be doomed if he told the truth? Would he and Joan be condemned to some miserable fate if he remained silent? Could he get away with telling only a half truth? But would that even matter?

Was the Drixi lying? Would he simply have them all killed in the end, whether they cooperated or not? As the Drixi waited on his reply Hae-jin found himself without an answer. Joan too remained silent. In all probability she was trying to sort out a similar dilemma in her own mind. Throughout the hall there was nothing but a tense, doleful silence....save for when an explosive sneeze erupted from one of the Wogs. At last, the Arbiter spoke again.

"I see I shall have to extract what I require without the convenience of your compliance. Perhaps after witnessing some of the powers which are mine to command you will be more inclined to cooperate." Here the Arbiter arose. "My Lord Arch-Haruspex, may I entreat you to approach?"

At this, one of the Drixi in sea green robes stepped forward, and ascended the dais. His gait was somewhat stilted, and his face and hands were gnarled and wrinkled. He appeared to be quite elderly indeed, and unlike the other Drixi, who were universally clean shaven, this one sported a long, thin silver beard. The Drixi approached the high table and bowed in a perfunctory sort of way, as if the observance wasn't really necessary but was done anyway out of tolerant indulgence. In contrast, the Arbiter rose to his feet and bowed deeply and respectfully, partially covering his eyes with one hand for a moment as he did so.

"My Lord Arch-Haruspex, I entreat you to call upon the powers at your command to bring light to that which is dark, to reveal that which is hidden, and expose that which is concealed, by Udar's most Holy Hand."

The Haruspex grunted. "I hear your plea", he said languidly, "and I do place my powers at the service of the Arbiters, so may Udar bless."

The Arbiter bowed again and resumed his seat. The Haruspex approached the edge of the dais and peered keenly at the prisoners with a pair of violet eyes which were so pale that they hardly had any color to them at all. Hae-ji suspected that the Haruspex might in fact be quite nearsighted.

The Haruspex then began to pace back and forth on the platform, muttering and moaning indistinctly to himself, his eyes rolled back in their sockets. He then began to execute a series of sweeping and dramatic gestures which caused his robes to billow theatrically. Every movement had an almost rehearsed sort of rhythm to it, yet the performance was somehow lackluster and slightly uncoordinated, as if he were executing motions which had been practiced and performed for a lifetime, but the performer himself was grown old and tired.

Suddenly, the Haruspex halted and cried out loudly. Immediately, four more Drixi in sea green robes stepped forward to ascended the dais, and gathered in a small group near the seer. Two of them carried large bowls, their arms draped with linens, while another held a small object tightly in his hands. It was a little grey dove, its wings and legs pinned closely to its body in the gentle, firm grasp of the Drixi. The Haruspex raised his arm slowly and pointed with a knobbly finger. The dove was then held over one of the bowls as another Drixi produced an ornate, razor-like knife. In an instant the bird was no more, its death throes contained by the iron grip of the Drixi handler as its blood was collected in the bowl beneath it. Its carcass was then slit open and its organs poured into the bowl as well. The Haruspex then approached as the acolytes stood aside deferentially, one of them handing the Haruspex a small golden rod not unlike a stylus. The Haruspex took the rod and then began to prod about the entrails with it, peering into the gory mass while reciting indistinctly. This went on for some minutes until at last the Haruspex grunted to himself in satisfaction. He then went over to another acolyte holding a water filled basin and washed his hands (which had nonetheless remained more or less clean throughout the ritual) and dried them on the linens proffered by the acolyte. He then approached the Arbiter, while the acolytes (whose hands were actually quite bloody) at last took their turn to wash their own hands.

The Haruspex raised his arm and pointed his gnarled finger again, this time straight at Hae-jin. "This one", the Haruspex said, as he continued to level his finger at Hae-jin. "This one is an alien from a distant land far to the east, which is called Ereph. He is a powerful warrior who is a traitor and an outcast among his own people."

The Haruspex now pointed at Joan. "This one has come from one of the human kingdoms which lie a several hundred leagues to the north, either Finnon, Renwall, Linster, or Tollardy. She is a witch, a traitress, and a murderess."

The Haruspex turned to face the Arbiter. "They have violated our lands in order to steal treasure, with which to further the wicked machinations of the woman. They have made the Wogs their servants. They breached our holy valances through the meddlesome arts of the Alva, who seek ever to undermine the will of the Arbiters and to diminish the glory of our sacred land."

The Arbiter's face flushed and he struck the high table with his fist. "I should have known it! The fairy folk care nothing for our sovereignty. They would impose themselves and their loathsome servants on us at every turn. They will not stop until they have obliterated every last shred of our autonomy."

The Arbiter then arose. "Worthy Emissary of The Speakers, will you approach the table?"

From the floor of the great hall a grey robed figure stepped forth from among the assembly. His gait was peculiar and unnatural, and as he ascended the dais he cast back his hood to reveal a terrible, reptilian visage, pebbly skinned with a long snout, with great sagging jowls which were lined with jagged spines. The scales of his face were a dull olive color, ornamented with various patterns of bright red paint. The creature bowed low and solemnly before the high table, and as he spoke he revealed rows of needle like teeth and a blue-grey tongue, and he spoke with a gravelly hiss.

"Most esteemed Arbiter of the Drixi, I am honored to be of assistance."

"Your assistance is appreciated, Emissary. What have you to tell me about these prisoners?"

The Zard cast a cold, inscrutable gaze over the prisoners. "They are servants of the Alva. They seek to do mischief against the worthy endeavours of my noble masters, as my masters have so informed the Arbiters."

Here, the old Haruspex grunted indignantly. "Endeavours with which your noble masters are ever wont to entangle all and sundry. You too sully our land with the evil fruits of your meddling and scheming."

The Zard hissed deeply. "My masters have been entirely forthright in all their dealings with Drixi, unlike others whom I need not mention. The Arbiter speaks rightly, the folk of Alfheim will never cease from molesting you with their relentless trespassing, unlike my masters, who desire only to live in friendship with you."

"Ha!", the Haruspex scoffed.

"I assure you", the Emissary insisted, "the Black Speakers unequivocally affirm the sovereignty of the Drixi. It is their spoken word."

"Only so long as Drixi sovereignty serves the interests of the Speakers", the Haruspex snarled.

The Zard hissed smugly. "You need only look at the present situation, old man. We have been entirely open and candid with the Arbiters.

Indeed, did we not warn them in advance of this very invasion which has now taken place? These loathsome prisoners before you are here in your power only because of our deep friendship and regard for the Drixi."

"Fiddlesticks! Arbiter, don't be taken in by this cold-blooded flunky of the Black Speakers. What is the word of one witch against another?"

The Arbiter cleared his throat restrainedly. "With respect, Arch-Haruspex, this is not the time to debate national policy. The night is waning and we've wasted too much time already. If the prisoners will not speak, I think it is time we compelled them."

The Arbiter arose and addressed Hae-jin and Joan. "I give you one last chance, humans. Will you speak to me?"

Again, Hae-jin and Joan remained silent.

"I see. Guards, bring forward the male."

Hae-jin found himself seized roughly by the arms and dragged closer towards the dais. The Arbiter leaned forward and looked Hae-jin straight in the eye. "Cut off his right hand."

From somewhere behind Hae-jin there was a gasp, and as one of the guards drew his sword the Arbiter abruptly waived his hand in abjuration, and the sword was returned to its scabbard. Twisting around, Hae-jin looked behind him to see that Joan had stepped forward.

"If you please My Lord", she said softly, "spare my friend's hand. There is no need to harm him, I shall speak."

The Arbiter smiled in satisfaction. "So the mute has a tongue after all. What have you to say to me?"

"If you please, My Lord, your Haruspex is partially correct. We came to this land with no intention of bringing harm or insult to the Drixi, but merely to conduct a small ritual needed to free my homeland from the oppression of the Black Speakers and their servants."

The Haruspex snorted. "Ha! You see Arbiter? The witches spread their chaos everywhere, even as they quarrel and fight amongst themselves, polluting our land with their foulness in the process!"

"So it please My Lord, I am no witch", Joan protested.

"Deceitful woman! I know what you are, I read it all in the entrails. You are tainted with witchcraft!"

"Indeed I may be so. Nearly all the poor folk of my land are tainted by the witchcraft of our oppressor."

"A pretty tale, witch, but if you think that....."

Here the Arbiter interrupted. "Again with respect, Arch Haruspex, there is much we still need to uncover. But I do believe more testimony is being offered." The Arbiter gestured towards the floor of the hall, where the Fox was now standing on his hind legs as high as he could and waving with his paws. "Speak, Bartholomew Fox-Goodburrow."

"If you please, your worship", the Fox said. "but I do believe the woman may be telling the truth, at least partially. When I saw them at the house of the Wogs, I also saw another creature, one not unlike his honor the Emissary. I saw him cast a mighty spell upon the whole party, and bewitch them all."

The Arbiter scoffed incredulously. "Are you talking nonsense, Fox? Why didn't you mention this earlier? Are you trying to make a mockery of this investigation?"

From somewhere near the high table another voice suddenly spoke up.

"I think the Fox is right!", the voice said. The Arbiter looked to see who had spoken, but suddenly another voice spoke.

"Nonsense! The Fox is clearly mad!"

"No, it must be true, the Zard have the prisoners bewitched!" retorted the first voice.

"Don't be a paranoid dimwit, you clod! The whole idea is nonsense!" the second voice shouted back.

"Is it time yet for a recess? I'm getting hungry!" said a third voice.

The Arbiter was still trying to identify who the speakers were when one of the teal robed Drixi sitting at the table stood up.

"Enough of these disruptions, this is getting out of hand", the Drixi said.

"Sit down, fool, you're making an ass of yourself!" cried one of the voices.

The Arbiter began to speak, but by this time the entire high table had descended into chaos as all the Drixi sitting there broke out into a graceless argument. Finally, the Arbiter beat his fist on the table.

"Enough! There is nothing to be gained by further argument. I will consult with the Haruspex on this matter in private. The questioning is suspended. Remove the prisoners, and we shall reconvene in the morning. This council is hereby adjourned."

And it was over. The Arbiter and the Haruspex made a grand exit in the company of their attendants while the rest of the Drixi began to disperse, and the prisoners were escorted out with all their limbs happily still intact.

13

"Of Birds and Foxes"

The fortress of the Drixi was not a prison by design. It was a military asset; a defensive bastion and a regional garrison which housed the provincial army. As such, it had no elaborate dungeon, as the fevered imaginations of bards are wont to include in every "proper" castle. It possessed only a small cell block, a place to temporarily detain the occasional bandit or petty delinquent while awaiting judgement. But today, it was being used to hold spies. Tucked away in the keep there was a short corridor which contained a half dozen small cells set three abreast to either side of the hallway. Each cell was sealed with a barred door, and contained a hard bed covered with straw, a stool, and a chamberpot. During the day the space would have been sparingly lit by the tiny barred windows which were set high in the walls, but by night the only light to be had was from a single candelabra placed near the door, which was there principally to ensure that the jailor could see what was going on inside the cell block before entering it. The Drixi were ever a cautious lot.

Hae-jin sat thoughtfully in his cell. Directly across the hall from him Joan was lying quietly on her own harsh berth. The Wogs had been piled into the next cell down, and Hae-jin could hear them quarrelling with one another. He was still perplexed by what had happened earlier in the great hall. Everything had been orderly at first, yet by the end things had devolved more or less into chaos. Having spent four days now surrounded by the Drixi, Hae-jin had developed a picture of them as meticulous, well disciplined, and very reverent creatures. Yet by the end of that evening even the officers had suddenly become flat out rude to one another. Perhaps they were simply a more volatile people than Hae-jin had given them credit for. Or perhaps there was something about the situation in the room just then which had led them to conduct themselves in a way which was foreign to their character. For one who had held such imperious command of the proceedings at the start, it seemed that even the Arbiter was baffled by the sudden outburst of discord. It was a mystery.

Suddenly, from outside the cell there was a polite cough. Hae-jin looked up and saw that he had a visitor. Standing on the other side of the door, his nose just poking through the bars, was the Fox who had given witness in the great hall earlier. The Fox sniffed slightly. "Good evening", the Fox said. "I hope you aren't particularly uncomfortable. The Drixi can be quite discriminating with their hospitality. I've got much nicer quarters. But then again, I'm not under arrest as a spy....no offense." The Fox gazed at Hae-jin with amber colored eyes which betrayed a keen, wild sort of intelligence. Hae-jin met his gaze evenly and shrugged. "It's not the worst place I've ever been in."

"Perhaps not, but it will likely get much worse soon enough. The Drixi are intensely fearful of humans, almost pathologically so. If you're lucky, they'll put you in a hole somewhere and keep you locked up forever like a rabid beast. I think it's more likely, though, that they'll just finish you off in some sticky way and then fumigate your ashes with a lot of hocus pocus."

"Are you taunting me?", Hae-jin demanded.

"I'm being realistic", the Fox said, with a sort of shrug. "Personally, I don't have anything against humans. I think they're interesting, especially when they travel around though magic and embarrass the Drixi. You're not from this part of the world, are you?"

Hae-jin shrugged again. "The soothsayer was more or less correct. I come from a place called Zhongyang."

"That's what you call it. On the elven maps it's called Ereph, but I suppose it doesn't really matter. What's in a name anyway, other than everything? I come from Zhongyang as well."

This caught Hae-jin by surprise. "You're from Zhongyang?"

"Indeed I am", the Fox said. "At least, I think I am..indirectly. They say that all talking Foxes such as myself come originally from the East. But my ancestors came here a long time ago, maybe hundreds of years past. You've only just come here, out of thin air as it were (quite literally in fact). I find that fascinating." The Fox paused to briefly scratch at an ear with his hind leg. "So I guess the problem right now is how to get you out of here."

Hae-jin was again startled. "What did you say?"

"I said we need to find a way to get you out of here. The Drixi certainly aren't going to release you."

"Um...that's very kind of you", Hae-jin said guardedly. "And unexpected. After all, you bore witness against us not long ago."

"Oh, that?", the Fox said airily. "Well, I lied about most of it. I mean, I really did see you all go off and disappear through a hole in the ground, but I never for a moment thought that any of you were going along unwillingly. The Wogs would sell out to anyone."

"Did you lie as well about having seen a Zard bewitch us?"

"Of course I did. It worked though, didn't it? It got the Drixi to suspend the interrogation, in a way that I thought was very funny. It was all I could do to keep from laughing at all those silly prigs arguing with each other. It's because of me that you're down here right now with both your hands still attached. You're very welcome!"

Hae-jin was taken aback. Perhaps this was an unexpected ally. Or perhaps it was all a Drixi trick of some kind. "Ah", he said cautiously. "Thank you for that. Are you saying you're going to help us escape?"

The Fox glanced over his shoulder briefly. "Oh, I think I'll manage to figure something out. Just don't let the Drixi kill you before I do (figure something out, I mean). If I help you, will you promise to take me with you?"

Hae-jin was confused. "What do you mean?"

"If I help you escape, will you promise to take me with you to wherever you are going?"

"Why would you come with us? Are you afraid of the Drixi?"

"No. I'm not afraid of them. I'm bored with them. They're superstitious, paranoid, and oppressive. And they're weak. You and your friends sailed right through their most powerful enchantments in order to get here. Whoever you are, or whoever you're working for, you're more powerful than the Drixi. Take me with you, and I'll get you out of here."

Hae-jin did not feel that he could trust the Fox. But in all honesty, he didn't have any better options. "If you keep your promise, I'll keep mine."

"Done! I'll be seeing you soon enough then, I'm off to go stir up some mischief."

"What kind of mischief?"

"No idea, really. But whatever it is, I'm sure it'll be funny."

And the Fox whisked away. Hae-jin leaned back against the wall of his cell, his mind a whirl. This was an unexpected development to be sure. Frankly, he didn't know what to make of it. True, he and his fellow prisoners seemed to have momentarily forestalled whatever fate was headed their way. But the Fox's story was remarkable, and Hae-jin wasn't at all sure he believed any of it. Nor could he understand why any of the Drixi should have believed the Fox either, or why they should have become so argumentative with each other over the Fox's lies. The Fox might take credit for having bought them some time, but Hae-jin wasn't so sure. There must have been something more going than just the wild stories of some flippant Fox.

"Do you think he'll really try to help us?"

Hae-jin snapped out of his reverie and looked across the hallway. Joan was pressing close by the bars of her cell door, looking anxiously at Hae-jin. Of course, from where she was she had probably overheard the entire conversation with the Fox. Hae-jin shrugged.

"I don't know", he said. "Maybe the Fox is on our side, maybe he's not. Either way, I don't know how he could ever manage to get us out of here....not on his own, at any rate. Something strange happened up there. Maybe heaven hasn't quite given up on us yet."

"Do you think the Bird was involved?"

"If the Bird were trying to save us, why wouldn't he just pop out of a hole in the air like he always does and get us out that way?"

"Maybe he can't. If the Drixi can lay an enchantment over their whole kingdom just in order to keep humans out, surely they could put even stronger enchantments on their castles? The Bird has got to have his limits."

"Of that I'm quite sure. He certainly hasn't helped us much so far. Besides, if the Fox were working for the Bird, why didn't he say so when he was here just now?"

They were both silent for a moment.

"What do you think will happen to us, Hae-jin?"

Hae-jin sighed. "Unfortunately, I think the Fox is right. I suppose it's possible that the Drixi may simply throw us out of their land and be done with us, but I'm inclined to doubt it. They seem too afraid, and too unsure. At best I think they'll keep us prisoners until they're certain they know how we got here, and then I suppose they'll make an example of us."

"I'm sorry", the woman said.

"What for?", Hae-jin asked.

"For getting you into this", the other replied.

"There's no need for you to be sorry. It was the Bird who got us into this."

"But you're here because the Bird asked you to help my people. To help me. It's still my fault. You'd be safe in your own land if it weren't for me."

"Nonsense", Hae-jin scoffed. "I was worse off there than I am here. The Haruspex was right about me....partially. I served my people as best I could, and refused to be an instrument of their oppressors. For this I was branded a traitor by my own king. Were I to have been captured I would certainly have been put to death. I suppose the Bird did save me from that at least, although I may wind up dying here instead."

"Is that why you're helping my people against our oppressor? Because you couldn't help yours?"

Hae-jin tensed a bit. Joan's words had struck an uncomfortable chord. "Maybe I did some good", he said. "I don't know. My whole life I was a loyal soldier to my king, who was, in the end, little more than a puppet of our enemies. So in some ways I suppose I was partially complicit. Maybe I achieved nothing at all for my people, even when I at last refused to go along with it any longer. All I know is that I did my best for them, and I paid the price for it. But at least I did something about it. I suppose you can understand that."

"Yes. Yes I do understand."

Hae-jin glanced at Joan. Her eyes were averted, and Hae-jin almost thought he could see tears in them. Hae-jin recollected the words of the Drixi Haruspex. He had called Hae-jin a traitor and an outcast, which was more or less accurate. And he had also called Joan a traitor, and a witch...and a murderess. If the Haruspex had been right in his assessment of Hae-jin, what did that say about Joan?

"What about you, Joan Greyflower?", Hae-jin asked. "What did the Haruspex mean when he spoke about you? Joan didn't reply. Her eyes were still averted, but even in the dim flickering light of the candelabra Hae-jin was sure now that he could see tears. "Joan Greyflower?" Joan sniffed, but made no reply.

Moonlight was beginning to filter through the tiny windows of the cell block. Outside, the moon was now high in the sky, bathing the world in eerie silver. Far below, the castle of the Drixi was largely asleep, the only wakeful persons being the sufferers in the Drixi cells and those assigned to keep watch through the night....as well as those who sought to carry out their business in secret.

Through darkened halls and silent corridors, the Fox lurked unseen. He'd always had an uncanny talent for this sort of thing. He had a way of dealing with people such that they never took him fully into account. It could be very funny at times, and it was always very useful. With the proper attitude and the right amount of cunning, a person who is never properly appreciated can achieve a degree of power which no other creature can. Right now, the Fox had a job to do. Since his arrival at the castle he'd made it his business to familiarize himself with it as much as possible, to know all of its paths and places, its secrets and its weaknesses. He was quite confident that he could arrange some humorous means with which to effect the escape of the prisoners. He had a plan in mind, and had already made some preparations. All that was needed now was to choose just the right moment to put it into action.

What was that? A cry? Had something caught the attention of the watchmen? The noise was faint, not enough to wake anyone, but Foxes have a keen sense of hearing and Bartholomew Fox-Goodburrow had always considered himself a particularly special Fox. He scampered off, following the noises to their source.

But Bartholomew was not the only creature who had heard the noise. High on a parapet somewhere in the castle a cowled, grey robed figure stood amidst the light of the stars, listening intently. He too had heard the sound, and as the noises grew steadily louder he smiled to himself. A few moments more, he thought, and it would be time to get down to business.

Guard duty is a delicate business, particularly at night. It consists of long, tedious hours of excruciating boredom, and very often it is all one can do just to keep awake. Along a lonely stretch of the castle wall, a Drixi watchman was pacing dolefully atop the battlements, dragging his feet with drowsiness as he went. Just a few moments before he'd been staring intently out into the darkness, thinking that he might have seen some obscure movement or other. But it seemed to have been nothing, and now his focus was lost again. His eyes were upon his shoes, and his thoughts were in his bed. What was that? A sound? Something at least had happened to once more arouse the watchman from his reverie. He caught up his spear in his hands and looked out into the darkness. Abruptly his vision was blocked by a great hairy shape looming before him. A massive paw swept out of nowhere and caught him at the side of the head, and the guard fell senseless. A tremendous bear now rolled over the parapet and onto the walk.

For four days now she had been tracking the Drixi, and each night she had waged war on their encampment. Though each time she had been thwarted, she had returned every night nonetheless to try again. Perhaps the Drixi had thought they were rid of her, now they were safely ensconced behind their stone walls. But they were wrong. People often underestimate the persistence and resourcefulness of even ordinary bears. They can reach places that many would think impossible for creatures of their size, and they will dare to invade places that many would think beyond the courage of any animal. And when a bear happens to be one of the greatest bear-wights of the Fairworld, there may be no limits to what such a creature might do. For three nights straight the Drixi had driven her from their camp. But tonight, she would conquer their castle.

The bear glanced to her right, and then to her left. So far, she had been undetected. That was about to change. It was time for mayhem. The bear began to casually saunter down the walk towards a covered turret. The door was open, and the bear squeezed inside. From within there then came a resounding crash and a series of startled cries, and suddenly two Drixi burst out the opposite door and ran pell mell down the walk, with the bear in hot pursuit.

The bear chased the Drixi across the walks, up and down stairs, through doorways and passages. As they ran more and more Drixi voices joined with the hapless cries of guards, as more soldiers were clamoring to arms. Soon the courtyards were swarming with bewildered Drixi, many half dressed and poorly armed. Lights were being called for, but in the chaos of the moment all order was lost as the bear careened through their midst, scattering Drixi in its wake.

"There it goes, stop it!"

"Where did it go?"

"It went that way!"

"Which way?"

"I've dropped my lantern!"

"Where's the captain?"

"What are we looking for anyway?"

"Lookout, it's coming back this way!"

"Quick, get out of the way!"

The chaos couldn't last forever though. Soon enough lanterns and torches were being passed around. Guard detachments from other parts of the castle were arriving, and these came fully armed and arrayed for combat, with their officers in the lead. Bit by bit they began to herd and corral the beast, until it was at last cornered in one of the courtyards. There the beast stood, swatting aside spears and knocking over Drixi whenever it could. Sporadic arrows were beginning to fall around it as archers mounted the surrounding walls. The situation was becoming desperate. For the moment the archers could only shoot intermittently, for fear of harming their comrades. But that was about to change. Suddenly there were multiple blasts from a horn in a precise, rhythmic staccato. It was a standard Drixi battle signal, calling for the frontline to fall back and make way for others to attack. In a moment the archers would have a clear shot of the bear, and would let loose a devastating volley. Then, somewhere else in the castle, a great bell began to toll.

It wasn't marking the passage of the hour. It wasn't the proper time, nor was it the proper cadence. It was a steady toll, rung as rapidly as the ringers could heave the ropes. It was the alarm for fire. From the walls of the courtyard someone shouted and pointed. All eyes now looked up to the great keep towering above them. There, silhouetted against the silvery moonlit walls, was a great billow of inky smoke. More cries now filled the air, along with calls for buckets of water and sand. The archers hesitated, their arrows still nocked. But this was all the bear needed. With a roar it leaped forward, ploughing through the ranks of the Drixi and barrelling off through the corridors again. The baleful tolling of the bell echoed throughout the castle, across courtyards and walks and through passages and corridors as the alarm was spread to every chamber. Hae-jin had fallen into a light doze, but awoke with a start as the sonorous ringing filtered its way through the tiny windows of the Drixi jails. He pressed his head against the barred door, trying to see as far as he could into the corridor to get some idea what on earth was going on. Failing this, he turned to face the rear wall, trying to guess whether he could stack up his meager furniture high enough that he could peep through the tiny window.

"Ahem."

The voice had come from behind him. Had the Fox come through with his promise? Hae-jin turned around. It wasn't the Fox though who stood outside the door. Instead, a cowled, grey robed figure stood there. Hae-jin looked at the face shrouded beneath the hood. For a moment he wasn't sure what was looking at, but in a flash the uncertainty had passed, and he could see the face of a Drixi. The Drixi met Hae-jin's gaze evenly. Then he grinned.

"Good evening", the Drixi said. "Pardon me while I unlock the door."

To Hae-jin's astonishment, the Drixi produced a set keys and opened the door.

"Please, do come out while I release the others.

The Drixi then set about opening the doors to the other cells as Hae-jin stepped into the hall. He took a furtive look into the guardroom outside, but it was empty. The Drixi had now bundled the other prisoners out of their cells. For once, the Wogs were speechless. Addressing them all, the Drixi smiled pleasantly. "Now that we're all together, I think it is time that we left. We only have a little time, please follow me."

Hae-jin looked at Joan. Her eyes were wide, but she met his gaze without speaking. They both knew that whatever was going on, this was the only chance they were likely to get to escape. The Drixi began leading the prisoners through various winding passages. Now and again they were obliged to duck into shadowy corners as groups of Drixi barrelled through the hallways bearing lanterns and buckets as the incessant tolling of the bell filtered through the halls. Bit by bit they made their way steadily through the castle, and Hae-jin had a sense that they were headed downwards towards the outer walls. Eventually they came to a place where the walls were thick and devoid of windows, and upon making a sharp turn they were met with a heavy, iron shod door. Again, their Drixi guide produced his keys and opened the door, flooding the passage with moonlight. The wogs could contain themselves no longer. The moment the way to freedom presented itself they bolted through the door. Joan and Hae-jin followed more cautiously. They were now outside the castle. They had stepped through a sally port at the foot of the walls. A narrow, precarious path sloped its way through the rocks beneath them. It would have been suicide to make such a climb while the walls were manned with archers, but for the moment the walls were deserted. The party began stumbling and scraping their way down the jagged hillside, while far behind them the tolling of the bell echoed through the night. Gradually they approached the bottom, making their way through the ever thickening trees. It seemed as though they were heading to the river, which soon enough they did.

Their Drixi guide led them to a place where the bank was a bit less rocky. Here there was a small boat drawn up onto the shore. The Drixi pushed the boat into the river and then began to usher them in. As the last of the prisoners stepped into the boat, the Drixi at last spoke again. "Take the boat a short way down the river. In a little while you will see a light in the forest. Cross there, your friends will be waiting for you in the woods."

"Aren't you coming with us?" Joan asked.

"No, my work here is finished for now, though perhaps we may meet again someday. In the meanwhile, I apologize for the inconvenience hitherto."

With that, the Drixi gave the boat one last shove, and it floated out into the river. As the prisoners bent to the oars, Hae-jin took a last look at the diminishing figure behind them. The Drixi was grinning, and raised his arm to wave casually. As he did so he suddenly appeared to shrink. At first Hae-jin thought it was trick of the light, but even as he watched the grey-robed Drixi's whole appearance began to change as he transformed into a small, green clad being with long willowy limbs, and a merry laugh floated over the river as the creature darted off and disappeared into the woods.

The current carried them swiftly down the river, and they hardly needed the oars. In a short while, Hae-jin spotted a glint of yellowish-green light in the woods. He directed the others to make for the shore. They crossed quickly enough, and once they'd all piled onto the river-bank they drew the boat into the woods and covered it with branches and rushes. They then made for the light. After a while of stumbling through the brambles and enduring the woeful cursing of the Wogs they came to a small clearing left by a fallen tree. There on the tree-trunk was set an iron lantern intricately wrought with pierced designs of stars and crescents. And beside the lantern, its golden feathers shimmering in the flickering light, was the Bird.

Hae-jin felt a wave of relief sweep over him, even as it was mixed with annoyance and suspicion. He doubled his pace, and as he and the others entered the clearing the Bird spotted them and began to beat his wings excitedly as he spoke. "Splendid!", the Bird cried. "Splendid splendid splendid! I see Elred found you, I knew he wouldn't let me down!"

"Who's Elred?"

"I'll explain all that later. But we must hurry. It's all up to us now, you know."

Alwog grunted petulantly. "Where have you been, Bird?", the Wog demanded. "We've been having an awful time."

"They would have eaten us for sure!" Berwog piped up.

"Shut up, Berwog. Drixi don't eat Wogs. But I'm thinking we're going to have to adjust our contract, Bird. We're going to have to move house now, that's for sure, probably to another country. That'll cost a bit. Then there's the loss of our equipment, plus acute mental anguish and additional hazard pay....I'm thinking five hundred silver marks at least."

"Five hundred and one!"

"Shut up!"

"Gentlemen, gentlemen!" The Bird said, beating his wings impatiently. "Gentlemen, I assure you that you will be duly compensated for your trouble. As for your equipment, Elred has already taken care of that." Here the Bird swept a grandiose wing towards the base of the log, where the prisoner's possessions were collected in a pile. "Your weapons and gear are all here. Elred saw to that as well, although he couldn't find Hae-jin's sword. I'm afraid it's probably still lying somewhere in the woods near Harin's Vault. Please, gather your belongings, we will be leaving just as soon as Ursilda arrives....aha! There she is now!"

A great dark shape was now looming into the light of the lantern.

"Ursilda! I'm so glad you made it out in one piece!"

"You expected any less, Bird?"

"No no, of course not. But I'm gratified nonetheless. I was flying overhead the whole time, keeping watch you know, and for a moment there I wasn't sure. That fire was a lucky stroke. If it weren't for that we might well have been in danger of losing our good bear."

"No you wouldn't have. I would have overcome them all anyway. I am Ursilda."

"Er, yes. Of course you would have. Never doubted you for a moment, my dear."

Here Hae-jin spoke up. For four days he'd kept his patience and his peace. Now that he was unleashed from captivity his anger was at last unleashed as well. "You may well have been in danger of losing us all!", he spat. "The rest of us were prisoners of the Drixi for four days, and Ursilda has risked her life every night to try and rescue us...at least I think it was Ursilda..."

"It was."

"Well then at least the Bear has been here trying to help us. And what about Lindsey, where is she?"

The Bird shuffled uncomfortably.

"Perhaps we'd better get a move on. I'll explain everything later...."

"No, you will explain it now. Where is Lindsey?"

The Bird coughed uncomfortably.

"I'm afraid I don't know."

"What!"

"Please, do try to keep quiet. We're not all that far from the Drixi castle you know."

"What do you mean you don't know? What happened to her?"

"I'm afraid I'm not quite sure. We had some unexpected complications, what with the Drixi and all...."

"We know all about the Drixi, thank you."

"...and I'm afraid that during the confusion we rather lost track of Lindsey."

"We?"

"Sorry. I'm afraid *I* rather lost track of Lindsey. I was busy you see..."

"Doing what?"

"...and there was so much going on, it was impossible to...."

"So you don't know what happened to her?"

"Yes I do....more or less. I found out where she went, and Elred went and talked to her and gave her a means with which to return to us, but then she disappeared again..."

"What do you mean she disappeared *again*?"

"...and that was four days ago and Elred's been looking for her ever since."

"And in all that time you didn't bother to rescue us?"

"We felt you were safe where you were for the time being. The Drixi would not have harmed you, not until after you'd had an initial interrogation with the Arbiters, and in the meanwhile I've been making other arrangements."

"What sort of 'arrangements'?"

"The Drixi who ambushed us at Harin's Vault were accompanied by the Zard, who are the servants of our enemies. Lindsey succeeded in opening Harin's Vault, and Gurth knows it. He has been calling upon all of his most powerful enchantments to stop us. For four days now the doors to Linster have been shut. I cannot take you there in my usual fashion, and as I said I have been obliged to make other arrangements. I commend Ursilda's earlier efforts to rescue you, of course, but there was really no point in doing so any sooner than we have, not without proper transportation to get you well away from the Drixi's clutches. They'd simply have caught you again right away. As it is, I think I've managed to arrange things remarkably quickly...Behold!"

The Bird hopped off the log and walked over to a long, dark mass lying in the underbrush. Grasping it with his beak, he dragged the object into the light of the lantern. It was a coiled, tubular object made of some heavy sort of material, and upon bringing it into the light the Bird unrolled it with a flourish to reveal a spacious, maroon colored rug. "I borrowed this from a friend of mine in Al Shati Ramal...well, sort of a friend anyway. Do be careful, he wants it back you know....at least, I'm quite sure he does. I suspect he made quite a fuss when he found out it was missing."

Hae-jin looked closely at the rug. It was staggeringly beautiful, intricately woven with many colored and metallic threads, bearing elaborate designs in a flowing script. Even without the gift of tongues Hae-jin recognized the writing, and with it he could read it all clearly. Like the majority of his people Hae-jin was a Buddhist, but he knew enough about foreign religions to see that the rug was covered in Quranic inscriptions which were blended with various magic spells and incantations, and although the whole thing put together was rather obtuse he was still able to get the general idea of it all. "This thing is supposed to fly?", he asked.

"And very fast too", the Bird said proudly. "Linster is many hundreds of leagues from here, but with the aid of this admirable carpet we should be able to get there in just a few hours. We should get going though, it won't be long before the Drixi discover your escape, although I suppose the fire will tie them up for a bit."

Hae-jin recollected the visit by the Fox. "I think I know how that fire came about. I'd wager it was the Fox that did it."

"Fox? What Fox?"

"There was a Fox in the Drixi castle. The Drixi had him there as a witness against the Wogs, but apparently he's not all that loyal to them. He offered to help us escape if we promised to take him with us to wherever we were going. The timing for that fire was far too convenient, I have no doubt it was he who created it. It seems we now have a promise to keep, if we can find him that is."

"What! But we can't hang around here trying to find some Fox!"

"You shan't need to." a voice suddenly interjected. "The Fox has already found you."

The voice had come from somewhere inside the woods. Upon hearing it everyone gave a start, even the Bird, and at that moment a small red fox sauntered into the light of the lantern and hopped up onto the log. The Fox sat down and casually scratched himself with his hind paw a couple times before speaking. "Well, here we all are" ,the Fox said. "You humans certainly keep some interesting company. Of course, as soon as I saw the Bear I figured it must be a friend of yours (which gave me the perfect opportunity to set the smoke off), but imagine my surprise when I came back to discover that your cells were already empty. But I found your scent, and I followed it as far as the river (which, I might add, is hideously cold and unpleasant to swim in). Your lamp guided me the rest of the way here. Anyway, I think we'd all better leave now. I was able to spot your light from across the river, then so can one of the Drixi's hawks."

The Bird looked imploringly at Hae-jin. "You're not seriously suggesting we take this Fox along?", the Bird said. "Our situation is very delicate at present!

"I gave the Fox my word, and he kept his part of the bargain", Hae-jin said firmly. "I shall keep mine."

"Oh very well, have it your way! Here, everyone gather your things and get together on the rug."

In a few moments the Wogs had donned their possessions and after a bit of jostling everyone managed to find a place somewhere on the rug. As large as it was, it was still dreadfully cramped with all of them on it together (including the Bear), and nobody wanted to sit too close to the edge. When everyone was finally settled, the Bird leaned down and pressed his beak to the rug and whispered instructions. Suddenly the rug began to quiver beneath them, and from within the woven fibres a sound emerged. It was a raspy, almost inaudible noise, like coarse cloth being rubbed together. You couldn't call it a voice, but it formed into words anyway: *"By Allah's grace, it shall be so."*, the voice said. With that, the carpet floated into the air and sailed high and away into the midnight sky.

14

"A Locked Door"

The sun was hidden behind a seamless sheet of pale grey clouds, bathing the world below in a hollow light. Below was a landscape of rolling uplands, with sloping plains carpeted by tall brown grasses waving gently in the breeze, disturbed here and there by pockets of leafy brush and scrubby trees. Zebra, antelope, and other grazing animals foraged in silence among the plants, while all around a soft chorus of insects filled the air, punctuated now and then by the gentle chirrup of birds. In all else the world was totally silent, for this was a place forsaken by man.

At the summit of a low rise there was a place where the grass was broken by a crumbled platform of worked stone, upon which there was a lonely stand of battered and bleached marble pillars, piercing the sky forlornly like an isolated copse of limbless stone trees. Many long years ago this had been a temple, but now all that remained were the fragments of a portico resting upon shattered foundations. At the foot of one of these pillars a lone girl was sitting, her back propped against the stone column and her elbows resting on her knees as she gazed pensively out across the savannah. A day had gone by since Lindsey had fled Dackery's house in Connecticut in the company of its proprietor.

Immediately after having passed out of the house Dackery had made another portal, which they then passed through as well. He then made another. And another. And still another. According to Dackery, if one were obliged (as they were) to make an escape via doormaking while likely being scried upon, the best approach was to create and pass through as many doors to as many places in as brief a time possible, so as to confuse anyone who might be watching by various arcane means. All day they had passed through one portal to the next, jumping from place to place, only ever pausing briefly to allow Dackery to rest between making doors, for channeling the energies needed to make a door was a physically demanding task. By nightfall they had come to this forlorn temple deep in the midst of a desolate savannah, at which point Dackery all but collapsed.

It was morning now, only a couple hours after dawn. Lindsey gazed out across the plains, idly watching the various animals as they grazed sedately not very far away from this desolate spot, yet never actually approaching it. Perhaps they were disturbed by the presence of two human wanderers. Or perhaps there was something about the temple itself which pushed them away, maybe some sort of enchantment or curse which repelled all living things. Either way, it was a hopelessly lonely place. A monument to the past, existing in the present yet cut-off from it, standing serene and immutable while everywhere the world went on without it.

Meanwhile, somewhere nearby, Horatio Dackery was likely still asleep. Lindsey hated the thought of waking him, but it was probably time enough all the same. She needed to talk to him. With a sigh she arose from where she sat and descended the crumbling steps. The only portion of the temple which still possessed most of its integrity was a small outbuilding just off the main platform. It was a small square block of mottled stone which stood a few yards away from the main temple itself, yet still within the protective aura which Lindsey suspected the temple possessed, for it was dry and clean and devoid of any vermin.

At one time it may have been a storeroom, or else might have contained some sort of secondary altar. In any event, last night it had served as an erstwhile bedroom for two weary travelers in need of a resting place far from the reaches of civilization. Lindsey approached the small structure and peeked inside. The interior was dim and cavelike, but in one corner she could still see Dackery's great shape stretched upon the floor, undisturbed in his repose, almost as if he were part of the temple itself. Lindsey was not about to bother him. She stepped back outside and sat down in the grass a few paces further down the hillside.

She was still determined to go on with her mission. Now more than ever, really. Yesterday she'd seen a man die while trying to kill her. If Gurth's agents were able to track her all the way back to her own world and ambush her there (as they'd already done once), there was no reason to suppose they'd ever let her alone so long as she remained a threat. There was a good chance she would be unable to get out of this now even if she'd wanted to. Which she didn't. As she was thinking her hand stole up and reached inside her dress to feel the medallion from Harin's Vault hanging there next to her skin. She was going to see this through. Gurth and his minions needed to be stopped, and Lindsey had made a promise which she was determined never to break. Not in a million years. Somehow she had to get to this place called Linster. She'd already lost the enchanted coin given to her by the mysterious individual who called himself Elred, so there was no getting there on her own. She was going to need help, and there was only one person in the universe who could provide it now.

A shadow fell across the ground before her. Lindsey turned and looked upwards to see Dackery standing behind her, gazing out across the savannah. Despite having spent the night bundled up on a stone floor he still appeared immaculate, fully dressed in a suit which hardly looked any worse for wear. Dackery looked down and touched the brim of his hat. "Good morning, Ms. Fluger. I hope you slept well."

"I guess. Do you think we've shaken them, Mr. Dackery?"

Dackery pursed his lips thoughtfully. "Having already underestimated them once, I'm hesitant to proffer any reassurances now. However, we couldn't have covered our tracks much more than we did yesterday. That being said, I'm not sure what should be done now. I'm sure they haven't given up looking for us, and were I to take you to your own home I doubt you'd be in any less jeopardy than you are now."

"Yes, about that. I've been thinking, Mr. Dackery."

Dackery cocked an eye at Lindsey. "You're going to go through with it then?"

"Yes."

Dackery remained silent. He didn't actually sigh, but his usually inscrutable countenance bore a look of resignation. "Well, that's that then. I respect your decision, of course."

"Thanks."

"But how do you propose to proceed?"

Lindsey hesitated. She felt she knew exactly what needed to be done next, but that meant asking Dackery for help. She hedged a bit. "I guess I'll just have to get to Linster somehow and figure it out from there."

"I will have to take you there then. You have no other means of reaching that place."

"Yes, I know. I'm sorry to be a pain. If you could just drop me off there I'd be really grateful. Once I'm there you can leave. You don't need to do anything else."

Dackery turned to face Lindsey head on and looked her straight in the eye. "What do you take me for, Ms. Fluger? You'll be in for a world of danger if you so much as set one foot in Linster. I will not permit you to go there alone."

"Well, I'm going. You don't have to permit me to do anything. This is my decision, and I won't drag you into it."

"Frankly, Ms Fluger, you won't have a chance without me. You won't survive on your own, and all your other allies have gone missing."

"I don't want anyone else to get hurt because of me."

"People are going to get hurt whether you want it or not", Dackery said bluntly. "Gurth's interest in Linster is significant. Even if you manage to lift the curse he won't let go of his hold on the country without a fight. People are going to die. It's not your fault that all of this is happening, but it will all be for nothing if you are foolish and try to tackle this on your own. You need my help."

Lindsey gritted her teeth and tried to keep from crying. She didn't like the way things were going, and she certainly didn't like hearing it from Dackery. Especially given that he was right. "I'm grateful, Mr. Dackery. I really am. Here I was thinking I would have a hard time talking you into taking me to Linster at all, and now I'm having to try and talk you out of coming along the whole way with me. I really appreciate it. You're a fine man."

Dackery seemed pleased, and just a little bit embarrassed. "Ahem. Well, it's not as if I haven't been in a sticky situation or two before. Gurth's men are following me now as well, and I'd just as well like to see his loathsome enterprises put to an end. Besides, there are other things to consider."

"Like what?"

Dackery made no reply. Lindsey looked at him and tried to meet his eye, but he avoided her gaze. Dackery cleared his throat. "Well, there's no point in remaining here any longer. It would be helpful if we got to Linster earlier than later. Our first order of business in Linster will be to establish ourselves in a secure place somewhere in the wilderness from which we can learn the lay of the land, and we would do well to have as much daylight as possible. If you're ready, I think we should leave immediately."

Lindsey took a deep breath. This was it; she'd committed herself. There was no going back now. "I'm ready, Mr. Dackery."

It didn't take long to gather up their meager possessions, and in a short while Lindsey and Dackery were standing together at the foot of the temple. Muttering some inaudible words, Dackery raised his walking stick and traced an arc in the air before him, leaving a trail of fire hanging on the breeze like an invisible burning thread. Dackery then tucked his walking stick under his left arm and drawing the curved saber which hung at his waist he stepped through the portal. Lindsey had a sudden feeling of dread as he did so, for the danger of their circumstance was quite apparent. Who indeed knew what might be waiting for them on the other side in Linster? Taking a firm grip on her own battle axe, Lindsey followed Dackery through. Suddenly, Lindsey felt as if the world had dropped out from under her.

It was only a momentary sensation. For a second she had felt completely disoriented, only to recover again almost immediately. Lindsey looked about herself. She and Dackery were standing inside what appeared to be a stone structure. It was a pentagonal room with a high vaulted ceiling and solid stone walls on every side, and on the floor there was the shape of a pentagram with each point touching one corner of the room. The place was dimly lit, yet no source of light was to be seen. And there were no doors.

Lindsey turned around and around bewilderedly. In every direction there were nothing but impenetrable walls, without an opening of any kind. Lindsey's heart began to race as she fought against the sense of dread and panic which was rising within her. Were she and Dackery trapped? Had they fallen into some kind of ambush, or bumbled into some impenetrable cistern? She calmed down as she reminded herself that whatever it was they were in, Dackery could probably just make another door and take them out again....at least, she hoped he could. Meanwhile, Dackery had been walking the perimeter of the room, feeling the walls while muttering thoughtfully to himself. "Interesting....very interesting indeed."

"Mr. Dackery, where are we?"

"Not in Linster. Or at least, not there in any meaningful way."

"What do you mean?"

"I believe we are somewhere between spaces. Not quite where we were, and certainly not where we were going."

"Come again?"

"This space, this room. It is sort of an illusion. Our minds are filling in the blanks with an image of something which is quite real, yet has no true existence on any physical plane."

"But what does it mean? What's causing it?"

"It means that the doors to Linster have been shut. All of them. While the enchantment lasts no one will be capable of making any doorways in or out of Linster, nor likely any doors within it. I've seen things like this done before, but never on such a scale. Quite a remarkable feat."

"So you mean nobody can enter Linster at all?"

"Not through doormaking."

"But how did they know....no, I guess that's a silly question. They knew about the Bird, and they know he's a doormaker. So they're trying to keep him and me out."

"Exactly."

"But how do you know they've sealed off the whole country? Couldn't we find some place that they don't have protected, or maybe make a door just outside the country and then walk the rest of the way?"

"Like I said", Dackery replied. "I've seen doormaking being blocked like this before. But only involving very specific locations. I'm afraid I don't know the geography of Linster, so our place of arrival would not have been in any way precise. As such, the fact that they've managed to snare us at all means that they must have cast their enchantment very wide indeed. The magic of doormaking is highly subjective in its operation, and a good deal of how it works depends on the intent of the user. The enchantment "knows" that we're trying to get to Linster, and as such it will block us out as far away as is necessary to prevent us from getting there. I doubt I could successfully make a door to anywhere within a thousand miles of the place."

"But what are we going to do?"

"I don't know. But we can't stay here. Come Ms. Fluger, I think it is time that we left." With that, Dackery took up his walking stick again, and traced out a pattern of flame in the stone walls, and he and Lindsey stepped through.

Suddenly they were plunged into darkness. Lindsey instinctively reached out to find Dackery. Instead, her hand struck against something hard and smooth which seemed to fly away the instant she touched it, followed a half second later by a ceramic sounding smash coming from the floor. Apparently she'd just knocked something over. Lindsey bit her lip to hold back a flow of curses as she reached out again more carefully this time.

Now there was a bright spot of light. Lindsey could now see Dackery a couple feet away, holding aloft a lit cigarette lighter which cast a faint golden glow over their surroundings. They were inside a short, tube-like room with a low vaulted ceiling of red brick which reached all the way to the floor on both sides of its length. At one end there was a vertical wall into which was set a small wooden door, and everywhere there was all manner of bric a brac; Barrels, crates, old chairs and neglected tools, and many shelves and tables piled with all manner of mundane items. Immediately to Lindsey's right there was a shelf stacked precariously with an assortment of small ceramic pots, one of which was now smashed on the floor at her feet. Lindsey spoke in a hoarse whisper, still shaken from the disturbance of the fallen pot. "Where are we now?"

"Inside someone's cellar."

"Yeah, I kinda guessed that. But where?"

"The kingdom of Ronymsia, which is a few thousand miles or so southwest of the temple where we slept last night. Pardon me a moment, I think a more permanent light is in order." Dackery was now picking his way over to a table and was rummaging through a small wooden box which was sitting on it. In a moment he had dug out a tallow colored candle and after a bit of fiddling managed to get it lit and mounted on a candlestick, after which he put away his lighter.

Suddenly, there was a gentle cough from the door. A woman was now standing there, wearing a heavy nightgown and shawl with her hair wrapped up in a nightcap. And in her hands was a compact blunderbuss, the gaping bore of which she leveled menacingly at the two intruders. The woman regarded them silently for a moment. Then suddenly a look of recognition came over her face and she lowered the muzzle of her weapon. "Good Lord, but if it isn't Horatio Dackery himself!", she said. "What on earth are you doing here?"

"My apologies, Mrs. Helwig, for intruding on your home unannounced", Dackery said.

"And hiding in the basement no less", the woman said critically. "Popped in out of thin air as usual, eh? You could at least have materialized outside somewhere and then knocked on the front door like a decent visitor. Fine thing sneaking about in people's cellars in the wee hours of the morning! I might have shot you just now! You're up to something, I'll warrant. Who's that with you?"

"This is Ms. Lindsey Fluger. She is under my protection."

Lindsey felt a bit uncomfortable as Mrs. Helwig ran a critical eye over her, with a particularly curious look being directed at the battle axe in Lindsey's hands. She felt she should say something. "I'm sorry, I think I accidentally broke one of your pots", Lindsey said apologetically

"Hmph!", the woman said. "I knew I heard something. Well, I suppose you'd better come upstairs the both of you. Come along, and mind you don't knock anything else over. I'll go tell Angela there'll be two more for breakfast."

Outside the door there was another room which contained a small staircase which led upwards through the ceiling. Mrs. Helwig led the way upstairs into the house as Lindsey and Dackery followed. For the moment at least it seemed that they had found a place of security.

15

"Residence at 26 Bodgerstreet"

The air was rent with the shrill cry of a steam whistle as the 1:10 Express slowed to a halt at Bodgerstreet station. A small, brightly painted locomotive headed a short train of cheerfully decorated railcars, which were now beginning to dispense an equally colorful assortment of persons. A grim dwarf dressed in blue livery stepped onto the platform first, blowing hard on a long whistle which was only just visible past the billowing mass of his copper colored beard and great waxed moustaches. Hardly anyone seemed to pay attention to him however, as the railcars were already rapidly disgorging their passengers, which quickly swallowed up the dwarf as he vainly attempted to direct the traffic of people about him. Most of the passengers were humans. The men were dressed in colorful doublets and broad brimmed hats festooned with feathers. Great sweeping capes barely concealed the massive rapiers which many of them bore, while the women were attired in brightly colored gowns of silks and satins. Dispersed within the multitude were also many dwarves dressed in a similar fashion as the humans, the men being further distinguished by their tremendous beards of coppery red or coal black. Here and there too, various animals could be seen making their way freely through the throng. At one place a Kangaroo wearing a messenger's bag was bounding heedlessly through the crowd, while at another a harried looking dwarf woman had stopped to ask for directions from a genteel looking Heron wearing a tall hat and a monocle. The crowd was now spilling past the platform and into the long porticos of the timber-framed station building as the clock surmounting the structure struck the quarter hour. Bit by bit the crowd thinned out as the people gradually filtered through to the street and went their various ways.

Further down Bodgerstreet things were a bit quieter. About a half mile or so from the railway station the rattle of a small handcart pushed across the cobblestones by a dwarf was about all the noise there was. Nearby a tall Stork wearing a scarlet tabard and a satchel bearing a royal seal made his way along the row of houses, carefully examining the addresses. The Stork paused now in front of a tall, narrowly built house and peered at the plate above the letter box at the door.

26 BODGERSTREET
CAMILLA HELWIG

Satisfied, the Bird reached into his satchel with one claw and produced a couple of envelopes, which he deposited in the letter box. He then moved on to the next house, humming idly to himself as he went.

High above the place where the avian letter carrier had just stood, Lindsey sat peering through a window in the attic of number 26 as she watched the quiet scene in the street below. Lindsey and Dackery had been hiding out at Camilla Helwig's house for almost a week now. During that time Dackery had been busy. He would vanish first thing in the morning, taking breakfast with Lindsey and Camilla and then making a door to somewhere or other. Some days he'd be back for lunch, only to go off again for the rest of the afternoon, while on other days he might not come back again at all until well after midnight. He didn't talk very much about his mysterious errands, but when he did he spoke of having made many attempts to enter Linster, probing Gurth's defenses and testing their limits. He had also been doing the rounds among his more trusted acquaintances, drawn from a long list of associations he had acquired during his lifetime of travelling in the Fairworld, in the hopes of somehow getting word to the Good Folk and reestablishing contact with either Elred or the Bird.

Throughout all this there was precious little for Lindsey to do, other than loaf idly about the house. It was a stressful and frustrating occupation (or lack thereof). Fortunately the company was pleasant and interesting. Camilla Helwig had been a considerate and gracious hostess in all respects, but initially she had remained rather cool and reserved towards Lindsey. It had taken a few days for her to thaw out, but by this time she and Lindsey had become proper friends.

Lindsey took a last bored look at the street below her, and then with a sigh she repaired from the window. Camilla was somewhere downstairs, and while Lindsey did her best to avoid being constantly in the good woman's hair, there was only so much boredom and solitude she could bear. Camilla's house was very tall and narrow, with each floor longer than the one below it. Lindsey wound her way down the tight stairways and made her way into the kitchen. Camilla was sitting at the kitchen table with a letter before her. Standing also at the table was Angela, Camilla's maidservant. More precisely, the maid stood *on* the kitchen table rather than *at* it, for Angela happened to be a large Pelican. She had black and white plumage and wore a small apron and mob cap of printed fabric as she stood solemnly on the table while Camilla spoke, her long yellow bill almost touching the tabletop as the Bird nodded silently now and then. Camilla looked up and smiled at Lindsey as she came into the room, and then returned to her conversation.

"Now for the next letter", she said, "it seems we have yet another order from Barnabas Johnson. This time he's looking to acquire some powdered ferimunger. I expect Vorelli's will have plenty in stock. Mr. Johnson only wants a quarter pound, but I think I should get two just the same. Be sure the grains are quite small and have a good green color to them, I'm sure Mr. Johnson needs the best quality. If you take the 1:37 train you should have plenty of time to do all the shopping and catch the 3:02 on your way back."

"It would be faster if I flew there directly, ma'am."

"But then you'd be passing over the foundries on the way, and I don't want you breathing in all that smoke. Besides, you'll have all the parcels to carry on the way back. The trains are much better."

"Yes ma'am. Will that be all?"

"I think so dear, thank you."

The Pelican nodded once more and then hopped off the table and waddled out the kitchen door. As the Pelican left the room Lindsey turned to Camilla.

"If you want I could go with Angela and help her carry her packages", Lindsey said hopefully.

"It's very kind of you to offer", Camilla replied. "but Horatio thinks it would be safer if you stayed indoors as much as possible, and I agree with him. Angela will be alright, so long as she takes the train that is. She's a dear soul, but hopelessly stubborn."

Lindsey sighed. It would have been nice to get out of the house. As it was, she sauntered over to the kitchen table and sat down across from Camilla. "I gotta say, I was surprised when I first saw that train. No offense, but I didn't get the feeling that anybody around here could make machines like that."

"Yes, we're uniquely blessed to have them", Camilla said. "Such things are extraordinarily rare elsewhere in the Fairworld."

"Why is that?"

"There are a variety of factors at play, but mostly it's because of the Good Folk."

"Why am I not surprised?"

"Yes, they can be quite assertive at times, in their own way. Steam technology first appeared in Ronymsia almost two hundred years ago. At the time I don't think the Good Folk were particularly happy about it, and they seem to have taken steps to ensure that no one else ever acquires it."

"But why would they do that?"

"I suppose they think it's for our own good. They prefer to keep the more disruptive sorts of technology contained. They also try to limit the general flow of human migration across their world, which keeps the various peoples in semi-isolation from one another. All of which makes it that much easier to prevent things like plagues and large wars. Everything comes at a cost, I'm afraid."

"Hmph. The Good Folk sure are a bossy bunch, aren't they?"

"Not really. They leave us to manage ourselves for the most part, and only rarely do they directly intervene in our own internal affairs. Indeed, there are many times when I wish they would actually do more. And then there are times when I wish they would do less. It's an imperfect universe. All things considered, I think that the Good Folk are doing a tolerable enough job in their own way. The Fairworld is a special place. I never wish to leave it."

"Yeah, it's not everyday you meet a talking Pelican....though come to think of it I suppose you actually do. Do all animals talk in the Fairworld?"

"Goodness no! No, the vast majority of the animals here are merely simple beasts, only the wightbeasts are capable of speech."

"Wightbeasts?"

"It's the word we use for such creatures. A wight is a term for a sentient being, like a human, thus a wightbeast is an animal which is sentient in the same way that a human is. The origins of the wightbeasts is a mystery. There was magic involved in it, that's for certain. The wightbeasts have many anatomical characteristics which are unlikely to have evolved naturally, such as specialized vocal cords which allow them to perfectly emulate human speech. And their brains are developed far beyond that of their respective counterparts among the simple beasts, to the point that they are very much equal to humans, dwarves, and elfkin. Intellectually, that is. Physically they can be quite disadvantaged at times. Our humanoid anatomy is ideally suited to ourselves as tool users, and there are many things which come naturally to us which can never be easy for the wightbeasts. Of course there are some things which wightbeasts can do much better than we can, but in general this means that their options for employment tend to be more limited, and there are only so many specialized jobs out there where wightbeasts are at a competitive advantage. Here in Ronymsia we have managed to live side-by-side with the wightbeasts for centuries, but in many other parts of the world that is not at all the case. In other places the wightbeasts live completely apart from humans and their like, while in others there are hardly any wightbeasts at all. Here in Meridiana the population of wightbeasts seems to be particularly high, which I think is part of the reason why we've wound up living on top of one another the way we do here. The other reason of course is the legacy of the Reman Empire."

"The Reman Empire?"

"Yes. Here, let me show you."

Camilla arose and stepped over to the other side of the room. On the wall there was a small framed picture, which she took down and brought to the table.

"This is a map of the Fairworld (well, part of it, anyway). It's not a very good one, quite old fashioned and out of date, but the new ones are hardly any better. However, it does give you a rough idea of where we are relative to the rest of the world.

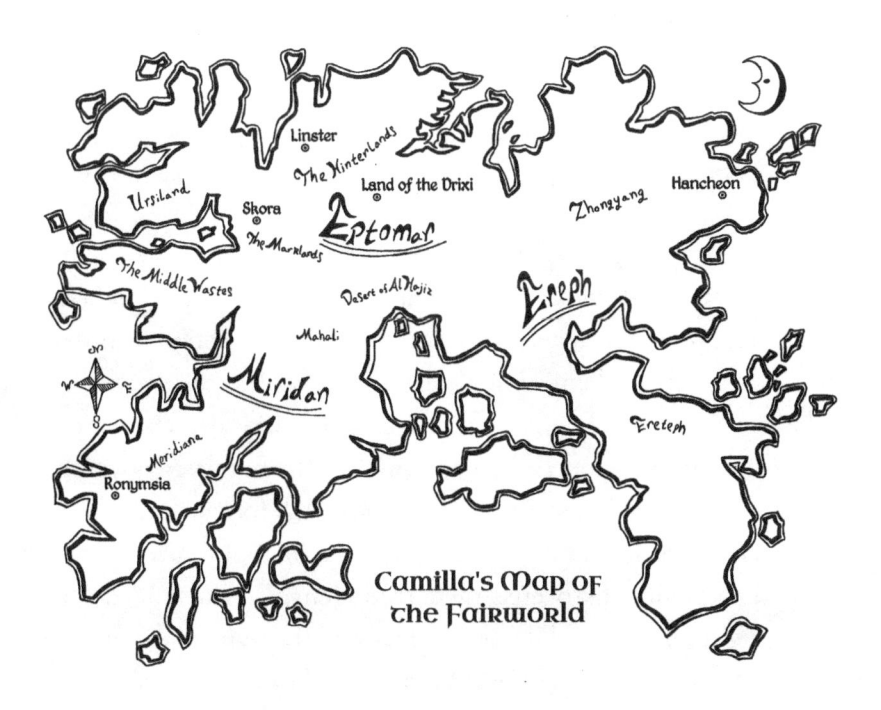

Camilla's Map of the Fairworld

We're here in Ronymsia, which is in the subcontinent of Meridiana. Long ago the Remans controlled most of the territory from here all the way up to the west coast of Ursiland. The Remans adopted a legal system through which the wightbeasts were integrated into mainstream human society. Most of our modern laws and customs pertaining to the wightbeasts have their origins somewhere in Reman law. For example, the Remans required that wighbeasts wear distinctive articles of clothing when in public. This is called The Mark of Wight, and it serves to protect the wightbeasts from being accidentally confused with simple beasts. The tradition continues to this day here in Ronymsia, and you'll notice that wightbeasts here always wear some kind of clothing, even if it's just a hat. This is but one example of the kinds of systems which the Remans created to ensure that wightbeasts and humanoids can live together in harmony, and their system has worked well enough at least to have lasted through the ages. Even elfkin like the Drixi have been heavily influenced by Reman tradition (something which I'm sure they would not be keen to admit, given how much they fear and despise humans)."

"I've heard of a *Roman* empire, but up to now I've never heard of a *Reman* one", Lindsey remarked.

"Well, the story is that there were twin brothers, Romulus and Remus. They were the grandsons of Numitor, a king who had been deposed by his brother, Amulius. When the brothers were born Amulius ordered them killed, seeing them as a threat to his stolen throne, but the brothers were rescued by one of the lords of the Uryads, who were the greatest among the Good Folk in those days. The boys were given into the care of the great she-wolf Vixitra, who cared for the children and raised them with the aid of a shepherd. At some point after reaching manhood the twins discovered their true identities and joined forces with their grandfather and deposed Amulius. The twins then set out to build a new kingdom of their own. However, the twins then quarrelled among themselves and Romulus tried to kill Remus. However, Remus was saved at the last moment when the fey wolf Vixitra returned and carried Remus away to the Fairworld. She then helped Remus to found the city of Reme here on Algard (that's the Elven name for this planet) while Romulus was busy establishing Rome on Earth. Plenty of Greeks had already come to the Fairworld in those days (brought here by the Uryads, who were more liberal in their dealings with Earth than the

Fairy Folk are today). Many of them joined Remus, or else were conquered by his successors. There must have still been some sort of special connection between Rome and Reme, for the two evolved in parallel with one another and were staggeringly similar, even across the chasm which divides the two worlds. Indeed, both empires even came to an end within a century or two of each other, and both left their profound marks on the worlds they left behind."

"You seem to know an awful lot about both worlds. Have you always lived in the Fairworld?"

"In point of fact, no. Like you, I grew up on our earth."

"Really?"

"Oh yes. 'Camilla Helwig' is not my real name. Or rather, it is my real name now, but it is not the name I was born with. I'm originally from Great Britain. I had a very ordinary sort of childhood, but when I was a young woman I found a way into the Fairworld. It was entirely an accident, really. Horatio discovered the Fairworld through years of research while you yourself were touched directly by the Good Folk. But with me it was purely random chance, or as random a chance as anything can ever really be in the universe. Doormaking is a specific technique for creating temporary portals between places, but sometimes portals (or rather fissures) open up on their own. I came across such a fissure once and quite literally fell through it. And there I was, stranded in another world. At first I had quite a time of it, as you might imagine. I somehow managed to survive on my own until the Good Folk eventually discovered me. They offered to take me home, but by that time I'd pretty much made up my mind that I wanted to stay. When you've been to this place once, it never quite leaves you, and likewise a part of you can never quite leave it. I found I could never leave it all. Instead I asked Good Folk to take me as one of their servants. And they agreed.

"I spent many years serving Good Folk in various capacities. It was a magnificent experience. I saw so many wonderful things and visited so many amazing places. But over the years I became frustrated with my employers. I would never say they were bad. No, never bad (though I suppose some might disagree on that score). But neither would I say they are as good as they could be. I met Horatio many years ago, and soon after that I finally left the Good Folk. I traveled with Horatio for a time, and then spent many years travelling on my own. I suppose I always was the footloose sort. Even before I came to the Fairworld I never really stayed in one place for very long or kept up with friends and family. But a proverbial rolling stone can only ever roll so far before it begins to slow down. I found myself getting on in years, and for the first time I finally felt like settling down somewhere. I acquired this house in Ronymsia a number of years ago, and these days I make my living as a dealer in petty magic.

"Sometimes I do wonder whether I made the right choices. I've only ever been back to our earth a couple of times in my life. I left everything behind in order to stay here and serve the Good Folk, and sometimes I feel that was quite a steep price to pay for the privilege of being their errand-girl. Still I have had a wonderful life and many remarkable experiences, and I hope I managed to do some good along the way. But it was a choice that I made, and I had to give a lot up in order to have that life."

Lindsey had been listening intently all the while Camilla had been speaking. On the one hand she had a new feeling of kinship with Camilla. Yet somehow Camilla's last comment had left her feeling slightly unsettled.

There was a noise from elsewhere in the house, and suddenly Dackery looked in through the doorway. "Good afternoon Ms Fluger, good afternoon Camilla", he said cordially. "I have a few things to attend to, but then I'll need to speak to you both. I will be back shortly." Dackery disappeared from view again, and Lindsey could hear his footsteps as he trudged up the narrow stairs of Camilla's slender house.

Lindsey turned to Camilla. There was something she needed to ask her, but she didn't quite know how to go about it. Not politely, anyway. "How long have you known Mr. Dackery?", she said finally.

"Oh my, I must have known Horatio for almost thirty years now."

Lindsey hesitated a moment. "Do you trust him?"

This time it was Camilla who hesitated. "I trust Horatio to be true to himself. And Horatio is a man who prizes trueness in others. In all the years I've known him he's never once lied to me."

"That's nice to know."

"Horatio's a good man, Lindsey. In fact, I personally would consider him one of the best. That's not to say he doesn't have his faults. He has a great many of them. But he's a good man. A very good man."

Camilla had taken on a wistful look as she spoke. Lindsey suddenly had the feeling that Camilla may not be entirely unbiased in her assessment of Dackery.

"Do you care for him?"

Camilla laughed in an embarrassed sort of way. "Well, I suppose I do in a way. We've known one another for a very long time. But we're both solitary individuals. I'm quite content as I am. Outside of Angela I really wouldn't want to bother with having someone else always around the house. Besides, Horatio's life experiences extend far before my own, and will likely continue long after I'm gone. I don't think I'd ever really be comfortable knowing that."

"What do you mean? I mean, I know Mr. Dackery is really old. How has he managed to live so long?"

"Actually, I think now would probably be a good time for lunch, given that Horatio is here", the other said. Camilla stood up and began rummaging about in the kitchen.

Lindsey was about to press Camilla further when a creaking sound from the stairwell outside the room announced that the subject of their conversation was soon to be rejoining them. Lindsey would have to wait for another opportunity. A moment or two later Dackery reentered the kitchen. His usual three piece suit was gone, and in its place he wore a medieval-looking ensemble consisting of a long, loose fitting tunic with a high collar and wide sleeves, which was cinched at the waist with a belt, under which he wore close fitting trousers and a pair of heavy boots. Dackery sat down, heaving his great form into a chair at the table, and then idly picked up the world map which Camilla had left there and perused it without speaking. Camilla had meanwhile sliced some bread and an assortment of cheeses, and bringing them over to the table sat down as well. Dackery then set the map down and tapped it in a didactic sort of way. "The Fairworld is a big place", Dackery said. "And this isn't even a complete map. It's missing an entire continent. But be that as it may, there's only one place that we really need to worry about getting to right now.

"The seal which has been put on Linster is a good one. I have made repeated attempts to create a doorway to Linster over the last few days, and thus far I've had no luck getting through. That being said, there is no such thing as an impenetrable defense. There are a number of potential options at our disposal. One way to get past this kind of barrier is to try and confuse the lock by taking a roundabout route to get there. The idea is to mask the intended destination by making a series of doors in rapid succession from one place to another, such that the lock isn't actually sure whether the area it protects is your true destination or if you are just passing through. The problem with this approach is that it is not very reliable. It could take us months of experimentation before we'd hit upon just the right way in which to fool this particular lock, and we don't have that kind of time. Gurth knows we are after him, and it is only a matter of time before we make it to Linster and break the curse. He's not going to wait for that to happen. The witches are investing a huge amount of resources to protect their supply of slaves coming from Linster. If they can't get what they want through black magic, then they'll do it through politics. Gurth has already been effectively blackmailing the whole country for years. In his current situation it won't take long for him to establish total political control of the country, after which it won't matter so much whether the curse is ever broken or not. I have picked up a couple of bits of information over the last few days which suggest to me that the witches are already on the move. I'd say we have only a few weeks at most before we will have lost whatever opportunity we had."

"Can't the Good Folk help us get there in time?", Lindsey asked.

"I've been trying to establish contact with them over the last few days. However the Good Folk are elusive even at the best of times, and neither I nor Camilla have maintained any direct connections with them for many years. I have other friends and associates in the Fairworld. However, of these I have thus far canvassed only those whom I trust with absolute confidence, and as such my list of contacts is a short one."

"But what can we do?"

"The way I see it, we can keep working at the lock and hope that we can get through before it's either too late or before the witches track us down. Alternatively, I can keep making the rounds among my associates until one of them manages to make contact with the Good Folk, during which time the witches will still be looking for us and Gurth will be free to make himself at home behind Linster's throne. We could of course try to fly there, but again that would mean procuring something that can fly, which could take a long time. It's not like there are griffons for hire on every street corner. In all three cases we are left with an uncertain timeline which may well conclude with our eventual discovery and capture. There is a fourth option though."

"And that is?"

"We walk."

"Are you serious?", Lindsey cried, aghast.

"Perfectly", Dackery said. "In my experiments over the last few days I discovered that although I could never actually make a doorway directly into Linster, I could manage to make a door to a number of points outside, much closer than I had initially thought possible. It would take time and I don't know the territory well, but with a good guide we could probably walk the rest of the way there in a reasonable amount of time."

"But wouldn't that be dangerous?"

"Very. But not necessarily any more dangerous than any of our other options. We'd be on the move, and quite possibly doing something which the witches won't expect. In the meanwhile Camilla can remain here and keep trying to establish contact with the Good Folk through our various associates. Personally I think it's our best option."

"But you said we needed a guide. Where are we going to find one that we can trust?"

"That's the riskiest part. It means engaging with people I don't exactly know and don't exactly trust. However, the truth is that the Good Folk aren't the only ones seeking to thwart the witches' schemes. In fact, in many respects they are the least of the witches' problems given the (shall we say) circumspect way in which the Good Folk prefer to handle political matters. The empire of the witches may be greatly reduced from what it was two millennia ago, but mark my words it is still a power to be reckoned with. The surrounding border regions have been greatly oppressed by them at times, and the witches have made many bitter enemies there. And some of them are rather well organized.

"In considering these facts I paid a visit this morning to an acquaintance of mine who lives in these borderlands. The man himself I would discount as a potential guide. I am not particularly inclined to trust him enough for that, and even if I were, I doubt he could be induced to help us, given his circumstances. However he *is* deeply involved with some individuals who may be much better suited to assist us. Unlike certain others whom I will neglect to mention, these people are utterly dedicated to destroying the witches."

Dackery paused for a moment and looked Lindsey directly in the eye. "At this point, if we want to reach Linster and bring the fight to Gurth anytime soon we're going to have to take a risk. A big one. And I think that if we are going to take such a risk, our best shot is to travel to Linster by foot as I have described. But the choice is yours. This is your cause now, and whatever we do your life is the one which is most in danger. Think about what I've said, but I would advise you to make a decision very soon."

Lindsey took a deep breath. On the one hand Dackery's logic made sense to her. On the other hand, she was also keenly aware of the fact that she knew very little about this world and the dangers which lurked within it. Dackery's plan could be suicide for all she really knew. Yet the choice was up to her. She could spend days fretting over what to do, but it wouldn't make a difference. She couldn't make herself into a superwoman by doing that, nor did she really expect she'd come up with any better ideas on her own. She could only work with what she had, and no amount of agonizing would change that. And in the end, she already knew what her decision was going to be. Lindsey looked Dackery straight in the eye.

"Let's take the fight to Gurth", she said.

16

"Falknir"

Lindsey and Dackery were standing on a dirt path outside of a small mud-walled cottage, with a tall roof of heavy thatch. To one side of the building there was a small enclosure in which a number of goats were milling about, while elsewhere nearby there were a couple of sheds and a small vegetable garden. The place was in an isolated spot deep in the middle of the woods. A few paths extended out from the homestead in various directions, but beyond that there seemed to be no other connection to the outside world.

Lindsey was dressed in a cloak and woolen tunic, wool leggings and sturdy leather boots. She carried a stout walking stick in one hand, while her vorpal axe was concealed in an oiled bag slung on her back alongside her knapsack. It was a nondescript sort of ensemble, calculated to be more or less unobtrusive in any of the places which Lindsey and Dackery were likely to visit along the way to Linster. The clothes were a little loose and baggy on Lindsey's thin frame, but not as badly as they could have been. Despite her adventures, Lindsey had the feeling that she'd gained a little bit of weight over the last week or so, especially under Camilla's generous hospitality. Dackery had spent the last couple of days making a few final visits to his most trusted associates, and had arranged a line of communication through Camilla in case any of them managed to make contact with the Good Folk. In the meanwhile, Camilla and Lindsey had been busy preparing kit and provisions for the coming journey. In the process, they had decided that Lindsey should be disguised as a boy. After all, the witches were looking for a man and woman from another world, who travelled in secret by way of doormaking. But they were not necessarily on the lookout for an ordinary man and his nephew traveling in the open on foot.

Before leaving Camilla's house, Dackery had had a long talk with their hostess in private. Lindsey had not been privy to the subject of their conversation, but before they departed that morning she had seen Dackery hand a small book to Camilla, which Lindsey recognized as the one which Dackery had taken from Harin's vault. Perhaps it wasn't any of her business, but Lindsey felt somewhat uncomfortable about the matter all the same. Up to now Dackery had said nothing about the incident and Lindsey suspected that he wasn't likely to either, especially now that they were at the doorstep of whoever this person was to whom Dackery was about to entrust their fate.

The area around the cottage was quiet. All that could be heard was the odd tinkle of a goat's bell and the songs of birds filtering through the treetops. Lindsey found herself feeling terribly uneasy as she stood there outside the cottage. At least she wasn't alone. Even disguised as a middling-status commoner, Dackery made for an imposing figure. A broad cruciform sword (borrowed from Camilla) was now strapped prominently at his side, while his pistol remained hidden inside a leather belt pouch where it could be easily reached in an emergency. It was easy to forget that the man was a capable killer, even though she herself had seen him kill on two occasions already. Despite the fact that in both instances he had killed in order to save Lindsey's own life, she still had a sick sort feeling come over her whenever she thought about Dackery in that way.

Dackery knocked on the door. A moment later the door was opened a crack, as the person behind it peeped through at the two visitors. The door then opened the rest of the way to reveal a thin, lithe looking man with closely cropped salt and pepper colored hair and a scruffy, unshaven face. The man looked them both up and down.

"You took your time getting here, Dackery", the man said. "I was beginning to think you weren't coming."

"My apologies, Kren", Dackery replied. "I thought I made it clear that it would take me a couple of days to get my affairs in order. Allow me to introduce my companion, Lindsey."

The man looked keenly at Lindsey, apparently sizing her up, but said nothing as Dackery continued speaking. "This is Kren", Daiquiri said. "The colleague of mine I told you about."

Lindsey nodded to Kren in acknowledgement while taking the opportunity to size him up in turn. The man was plainly dressed, and a bit rough around the edges, but otherwise he had a clean and orderly appearance. Despite being in his own house the man nevertheless wore a large, unpleasant looking dagger on his belt, and peeking just past the collar of his tunic Lindsey could see the fringe of a mail shirt hidden underneath his clothing. Kren grunted. "Well", he said, "your timing caught me a bit unprepared. Let me get a couple of things, and then I'll take you to The Keep. Come on inside." Kren opened the door the rest of the way and led Lindsey and Dackery inside his cottage.

The interior of the place was much more comfortable than it would have seemed from the outside. The whole building consisted of a single room, and smelled strongly (but not altogether unpleasantly) of smoke and cookery. The walls were painted white, the furniture was well made, and overall the place was clean and fairly well appointed. On one side of the room there was a fireplace and cooking range, while opposite this there was a table and a set of benches. A compact bed was drawn up near the warmth of the fireplace, and above this there were a couple of shelves containing a small assortment of books and various personal items, and sitting in one place on the mantelpiece there was the bleached white dome of a humanoid skull, it's empty sockets casting a macabre gaze across the room. Kren bade his guests sit down at the table, and then took a seat himself. "Can I get you both something to eat?", he asked.

"Thank you, but no", Dackery said. "I think it would be better if we departed as soon as possible."

"Of course, of course. But we've got plenty of time. The meeting doesn't start until noon and The Keep is only a couple hours walk from here. You sure I can't get you something?"

"Yes."

"Very well. However, before we leave is there anything else I should know about this mission of yours? The others are going to be asking a lot of hard questions before they'll let me introduce you to them. Fortunately I can vouch for you personally, but it would help if I could give them more details in advance."

"As I've already said, Lindsey and I are engaged in an undertaking which will inflict considerable damage to our mutual enemies. But in order to succeed we must travel to the kingdom of Linster, and we need a guide to get us there on foot in order to get past the defenses of the witches. There is nothing more I can tell you at this time. I'm sure that you of all people understand the high degree of discretion such matters require. I would never wish to further burden your circumstances with such dangerous knowledge."

"Oh, I can manage alright. I have for years now."

"Nonetheless, it would be better if I said no more at this time."

"Ah well, as you wish. It's your affair, after all. I'll still do my best to help, of course."

Kren hesitated a moment longer, but Dackery remained silent.

"Well then, let me get a couple things together." Kren arose and retrieved a small satchel from elsewhere in the house, into which he placed a couple pieces of bread and cheese. He then collected his cloak and hat, along with a staff which was leaning beside the door. "I suppose that's it. If you're ready leave...."

"Yes, we are quite ready."

"Right, yes. Well then, follow me." Kren led the way outside, closing and locking the door behind him as Lindsey and Dackery followed him out. He then headed down one of the trails which led away from the house. The path was very narrow, and would have been difficult to find if one didn't already know it was there. They continued in this way for nearly three quarters of an hour, taking a number of odd twists and turns along the way, until at length the trail ended at the verges of a wide, well trodden road. Kren paused briefly and glanced reflexively in both directions before stepping onto the road, like someone who is habitually furtive. They continued along the road for at least another hour, walking in silence the whole time. As talkative as he was inside his own home, out in the open Kren hardly spoke at all, instead paying keen attention to his surroundings. Lindsey was dying to take Dackery aside and pry him for information about this obscure individual they had thrown in with, but no such opportunity presented itself.

Eventually they came to a turn. Here a smaller path split off from the main road. The place was completely unmarked save for a slender wooden cross which was engraved with a blessing and invocation addressed to some hallowed name or other. Kren quickened his place as he turned onto the path, almost like one who is anxious to reach a place of shelter. It seemed that the man hated being out in the open.

The side road was well kept and was obviously maintained on a regular basis. The surrounding underbrush was cut back and it was clear of weeds and obstacles. Soon enough the trees gave way to reveal a few small fields to either side which were ploughed and planted with cabbages and hops. The ground was moving steadily uphill as they went, and after another quarter hour or so of walking they came upon a farmstead nestled at the foot of a craggy hillside. The central feature of the farmstead was a single timber-framed structure coated in white stucco and surmounted with a great vaulted roof of thatch. This voluminous structure seemed to combine the functions of both main living quarters and a barn, and dominated the small buildings around it. Its only competition came in the form of a tiny chapel which stood apart from the other buildings. The road wound past the chapel and continued onward until it disappeared into the trees which blanketed the hillside. At the door of the chapel there stood a tonsured man in a brown robe and white scapular, who waved genially to Kren as he approached. Kren waved back and addressed his companions as he did so. "Well, here we are. Welcome to The Keep.", Kren said.

Lindsey glanced about the farmstead. "It looks like a farm", she replied.

"It is."

"But who builds a farm in the middle of the woods?"

"Monks do. So far as anyone else is concerned this place is a cloistered monastery. But for us it's as good as a keep."

Dackery cast a scowl about him. "Can the monks be trusted?", he asked suspiciously.

"As much as anyone can be", Kren replied. "They're supporters of the cause and they allow us to use their property for our purposes, but otherwise they're just a gaggle of hermits. They do nothing but pray, farm, and dig holes. The hills behind the hermitage contain a lot of quartz, which the monks have been mining away bit by bit for probably a hundred years or more. The sale of the crystals provides the monks with a small trickle of income, and gives my associates a handy excuse to be always coming and going."

"Is the output of the mine enough to justify all the traffic?"

"No, but we keep it pretty discreet, and for their part the monks keep their mouths shut and hardly interact with the outside world at all, so nobody knows for sure how much they really put out."

They group had reached the chapel by now and the monk sauntered forward with his hands cradled in his sleeves. "Afternoon, Kren", the monk said jovially.

"Afternoon, Brother Dominic. Has everyone else arrived?"

"Oh, I'm sure I know nothing about that, Kren", the monk said. "I never do. But if you want to talk to the 'merchants', I suspect you'll find them all inside the mine. Pax vobiscum." The monk grinned and winked, and Kren led on with a nod. The road wound steadily up the hillside as the trees closed in around them. For the first time since they left his cottage Kren seemed somewhat relaxed, and began to chat again.

"Things have been busy of late" he said. "Something's been brewing for months, the witches have been shoring up their forces everywhere, and then about ten days ago all hell broke loose. It seems as though something must have happened recently to alarm them, as all of a sudden they've gotten very aggressive and are coming down hard on everybody. We scheduled this meeting weeks ago, which is just as well, since pretty soon a lot of us are probably going to have to go underground for the time being. I'm not sure you'll find the kind of help you're looking for."

Lindsey and Dackery digested this bit of information as the road ahead of them began to narrow. Abruptly they came to a place where the road took a steep incline and turned straight into the hillside itself. Here a portion of the hill face was cut away and filled in with a rough stone wall, with a square opening lined with heavy timbers. The road led straight through this entrance and into the hill. Inside the gloom, Lindsey could just make out the shape of a man lurking inside the passage, with a stout longbow in his hand, who tensed and nocked an arrow as the trio approached. Kren must have seen the man as well, for suddenly he made a rapid hand sign and gestured quickly to Lindsey and Dackery. The man in the door relaxed again. Kren silently motioned for Lindsey and Dackery to remain where they were, and then proceeded alone into the mine. He stopped at the door and conversed with the man there for a moment, and then disappeared inside. For the moment, Lindsey and Dackery were more or less alone. Lindsey leaned over and whispered to Dackery. "So, just who is this guy anyway?, she said huskily. "How do you know Kren?"

"Kren is an interesting individual", Dackery replied darkly. "Rather unique among my associates. He's a witch, you see."

"A what!"

"Well, shall we say a former witch. He ran afoul of his masters years ago, and as such found it rather imperative to remove himself from their influence with all expediency. He defected to the other side, and is now more or less completely reliant on them for protection and support. In exchange he gives them all the inside information and dirty secrets he can. Besides keeping his skin intact it also gives him an opportunity to take some revenge on his former associates."

"Charming", Lindsey said through gritted teeth. "And you trust this guy?"

"No. Which is why I didn't tell him any more than I absolutely had to. I checked up with him a few days ago in the hopes that his current allies might be able to help us, and when he told me their leaders would be meeting today I felt it was an opportunity we couldn't afford to miss, even if it was risky."

"I sure hope you were right."

"As do I."

Lindsey and Dackery remained standing there at the base of the mine entrance for quite a while, all the time under the wary gaze of the guard hiding in the shadows. It seemed like ages had gone by before Kren finally reemerged and beckoned for them to come in. Lindsey and Dackery at last trudged their way up the last portion of the slope and passed inside the mine. The walls were supported by heavy timbers and were lined with wooden boards. Directly inside the guard stepped aside, eyeing them suspiciously as they continued on through the tunnel. Further down there were lanterns hung at various points in the ceiling, and here and there other passages went off in various directions. Deeper still within the hillside were the portions of the mine which were currently active, but here nearer the entrance most of the space had long been converted into cellars and storerooms; some filled with tools, others with grain, and some with crates and barrels piled high with quartz. And then there were some rooms which were filled with outlaws. They had gone a considerable distance into the mine when Kren took a sharp turn down one of the side passages, which led into a long vaulted chamber. It was a sort of common room, practically a miniature tavern in fact. A large wooden chandelier bedecked with candles hung from the ceiling while many shelves stocked with goods and supplies lined its walls. Various chairs and tables were scattered about here and there, and taking up the middle of the room was one particularly long table set with generous portions of food and drink. Seated at the table were about fifteen to twenty men. And all of them were looking at Lindsey and Dackery.

It was a grim, surly looking assembly to be sure. Lindsey felt like she'd never before seen such a motley collection of tough customers. Most of them wore what looked like traveling clothes of some sort, and there was enough variation among them to suggest that they had come from a wide dispersal of places. All of them carried weapons of some kind on their persons, while still more arms and equipment were piled up throughout the room. Many of them also wore padded jackets or else had bits of chainmail slipping out here and there from underneath their clothing, and one or two of them had prominent scars on their faces. One of these, a particularly grizzly looking character with a great patch over one eye, stuck out a thumb in the direction of the newcomers and addressed Kren. "Well Kren", barked the man with the eyepatch, "explain what this is all about. Who are these two, and what do you think you're doing bringing them in here?"

Another man, a swarthy looking fellow in a turban, piped up as well. "Whatever it is, it had better be important. This is no time to be bringing in strangers. I hope for their sake that your friends can make a good account of themselves." The man followed his remark with a forbidding glare directed at the newcomers.

Kren fidgeted a bit. "As I explained", he said. "I can personally vouch for..."

At the head of the table another man now stood up. He was a bearded, grey haired man wearing a dark colored cloak with a scarlet cross sewn prominently on it. A great war sword was buckled at his side, and his words carried an aura of command when he spoke. "We've heard your explanation, Kren" the bearded man said. "Now let us hear theirs."

Dackery cleared his throat. "I will gladly provide a full account of myself and my companion and answer all your questions....in private."

Here Dackery cast a significant glance at Kren. The grey haired man followed Dackery's gaze, and nodded. "Of course. Kren, please step outside and wait in the outer passages."

"But..."

"There will be no buts, Kren. Please step outside."

Kren reluctantly obeyed, and one of the men at the table stood up and saw him out. Once the door was closed the grey haired man turned and raised an eyebrow at Dackery. "What have you to say to us, then?"

Dackery cleared his throat, and began to relate the tale of their mission to Linster. The outlaws listened attentively to the story from beginning to end, murmuring incredulously among themselves from time to time. When it was all finished a stunned silence hung over the whole assembly. The man with the eyepatch broke it first.

"What a lot of rubbish!" the man said. "Kren is an idiot. These two are either agents of the witches, or loonies."

The man in the turban stroked his chin thoughtfully. "Not necessarily. Much of it fits in with what we've been experiencing over the last month. Something has suddenly made the witches very, very nervous, and if the Good Folk are finally stepping in and threatening to cut off their supply of slaves...."

"Bollocks! The Good Folk don't give a damn about people like us. Besides, why would they bother with Linster? It's just one kingdom, and a damned far away one at that."

"But Linster isn't the only place where Gurth operates. We're all very familiar with him, he has gathered slaves from all across the border countries and beyond. If he loses his grip on Linster, maybe others will follow."

"Fat chance!"

A heated discussion then broke out at the table. Back and forth the outlaws argued and debated amongst themselves. Finally, after well over an hour had gone by, the grey haired man at last arose and addressed Dackery and Lindsey.

"Your story is very convincing. It corresponds well with what we already know. I believe your mission to Linster may have great potential. However, I'm afraid we cannot help you."

For once Dackery seemed at a loss. "I don't understand", he protested. "You've heard our story and you say you believe it. Why can't you help us now?"

"The situation is more serious than you realize. The witches have been expanding steadily for a long time now. Every year their power increases. They are enlarging their slave networks and shoring up their supply lines at every level. They are levying more and more taxes from their tributaries and are raising more and more troops, including the Zard. Just a few years ago everyone thought the Zard had been extinct for centuries, and now they are everywhere. It won't be long before the witches will be strong enough that they'll be in a position to embark on a new wave of conquest, the likes of which haven't been seen in a millennia. This situation in Linster comes at a critical time for them, and any significant disruption in their supply of slaves will be a huge setback. They'll stop at nothing to prevent that from happening, and at this time we are not strong enough to resist them. The witches are hounding us everywhere, our forces are on the run, and at present we are all but immobilized. As much as we would like to help you, we can't. Our own survival is at risk. I am sorry, but there is nothing we can do to help you."

Lindsey looked despairingly at Dackery. His jaw was set, and there was a grim look in his eye. Then, from a neglected corner of the room, there was a polite cough. A tall, sharp featured man with a dark beard and straggly dark hair dangling from the back of his otherwise bald head had stood up from where he had been sitting, and was now casually shaking out a white clay pipe. He had remained silent throughout most of the previous proceedings, smoking languidly in the shadows while the rest of the assembly had been engaged in heated dispute.

The grey haired man cocked another eyebrow at the interloper. "Did you have something to say, Falknir?"

"In point of fact, yes", the other man said. "Unlike most of you, I am not tied down to anywhere in particular. The rest of you all have your own personal nests to protect at present, but I do not. I will be quite useless if I am obliged to remain cooped up here until everything blows over. However, since my usual work takes me more or less everywhere, I'll wager I know the routes from here to Linster better than anyone else in this room. I am ideally suited to assist these people."

"I don't want to risk it.", the grey haired man said.

"Ah, but you see I *do* want to risk it", the man called Falknir replied. "I think I can speak for all of us when I say that the reticence of the Good Folk as regards the witches has been a source of profound discouragement for many a long year. The thought that they may have finally gotten involved is frankly the best news I think I've ever heard. Unlike most of you I've actually met some of the Good Folk. They like to stay out of human affairs as much as possible. The fact that they've gone and started meddling in Linster is significant. Very significant indeed. Ibrahim here had an excellent point earlier. Gurth is probably the most important slave dealer the witches have. I guarantee you that breaking Gurth's hold on Linster will have a profound impact far beyond the borders of that land. I doubt the Good Folk would have done anything about it otherwise. As it is, the Good Folk have made an extraordinary move by taking an active interest in the matter, and we would be mad not to embrace their aid. Moreover, the very fact that they have become involved at all suggests to me that the situation is even more serious than we ourselves realize. In point of fact, I'd say it must be positively dire. Again, we would be utterly mad if we did not embrace the Good Folk now, while we still can. We simply must help these people reach Linster!"

"I won't allow it, Falknir."

"You won't have to. I'll do it anyway."

"Damn you, Falknir!"

"We're all damned, Casimir. Unless we act now to prevent it."

The table erupted with a chorus of loud protestations from the other outlaws, and the argument started all over again. For two more hours the outlaws argued back and forth. Dinner came and went, and the outlaws went on arguing. But in the end, they finally reached an agreement. They would all depart to their respective strongholds and shore up their defenses in order to weather the coming storm and discommode the witches as much as possible. In the meanwhile, the man called Falknir was to guide Lindsey and Dackery all the way to Linster and assist them in the completion of their quest.

Throughout all this time the passages of the mine were quiet, save for the muffled voices of the outlaw's council. All was stillness, save for the occasional rat which skirted about cadging for whatever scraps it could find. And in a secluded corner, in a place where the sounds of the mine echoed and reverberated with a peculiar kind of clarity, a man called Kren had been sitting quietly all the while, listening. Just listening.

17

"The Kingdom of Linster"

Between the domain of the Drixi and the Kingdom of Linster were many and varied; small kingdoms and settlements crowded together along bounteous rivers and precious tracts of fertile land, while elsewhere there were vast empty spaces. Empty, that is, save the wild and solitary beings who make such places their homes. On the off chance that one of these sundry beings had happened to glance at the sky, he might have espied a tiny squarish object passing high above him. And if he'd had particularly good eyes, such a being might well have observed that the object was more or less flat, and that huddled upon it was the queerest assortment of characters.

It had been just over a day since Hae-jin, Joan and the others had made their escape from the fortress of the Drixi on their borrowed flying carpet. It was truly a remarkable contrivance, and the complexity of the magic which was woven into it went far beyond just being able to fly, not the least of which was safeguarding its passengers. Despite hurtling through the air at tremendous speed, there seemed little danger of anyone being blown off the edge. Even so, the wind was still strong and frankly unpleasant as it whipped around the bodies of the passengers. Likewise, even as there was clearly some force which prevented the carpet from collapsing completely under the weight of its passengers, it still yielded alarmingly beneath them. Ursilda's weight in particular created a substantial depression in the carpet, and the other passengers quickly found themselves pressed around her as they inevitably slipped into it. Not that they would likely have chosen otherwise, for with a complement of two humans, three wogs, the Bird, a Fox and a Bear there was not much room to go around, and nobody was inclined to sit near the edges if they could help it. At first the Bird attempted to fly on his own rather than ride, but finding it next to impossible to keep up he soon abandoned this course and remained huddled on the carpet with the others. All in all it was a tedious mode of travel. There was hardly room to move, and conversation was all but hopeless due to the wind. Thankfully, the Bird had the foresight to prepare a basket of provisions, and periodically he would instruct the carpet to set down in some deserted spot or other to give the passengers time to eat and refresh themselves before carrying on again. All this took more time though, and despite the wondrous speed of the carpet the journey to Linster still took many hours. They had left the fortress of the Drixi in the middle of the night, and by the time they arrived in Linster it was nearly sunset on the following day.

Hae-jin, of course, hadn't the foggiest idea where he was. During the night there had been nothing to look at except a sea of stars above and the empty blackness below. Once daylight had broken, Hae-jin could now watch the forest and fields which passed slowly beneath him. It was a dazzling view nonetheless, and quite informative so far as the lay of the land was concerned, although this knowledge would likely be less useful to Hae-jin until their destination was nearly upon them. It was not until the Bird at last let forth a jolly whoop and announced that they were over Linster that Hae-jin could really make use of his vantage point and attempt to familiarize himself with this new land.

Beneath them was a pleasant enough looking countryside. Most of it was cultivated in some way, the land being composed largely of vast networks of fields which were divided into many long ribbon-like strips of ploughed land, each many hundreds of feet long. Between these fields there were pastures and meadows, as well as orchards and carefully tended woodlands. Every scrap of land seemed to be developed in some way, and even the wastes and defiles were dotted with grazing livestock. There were of course many habitations as well. Most of the buildings seemed to be clustered in small, dense villages, although here and there were also scattered farmsteads or monasteries which were more isolated, and every so often Hae-jin would catch sight of a full sized town. Indeed, just visible now through the haze of the horizon was what appeared to be a particularly large town, a proper city in fact, the skyline of which was dominated by a single, massive cathedral alongside a castle. From the density of the buildings, Hae-jin guessed that it might have a population of several thousand persons, far greater than that of any of the tiny villages he had seen hitherto. He didn't get a much closer look at it though, for at this point the carpet began to descend, apparently headed to a point in the countryside several miles from the city.

The ground was coming up on them fast. They were now passing over a small village, and as it sped by beneath them Hae-jin caught a glimpse of timber-framed cottages clustered around a central green containing a small church and a manor house. In a moment the village was behind them as the carpet hurtled silently through the air, with a fleeting shadow as the only hint of its passing. Suddenly the carpet took a sharp turn, fearfully jostling the passengers against one another and nearly catapulting the lot of them off. The carpet abruptly halted just a few feet above the earth and then gently floated the rest of the way to the ground. The moment it touched the earth, the carpet lurched, and a violent wave rolled along its length, unseating the passengers and sending them all to the ground in a tumble. It then took off again and hovered nearby, quivering slightly. The magical object seemed to be aware that it had been "borrowed" under dubious circumstances, and was now being missed.

Hae-jin scrambled to his feet and looked around. He and his comrades had landed in a field of barley, which grew to well past Hae-jin's knees, and was intermixed with an assortment of other weeds and grasses. From what he had seen on the way down he guessed they were maybe half a mile or so from the village, and several miles more from the larger city. Near to one side of them were the fringes of a small patch of woodland, while on the other side of the field Hae-jin could see a substantial looking homestead, which contained what appeared to be a dilapidated watermill.

Abruptly, Hae-jin realized that while he had been taking stock of his surroundings the Bird had been speaking with the magic carpet. Hae-jin turned just in time to see the Bird make a parting remark, perhaps dictating a message of apology to the owner, and Hae-jin was suddenly horrified as the carpet leapt into the air and rocketed away into the sky. "Hey!"

The Bird turned to look at Hae-jin. "Something wrong, General?"

"Yes, something is very much wrong", Hae-jin barked. "That carpet would have been invaluable to us. I assume you've sent it back to its owner?"

"Why yes, of course I did. Made a promise (well, more of an IOU, I suppose), and I always keep my promises."

"Do you indeed? Well, your fidelity has cost us dearly now."

"Perhaps. But I must keep my promises."

"Hmphf!"

Hae-jin cocked an eye at Joan. "Do you know where we are?", he demanded.

"Yes", the woman replied. "The village we passed over just now is

Tresham, my home. That group of buildings just across the field is Mortimer's Mill. The miller Hugh Mortimer is one of us."

"How do you mean, 'one of us'?", Hae-jin asked, momentarily puzzled.

"There are four of us you see", Joean explained. "Myself and three of the local yeomen: Hugh Mortimer, Will Little, and Rob Sykes. These men have been my allies throughout this endeavor, and they are the only ones in Tresham who know about our mission. Mortimer's place will likely be our best refuge at present, there's plenty of room, and ever since the mill failed few people ever come here."

"Can Mortimer be trusted?"

"Absolutely. As I said, he's one of us."

"Yet someone has clearly betrayed you", Hae-jin cautioned. "Gurth knew exactly where we were when we opened Harin's vault. There must be a traitor in your midst."

"I can't believe that!", Joan protested. "Neither Mortimer, Little or Sykes would ever have sold us out to Gurth."

"Yet one of them must have."

The Bird flapped his wings impatiently. "Please my friends, this is no time to bicker!', the Bird said. "Before anything else I think it's time we took shelter; there is no need to advertise our presence in the country prematurely. I suggest we relocate to yonder woods, and then we can all argue to our hearts content."

The Bird's point was well taken, and a short while later the lot of them were under the shade of the trees, squatting as best they could among the sparse brambles, for there was surprisingly little cover to be found. The forest itself was as much a part of the rural economy as the fields were, with the floors cleared and harvested regularly and the trees regularly coppiced and pollarded. And there they were, man, woman, wightbeast and wog, huddled together beneath the trees as they discussed the situation before them. There was now no doubt in anyone's mind that their circumstance had long been compromised. Exactly how much Gurth knew of their plans was not known for certain, however it was clear that he had been informed well in advance of their intent to open Harin's vault, and consequently he must be equally aware that the curse was now in danger of being broken.

"The question is", remarked Alwog, "what the devil the Bird thought he was doing bringing all of us here in the first place? I assume there's no breaking the curse now that the girl Lindsey has been misplaced. Just precisely what do you expect my brothers and I to do in this dratted country? We can sit around in the woods all you like, but that'll still cost you an extra twenty-one marks a week."

"Twenty two!"

"Shut up. How about it, Bird?"

The Bird ruffled his feathers a bit, looking just slightly self conscious. "As I have already explained, my associates are at this moment searching assiduously for our missing member. I have the highest hopes that she shall soon be restored to us and we can get on with breaking the curse. However, there is still quite a bit to be done in the meanwhile. The fact is, breaking the curse simply won't solve our problem, not entirely."

"Ha! I might have known it. You've messed up again Bird, haven't you?"

"Not in the least", the Bird said coldly. "It was always understood that more would be required than simply breaking the curse. It's not as if Gurth and his minions will simply evaporate the moment the curse is lifted. They must still be dealt with. Hae-jin and I have already spoken about this."

"Oh really? So you and the Zhongling have been holding out on the rest of us?"

"Oh no, not at all! Er, not intentionally, at any rate. I merely contracted your services for assistance at Harin's vault, the rest is a private matter between Hae-jin and myself. It was not originally intended that you and Ursilda would need to be involved any further."

"So you *have* messed up again, haven't you?"

"No I haven't! Not *again* anyway. But I think we will be needing all of your services for a bit longer than intended. You will all be properly compensated of course, and my associates have seen to it that Ursilda's cubs are being properly looked after. I've contracted a pair of dryads to look after them in her absence."

"What, a pair of silly dryads looking after my cubs?", Ursilda grumbled. "I suppose they'll do well enough, though I shouldn't wonder I'll come home to find my poor cubs hopelessly fat and spoiled. All dryads are frivolous creatures."

"That's all well and good", Alwog interjected, "but what do you want us to *do*? If you're really just going to have us sit in the woods I'll have to charge an additional fee for boredom."

Hae-jin now spoke up. "The Bird is correct", Hae-jin said. "He and I spoke on this matter many days ago, back when he first approached me with this venture. We have a job of our own to do here, and I will certainly be grateful to both Ursilda and the Wogs for their aid in carrying it out. Likewise, if the Fox wishes to join our cause I would be equally grateful."

The Fox had been sitting quietly all this time, sniffing the air about him and licking his paws idly now and then as the conversation went back and forth. Now he looked up and winked humorously. "I should be delighted to help out" ,he said, "if only I knew what I were helping out with. So far you've said a fair bit about this curse of yours that needs breaking, but there seems to be another side of this business you haven't spoken much of yet. I'm quite fascinated. I presume that once the curse is broken you're next move will be to do away with this man Gurth?"

Hae-jin and the Bird exchanged a look. So far Hae-jin hadn't spoken with anyone else about the things he and the Bird had discussed in the beginning, before Hae-jin had even left Zhongyang. Just how much of that should he reveal now? "In essence that is correct", the Bird said cautiously. "I'm sure Gurth's demise would be welcomed by most everyone in Linster, but the fact is that the situation is more complex than that. Things have become, shall we say, volatile. To put it bluntly, Linster is getting quite close to exploding."

"How do you mean?", the Fox asked curiously.

"I think we can discuss that in more detail another time. Suffice to say, we could be in for rather a long haul. For the moment, I think our principal concern should be to establish a secure base of operations. I had hoped that Mortimer's Mill would serve that purpose."

"But we still don't know that this man Mortimer can be trusted", Hae-jin interjected, "For all we know it was he who betrayed us to Gurth."

"Quite right", the Bird said. "I propose that we wait here until nightfall, at which point I'll fly over to the mill and see who's at home. If Mortimer is there alone we can perhaps interview him."

Ursilda grunted. "And if Mortimer is a traitor or if Gurth's men are keeping watch on the mill you and your golden feathers will be spotted for sure, and you'll come back with an arrow in your gizzard. Send the Fox instead. Even if he's seen he won't raise any suspicion (surely there are other foxes hereabouts)."

This comment was followed by a bit more discussion and bickering, but at length an accord was at last reached, and at dusk Bartholomew scampered across the field towards the mill while the others waited anxiously in the woods. The Fox was a long time gone. It had been agreed that he would scout around the area a bit to ensure that no one was spying on the property, but Hae-jin feared that when dealing with someone of Gurth's resources they would be hard pressed to have any true assurance of secrecy. The Fox might perhaps spot a man or a Zard lurking around the house somewhere, but what if Gurth were employing owls, or even bats? Or what if the trees themselves were serving as his eyes? Hae-jin shivered.

Finally, after a very long wait indeed there was a rustle at the edge of the field and Fox bounded out from among the tall stalks of barley. "I'm back!"

Ursilda snorted derisively "So we noticed", she rumbled. "Well, don't just stand there, what have you to say for yourself, Fox?"

Bartholomew paused and licked himself with deliberation for a moment. He wasn't about to be hassled by some imperious Bear. "The farm is largely deserted", he said. "I didn't see anyone spying on the place from the outside, and on the grounds itself I saw only two people, both humans. One is an older man, grey haired and a bit frail looking. The other is a young boy with red hair. I'll admit that I'm not very good at guessing the ages of humans, but I'd say he's far from full grown while still far too large to be a mere kit."

"That would be Tom Oates.", Joan observed, "He's an orphan who Mortimer took in years ago. The other is Mortimer himself. But I'm surprised they were the only ones you saw, I would have expected Watt the farmhand to have been there as well. Are you sure there was no one else?"

"Quite sure. It was definitely just the two."

"Hmm. That seems odd to me. Still, I suppose there's nothing for it now but to go and talk to Mortimer."

"I'm still not sure you should go in alone", Hae-jin interjected.

"We agreed I should go first. Don't worry, Bartholomew will follow and keep an eye on me."

With that, Joan ducked her head down low and began to creep slowly across the field, followed by the Fox as the others stayed behind beneath the trees. Joan and the Fox crept together as far as the farmhouse, at which time they agreed that Joan would go in alone to talk to Mortimer while Bartholomew kept watch outside. With that, Joan softly opened the door of the house and slipped inside.

But Bartholomew did not remain to keep watch. Bartholomew had always fancied himself a particularly clever and talented sort of Fox. He was accustomed to observing things which ordinarily escaped the attention of others. And Bartholomew had caught a scent. It had been a subtle thing, exotic and tantalizing, and hardly a proper smell at all really, which made it all the more fascinating. He noticed it the moment he set paw inside the farmyard, and while Joan was busy talking to Mortimer, Bartholomew resolved to find it.

The Fox began to rove stealthily around the farmyard, dipping his nose to the ground now and then as he came across some hint of the elusive odor. Suddenly, there it was. Bartholomew began following the trail now, moving at a trot as his nose almost scraped the surface of the earth. The trail proved to be a confusing one, crisscrossing in all directions across the farmyard. But there was one thread which was stronger than the others, and bit by bit the Fox was able to pick it out and at length he tracked it to a place right at the base of the barn. The barn's walls were composed of bare wattle made from springy strips of wood woven together like basketwork. Here the scent was stronger than ever, though by now it was quite clearly something which was more than a simple odor. Bartholomew was sure he was smelling magic. He ran his nose along the length of the wattle, trying to find the source of the odor. And soon enough, he found it.

Crammed in a gap between the wattle, was a small dark object. It was black and irregularly shaped, and even with his own keen night eyes the Fox could hardly make out what it was. He felt it gently with the tip of his nose. It was hard and just a little bit sharp, like a large piece of flint. Gingerly he tried biting at it to see if he could get it out. It wasn't easy, for the stone was smooth and hard. But it wasn't set very tightly in the wattle and a fair bit of it was sticking out, as if someone had put it there in the hopes of being able to remove it again easily. Twisting his head this way and that while carefully prodding the object with his teeth, the Fox finally managed to knock the thing free of the wattle and onto the ground. The Fox looked at it keenly for a moment, and then gingerly picked it up in his jowls and carried it away from the barn. Casting about himself for a moment he spotted a place where he was sure he could find it again quickly. Depositing the stone there, Bartholomew then made his way back to the farmhouse, for by now he could just hear the sound of Joan's voice softly calling his name.

Across the field, Hae-jin was anxiously watching the mill, looking for any sign of either Joan's return or the Fox bringing word that disaster had struck. Yet all remained quiet and still. Finally, after what seemed like an eon, Hae-jin was certain he saw movement around the house. At first Hae-jin wasn't sure whether his eyes were playing tricks on him or if someone were indeed moving around the farmyard. Then abruptly the sound of a whinney floated from across the breeze, and out of the homestead there came a rider on horseback. The rider was a smallish sort of person, and Hae-jin caught a glint of red hair as the rider paused briefly in the night and looked around before spurring his mount on again into the darkness. Suddenly the fringes of the field rustled before him again, and the Fox popped out of the barley.

"Hullo Hae-jin!", the Fox said cheerfully. "It's alright, Joan says for the rest of you to come inside. Oh, and she says to hurry and also to be sneaky about it. Apparently there have been some disturbing developments as of late, much as we already suspected. I'll see you at the mill!" With that the Fox darted back into the barley. Hae-jin and the other followed shortly thereafter (after a bit of the usual bickering between Ursilda and the Wogs).

Besides the mill itself there were several more buildings on the property, including a barn and byre and a fine looking house. Hae-jin guessed that this man Mortimer was fairly rich, or at least he had been once upon a time. Though it was difficult to tell in the darkness, Hae-jin was left with the impression that the shadowy structures around him were in poor state of repair. The windows of the main house were shuttered, but as they drew close Hae-jin could now see faint cracks of light behind them. It seemed that the householder was awake. Suddenly there was a blaze of light as the door to the house was opened and Joan appeared, her graceful shape silhouetted against the firelight behind her. Hae-jin quickened his pace as he approached the woman at the door. Joan had a tense sort of look on her face, and as Hae-jin approached she beckoned him inside urgently. "Come inside quickly",she said. "Mortimer has sent Tom off to fetch Little and Sykes. The rest of us should stay out of sight. Things aren't safe anymore. Gurth is on the move, and Watt has gone missing." As Hae-jin stepped across the threshold Joan's hand stole out and tightly grasped his own, her slender and soft fingers entwining tensely with his as the woman's whole manner exuded a peculiar mixture of iron willed determination and barely contained terror.

The interior of the house was bathed with flickering red light. On one end was a fireplace, recently renewed with freshly stacked logs, which cast dancing shadows on the walls. The room was modestly well appointed, if plain and stark by comparison to the Zhongish palaces to which Hae-jin had once been accustomed. In one corner stood a brightly painted cupboard, while in another there was a sturdy chest (also brightly painted with simple floral and geometric patterns). Removable panels shuttered the windows from the inside, which possessed no glass. Various well stocked shelves lined the walls, and in the middle of the room there was a good sized table set with benches. Lastly, but perhaps most notably, was a simple but well made and elaborately painted high backed chair, which at the present moment was set beside the fire and occupied by a gray haired man who was regarding the newcomers keenly. "Good Lord, Joan, who is this you have brought here?", the old man said.

"This is General Moon Hae-jin, Hugh", Joan replied. "The Good Folk have sent him to help us."

"Looks like the Devil himself, old Robin Goodfellow come to haunt us", the other remarked. As Mortimer looked Hae-jin up and down quizzically, Hae-jin was suddenly very conscious of the fact that his features were very alien to those of Joan and Mortimer, marking him instantly as a foreigner. Apparently he was going to have to get used to standing out in a crowd while here in Linster. Mortimer was now looking past Hae-jin, and his eyes had widened as the wogs just shoved their way through the door. "Make that the Devil and three of his imps!", the old man gasped. "And are those some animals I see out there? Has this demon brought with him a legion of his familiars? What on earth have you done, Joan?"

"These are the persons the Good Folk have sent to help us", Joan said frustratedly. "Hae-jin is foreign but he is as human as you or I, and I assure you that none of the others are demons, but friends come from many far places to aid us in our hour of need."

At this point Hae-jin caught a glimpse of golden plumage as the Bird pushed his way past the others and hopped up onto the table, which wobbled and creaked alarmingly beneath his weight. Mortimer stared wide eyed at the dazzling creature before him as the bird's iridescent feathers glinted in the light of the fire. The Bird skewered Mortimer with a glittering black eye and spoke softly. "Gaze upon me, Hugh Mortimer", the Bird said dramatically, "and know that I am a true servant of the Good Folk. I have been commissioned by them to secure your deliverance, and to the consummation of that end myself and my fellows do pledge our lives."

"Hoy!", cut in Alwog. "I'll have you know a pledge like that'll cost you a full sixty silver marks a day!"

"Sixty-one!"

The Bird flapped his wings impatiently. "Oh, do shut up the both of you!", the Bird said crossly. "The Good Folk will see to it that you are properly paid when all this is done. Well, Mortimer, what say you? Will you accept our aid?"

Mortimer looked helplessly to Joan, who set her hand on his shoulder reassuringly. "Listen to the Bird, Hugh", she said. "We are all allies here."

Mortimer threw up his hands resignedly. "Fine", he replied weakly. "Who am I to argue while a *thing* like that sits on top of my table? But you'll have to convince the others. Tom is making the rounds to Sykes and Little now. They should be here soon enough. Tell the rest of your menagerie to come inside, no need to have them wait outdoors and be spotted by someone."

18

"Of Millers and Yeomen"

Mortimer's Mill wasn't particularly far from the respective abodes of the other yeomen, but it took a fair bit of time nonetheless for young Tom Oates to reach them and arouse their occupants. In the meanwhile, Hae-jin and his fellows waited beside Mortimer's fire, while the miller recounted the events in Linster over the last week since Joan had departed with the Bird for Harin's Vault.

The last time anyone had seen Watt the farmhand was the day Joan had left Linster in the company of the Bird. The very next day a detachment of Gurth's men had come to Mortimer's Mill, demanding to know the whereabouts of Joan. They ransacked the mill quite thoroughly before they left, and had returned twice in the days since then.

In the meanwhile, Gurth had been very busy elsewhere. It started when Gurth's men seized the granaries at Leighshaw and Elmstead, occupying them and preventing any of the food stores from being removed. Other bands of Gurth's men had since begun roving the countryside, seizing food and burning crops wherever they went. Anyone caught working the fields or transporting food would be waylaid and seized, with the food taken to the occupied storehouses and the farmers themselves being thrown into Gurth's slave pens. Reportedly this pattern was being repeated all across the country. The slave pens were close to bursting now, and at the rate at which Gurth was seizing food and laborers, half the country would soon be on the brink of starvation. According to rumor, Gurth had recently issued an ultimatum to the king, demanding the surrender of several key castles and armories in exchange for releasing a portion of the captured food back to the population. All of this, however, was coming on the heels of a situation which was already getting out of hand. For months Gurth's demand for slaves had been steadily increasing. The supply of labor had become more and more strained as the slave pens became ever more full. Gurth's crackdown over the past week had finally driven the common folk to desperation and the entire countryside seemed on the verge of boiling over.

"Frankly, I don't see what option the king has but to give in to Gurth", Mortimer speculated, "It's the only way he can avert a general uprising. The king and the nobles are scarcely more popular than Gurth these days. Their own necks are as much on the line as his. Much as it will harm their own interests, I don't think they have any choice other than to acquiesce to Gurth's demands, which won't end at a few castles, mark my words. I'll warrant Gurth won't stop until he's blackmailed the king into handing over the privy seal itself, at which point it won't matter much whether the curse is ever broken or not."

Joan shivered in the firelight. "I still can't believe that Watt would have betrayed us to Gurth", she said.

"Neither can I", the other replied. "But he disappeared right before Gurth's men first came around looking for you. Why else would have fled, unless he'd betrayed us?"

"Did he take anything with him?"

"Nothing but the clothes on his back, so far as I can tell. Most of his belongings are still here."

"Perhaps he was kidnapped by Gurth instead. Perhaps he was tortured and forced to betray us!"

"If that were the case, it would have been a remarkable timing indeed. It wasn't very long after you left that it happened."

"But by that time Gurth might already have known what was happening; his men were at the vault after all."

"Which means that they must have known in advance exactly where you would be. If Watt is not the betrayer, then it must be one of the others. And if that were the case, then why has Watt gone missing? No, I'm afraid we must accept the fact that Watt has indeed betrayed us, as incredible as it seems."

Suddenly from somewhere outside there came the sound of a faint whinny and the muted clop of hooves, announcing the arrival of a man on horseback. Joan quickly arose and made her way silently to the door. She peered out tensely for a moment, and then with a quick sigh of relief she flung the door wide to admit the newcomer.

The horseman proved to be a man who looked to be in his mid to late thirties, of medium height and a compact, athletic build. He was dressed in tight-fitting red hose and a padded linen jacket, over which he wore a russet colored leather coat covered in a pattern of brass studs, which clinked and shifted in a peculiarly rigid manner which betrayed a layer of overlapping steel plates beneath the leather. At his side he carried a broad, machete like sword of the falchion type, along with a small round shield, while opposite this he sported a large, nasty looking dagger. The man had clearly come prepared for trouble. He abruptly halted in his tracks as he observed the room before him packed with a bizarre assortment of creatures (not the least of which was a colossal bear). On the other side of the room Mortimer stood up and waved languidly to the stranger.

"Come on in, Sykes", the latter said. "Nothing to worry about here. The Good Folk have sent Joan back to us along with Robin Goodfellow and an army of demons and familiars."

The man called Sykes made his way cautiously into the crowded room, warily eyeing the peculiar beings which were now surrounding him. Sykes picked his way carefully past the animals and wogs, but paused when he came to Hae-jin. For a moment the two men regarded one another. There was something about Sykes which seemed at once familiar; his features and attire were foreign, but there was something about his deportment which Hae-jin instantly recognized. The quality of the man's weapons and armor, the manner in which he bore them and carried himself, all suggested to Hae-jin that the man before him was a professional soldier (or had been one in the past). A man of his own kind. Sykes too, seemed to recognize the familiar bearing of a fellow soldier, and addressed Hae-jin cordially.

"Robin Goodfellow, I presume?", Sykes asked.

"My name is Moon Hae-jin", Hae-jin replied.

"Well met, Moon Hae-jin!", the other said. "You're a long way from home, I'll warrant."

"I come from Zhongyang."

Sykes whistled. "That's a long way off indeed. You might just as well be Robin Goodfellow to have come all that way. What in the name of The Twelve Kingdoms of Arthur is a man like you doing out here in the Hinterlands?"

Hae-jin shrugged. "Apparently the Good Folk felt you needed the help of a soldier."

"Frankly, the way things are going we could do with a thousand soldiers. Your company is welcome of course, but one man will hardly be enough to sway fate in our favor. Unless you're one man who is equal to a thousand men."

"I would never claim to be that, although once upon a time I commanded upwards of ten thousand men."

Sykes whistled again. "That's quite a host indeed. I served the king as a bowman during the last war with the Tollards, and even in those days the largest army we ever mustered was scarcely twice that. The Good Folk have sent us more than a soldier, they've sent us a captain! Consider yourself very welcome indeed, *Sir* Robin Goodfellow."

It was a while longer before the last yeoman arrived. Will Little proved to be a man in his early thirties, the youngest of the three yeomen and likewise the poorest. He came wearing a sword and carrying a longbow, but he possessed no armor and his sword was rather old and pitted. And unlike Sykes and Mortimer he did not own a horse, and had been obliged to ride to the mill with young Tom Oates. The latter was a red headed stripling of about thirteen, the foster son of Mortimer. Tom Oates was skinny but strong for his age. For many long years now, the burden of maintaining Mortimer's homestead and mill had been largely up to the boy and Watt, for Mortimer himself was frail and a widower, whose health and family had been taken long ago by the want and pestilence brought by the Curse of Gurth. The yeomen were dismayed at the news that the Curse of Gurth was not yet broken. It had been three years since Joan and the yeomen had first come together to seek the aid of the Good Folk, and the news that the culmination of all their efforts had yet to bear fruit was taken hard. Of all of them, Sykes was at first the most bitter about the matter, for he had spent many long and weary days and nights roving the countryside alone in search of any sign of the Fairy Folk. Still, Joan's return in the company of such an extraordinary ensemble of characters proved decisive in convincing them that the Good Folk hadn't abandoned their cause. Although Linster was a place where wightbeasts and other fey creatures were largely unknown (although for their part, the Wogs would likely raise eyebrows wherever they went), it was ultimately the Bird himself who made the greatest impression. His eloquence notwithstanding, his extraordinary appearance alone was quite enough to dazzle the four Linstermen. In the end, it was Sykes who rebounded from his disappointment the fastest.

"Whether the Good Folk come through for us or not", Skyes said, "the fact is that something has to be done, and done now. We can no longer wait. If we do we will surely lose any chance we have of ever being free from Gurth."

"We all realize that", Little interjected, "the problem is, what can we do? If the king and the nobles can't resist Gurth, how can we?"

Up to now Hae-jin had been listening attentively to the conversation, observing the yeomen carefully and attempting to gauge their reactions to the news which had been brought before them. One of them could still prove to be a traitor, although there was nothing in anyone's manner thus far to rouse his suspicions. But more than that, Hae-jin wanted to assess the character and personality of each man as much as possible, for he knew that he would be relying on these men in the near future. But now, it was time. Time for Hae-jin to begin what he had been brought to Linster to do. Hae-jin now arose and spoke.

"The present situation in this land may be dire, but Gurth's malevolence is also our opportunity. At this moment, Gurth's men are ravaging the countryside and driving the people to the brink of starvation. This must be stopped, and the desperation of the people is the weapon with which we will do it. Desperation breeds valor, and the desperation of one breeds the valor of one. But when harnessed together, the desperation of many can be forged into the valor of a nation. The fire has already begun to burn. It must now be fed, and its path guided, until it blazes like an inferno at the very gates of the enemy. If the king will not oppose Gurth, then his hand must be forced. If he will not be forced, then the king himself must be overcome."

Sykes was looking keenly at Hae-jin as the latter spoke. "That's all well and good, my friend", Sykes said. "But how do you propose that it be done? Who is to guide the blaze?"

Hae-jin looked Sykes in the eye. "Look at my face", he said. "I am an alien, I am not one of you. But I will pledge my own life to you and your kingdom's cause. The question is, will you follow me?"

There was a steely glint in Sykes's eye as returned Hae-jin's gaze, and a resolute smile began to play across his lips as he spoke. "Aye, I'll follow you", the man said. "My sword and bow shall be yours to the bitter end. What say you, my fellows? Will you also follow our Robin Goodfellow?"

Mortimer stirred uncomfortably, but Little slammed his fist into the table with a hearty "Aye!", and the boy Tom belted out his assent as well. Hae-jin looked at the Bird, and though the avian's features were by nature a bit inscrutable, the creature nonetheless replied with half a wink, as if to say he knew what Hae-jin was thinking: It had begun. In that very moment, a rebellion had been born. They spent the remainder of the night in deep discussion. There was much to be talked and argued over. But in the end a consensus was reached, and a plan had emereged.

Hae-jin stepped out of the house into the starlit night and heaved a sigh. It hadn't been precisely easy, but in the end he had succeeded. His army was a tiny one, but that night it had been forged into what he hoped would become the core of something much bigger. Much, much bigger. Though where it would ultimately take him he couldn't guess. For a moment, he simply had a job to do. And so far he had done it. The yeomen had returned to their homes, Sykes having taken Little with him on his horse. There were still a few hours of the night left to them, which was a good thing as they would all be in need of sleep. There was much to be done over the next few days. Mortimer was to put Hae-jin and the others up in his barn for the night. Joan herself possessed a cottage in the village, but it was agreed that she would be safer if she remained with the others at the mill. She, Hae-jin, the wogs and the Bird clamored up a rickety ladder into a loft filled with hay, while Ursilda stoutly refused to entrust her weight to such an inferior device and curled up in a corner on the ground floor, while Bartholomew volunteered to sleep by the door.

Hae-jin stretched himself out onto the hay, grateful for what little comfort it provided. A pile of hay and a drafty barn was luxurious compared to the sort of lodgings he'd been accustomed to over the last several days. Come to think of it, Hae-jin hadn't slept in a proper bed since he left his own home in Zhongyang for the last time. True, there had been that cot in the Drixi jail, but it had also come with a locked door and more or less certain doom, so he supposed that didn't really count. Here in Linster, at least, Hae-jin had a second chance. Hae-jin had tried to overturn tyranny once, and had failed. Whatever else happened, he was determined that this time he would succeed. Victory was never so sweet that it did not carry the taste of righteousness, and it was for the sake of righteousness that Hae-jin had lost everything. And only the continued pursuit of righteousness could make that loss have meaning. A home, a fortune, a rank and reputation, a nation, and even a wife. Hae-jin's choices had ultimately cost him all of these things. And unless he remained true to those choices, it would have all been for nothing. It wasn't the rosiest future he could imagine, but without it what else was there for him?

The loft was faintly lit by the moonlight poking through the gaps in the wattle walls of the barn. Hae-jin could just barely make out the glittering feathers of The Bird, perched with his beak tucked under one wing as he slept, while elsewhere in the darkness Hae-jin could hear the coarse snoring of the Wogs. Suddenly, Hae-jin felt a shift in the weight of the hay around him, and he realized that someone was now lying close beside him in the darkness. A soft hand stole up and clutched his arm tightly as a woman's lips pressed close to his ear.

"Are you still awake?" There was a tense hush in Joan's voice as she whispered.

"Yes", he replied.

"Are you really serious about starting an uprising against Gurth?"

It was too dark for Hae-jin to properly see Joan's face. He shrugged. "That is what I was brought here to do."

Joan remained silent, but Hae-jin could sense her body tensing beside him. Perhaps she had never really realized that the path she had taken would have led to such an eventuality. Or perhaps she had never wanted to realize it. Joan now heaved a sigh. "That's what the Good Folk were planning all along then?"

"So it seems."

"I wish it didn't have to come to that."

"Frankly, I don't see that there was ever any other way. Breaking the curse simply wouldn't have been enough, not on its own. Not with Gurth himself still being free to cause mischief."

Joan was silent again. Her hand stole down now to nestle into his as she shifted her weight to rest closer beside him, and Hae-jin could feel her body now pressing deeply into his with each breath. "I'll stand with you, Hae-jin. Whatever happens, I'll remain beside you."

Hae-jin made no reply. But he closed his hand tightly around hers.

Downstairs, the Fox pricked his ears up. He could hear soft voices above him, but he had no interest in what they were saying. They were busy, and he had something to tend to. Creeping softly through the door and out into the night, Bartholomew made his way to where he had hidden the mysterious object he had found earlier. He couldn't see it any better than before, but he was quite sure it was some kind of stone, like flint or obsidian. And it was imbued with a dark and powerful magic. He was sure of it! Whoever had hidden it near the barn had done so for a reason, and no doubt would be back to retrieve it. But they wouldn't find it. Bartholomew gingerly picked the stone up in his jowls and trotted out into the field. In a short while, he found a place that he liked and there he buried the stone. Chuckling softly to himself he then darted back into the barn and curled up again beside the door.

The moon had long sunk below the horizon as the night passed into its final few hours. All was still across the farmyard. Then, the door to the farmhouse was stealthily opened. A shadowy figure peeked furtively outside, looking this way and that. The figure then crept its way warily across the farmyard towards the barn, coming to a stop at a very particular place along the barn wall. He then began to feel the wattle, looking for something which would be invisible in the darkness. But whatever it was, he couldn't find it. He began frantically casting about, feeling everywhere along the walls and crawling about on the ground, but to no avail. Whatever it was he was looking for, it was gone.

Finally, at long last the shadowy figure made its way back into the farmhouse, as somewhere in the distance a cock crowed.

19

"Robin Goodfellow"

The sun rose the next morning amidst a clear blue sky, as a cool breeze gently swept the countryside. In the village of Tresham, the people arose and began to go about their daily labours. Yet there was a sense of disquiet everywhere, many of the villagers tarried as they went about their business, pausing at every turn to speak anxiously to one another. By the time the red glow of dawn had passed away the village green was dotted with small knots of people conversing with one another as their tools rested idly beside them. The people were uneasy. Gurth's men had been on the prowl for days, seizing food stores and waylaying farmers. Several people from the village had already been taken and thrown into the slave pens, and the remainder were now afraid to go out into the fields, lest they themselves also fall prey to Gurth's marauders. Not that there was much reason to work the fields anyway, for many of them had been burned to the ground by Gurth's men, and whatever was left would surely be seized or destroyed soon enough anyway. Food was becoming scarce and the people were growing more hungry by the day. Yet there was a curious sort of uncertainty about their mood this particular morning, teetering back and forth between dread and hope. For on the previous day, not long before sunset, an omen had appeared in the sky: The Dark Comet.

That's what people were calling it, at any rate. It had passed briefly overhead, casting a fleeting shadow across the village as it did so, like that of some monstrous bird. Several persons swore to have seen the object itself, a dark square which had passed low over the village. One woman even claimed that the comet had in fact been a black shield ridden by seven men. Everyone had an opinion on what the comet meant, what sort of omen it was, and so on. Opinion had largely become divided between those who believed the omen spelled doom for everyone and those who were cautiously hopeful that the comet might be a sign that deliverance was coming. The people speculated on these things in animated tones, debating back and forth between the various fates which might soon befall them, until at last the reeves emerged from the manor house and began shooing the people out of the green and hustling them off to work reluctantly in the fields. Of course, unbeknownst to the villagers, the thing they'd seen in the sky had in fact been a carpet, whose passengers were presently ensconced at Mortimer's Mill and were at that moment commencing their own particular tasks for the day.

Skyes had arrived on horseback early in the morning, and was followed not long after by Little, who came on foot along with his two sons, a pair of sinewy lads of thirteen and fourteen, each with a quiver of arrows and a longbow which was only slightly lighter than that of their father. Everyone already knew what was expected of them, and it didn't take Hae-jin long to set everyone to order and see them off on their respective tasks. Bartholomew and the Littles were dispatched to scout the roads, keeping watch for Gurth's men and carefully observing their movements, while the Bird was to do the same from the air. Meanwhile, Mortimer had been sent to the village to gather news from further abroad, taking Tom with him. Gurth's men were already known to be seeking Joan's whereabouts, and as such it had been decided that Joan should remain hidden at Mortimer's Mill and direct the activities of Ursilda and the Wogs, who had been tasked with digging out a hidden cellar beneath the barn. The great Bear had spent the morning burrowing a gaping cavern in the dirt, while the Wogs busied themselves shoring up its roof and walls and carting the dirt away as discreetly as they could, and disposing of it in the woods. As usual with anything involving the Wogs, there was a good bit of quarrelling, particularly as regards the overall quality of the excavation. The Wogs complained that being experienced mine workers they had professional knowledge of the matter, and that the disgraceful hole the Bear was digging was the most dreadful and unsafe thing they'd ever seen. Ursilda retorted in turn that she had dug a hundred dens for a hundred winters, and the Wogs had no idea what they were talking about as usual. For his part, Hae-jin had borrowed Mortimer's horse and had spent the morning riding around the countryside in the company of Skyes, acquainting himself with the lay of the land.

It had been agreed that Hae-jin was to rendezvous at noon with the Bird at Mortimer's Mill, as Hae-jin wanted a preliminary report from the Bird's vantage point as soon as possible. The morning passed and just as the sun reached its zenith, Hae-jin and Skyes rode into the mill yard and dismounted. In addition to the what he had worn on the previous night, Sykes was now bearing with him a great knobbly war bow nearly as tall as himself. Hae-jin meanwhile carried only a heavy staff, having lost his own sword days ago at Harin's Vault. Otherwise he was dressed in the same Zhongish clothes had been wearing for days, and both men also wore cloaks and hoods to conceal their unwonted appearance to the casual observer. The two men entered the barn, where in one corner there was now a massive hole, from which Ursilda's great posterior protruded gracelessly as bits of dirt were tossed out behind her. From beneath, the voices of the Wogs could be heard complaining loudly that the entrance was still too small. Joan was sitting in one corner on a stool, watching the proceedings pensively. She arose when she caught sight of Hae-jin, and made her way quickly to his side. "Thank heaven you're back", she said. "Have you seen any of Gurth's men?"

Hae-jin nodded. "We caught sight of a group of them about three hours ago. They had two carts of grain with them, and were headed westward along the road to…where did you say it was, Skyes?"

"Elmstead", the yeoman said. "The Bishop of Larchester has a large granary there, which Gurth's men occupied several days ago."

Hae-jin looked back at Joan. "Any sign of the Bird?", he asked.

"No, he hasn't turned up yet", the other replied.

"Let's hope he doesn't go missing again. Having him scouting for us from the air is a critical advantage for us. It is imperative that he be reliable."

Silence hung for a moment. Then Joan reached out and took Hae-jin's hand. "Come, walk with me for a while."

Joan and Hae-jin wandered out into the mill yard. In the light of day, Mortimer's Mill exhibited much clearer signs of want and neglect. In many places the plaster walls of the buildings were crumbling away, exposing the wattle and mud daub beneath. The barn itself was built on a foundation of finely cut stone, yet its walls were composed of bare wattle entirely devoid of any covering. It seemed as though the barn had once been a fine structure, which had since perished and been rebuilt quite cheaply. The mill itself wasn't much better. It was a sagging, crumbling, motionless heap, with the great water wheel bleached and dilapidated as it loomed idly above a shriveled and dried up creek bed. Just beyond the wheel there was a small footbridge which passed over the deepest part of the creek. Here Hae-jin and Joan paused. The creek was mostly dry. It was wide and deep, yet the only water which remained were a few small pools teeming with small, insignificant fish, which schooled aimlessly back and forth between the ever contracting edges of the water. There was a cracked and fragile railing on the bridge, and Joan leaned carefully against it as she gazed down at the empty creek bed.

"Mortimer was a rich man once", she said. "The mill used to be very profitable, before the Curse of Gurth. After that happened, the water began to dry up. Nowadays the creek is only full after a heavy rain, and even then it's hardly enough to turn the wheel, and Mortimer has been quite destitute for many years now. The franklins and yeomen are hardly any better off than we are."

"What do you mean, 'we'? Aren't you all part of this same conspiracy?"

"Oh yes, but that's only because I am a midwife. I birthed all of Mortimer's children, and I helped bury all of them as well, along with his wife when she finally died too. I suppose I'm all the family he has left, except for young Tom. But Mortimer, he's a freeman. All of the others are. Sykes and Little are both yeomen, and Mortimer himself is practically a franklin in his own right...or used to be anyway. As for myself, I was born a serf in Tresham, which is part of the demesne of the Bishop of Larchester. I suppose I would have remained bound to the estate had my talents not been discovered. I've always had a certain sensitivity to magic. Not much, but just enough. People realized I was of cunning when I was still a little girl, and in those days the king had ordered that all cunning folk should be enrolled and educated by the church. When I was twelve years old I was sent to the Abbey of St. Etheltrude for two years. The monks taught me to read and write, along with a smattering of philosophy and a thorough catechising. After that I was sent home and given over to our village midwife, who taught me her craft. Things weren't ever the same after that. Technically I am still a serf, but after having been educated by the clergy I felt like I'd become something more, and it's been rather awkward living among the illiterate villeins. I don't feel as though I belong to them, but neither do I belong to the clergy. It is as though I belong to no one now. If anything, it is among the yeomen that I feel the most at home. But even with them, I am still technically an outsider. The freemen and the nobles blame the serfs for bringing the Curse of Gurth on the land, and in some ways they are right. It wasn't hard for Gurth to seduce us with his dark arts. The common folk have always been inclined to embrace simple magic, whether black or white. I was taught to know the difference, but others of my station neither know nor care. It's how we've always survived. Look at the fish in the creek below us. Each time it rains the creek fills up and flows again. For a while there is plenty, and the creek is full of life. But bit by bit it begins to dry up again, and the animals leave. First the birds, then the frogs and turtles. But the fish are left behind. The things which have wings and legs can go elsewhere, but the fish cannot escape and must remain until the end. And we serfs, we are like the fish.

"Years ago, a fever tore through the village of Tresham, killing many. It took mostly the children, who died within a few days of catching the fever. None of my remedies worked, and I was powerless to do anything to save them. So I sought out Gurth. Gurth had only recently come to Linster in those days. The last harvest had been poor, and the serfs were suffering greatly. Then Gurth came, and the people flocked to him. And I flocked to him too. Gurth gave me a potion which he promised would cure the children of our village. But it required an ingredient which Gurth did not provide: the life-essence of another human being, taken through blood. I had to acquire this ingredient for myself, and I knew the perfect candidate for it. There was a monk who lived in a hovel not far from our village. He claimed to be a holy hermit and lived alone in a cottage well outside the abbey, where he did nothing but grow fat on the tithe. He was as useless a creature as had ever been born; the monks at the abbey disapproved of him, and the villagers hated him. He was perfect for what I needed. If I could only take just a little bit of what was his to give to those who needed it more. It was black magic (technically vampirism in fact), and I knew it, but I believed I had justice on my side.

"One night I took some strong ale and a knife and crept out to his cottage. At first he wouldn't let me in, insisting that his vow of chastity prevented him from entertaining a woman in his home, but I wouldn't leave and at last he admitted me. I then amused him. I entertained him and pressed him with drink until he was asleep, and then I took what I came for. One prick was all I needed to complete my crime, and I left my victim sleeping peacefully none the wiser. That night I went around the village and gave Gurth's potion to the sick children in our village, and it worked perfectly. All of them had recovered by morning and the fever never returned. But it had come at a price. That same morning the monk I seduced was found dead in his hovel, shriveled almost to nothing. The villagers saw it as divine justice, but I knew better. I was responsible for that man's death. In hindsight he wasn't an evil man. Not really. He'd never wronged anybody, so far as I know he'd never even violated his vows (not in any serious way). His only sin was being a lazy glutton. And I stole his life from him. I hadn't meant to kill him, but the guilt is mine anyway. That was more than ten years ago. It wasn't long afterwards that the Curse of Gurth was upon us. And I, a murderess, am partly responsible for it."

Hae-jin looked silently into the water as Joan finished speaking, gazing at the fish as they darted about hopelessly in the tiny confines of the shrinking pool. Hae-jin then looked at Joan. "Why have you told me all of this?", he asked

Joan was looking pensively into the water as well. Now she looked away into the woods as she spoke. "I'm fond of you, Moon Hae-Jin", she said. "I would rather you knew what sort of woman I really am."

From the direction of the mill there now came a great beating of wings, and with a sudden flurry of golden plumage the Bird was among them. "Aha!", the Bird said cheerfully. "There you are! Sykes said you had gone this way. I've been very busy."

Hae-jin took a deep breath and turned to address the interloper. His earlier annoyance at the Bird's tardiness had now become annoyance at his inopportune arrival. The Bird seemed to have a unique talent for inconvenient timing. "Well, what have you seen?", he demanded.

"Gurth's men are everywhere. They keep mostly to the roads though, which is helpful. Once you know what to look for they're rather predictable. It shouldn't be too hard to keep track of them."

"Are they traveling on foot or mounted?"

"Some are on foot, but quite a lot of them have horses."

"Good. We'll be needing those."

"Ahem"

Hae-jin started briefly, as suddenly he caught sight of Bartholomew the Fox sitting primly on the foot of the bridge. Hae-jin felt a fresh surge of annoyance. "What are you doing here? I wasn't expecting your report until nightfall."

"Quite true", the Fox said. "However, since you and the Bird were supposed to meet at noon I thought that this was an excellent opportunity to speak to you both in private, without anyone else knowing about it."

"What for?"

Here the Fox arose, and turning around he scooped up a small object from the ground beside him, which he carried over in his jaws and deposited at Hae-jin's feet.

"Last night I found this hidden near the barn", the Fox said. "I thought you would want to see it, so I took it and buried it in the field to show to you later. Rather interesting, isn't it?"

Hae-jin picked up the object and examined it, pausing to wipe a bit of the Fox's saliva off it as he did so. It was a thick flake of jet black stone, smooth, and almost iridescent. It looked very much like obsidian, though there was a certain quality to its color which seemed unnatural and unwholesome, almost sinister, and the mere sight of the thing gave

Hae-jin a shiver. Hae-jin proffered the object to the Bird. "Do you know what this might be?"

The Bird looked keenly at the stone, peering closely at it with an air of both fascination and growing distaste. "Why bless me, but I do believe...yes, yes I think it is! Yes, yes, I can see it now quite definitely. This thing is a scrying shard. How ever did you find this?"

The Fox twitched his head slightly in a way that looked rather like the canine equivalent of a shrug. "I smelled it."

"How extraordinary. And you found this hidden near the barn you say?"

"So what is this thing, then?" Hae-jin interjected. "You call it a scrying shard, what is that?"

"A scrying shard is a fragment of a larger scrying stone", the Bird explained. "Whoever carries the shard can speak directly to the possessor of the original stone, wherever he may be. This particular shard is a bit small, I suspect that you'd have to put it inside a bowl of oil or water to get anything near the effect of having a full sized crystal, but in a pinch you could certainly use the thing just on its own. It's a very straightforward method of communication really, and a relatively common one at that, at least among people with sufficient means and the just the right kind of connections."

"People such as Gurth, you think?"

"Oh yes, I do think so indeed. The dratted thing positively reeks of black magic."

Hae-jin turned the shard over in his hand thoughtfully. "Well, if we weren't sure we had a traitor among us before, we are now."

"Do you think Watt left it behind?", Joan speculated.

Hae-jin shrugged. "It seems odd to me that he would, but perhaps he panicked and neglected it. That is, of course, assuming that Watt is our man."

"I can't believe that any of them would do such a thing!"

"You said yourself just now that the freemen blame the serfs for bringing the Curse of Gurth. Maybe their lack of sympathy is more profound than you thought. Or perhaps one of them is simply desperate."

Hae-jin glanced thoughtfully at the dilapidated mill a few paces away. As he did so, he caught sight of Mortimer crossing the mill yard. Hae-jin had just enough time to surreptitiously tuck the shard into his waistband before Mortimer caught sight of them and walked over. There was a certain wariness in his manner as Mortimer approached, and he eyed Hae-jin quizzically as he spoke.

"Afternoon, all", Mortimer said. "What are you all doing over here?"

"I was speaking with the Bird", Hae-jin replied casually. "I see you are back from the village?"

"Yes. There's no news really, except that the people think they've seen an omen or something. Nothing at all about the king or the situation at the capitol. I left Tom behind to pick up anything else that might be said. I myself was going to go to Elmstead to see if there is any news there. Tresham is such a desolate place. At least in Elmstead there is a proper tavern. If there's any news to be had, it'll be there."

Joan eyed Mortimer keenly. "You've gone a fair bit out of your way", she said. "Elmstead is the other direction up the road you know. What brought you back to the mill?"

Mortimer fidgeted a bit. "Er, well, I came to pick up my horse."

"But Hae-jin has it."

"I know that", Mortimer snapped, "I remembered that our Robin Goodfellow here was going to meet with the Bird at noon. I thought perhaps I could get my horse back so I wouldn't have to walk all the way to Elmstead."

"I'm sorry Mortimer, but I'm afraid Hae-jin will continue to need it over the coming days, at least until we acquire more horses."

Mortimer threw a sharp look at Hae-jin. "What do you mean, more horses?"

Hae-jin met Mortimer's eye. "I will tell you more about that later. In the meanwhile I will be grateful for whatever news you can bring from the town, but I'm afraid I cannot spare you your horse at the moment; Sykes and I will be leaving ourselves again shortly."

Mortimer grunted derisively, but said nothing and walked off in the direction of the farmhouse. As Mortimer withdrew, Joan threw a concerned look at Hae-jin. "Do you think he saw the shard?", she asked softly. "I don't think so, but I can't be sure", Hae-jin replied. "However, whoever the owner of the scrying shard is will likely be trying to find some other way of contacting Gurth, now that he's lost the shard. We will need to keep an eye on our friends from now on. I will be departing with Skyes shortly, and I'll need the Bird to return to the air and continue tracking Gurth's men. Can I ask our good Fox to dog Mortimer's footsteps for the moment?"

"You can ask", the Fox said. "I'll probably say yes."

The rest of the day went as planned, as did the following day and the day after that. During that time Ursilda and the Wogs had managed to hollow out a sizable cavern beneath the barn, and even more remarkably, had managed to agree that it was a more or less sound piece of construction. In the meanwhile, Hae-jin felt that he had gathered enough information about the surrounding land and the movements of Gurth's forces that he could begin real action. It was now time to strike back.

The sun was lowering on the horizon as a column of armed men marched dolefully along the road between Tresham and Elmstead. There were seven men at arms on horseback, all wearing the scarlet and black livery of Gurth. The design looked rather like a horseshoe from a distance, but it was in fact a pair of scarlet shackles on black field, connected by an arched chain. The soldiers were leading a wagon full of grain, along with a wretched group of farmers bound together on a rope like a string of fish. They were just coming up on a line of poplars beside the road, which caught the sun and cast a macabre shadow, like a barred window over the sorrowful procession. Suddenly there was a cry, as one of the men at arms jerked and fell off his horse, clutching at an arrow which was embedded in his breast. More arrows quickly poured forth from the treeline, and as this was happening a tremendous bear burst from out of concealment with a bellow, followed by several Wogs making bloodcurdling yells. Pandemonium ensued as several men now joined the melee from behind the trees. In a few moments the contest was over. Two more of the men at arms had been unhorsed and killed, while the others had fled in disorder down the road, abandoning their prisoners and booty.

Hae-jin strode confidently down the road towards the cart, where the Littles were busying themselves releasing the farmers. The Wogs were busy looting the dead men at arms of their weapons and armor. Joan was trying to contain one of the horses which had been abandoned by Gurth's men, while Sykes had already mounted another of the horses and was attempting to chase down a third. Things had gone exactly as planned, and Hae-jin was quite pleased. Hae-jin now approached the farmers, who were trembling with a mix of fear and bewilderment. He paused to look each man in the eye before he spoke. "You are all free to go", he said. "Take your grain and be gone. And tell all you meet that it was Robin Goodfellow who saved you."

20

"The Battle of Mortimer's Mill"

Along a dusty road, an eccentric party of bandits made their way brazenly under the shining light of the sun. First four men, three boys and a woman. Then three Wogs, and finally a Bear trudging along in the rear. All of them rode horses (save for the Bear), and they bore with them as well a motley assortment of looted weapons and armor as they made their way confidently through the countryside. And one of the Wogs carried a tattered and bloodied surcoat bearing the livery of Gurth, hung upside down on a pole as a makeshift banner.

For many days now Hae-jin and his followers had been waylaying Gurth's men along the roads. By this time they had refined their methods down to a well drilled system. The Bird would scout from the air, using this vantage point along with his extraordinary vision to spot roving bands of Gurth's men (particularly those with prisoners and seized food). He would then return to Hae-jin and the others, who would quickly ride to a suitable location and prepare an ambush. All of them had horses by now, save for Ursilda (whom no horse could hold), but the great bear kept up perfectly well with the others all the same, even at a gallop (for she was after all no ordinary bear, as she was ever wont to point out). Even the Fox came along, doubling as a backup scout and riding in a suitably configured sack on Hae-jin's saddle when not otherwise required. Thus far their enterprises had been eminently successful. Gurth's men tended to move in groups of ten or less, and Hae-jin always had twelve (one of whom was a colossal bear), or even thirteen if the Bird joined them and swooped in from above to claw at heads and shoulders and pull people off their saddles. They usually had the element of surprise on their side, and if they ever felt themselves inadequately advantaged by either terrain or numbers they would simply leave that particular party unmolested and seek out another. And thus far none of their own number had been seriously injured, though they had slain and scattered many of Gurth's men. The mill itself they kept locked but otherwise unguarded, with their supplies tucked away inside the hidden cellar built by Ursilda and the Wogs, while their spare horses were concealed in a makeshift corral in the woods. They would visit the mill from time to time, depositing weapons and booty and replenishing their own supplies. Most of the food they captured from Gurth was released back to the population (either dropped off at a village or farm or sent along with newly released captives), but a portion of what could be readily consumed they kept for their own sustenance, which they stored in the cellar as well. By now many wagons of food had been liberated, as well as many scores of laborers. And the name of Robin Goodfellow was being spoken far and wide across the countryside.

Hae-jin rode at the head of his small column now, and suddenly he commanded his followers to halt. Up ahead in the sky, a small dot was swooping down in their direction. The Bird, as usual, bringing Hae-jin the latest intelligence. Hae-jin steadied his horse as the Bird lighted on the ground beside him. Hae-jin had gradually been getting better at reading the avian's emotions, and the Bird seemed unusually excited. "What news, Bird?", he asked.

"It's finally happened!", the Bird said. "I spotted a column of Gurth's men a few moments ago, and they are headed for the mill."

Hae-jin felt a knot form suddenly in his stomach. "How many of them are there?"

"Nearly thirty."

The knot in Hae-jin's stomach became quite a bit tighter. He'd always known it would only be a matter of time before Gurth's men turned their attention to the mill once more, and Hae-jin had made advance preparations for such an eventuality. But against thirty men, outnumbered more than two to one....

There was nothing for it though. Hae-jin had a plan, and it had taken into account the possibility of being outnumbered. The mill was their refuge and their storehouse, and its loss would be sorely felt. And besides, this was also an opportunity, one which Hae-jin had been keenly waiting for. "It's time we met our enemy head to head. We will proceed with the plan."

"But against thirty!"

"We are prepared to be outnumbered, even against thirty. This is what we've been waiting for." Hae-jin called back to the rest of the column, and as they gathered around he issued his orders. The plan was already known, and each already knew his place and task, and in a few moments they were all of them barrelling down the road at a gallop, while somewhere ahead the enemy was waiting for them.

The sun shone balefully down on the scene at Mortimer's Mill, where more than two score men at arms dressed in black and scarlet livery were milling about. Some of them were on horseback, sauntering around the perimeter of the farmstead like circling wolves. Others stood casually by, holding the horses of those who had dismounted and had been busy ransacking the farmstead. The doors were broken down, and everything had been turned out and broken into. Yet there was no sign of their quarry. A group of them were now gathering sticks and twigs as others built a fire in the middle of the yard, for they were preparing to burn the mill. Suddenly, a shout rose up as one of their number pointed, and all heads turned towards the road. There, at last, was their quarry. Joan Greyflower, sauntering up the road on horseback. With her were also three impish creatures, looking comically small riding on full grown horses. And there also rode a man, of alien countenance and foreign garb, and carrying in his hand a quarterstaff.

The captain of Gurth's men eyed the newcomers warily as he sat on his horse. Here at last was their quarry, yet something seemed surely afoot. Hae-jin brought his horse to a stop just out of reach of the captain. For a moment there was silence, broken only by the odd grunt of a horse as the rival parties eyed on another. Hae-jin then spoke. "What have we here at Mortimer's Mill on this fine day?", he said. "A lot of misbegotten churls looking for something they cannot find?"

The captain stirred, but did not speak. Hae-jin now reached into his clothing and produced a small, shiny black stone, which he now held out to the captain. "Perhaps this is what you are looking for? A pretty trinket with which to tie a bratling to his nurse's skirts?" The captain's eyes lit up when he saw the scrying shard. He clearly knew what it was, and he instinctively began to reach out for it before withdrawing his hand again. Hae-jin tutted. "Fancy that", he said mockingly. "Thirty strong men at arms frightened of a mere five persons. Perhaps I should keep this little toy for myself, for there is no one who will dare take it from me."

The captain swore inaudibly. He knew he was being baited, even as he succumbed to the bait in the same instant. Suddenly, the captain spurred his horse forward, and snatched at the scrying shard. In a flash, Hae-jin swung his staff and with a crack struck the captain upside of his helmet and nearly unhorsed him. With a shout and a laugh Hae-jin reared his horse, and spurring it forward he bolted off down the road with Joan and the Wogs galloping beside him. The captain was cursing profusely now as he ordered his men to mount. Soon thirty men of Gurth were astride their horses and tore down the road after their quarry.

Hae-jin rode at a slow gallop at first, just enough to allow Gurth's men time to collect themselves and give chase. Down along the road they went, with great plumes of dust rising in their wake as the chase went on. In a short while they came to the bank of a swift river, at which there was a crossroads. In one direction was the village of Tresham, but Hae-jin went the opposite way, galloping down the road beside the river bank as Gurth's men followed. Soon they came to a slight bend in the river. To one side there was a copse of woods which blocked the view ahead, and Hae-jin disappeared around the corner as his enemies sped to catch up. In a moment Gurth's men rounded the bend, and abruptly came to a halt.

The road continued straight ahead to a bridge which lay across the river. The bridge was stone and steeply arched above the surrounding terrain, and sitting upon its crest there was a heavy wagon armored with thick wooden boards which was blocking the way. Here their quarry had stopped, and Hae-jin, Joan and the Wogs were now cantering around to one side of the road along the river bank. Suddenly with a shout, six bowmen stood up from the bed of the wagon and unleashed a hail of arrows upon the men of Gurth. Then with a bellow a tremendous Bear came barrelling out of the woods, hemming Gurth's men in from one side while Hae-jin, Joan and the Wogs penned them in from the other. The road quickly became a killing field. Several men had fallen in the first couple volleys of arrows, and now they milled around in pandemonium as man and horse alike flew into panic as more men continued to fall beneath the yeomens' arrows. A few of Gurth's men tried to charge the wagon, but were shot down to a man as they approached. One or two tried to make a break for the river to swim across it and attack the wagon from the opposite side, but these were quickly struck down. The Wogs wielded their own peculiar hooked pole weapons with great effect, grabbing at Gurth's men and pulling them off their horses as they attempted to escape and then circling back to skewer them with the points.

Finally there was a cry from the captain. Gurth's men had lost, and the survivors now turned their horses around and began tearing back up the road. Hae-jin wasted no time. As the yeomen released their last volley of arrows Hae-jin gathered up his own horsemen and the Bear and began to give chase in turn. Now the positions were nearly reversed, save that Gurth's men were in full flight. Back along the road they ran with Hae-jin and his comrades at their heels. The battle of Mortimer's Mill had been decided, and Robin Goodfellow had proved the victor. They were nearing the outskirts of Tresham now, when Alwog brought his horse alongside Hae-jin's. "How much farther do we chase them?", the Wog shouted, "We've thrashed them enough already."

"We already discussed this!", Hae-jin barked back. "We are going to chase them clear through the village."

"But why!"

"Because I want the villagers to see it happen, that's why!"

The village was now nearly upon them. Gurth's men barreled through the green, scattering the villeins in their wake as Hae-jin's men rode close on their heels. Men and women scrambled to get out of the way as others ran to the green to see what the commotion was about. In a few minutes the riders had passed through, and went on down the road in the direction of Elmstead.

Finally, Hae-jin called a halt and turned his followers back. Gurth's men remained in full flight, while Hae-jin and his followers headed in the opposite direction, back towards Tresham. The village green was all atwitter as men and women milled around, collecting upset handcarts and setting things back to order here and there, but mostly they talked in animated tones about what they had just seen. More people were filtering in from the outskirts of the village, brought by the noise and commotion, asking questions and getting only half responses. Suddenly a hush fell upon the people as a group of riders entered the green at a relaxed trot. Joan Greyflower was riding a fine horse in their midst, with a foreign looking man at her side, and a bear and three mounted imps in her wake. A few people approached and attempted to speak to her, but Joan made no reply. The riders paraded through the green, and Hae-jin watched as the villagers gathered in stunned silence along their path, their faces displaying looks of wonder and curiosity, and as Hae-jin passed he attempted to make eye contact with as many of the villagers as he could. In a few minutes the riders had crossed the green, and continued out of the village in the direction of the mill, while behind them in the village, the people began murmuring excitedly to one another.

The fire had now been lit, but Hae-jin had resolved to allow his brew to simmer for a while. For a day or two he and his fellows continued as they had before, waylaying Gurth's men where they found them. Meanwhile, word of the incident at Tresham was spreading quickly, and soon all the neighborhood from Tresham to Elmstead was afire with the news. It was on the third morning after the battle at Mortimer's Mill that a group of villagers from Tresham were half heartedly tilling their fields. Suddenly there was a great beating of wings from above, and a marvelous golden Bird was now circling over their heads, crying out in a loud voice.

"Attend me, people of Linster!", the fabulous creature said. "Hear the news that I bring! All good men and true, come hither to the village green at noon, and bear witness to the fate of a nation! Leave your fields and come to Tresham at noon!" As soon as all the farmers had heard the message at least once, the Bird soared off again and disappeared into the sky, leaving the startled farmers in its wake. All across the neighborhood that morning the farmers and laborers were accosted wherever they were, as the great bird appeared from the sky and called them to the village. By noon, a very large crowd indeed had assembled at the green in Tresham, waiting expectantly for whatever was about to happen. Practically everyone who lived in Tresham was there, but likewise too were serfs and freemen from other parts of the area who had heard the summons.

Suddenly a loud murmur spread through the crowd, as a group of horsemen entered the green. At the front was Hae-jin, wearing various bits of armor and carrying in his hand a sword. Behind him rode ten armed horsemen and a bear in a single, widely spaced rank, while the golden Bird soared above the heads of the crowd. Hae-jin and his followers had donned as much of their looted armor as would reasonably fit them, and one of the wogs carried aloft their banner with Gurth's inverted livery, now further embellished with a number of familiar looking golden feathers sewn to its surface. The horsemen crossed the green and headed for the church, and the crowd slowly followed them. Upon reaching the building the horsemen lined up at the door of the building with Hae-in at their head as the villagers gathered around them. Hae-jin then spurred his horse forward and addressed the crowd.

"By now many of you have heard my name", he said in a loud voice. "I am he who is called Robin Goodfellow. For many days now my fellows and I have made war upon Gurth's men. It is now time to rout them completely. I call upon the good people of Tresham to join in our cause, to seize the yoke which is upon them and cast it off forever. The reign of Gurth is come to an end! Follow me, and we shall soon rid this good land from the rotten pestilence of Gurth!"

Somewhere underfoot, strangely unnoticed by anyone in the crowd, a Fox crept between the legs of the people. Suddenly, a voice rose up, as if from someone in the crowd. "Three cheers for our champion! Long live Robin Goodfellow! Hip hip...." The crowd then burst out into a chorus of cheers. Hae-jin addressed the crowd again, but his work had largely already been done. Every now and again a voice of assent from somewhere in the crowd would punctuate his words, as the Fox crept to and fro among the people, unobserved and undetected, almost as if the creature were invisible. The only one who ever saw Bartholomew was The Bird with his extraordinary eyes, who now watched the Fox with a sudden new interest.

More voices arose from the crowd now, and soon nearly every remark was punctuated with a resounding chorus of cheers. Then the elders of the community came forth, led by the village priest. They were a hungry, angry looking lot, with many long days of famine reflected in their eyes and long years of suffering etched into their faces. They pledged themselves and the entire village to the service of Robin Goodfellow. And thus Hae-jin conquered the village of Tresham.

All that was required to make the conquest complete would be to seize the manor house itself. It was by far the largest building in the village, and the only one which was built of stone. It was the seat of government in the village, and nominally the residence of the lord of the manor. However, the lord of Tresham was in fact the Bishop of Larchester, whose actual residence was in the city of that name, and the manor house was occupied by the Bishop's steward and his reeves, who managed the village in the Bishop's absence and was in all practical respects the ruler of the village. Hae-jin had no difficulty in persuading the villagers to march on the house. Indeed, they surged upon it themselves, as years of pent up wrath and desperation all burst forth at once. By the time Hae-jin himself managed to reach the place, the villagers had already stormed the building and dragged out the steward and the reeves and hurled them on the ground before Hae-jin.

One of the village elders now turned to Hae-jin. "Give us the word, Robin Goodfellow", the man said, with bloodlust in his eyes, "and we shall put these men to death at once."

Hae-jin felt a knot form in his stomach. He looked at the Bishop's steward, a well dressed man about Hae-jin's own age, with a faint suggestion of efficiency and respectability about him which was wholly overwhelmed by the terror that was in the man's eyes as he faced death on the threshold of his own home. Hae-jin turned now to the elder who had spoken. "Release this man", Hae-jin said. "Our quarrel is with Gurth, not with the nobles or their servants."

The elder spat on the ground. "The nobles and the church are no better than Gurth", the man growled. "All of them deserve death." For a moment Hae-jin was at a loss. Then a voice piped forth from somewhere near the ground amidst the crowd.

"Obey our captain! Release the steward, slay Gurth instead! Slay Gurth! Slay Gurth!"

Other voices then joined the cry, and the elders reluctantly released the steward and the reeves. And as Hae-jin crossed the threshold of the building and occupied the manor house, he reflected to himself that his new army was already proving to be a dangerous force indeed. And not just to the servants of Gurth. Hae-jin feared that the peasantry were inclined to unleash their fury upon whoever they might happen to take a dislike to, innocent and guilty alike. For the first time since coming to Linster, Hae-jin felt a sense of genuine fear at the thought that his own burgeoning army might prove the equal of his enemy in more ways than were desirable.

Hae-jin established his new headquarters in the manor house. From there he organized the disposition of his ragtag army, though in practice he found himself working directly in the people's midst more often than not, for it soon proved that very close leadership indeed was essential if the efforts of the villeins were to be productive in any way. And there was a great deal of work to be done. Hae-jin's diminutive empire now consisted of the village and Mortimer's Mill, which were garrisoned and fortified with trenches, overturned carts, and wooden palisades. Their herd of stolen horses was moved into a newly built corral in the village green, while likewise their tiny stockpile of stolen weapons was brought to the manor house and distributed as efficiently as possible among the more capable men of the community. Those of the yeomen who joined Hae-jin always possessed weapons of their own of some sort, for such was required by law for all freemen. But the serfs had very little in the way of arms, and the village smithy was now operating day and night sharpening sickles, rebuilding scythes into crude polearms, mounting billhooks on staves and fitting threshing flails with iron spikes. When they were not occupied with constructing weapons and fortifications, the villagers were being drilled in the use of arms under Hae-jin (or whoever else who happened to be available, for Hae-jin's presence seemed to be in demand everywhere at once). It was imperative that the villagers be readied for combat as quickly as possible, for Hae-jin knew that battle was not far away.

Word of the rebellion was sure to reach the king swiftly, and it was only a matter of time before his forces could be assembled to march on Tresham and suppress it. How much time Hae-jin couldn't guess. What with the paralyzing political situation being created by Gurth and the potential threat of more rebellions elsewhere among the disgruntled peasantry, it might even be as much as a matter of weeks. But it would happen. It would surely happen. But that wasn't Hae-jin's most immediate problem. Gurth's men had thoroughly ravaged the countryside, and were continuing to do so. Though Hae-jin now had numbers on his side, his army consisted mostly of the farmers. While they were soldiering, they were not working the fields. And while they were working the fields, they would not be soldiering. And Hae-jin needed them to spend every waking minute as soldiers, or at least the seedlings thereof. Food was therefore a problem. Sykes continued to lead sallies against Guth's patrols, liberating more food and laborers with each day. But it wasn't enough. A substantial infusion of food was needed, and quickly. This therefore gave Hae-jin his next military objective. The largest stockpile of food nearby was the Bishop's granary in Elmstead. It had been occupied by Gurth many days ago, and was the central repository for all the food which Gurth's men had seized from the local area. Elmstead was a substantially larger settlement than Tresham, a proper town in fact. To capture it was risky, but Hae-jin's entire enterprise was nothing if not risky and ambitious. Elmstead would be his next conquest.

Several days after the occupation of Tresham, Hae-jin was scouting the road to Elmstead. With him was Bartholomew, sitting comfortably in a carefully positioned sack hanging from Hae-jin's saddle. Bartholomew had proved to be extraordinarily helpful over the last few days, demonstrating an uncanny ability to collect information and move about unnoticed, and Hae-jin had come to frequently rely on the Fox. The Bird was nearly always occupied scouting out Gurth's men while Sykes hunted them down, and Joan was usually engaged in maintaining cordial relations with the villagers and hearing out their many and varied grievances, which left the Fox as Hae-jin's chief resource. Over the last week Hae-jin had become very familiar with the countryside. At the moment he reckoned he was about a mile from Elmstead. It was morning, and a cool breeze whipped through the green grass, while the sun cut through the windswept treetops and cast magical beams of gold on the ground, waving and undulating in the wind between murky patches of dark and sinister shadows. Suddenly, from his perch on the saddle the Fox hissed a warning. Hae-jin looked down at Bartholomew, who returned his gaze and then pointed with a paw at a place under the trees just off the road.

A lone horseman stood there, sitting calmly on his animal as he watched Hae-jin from a distance. As Hae-jin looked back in turn the rider casually spurred his horse to a walk, and approached Hae-jin. There appeared to be no immediate threat emanating from the man, but the sight of him filled Hae-jin with a peculiar sense of loathing, and likewise Bartholomew quickly ducked down to hide at the bottom of his riding bag. The rider stopped when he was about ten feet from

Hae-jin's horse, and there the two men regarded one another for a moment. The newcomer was a muscular, broad shouldered man dressed in fine clothes, thoroughly resplendent by comparison to that of the serfs and yeomen with which Hae-jin had largely associated since coming to Linster. Otherwise, the man nonetheless gave the impression of an ordinary Linsterman, albeit from the higher echelons of society, wearing a finely embroidered tunic and feathered bycocket cap on his head. Yet simultaneously there were things about him which spoke of something weird and foreign. A strange looking sword hung at his side, and his frame was wrapped in a dark colored cloak trimmed with speckled hyena fur. About his shoulders was a polished iron chain which he wore like a livery collar, and hanging from it in lieu of a badge of office were a miniature pair of golden manacles. "Good morning", the man said, "A fine morning indeed to be out riding."

The man's face was thoroughly inscrutable. His features were boring and nondescript, and his complexion was dull and ambiguous. His expression bore a look of banal pleasantry, but his eyes were sunken and glazed, like hollow receptacles which irresistibly drew in the light of the world around them and sucked it into a crushing abyss. Hae-jin felt an instinctive urge to reach for his sword, but he merely gripped his reins a bit tighter and replied. "What do you want from me?"

The man shrugged. "Merely to speak with you. I have heard a great deal about you, Robin Goodfellow. Your reputation has spread far and wide, and I will own that your activities have caused me no small amount of inconvenience."

Hae-jin was already beginning to suspect the identity of his erstwhile companion, but now he was sure. "I presume then that you are Gurth?"

"I am."

And there it was. Right there, before him at that very instant, was

Hae-jin's enemy, conversing with him politely. "You are quite bold to have sought me out alone", Hae-jin said.

"No bolder than yourself, traveling alone as you are without the protection of your little band of peasants. Your achievements thus far have been surprising, and quite troublesome."

"I aim to be both troublesome and surprising, particularly to those who have enslaved and persecuted the people."

Gurth shrugged again. "What is one creature that it doesn't persecute another? The wolves devour the sheep, the sheep devour the clovers, and the clovers devour the sunlight. I perceive that you are an idealist, Robin Goodfellow. And a fool. Or perhaps you are merely leading the peasants in a dance of your own design. For a wise man would know that the wretches who become the prey of the wise would gladly prey upon them in turn, if they had but the wisdom to do so."

"If that is the case, then the wise man would know that he cannot press his yoke upon others without one day suffering a reversal, and that to truly command men he must first command their hearts."

"I am told by my associates that you are a professional soldier", the other demurred, "one who has fallen from great prominence no less. I too am a professional. I do my work, and I excel at it. The only difference between you and I is that I remain at the top of my profession, while you have fallen to the bottom, where you will no doubt remain so long as you turn your back on true wisdom."

Hae-jin shrugged. "Only when one has stood at both the pinnacle of fortune and its abysses does one truly comprehend the path which lies between."

Gurth tutted. "A wise man would have reached the pinnacle and remained there", he said. "You may have the veneer of wisdom, Robin Goodfellow, but you are still a fool at heart. I am glad to have seen that for myself. Good day." With that, Gurth turned his horse around and spurred it to a gallop. For a moment Hae-jin considered giving chase and perhaps slaying the man, but Gurth was already far in the distance as he rode at a seemingly unnatural speed. Gurth was bold, but only just bold enough.

Hae-jin turned his own horse around, and began to make his way back to Tresham. He still had the entire day before him, but at the moment he felt the need to take council with his comrades. The fact that Gurth was personally in the area was surely not a good sign. Hae-jin had only gone a brief way when he realized that he had forgotten about the Fox who had been riding with him. He looked down into the sack at his saddle. The Fox was gone.

21

"Gurth the Witch"

The town of Elmstead was a finer place by far than the little village of Tresham. Neat rows of well built timber-frame houses with tiled roofs and whitewashed walls lined its streets, while a few shops and businesses could be found here and there near the fine marketplace which occupied the main square. Just off this was a spacious tavern, and next door to that there was a modestly appointed inn. Also near the marketplace was the Bishop's granary. Even under normal circumstances it would have been kept locked under the watch of the constables, but these days it was thoroughly fortified, its wide doors cordoned off by overturned wagons, its yard bustling with soldiers wearing the scarlet and black livery of Gurth.

A lone horseman was now passing by the granary, and several of the soldiers straightened when they saw him and touched their brows deferentially. The horseman nodded curtly in turn, and proceeded on his way. He stopped at the inn, where more liveried guards stood at the door. All of them saluted the rider respectfully while two of them quickly stepped forward to take his horse as the rider dismounted and entered the inn, where he was met by an officer. "My Lord Gurth, you have a visitor from Tresham", the officer said.

"Good", replied the horseman. "His report is long overdue. Have him brought up to my chamber." The officer bowed in response as Gurth mounted the stairs of the inn. The rooms were all quite small, and Gurth had simply turned out the innkeeper and occupied the latter's own personal apartments, which were barely spacious enough to serve Gurth's purposes. The main room was strewn with Gurth's accoutrements, including many books and scrolls and a variety of weird and sinister looking artifacts of occult appearance. Gurth made his way to a central table, on which there was set an object covered in a velvet cloth. Gurth pulled the cloth away to reveal a large block of iridescent black stone about a foot high, with its surface marred and gouged from the many flakes which had been broken from it. As Gurth breathed upon it, a faint glow seemed to emanate from inside the stone, shifting between unwholesome colors like a dying chameleon. In a moment a face appeared within the mists of color, a horrible reptilian countenance. A voice now arose from the stone, smooth, hissing, and slightly muffled, like one speaking through a wafe-thin membrane of rock. "I have good news, my friend", the face said. "Five hundred Zard will be crossing the border in the next few days, and a thousand more will follow soon after. And I have spoken with the Black Speakers, and they have been in dialogue with the Drixi."

"Drixi?", Gurth said, momentarily puzzled. "What do I want with Drixi?"

"Soldiers, that's what" the other said. "That's what you've been asking for, isn't it? The Drixi are furious that the Alva have run circles around their little enchantments and permitted humans to infiltrate their country. The Speakers had to promise them that our business will not spill over into their territory again. Furthermore, the Speakers also promised the Drixi that if they support us in Linster now they will be left alone in the future, and will be kept out of the war when it finally comes."

"And the Drixi believe that?", Gurth scoffed.

"It doesn't matter whether they believe it or not", the other said flatly. "They agreed to it and their troops are already on their way to you. Three hundred Wind Helms are flying to Linster at this moment, and should be there within a fortnight. The Black Speakers are determined that you shall get everything you need to retain your position in Linster."

"I'm glad The Speakers appreciate the importance of the services which I render to them."

"I assure you they do. Things are developing quickly. We cannot possibly allow anything to disrupt the supply of slaves at this juncture."

"Not if the Speakers hope to be able to launch a full scale offensive any time in the next ten years."

"Mind your tongue, my friend. We should still be discreet even amongst ourselves. Besides, if such a thing were to occur it would be much sooner than that, no matter what happens. What is your latest report regarding the peasant rebellion?"

"It will be suppressed soon. I am on my way to Larchester to speak with the Bishop there. The rebellion is centered in his lands. It shouldn't be too difficult to pressure him into committing troops to put it down, particularly once the king becomes involved. In a few days there will be nothing left of the rebels."

"That's good news indeed. I hope the matter is resolved as easily as you imagine. You must solidify your hold on the kingdom as soon as possible, you cannot afford any distractions."

"What about the girl? I assume the Speakers haven't caught her yet?"

"The Speakers are confident that she shall soon be brought to ground, but in the meanwhile you must take every precaution to ensure that Linster remains bound to the empire. We shall speak again soon." With that, the image in the stone disappeared as the mist of colors faded away. Then, there was a knock at the door. Gurth covered up the black stone again. "Enter", he said.

The door opened, and one of Gurth's officers stood outside. "Tom Oates is here to see you, My Lord." Gurth scowled. "Send the boy in." The officer made way for a skinny, redheaded lad. Tom Oates was more near twelve than thirteen, and he fidgeted and shuffled uncomfortably in Gurth's presence. Gurth looked silently at Tom, letting his gaze sink into the boy for a moment before he spoke. "Come here, boy", he said gently.

Gurth sat down on a chair and took the lad's hand as he approached. Gurth looked him in the eye. "Why have you failed me again, Tom?", he asked softly. The boy sniffed, the nascent man inside him fighting to hold back the child's tears which were beginning fill his eyes. "I'm sorry", he blubbered. "I've been trying for days to get away, but they make me do things for them all the time and if I went away for long I would be found out right away, I just know it!"

"Why didn't you use your shard?"

"I'm sorry, I lost it. I didn't mean to, I tried to find it, but I couldn't."

"You lost it!" Gurth almost bellowed as his hand snapped out of nowhere and slapped the boy across the face. Tears were now pouring liberally down the boy's cheeks, and suddenly Gurth's manner changed, and he held the boy's hand tenderly now. "Tom, my boy. You have a terribly important task. I know you can do it. Don't make me doubt my faith in you again." Gurth then arose and stepped over the table bearing the black stone, and uncovered it once more. Beside it there was a smaller stone of smooth grey, and cupping it in his hand Gurth struck it against the black stone several times until a black shard broke off, leaving yet another gouge in the body of the larger stone. Gurth scowled briefly at his ever diminishing tool before turning again to

Tom and resuming his gentle tones. "Here is another shard, Tom. Don't lose it this time, and be careful not to be caught using it." Gurth then looked to the officer still standing in the door. "Send the boy back to the village", the wizard said. The officer acknowledged and led Tom out of the room. Gurth then rummaged about among some parchments for a few moments, and then stepped out of the room himself.

For the moment, the room was empty. Then suddenly, as if from nowhere, a Fox crept out from behind a pile of bric-a-brac and into the middle of the room. Bartholomew's ears twitched and his nose quivered as his senses were all but overwhelmed. He could smell magic everywhere around him. In the great black stone, in the books and scrolls and the many other arcane objects which were scattered about. Everywhere, everywhere magic! The Magic of the Bird had enthralled him many days ago. But this, this was more magic than he'd ever smelled before! The Fox turned round and round on the floor, unable to decide what to smell next. He finally lighted upon a half open volume cast carelessly in the corner, and gleefully Bartholomew pounced on it and began poring over the leaves. His eyes widened and his nostrils flared as he began to read, turning one leaf over another faster and faster as he picked up little bits of knowledge from a single glance.

Suddenly, the Fox felt a funny sort of tug at his tail. He looked back over his shoulder, and nearly barked with excitement as he did so. For there, right beside the first one, was a second tail growing out of his body. Bartholomew leaped into the air with joy and began running around in circles as he looked at his new pair of tails. He was only just shy of a hundred years old, but already he had become wise enough to have grown a second tail! The Fox turned again to the book before him, a steel resolve taking over his heart. Here before him was enough knowledge to give him power and wisdom beyond anything he'd ever imagined. He would possess Gurth's book. He would possess all of Gurths books. Not now, not yet. But soon. Soon, when Gurth was defeated, he, Bartholomew Fox-Goodburrow, would take all of Gurth's treasure for himself. And then, who knows how many more tails he might grow? Perhaps he might even reach nine one day, perhaps even before his one thousandth birthday (as was more usual for his kind). The Fox was about to turn his attention back to the book when a noise from outside the door told him that Gurth would soon be returning. The Fox dove into hiding and vanished from sight like a wisp. A moment later Gurth stepped back into the room, and by then the Fox was long gone.

The day passed, and night had fallen. But the village of Tresham was alive and awake, with fires set at intervals across the green as men continued to bustle to and fro. In one corner of the green a man, who was a simple farmer a few days ago, now stood awkwardly with an iron shod flail, trying to imitate the soldierly stances he'd been taught over the last few days. Not far from him were a group of farmers carousing together over free flowing ale, having already forgotten everything they'd learned during just the afternoon (let alone the day before). From the smithy came the ringing of hammers as more and more makeshift weapons were being turned out as fast as the tiny forge could manage. In a corner behind the smithy, where the dancing red light of the fires reflected across the white stucco of the surrounding buildings, Tom Oates sat curled up miserably. Gripped tightly in one hand was a small shard of black stone. Tom looked into the shiny blackness of the stone in his hand. In its surface he could almost imagine that he could see the reflection of Watt, the farmhand. Tom had hated Watt, almost as much as he hated the senile old miller Mortimer himself. Ever since he'd been taken in at the mill they'd both treated Tom like a mean servant. Well, that wasn't going to happen anymore. Mortimer would soon be dead, just as soon as Gurth came with his soldiers to kill him, along with Hae-jin and everybody else. And of course, Watt was already dead.

Tom felt a terrifying thrill go through him as remembered the night he'd killed Watt. Mortimer was an old dunce, but Rob Sykes was clever. And when Joan left and didn't come back they would have realized that someone had betrayed them, and then Tom would have been found out for sure. Someone else had to take the blame, and that someone else had been Watt. As Gurth said, all creatures prey on other creatures, and from now on Tom was going to be the one that preyed on others. It's what Gurth would want him to do. And besides, Tom rather enjoyed it. Suddenly, he realized that the shard in his hand was gone. Had he dropped it? No, no he couldn't have! Not again! Frantically he cast about him.

"Ahem. Were you looking for this, Tom?"

Tom tore his eyes away from the ground and looked up. There before him was the Fox, sitting primly on the grass with Tom's shard at his feet. Tom was about to lunge for the shard when the Fox calmly raised a paw, and Tom stopped dead in his tracks. "Aha, no you don't", the Fox said slyly. "I think I shall take care of this trinket for now. You seem to have a habit of losing things." Suddenly from behind the Fox a pair of tails flicked out, catching up the stone and tossing it spinning into the air before catching it again. The instant the stone touched one of the tails again it melted away like water and was absorbed into the Fox's fur. The Fox winked at Tom. "I'll carry the shard from now on", he said. "You just behave yourself, and we'll keep it our little secret, shall we?" With that, the Fox darted off into the darkness as a faint, canine laugh floated on the air behind him. And Tom Oates despaired.

The Fox trotted merrily through the shadows towards the manor house. On a sudden thought he looked back at his two tails. They were beautiful to behold together, but for the moment it would be better if there were only one to be seen. There was no need to provoke questions. The Fox thought for a moment, and then tried pressing his tails together. Suddenly, where there were once two tails there now seemed to be only one. There, that should do it! With a merry laugh, the Fox continued to the manor house, as all around him the preparations for war continued on through the night.

22

"The Occupation of Elmstead"

The moon had sunk below the horizon as the night passed into its final hours. Above the township of Elmstead, a dark shape drifted silently through the sky, with keen eyes piercing the inky black of the night and searching out the streets and alleys below. There! Right there was a nice sheltered spot quite close to the town gates. The dark shape dove and circled stealthily to the ground, and the Bird entered the streets of Elmstead. As the Bird was just grazing the cobbles he gingerly deposited a sack which he had been clutching in his claws, which tumbled lightly onto the street and rolled to a stop on the ground as The Bird himself landed a few paces ahead. The Bird looked furtively around him as the sack twitched and jostled for a moment before a furry red snout poked out of its opening and sniffed the air. Then the Fox stepped out, shaking the sack off his tail behind him.

The town of Elmstead was defended by a high wall of stout wooden timbers which enclosed it on all sides. The wall possessed only two gates, each flanked by fortified wooden towers. For two nights straight, the Fox and the Bird had paid nightly visits to the neighborhood near one of these gates, and by now they knew the area well. The two wightbeasts made their way stealthily now to the gate. Up in the tower there was a double guard of watchmen, but the two animals knew how to approach the place from just the right angle in order to stay out of sight. In three quarters of an hour the next watch would begin, by which time the intruders would be finished with their work. They were coming very near the gate now, which consisted of a pair of stout wooden doors with a great bolt shot across them which was held in place with a padlock. Fortunately, the two burglars didn't plan to bother with the gate for the moment.

Several yards further down the wall they stopped at a prearranged location. With a furtive look about him, the Bird flew to the top of the wall and disappeared on the other side while the Fox kept watch from the street. An uncomfortable wait then followed, which felt a bit longer perhaps than it ought to have. But soon enough the Bird reappeared over the wall, this time carrying a stout rope in his beak. Glancing about him again, the Bird then tied the end of the rope down on a convenient place on the scaffolding, and then disappeared back over the wall again. A moment later the rope went taut, and shortly after that the head of a Wog appeared over the top of the wall, climbing the rope. The first Wog was then followed by two more. Last came the Bird, fluttering up onto the wall bringing the other end of the rope with him. In a few moments the rope was coiled up and stowed away, leaving no trace of the intruder's presence. Then, the Wogs and the Fox slipped into the city and headed to a place which had been prepared in advance as behind them the Bird soared away into the night sky.

Hours went by. Then bit by bit a faint amber glow spread across the horizon, followed by the blood red band of dawn. In the wooden tower above the town gate, a pair of watchmen stood wearily in the waxing light. The town guard had been obliged to serve double and triple shifts for many days, and the strain was beginning to be felt even as the possibility of action drew inexorably closer. Gurth's men had been occupying the granary for over a fortnight now, and there they remained (with Gurth himself having relocated to the city of Larchester). Fortunately (so far as the town council was concerned, at any rate), Gurth's forces were spread so thin while they marauded the countryside that the defense of the town itself had by necessity to be left up to the locals. Wary of a popular insurrection, Gurth had ordered that the militia be disbanded. But the regular watchmen themselves were retained and were being worked to exhaustion. Suddenly, one of the watchmen shook his drowsy companion and pointed out towards the road.

Before them the rolling green downs were bathed in the cool grey light. The wind rippled through the bright banners which hung from the town wall, carrying with it the faint snatches of mens voices raised in song. It was an old folk song, a sentimental ballad known to everyone. But its rhythm was somehow different, as if it were being sung to a steady cadence of marching feet. And indeed, coming now down the road from the direction of Tresham was a thick, dark column. Nearly three hundred men marched together in step (or more or less in step anyway), led by a small detachment of horsemen. The singing grew louder as the army approached, and the men could be seen clearly. They were peasants mostly, many of them armed with makeshift weapons, while a few were yeomen who were well armed and equipped. They had a motley appearance overall, yet they sang and marched together in grim, barely sustained unison which was terrifying to behold, like a wild animal on a leash. A shout rose up from the tower as one watchman called to the men in the next tower while the other pressed his lips to a horn and let forth an asthmatic blast, sounding the alarm. For Robin Goodfellow and his army were marching on Elmstead.

The watchmen were still blowing frantically on their horns as the hostile column halted before the gates. At its head were several horsemen, armed and equipped with the best gear of the army and bearing the most soldierly deportment. And waving high above them was a banner, the livery of Gurth insolently inverted and trimmed with dazzling gold feathers. Now the lead horseman stepped forward, and called up to the guardsmen in the tower. "Here me now, men of Elmstead", the horseman said. "I am Robin Goodfellow, and the gates of this town shall open for me." Suddenly there was a sharp clack of a great bolt being shot, and beneath the feet of the astonished guards in the towers the gates of Elmstead creaked and opened at Robin Goodfellow's command.

The army marched in an orderly fashion through the gates and into the streets of the town as the gates were held open by the three Wogs, who grinned insolently as they slouched against the doors (one of them twiddling with a set of skeleton keys). The column proceeded down the winding streets of the town, singing again as they went. Shutters were now being opened around them as the townsfolk looked down in anxious surprise at the events unfolding before them. The town watch, armed and awakened by the alarm coming from the gates, were converging on the scene only to stop in their tracks before tens of scores of armed men, and they allowed the army to pass by unopposed.

The army marched clear to the town square, where it halted just outside. To one side of the square was the great hall of the town, but on the other was the Granary, where Gurth's men were now scrambling to assemble behind their makeshift barricades. Word was then passed to the watchmen and townsfolk nearby that Robin Goodfellow demanded to address the town council. Messengers then went round to the homes of the councilmen, rousing those who had not yet been awakened by the commotion which was quickly taking grip of the whole community. Barely half an hour later the council were gathered in the square, and Robin Goodfellow issued his ultimatum: The town would be spared and its folk left unmolested, but the council would swear loyalty to Robin Goodfellow and support him in the occupation of the town and seizure the granary from the forces of Gurth.

The councilmen briefly deliberated among themselves in the street, but their decision was forgone as they looked about at the host of grim and volatile men all around them. The town watch was already vastly outnumbered, and it was too late for the militia to be called (even if the townsfolk had been inclined to support Gurth...which they weren't). And besides, they could always swear (quite truthfully) to the king that their cooperation had been coerced. Their agreement was unanimous, and there upon the cobbles they swore their fealty to Robin Goodfellow. Now the army of Robin Goodfellow occupied the square, and made their way to the granary. Gurth's men were ready for them, but Hae-jin had judged it better to ensure the cooperation of the townsfolk first before doing battle. It took nearly three hours to capture the granary, as Hae-jin cautiously directed his forces against the small band of men making their stand there. Numbers were on his side, but Hae-jin knew the morale of his army could prove fragile, and he was not prepared to take unnecessary losses. Not yet. When it was all over Gurth's men were slain to a man, the very last of them taken with Hae-jin's own hand in the final assault. The wrath of the peasants was thus unleashed and expended on the servants of Gurth, while the townsfolk were completely spared in fulfillment of Robin Goodfellow's promise. Not even so much as a stray coin was taken by the invaders.

With the conquest of the township complete, Hae-jin moved his headquarters yet again, and began to direct his newly expanded empire from the town hall of Elmstead. With the Bishop's granary in his possession, Hae-jin now began to distribute the fresh injection of food, both to his own army as well as further afield across the countryside to anyone who would pledge their loyalty to Robin Goodfellow. In this way, the ravages of Gurth became oddly mirrored and reversed. Now the men of Robin Goodfellow were roving the countryside, seizing food, arms and treasure from Gurth's men wherever they were to be found, and redistributing it at Hae-jin's direction. Rarely was food withheld from those who pled for it, but it was never given liberally without a pledge of loyalty. For Hae-jin believed that mercy must be the servant of necessity, and his success depended on the people flocking to his cause in overwhelming numbers, and remaining faithful thereafter. Food was offered to all, but to take food from Robin Goodfellow was to become a party to his rebellion, and all who ate at the table of the outlaw would be obliged to defend that table in order to preserve his own skin. And thus far Hae-jin's plan seemed to be working, for every day that followed more and more people poured into Elmstead to swell the ranks of his army, and even whole villages began to pledge themselves to Robin Goodfellow.

Word was even starting to come in from further afield across the kingdom. Far and wide men had heard of the successes of Robin Goodfellow, and many sought to join the revolt. Some were making their way to Elmstead, but others had begun to engage in banditry and pillaging, looting freely and slaying whomever they were inclined to. Hae-jin's worst fears were already being realized, and it was all he could do to keep his own army from descending to the same levels of villainy. Above all else, Hae-jin did everything to ensure his army remained in discipline, directing their violence and avarice towards the forces of Gurth alone while leaving all else untouched. It was imperative that Robin Goodfellow be a fulcrum of order if the greater powers of the land were ever to take part with him against Gurth. For Hae-jin knew he could never win. Not on his own. Hae-jin had seen his own men in action many times now, and their limits were quickly becoming apparent. Many were content to be idle and remain carousing in the towns and villages while they feasted on the dole of Robin Goodfellow. Others looked greedily on the plunder which was to be had all around them, chafing and grumbling that they were not allowed to take their fill in pillage. It was only a matter of time before the peasants could be contained no longer, and would either disperse or mutiny. And those who remained faithful were often poor fighters. Those among the yeomen who were trained or experienced as soldiers performed well, but the serfs seemed to remain miserable no matter how hard Hae-jin dared drill them, and they usually held back and allowed the yeomen to do most of the fighting.

Meanwhile, Robin Goodfellow's enemies had not remained idle. The unopposed capture of Elmstead seemed to have taken Gurth by surprise, but now he was springing back. His patrols moved with greater cunning and in larger numbers, deftly avoiding conflict where they could and striking back ferociously when attacked, while elsewhere others of his men were gathering from all parts of the land and were assembling near the city of Larchester. And far away in the capital, the King was at last taking action. The situation with Gurth had left the royal court in a political paralysis. Discord was spreading among the nobility as the King wrestled to resist the ultimatums of Gurth while seeking vainly for support among the peers of the land, who were themselves boiling over with long years of discontent of their own. But after nearly three weeks of indecision and impasse, the King had at last assembled an army and had departed the capital. And according to rumor, the King was headed to Larchester to join with the men of Gurth. From there, the combined forces of Gurth and the King would surely come next to Elmstead.

It was several days after the capture of the town, and Hae-jin was ensconced at the town hall from which he commanded his army and held a kind of de-facto court. A great table was set at the threshold where Hae-jin and his officers now sat and held their daily conference. A sheet of linen had been laid across the table and painted with a crude map of the area, while all around were rolls of parchment containing lists, inventories, reports, and all manner of clerical flotsam that comes with a properly managed army. Suddenly there was a beating of wings and the Bird descended onto the table, nearly upsetting it as he did so. "Hae-jin! I have news!"

"Good, we've been waiting for your report for a while now....is something wrong?"

"I fear it may be so. An army is approaching the town. I reckon it's easily four or five thousand strong, and they are perhaps half a day's march away. A chilled silence took hold of the table. Everyone had known this was coming, but up to now their information had suggested that the King was still many days away. Yet already, there was an army almost upon them. Sykes piped up now. "Well, who's army is it?", he asked shrewdly. "Gurth? The King? The Bishop? Did you see any banners or livery?"

"They bore many banners with them", the Bird said.

"Well, what did they look like!", the veteran barked. "Did any of them particularly stand out?"

The Bird thought for a moment. "I remember one that I saw being carried in several places. It was a blue and yellow check with a vertical white band in the middle bearing three black stars."

Sykes looked sharply at Hae-jin, an odd gleam in his eye. "That's the arms of the Earl of Wickhowe", he said slyly.

"And who is the Earl of Wickhowe?", Hae-jin asked, intrigued by the other's manner.

"Only one of the largest landowners in the kingdom", Sykes said excitedly. "And among the nobility he is the king's greatest nemesis. Tell me Bird, how many other banners did you see? Describe as many of them as you can remember!"

"Goodness, I don't know. There was a yellow one with three red boars on it."

"That'll be the Earl of Swinstoke."

"Then there one that was half white and half blue with six oak leaves on it"

"That's the Earl of Donnock."

"There must have been at least a dozen more, do you really expect me to remember *all* of them?"

"Yes!"

"Well I can't."

"Then go back and look again! Look for a banner with two gold leopards on a blue field bordered with red and white. Those are the king's arms. If the king's there then his banner will be displayed. If he's not, then that will be very interesting indeed. Hurry, and get back as quick as you can!"

The Bird looked imploringly at Hae-jin, but Hae-jin merely nodded. "I agree with Sykes", Hae-jin said. "Go back and find out as much as you can." The Bird took off and Hae-jin turned to Sykes. "You've got an idea, Sykes. What are you thinking?" Sykes pursed his lips thoughtfully, an excited light still in his eye.

"It seems almost too much to hope for, but honestly I think it's well within the realm of possibility. Over the last few days our ranks have swelled to well over eight hundred, but that'll never be enough to face both Gurth and the King."

"We all know that. You think that the army that's approaching is not from the King?"

"It's possible. The nobles aren't particularly happy with the King, and haven't been for a long time. I served as a bowman under Simon the Second back during the wars with the Tollards, and taxes were heavy in those days (in order to finance the war). Then the curse came, and we lost the war. Now we pay tribute to the Tollards, and things are even worse. Taxes are still heavy and the landowners constantly lose workers to the Due of Gurth. Simon was a gallant man in his youth, but by the time he died eight years ago he was despised by nearly everyone. He was succeeded by his nephew, William of Bradlaw, who is now

William the Fourth. William may have merely inherited the mess left behind by his uncle, but that hasn't saved him from being any less unpopular. Dissent has been growing among the nobility for a long time, and Wickhowe has usually been in the middle of it. It still seems too much to hope for, but I wonder. Indeed I wonder."

Hae-jin and his council continued with their discussion as best they could, though they were reduced mostly to more rounds of speculation as they waited on the word from Bird. No one was ever quite sure exactly just how fast the Bird could fly, but it was reckoned by most that it would be some time before he returned. They were therefore taken aback when the Bird returned not thirty minutes later with a fresh report. Six horsemen were on the road to Elmstead well in advance of the rest of the army. They bore with them the banners of the earls of Wickhowe, Swinstoke and Donnock, and were now scarcely an hour's ride from the town gates. Sykes shot a glance at Hae-jin. "Well, if we weren't sure before", Sykes said, "I think it's quite clear now. I do believe the earls want our attention."

"Indeed", Hae-jin replied. "These developments bode well. But muster the men nonetheless. We still can't be sure of the earls' intent, and in any case I would prefer to meet their emissaries with a suitable exhibit of our strength. Assemble the men!"

Orders were given and criers were dispatched throughout the town as they summoned Hae-jin's army to assemble at the square. Within an hour Hae-jin's forces were put to order, some sent to man the walls while others remained massed in the square, with Hae-jin himself holding court before the town hall. Word then came that the six horsemen had arrived at the gates and requested an audience with Robin Goodfellow, and Hae-jin commanded that they be admitted and brought to the square. The horsemen entered the square at a walk, three heralds in voluminous tabards sumptuously embroidered with the livery of their masters, each accompanied by a sergeant carrying a banner bearing the same. They made their way through the square past the semi-ordered ranks of Hae-jin's army to the great table where Robin Goodfellow awaited their approach. The horsemen stopped before the table, and the most senior of the heralds now saluted Hae-jin, who nodded in acknowledgement as the herald spoke.

"Their Lordships the Earls of Wickhowe, Swinstoke and Donnock greet Robin Goodfellow, and salute him for his achievements against the forces of the wicked tyrant Gurth and his followers. In accord with their noble peers, Their Lordships have vowed to rid Linster of the despot's yoke, and do therefore pledge their friendship to the valiant Robin Goodfellow and do entreat him to ally himself with Their Lordships in their most worthy enterprise."

The herald then produced a scroll, which was taken by Sykes and handed over to Hae-jin. The scroll bore the seals of about a dozen noble names, all earls, counts and barons, representing both themselves as well as their respective vassals. Accompanying the signatures was a pledge which was a bit more loosely worded than Hae-jin would have preferred. However, as things were Hae-jin had no intention of rejecting the overture. His army would more than quadruple in size, and with it came an alliance with a sizable contingent of the Linsterish nobility. The choice was not without its own attendant risk, but with the forces of both Gurth and the King massing together only a few miles away, it was nothing short of a miracle which he could not possibly refuse. Hae-jin silently praised heaven as he closed the scroll and addressed the heralds.

"You may return to your masters and tell them that Robin Goodfellow accepts their friendship gladly. The gates of the town are open to them, and Robin Goodfellow eagerly awaits Their Lordships' arrival." With that, the heralds departed and sped swiftly to their masters who were drawing nearer with each hour. As the sun was lowering the first advance columns of soldiers could be seen from the walls of the town. And the army of the earls marched now on the town of Elmstead as the gates stood wide before them.

23

"Three Earls and an Outlaw"

The air was rent by trumpet blasts as the army of the earls approached the gates of Elmstead. Beneath the gates, Hae-jin sat on horseback beside Sykes, Joan and his other chiefs, along with a detachment of his best fighting men (and fighting Wogs and Bear), all arrayed in the finest armor and accoutrements they could manage to assemble. Beside him Will Little carried the banner of Robin Goodfellow, while above the gate the glittering Bird was perched beneath the splendor of the setting sun, doing his best to look impressive as Robin Goodfellow and his captains waited to receive the army of the earls.

Trailing along the road before them was a long column of soldiers, just shy of four thousand men at arms, attended by an even longer baggage train. Archers, halberdiers and armored horse were arrayed in polished plate which glowed like amber beneath the golden light of the sunset, while above them a sea of banners and pennants in all manner of colors drifted in the breeze. At the head of this multitude were the nobles themselves; fifty or more men on horseback along with scores of attendants, all lavishly attired in fine silks and brocades. Earls, counts, baronets and knights, all assembled before gates of Elmstead opposite the ragtag band of Robin Goodfellow. Three men now detached themselves from the head of the column as Hae-jin in turn rode out to them at a walk. Midway between the two sides the three earls at last met with Robin Goodfellow.

The Earl of Wickhowe was a man about Hae-jin's own age, with streaks of grey intruding upon a neatly groomed beard of otherwise youthful hue. He wore a voluminous cloak over one shoulder, lavishly embroidered, and lined with square sections of grey and white squirrel pelt, beneath which he wore a tunic of brilliant silk which was covered with yet more embroidery. A great golden chain set with pearls and dark sapphires crowned his shoulders, on his head was a round, turban like hat with a long trailing tail which was draped around his shoulders, and on his fingers were many jeweled rings. His features were finely chiseled and craggy, weathered beyond their years by the storms and winds of responsibility and machination. And his eyes were like steel daggers, bright, sharp and lethal within a sheath of civility and decorum.

To either side of Wickhowe were the earls of Swinstoke and Donnock. Swinstoke was a large man who sagged and drooped in every direction, with a great puffy beard which could hardly conceal the wattle of skin which hung beneath his chin like that of an aging cockerel. His clothes were of comparable finery to that of his fellows, but they were a little too large for him, suggesting that the man's girth had shrunk a bit since he had last seen a tailor. He was in every way a picture of wealth and plenty which had been slowly sapped of its bounty and vigor. Yet there was yet a bright gleam in his eyes, like that of an old dog which still had a spark somewhere inside its hide, wanting only the right opportunity to leap to its feet and chase something. The Earl of Donnock was something of a surprise. He was quite a young man, hardly more than a boy. Sitting on his horse beside his wizened peers and dressed in matching finery he carried himself with an uncertain air of distinction, as one who is only recently accustomed to authority and status, and though his limbs looked strong his frame was spare and seemingly fragile. His features were smooth and set with an aristocratic air of dignity, while his wide eyes betrayed inexperience as they drank in the scene before them.

The Earl of Wickhowe regarded Hae-jin critically for a moment, and then spoke. "So you are Robin Goodfellow", the man said in smooth, formal tones. "Some have said you are a foreigner, and that much I see is obvious. But I would hardly call you a demon or a sprite, as the more colorful rumors would have you. Goodfellow the man you are, but Goodfellow the elf I think not. Pray sir, what is the true identity of the man who has named himself after Puck?"

Hae-jin shrugged. "In an age past I was called Moon Hae-jin, but that name has died along with the life which perished before it. The people call me Robin Goodfellow, but I have now no proper name of my own, unless it is Nemesis." An amused smile played across Wickhowe's lips. "Boldly spoken, Nemesis. But you contend now with the named, not the nameless. To the peasants you are Robin Goodfellow, but to me you are yet an enigma. I deal with men, not mysteries." Hae-jin hesitated for a moment. "Then know me now as Robin Greyflower", he said.

Wickhowe nodded. "Very well, Robin Greyflower. We are well met at last."

It had been agreed that the three earls would represent their fellow peers in their negotiations with Robin Goodfellow, and as such the earls of Wickhowe, Swinstoke and Donnock entered the town in the company of Robin Greyflower and made their way to the town hall. Here they met privately with Hae-jin, and discussed the details of their arrangement in depth. They did not emerge until after the sun had long since set, but their discussion had been fruitful. And thus it was that Robin Greyflower and the earls pledged their allegiance to one another on the steps of Elmstead hall, and the army of Robin Goodfellow joined forces with that of the nobles to rid the land of Linster from all tyranny.

Of course, there remained much yet to be discussed and determined.

Having banded together and unified their forces, everything now needed to be reassessed and reorganized. The town of Elmstead was far too tiny an affair to accommodate such a host as the nobles had brought, and the army of the nobles instead remained encamped before the gates of the town. By nightfall Elmstead had virtually tripled in size, with a great tent city having suddenly blossomed beside it. Men bustled to and fro among the forest of canvas dwellings, from the brilliant pavilions of the knights and lords with their great pennants curling in the breeze, to the scant shelter of an archer's lean-to, creating virtual streets and neighborhoods which were weirdly reminiscent of an ordinary township, though dominated by that unique sense of purpose and direction which is common to all military establishments. As Hae-jin made his way through the camp, its distinctive atmosphere carried with it a particular kind of familiarity to him. The men at arms respectfully made way for him as he passed, while the varlets bowed and proffered their services. As Robin Goodfellow Hae-jin may have been a folk hero, but as Robin Greyflower he was again a true captain, with status and authority commensurate to his responsibility and rank. Here were all the things which came with a proper military command, and Hae-jin felt almost at home. Accompanying him was Sykes, who came as his squire. The Earl of Wickhowe had invited Robin Greyflower to dine with the nobles in their camp that evening, and the invitation had been addressed to Hae-jin personally, not his comrades. However, Hae-jin felt it would reflect poorly on the credibility of Robin Greyflower if he were to appear before the nobles without a personal attendant of his own. More importantly, though, Hae-jin was anxious to have his chief lieutenant at his side at all times. Being a veteran fighting man of Linster, Sykes was even more at home in the camp than was Hae-jin, and indeed there even proved to be more than one person they met along the way whom he recognized from his previous career. Hae-jin knew that Sykes's insight was invaluable in this regard, and later on he intended to confer with him at length on everything they observed throughout the coming evening.

The nobles had assembled in a grand pavilion, hung with their many banners and appointed more finely than anything which could have been found in the town. Two long tables were placed inside with seats for about fifty or so high ranking nobles. Wickhowe himself sat at the head of one of these, with Hae-jin at his right and the earls of Swinstoke and Donnock on his left. Squires waited on their respective masters while minstrels and a few of the more talented squires entertained the nobles as they dined in the light of the many lanterns that were set on the tables or hung from the tent's supports, filling the space with a warm red-orange glow. The food was quite different from the sort of fare Hae-jin had been accustomed to in Zhongyang, and the manners and deportment of the nobles had their own flair of the exotic in Hae-jin's eyes. Yet, like the camp itself, there was an air of familiarity to it all. In Zhongyang, Hae-jin had spent a career in the company of captains and courtiers, and here among the warrior elite of Linster he was perhaps more at home than he would ever have been had he instead lived out the remainder of his days in hiding among Zhongish peasants. Here with the earls and barons Hae-jin was playing a game that he knew well, and he conversed easily with them. Through the course of various conversations, Hae-jin learned more of the nature of the nobles' insurrection. Some of it he and his fellows had already guessed at, but hearing the details from the peers themselves was another matter. Each of the nobles it seemed had his own idea of how it all had come together. But it was clear that Wickhowe had been at the center of it all. He was more than simply their chief. It was he who had really begun the whole thing in the first place, seeking out and uniting the nobles in their various grievances and directing their wrath against the king. Second only to Wickhowe were the earls of Swinstoke and Donnock, who had been among the first whom Wickhowe had approached to join his conspiracy. Now Hae-jin sat at the head of the table with Wickhowe himself and the men whom Wickhowe had sought out to be the pillars of his rebellion.

The Earl of Swinstoke proved to be among the more gregarious of

Hae-jin's fellow diners, his earlier appearance of lethargy vanishing before the presence of rich victuals. The earl spoke in loud and animated tones as he cheerfully aired his grievances while digging into the banquet with relish. "Damn near impossible to find a good roast these days", the earl said between mouthfuls. "The animals are all thin and stringy. Even during the war with the Tollards the beef was better, and the pork...don't let me start on the pork! Back in those days there was still plenty of wild boar around, and there was fine hunting to be had. Now there's hardly a sniff of boar, deer, or even rabbits for that matter. Can hardly find a good, plump rabbit these days! Labour isn't any better. If the peasant's go and bed with swine then it's their own fault if they get themselves accursed for it. But now they've gone and ruined the whole bloody country in the process! We're all stuck with their bloody curse. A good worker is as hard to come by as good beef anymore. Those that don't die off get hauled off to Gurth's slave pens instead, and I'm nearly made a pauper from having to buy them back from that cursed devil. And the taxes! By my faith, the taxes! They were high enough during the war, but I don't mind paying for a war, so long as it's won. But we didn't win, you know. Once the curse was upon us people lost the will to fight, the Tollards thrashed us thoroughly, and now we pay them tribute. Now the taxes are higher than ever. And the king? Bah! Don't let me start on the king. He's half the man his uncle was, and twice as greedy. He won't oppose the Tollards, and he won't oppose Gurth. But he'll oppose us. Oh yes, he'll do whatever it takes to keep Gurth happy and keep his own purse full. Our workers go to Gurth, our treasure goes to the Tollards, and the king keeps whatever is left. If the peasants brought this curse on us, then it's the king who's kept us from casting it off. Hoy, Squire! My cup is empty again."

Hae-jin pursed his lips as he cocked an eyebrow at the earl. "I wonder who you loathe more, Gurth or the king",he said.

Swinstoke paused as he raised his newly refilled cup to his lips, and fixed a beady eye on Hae-jin. "I am against Gurth", the earl grunted.

"If the King is with Gurth, then I am against the both of 'em! Damn! The wine around here isn't what it used to be." Swinstoke took a deep draft of his beverage nonetheless, and Hae-jin took the fleeting respite from the earl's loquacity to shift the conversation elsewhere.

The young earl of Donnock had remained silent as Swinstoke dominated the conversation, appearing to listen attentively all while discreetly observing Hae-jin across the table. Hae-jin now looked the young man in the eye and addressed him. "And what say you, my lord?", Hae-jin asked of the young earl. "Is your enmity greater for the king, or for Gurth?"

A flicker of emotion passed over the boy's face for a moment before it was buried beneath a quickly assumed air of hauteur. "My father, the previous Earl of Donnock, was taken by sickness just a year ago, brought on by the curse of Gurth. Taken with him also was my mother, who succumbed to the same ailment." The earl gestured towards a jeweled brooch pinned on his shoulder, a simple gold ring to which a cluster of oak leaves had been affixed. "I have taken a vow that I shall not rest until Gurth is driven from this land and his pestilence purged from my country and its people. Only then shall I forsake this badge and account my family avenged."

"A worthy vow indeed, my lord", replied Hae-jin, " But what of the king?" The young earl's eyes flicked irresolutely for a moment toward the other two other earls before returning his gaze to Hae-jin. "I have taken a vow to vanquish Gurth at all cost. If my loyalty to the king is the price for fulfilling that vow, then so be it."

Throughout the conversation, the Earl of Wickhowe had been sitting regally at the head of the table, presiding serenely over his guests like an indulgent monarch in his own right. Now at last he spoke. "Gurth is, of course, a deplorable individual, whose cancerous influence has caused incalculable misery. But for our enterprise to be successful we cannot content ourselves with merely expunging Gurth and neglecting the greater problem."

"And what is the greater problem, my lord?", Hae-jin asked. The earl took a sip of wine from his cup before setting it down again and speaking. "In the words of St. Etheltrude of Hempt, 'there is no piety so pure that it does not exalt the poor'. The common folk of Linster have suffered greatly for over a decade, suffering and hardship which has been the result of corruption and greed. Over many long years I have watched as the people in my care have starved and slaved without hope or relief, and I have watched for long enough. I felt that the time had at last come for the peers of Linster to band together for the sake of justice and to rid our kingdom of this pestilence."

"By that do you mean Gurth?"

"Indeed. But Gurth is merely a symptom of the greater problem. Gurth we could moderate and dispense with as we wished, if it weren't for those who have given him unfettered license to do entirely as he wills. If we truly wish to free our country we must excise the problem at the root. And unfortunately, the root is presently entwined with the throne. King Simon was a valiant man, but he failed to defeat the Tollards, and in doing so failed our people. His successor is little more than a puppet of our enemies who feeds on their leavings. King William will do anything to please the Tollard louts who fill his coffers, while doing nothing to regulate Gurth and his servants. We need a ruler who will pursue justice with the Tollards and is capable of containing Gurth so that he may be dealt with in due course. If the king will not listen to reason, then he must be made to listen, or else cast aside. Which is why we need men like you, Greyflower. You have captured the hearts of the common folk and set the country ablaze in a way which my brethren and I never could. It was you who lit the spark and gave us an opportunity to take action. With our combined resources we will soon become an irresistible force with which to at last bring the king to account, for the good of the nation."

The remainder of the evening passed pleasantly enough, and it was past midnight by the time diners returned to their tents, for there was much to do upon the morrow. Hae-jin and Sykes were making their way through the dark masses of tents back to the town proper. They had not gone far when they were accosted by a squire dressed in blue livery with a white oak leaf embroidered on his left breast. The squire bowed low and spoke. "If you please, sire, my lord the Earl of Donnock desires an audience with Robin Greyflower at his pavilion." Hae-jin was taken aback by the unexpected invitation. Precisely what the young earl wanted he couldn't guess, however he saw no reason why he shouldn't assent. "Very well. Lead me to his lordship then."

Donnock's pavilion was much like those of the other nobles, being very nearly a tiny manor house in its own right, made of brightly colored canvas. The young earl welcomed Hae-jin inside, where the finely appointed interior was bathed in the red light of a comfortable fire. The earl's squire stepped forward now, carrying a long object wrapped in a velvet cloth, which the earl then took and unfolded to reveal a sword, which he carefully drew from its scabbard and handed to Hae-jin.

"This sword was made for my great uncle", the young earl said, "who was renowned for his valor and integrity. It is a weapon befitting a champion of your standing, and I should like you to have it."

Hae-jin briefly examined the sword in his hands. It was a straight, double edged sword of elegant proportions, with a blade which tapered substantially along its length to terminate in a wicked, awl-like point. Although the leather covered scabbard was richly embossed with brightly painted floral patterns and fitted with fine metalwork, the sword itself was quite simple, its only decoration being an image of an oak tree painted in enamel in a recess of the pommel. Yet the weapon hardly needed adornment to recommend itself. Having handled many swords in his life, both in his homeland and more recently in Linster, Hae-jin could tell that the earl's gift was a weapon of extraordinary craftsmanship and lethal utility, and was the match of any of the finest swords Hae-jin had ever possessed. Hae-jin looked to the young earl.

"I am truly honored to receive this, my lord", he said. "The honor is mine to give", the other said gravely. "You have distinguished yourself, Robin Greyflower, as a man beyond the ordinary scope of men. Your achievements are extraordinary, and speak of a wisdom which envelops both prudence and compassion in a way which is irresistible to the hearts of men. I pray that you shall weather the storm which is before us, and that I may come through it also as your friend."

Hae-jin then gripped the young earl's hand. "Then let it be so, my friend."

It was some time later that Hae-jin and Sykes were making their way back through the streets of Elmstead. They were walking through a quiet alleyway, and Hae-jin at last had an opportunity to speak privately with his comrade. "Well, my friend, we've had quite an evening. What do you think of our new allies?" Sykes pursed his lips thoughtfully. "Swinstoke is an old soldier", he replied. "He was always a bit of a blowhard, but in days gone by he had a reputation for valor and obstinacy in the field which earned him the admiration of many. He's well respected, but he's also loud, opinionated, and dauntless. A perfect rabble rouser. No wonder Wickhowe sought him out. Young Donnock, now, that's another matter. I don't know much about him personally, but I don't think he could be more than fifteen years of age, and so far as I know has no particular achievements to boast of. However, the Donnock estate which he has inherited is large and significant, and that in itself ought to make him a very powerful man indeed. As it is, he seems to be rather impressionable, the sort that is easily dominated, which Wickhowe seems to have managed to do quite handily up to now."

"And what of Wickhowe himself?"

Sykes hesitated again for a moment. "It is inspiring to see a man like the earl use his position to help the common folk. But I suppose I am a cynic. I can't help feeling that he is in it for himself somehow. Men like Wickhowe don't do anything unless they think they will profit by it in some way." As the pair made their way through the streets, Hae-jin and Sykes continued to talk over the things which had occurred that evening. A stillness hung over the town, broken only by the odd cry of the watch, as the town of two armies slumbered in the night.

Somewhere in the darkened streets, a red headed youth crept furtively through the shadows, headed towards the wall. As he approached the gates he stopped just out of sight around a corner. There for a moment Tom Oates stood, trying to figure out how best to sneak out of the town without being seen by the sentries. Suddenly, there was a faint cough from behind him. "Going somewhere, my lad?" Tom whirled around, a sense of helpless rage welling up inside him, for he was already certain of what he was about to see. Sure enough, sitting there with his tail swishing idly in the dust and detritus of the street, was the Fox. The Fox yawned and cocked a wily amber eye at Tom. "Tut tut, my boy. We've been over this before. We can't possibly have you wandering off to visit your master, not now. Next time, I may just tell Hae-jin all about you. Or better yet, I'll tell the Bear. I don't think bears ordinarily eat human whelplings, but then again Ursilda is no ordinary bear, and she might just make an exception in your case. And I would hate to see something like that happen to a useful lad like you. Speaking of which, I have a couple little odd jobs for you. Go to the granary, and wait there for me. And don't disappoint me again." With that, the Fox turned around and vanished, leaving behind only a few stray leaves fluttering on the ground in his wake. Tom bit his lip in fury, as an intense hatred for the Fox washed over him. Then he sighed and made his way dutifully to the granary. Somehow, he'd figure out a way to outsmart the Fox and reach Gurth. It was only a matter of time.

24

"There's Always Politics"

The brassy bark of a trumpet sounded on the breeze as the wind whipped around the tents and banners of the fortified town of Elmstead. Nearly a week had passed since the army of the earls had joined forces with that of Robin Goodfellow, and Elmstead had since become a kind of warrior's crossroads, a central depot through which a constant stream of military activity passed in and out. Having grown fourfold overnight, their sallies had expanded commensurately, and likewise had increased in effectiveness, for Hae-jin now had professional soldiers at his command. No longer did Hae-jin need to rely on the dubious talents and unreliable committal of the rebelling peasantry. By now nearly all of the actual fighting was being conducted by proper men at arms (both of the earl's men and the yeomanry), while the serfs and villeins had become largely relegated to auxiliaries.

Marching up the road to Elmstead now was a column of troops, with Hae-jin riding in the lead. He and the Earl of Donnock were just returning from having liberated the slave pens at Willowham, one of Gurth's last remaining strongholds in the area. In the wake of the column there was a long line of disheveled but buoyant looking people, who until today had been fated to exportation and a subsequent lifetime of exile and bondage. There was no small amount of laughter and singing as they trotted along behind the soldiers, with their former prison left behind and reduced to a pile of smouldering ashes. Hae-jin had insisted that the vacated slave pens be burned to the ground as a clear statement to the people that the reign of Gurth was coming to the end. This had been much to the annoyance of Wickhowe, who had desired that the slave pens be instead occupied and repurposed as a supply depot. However the earl had acceded readily enough to Hae-jin's wishes, for indeed things had been going very well of late. Gurth's men were in full retreat now, his marauding bands evaporating as they clung to a handful of diminishing strongholds.

Yet, the glimmering rays of success were tempered by shadows of the impending threat before them. Many of Gurths men had regrouped and were now massing at Gurth's encampment near Larchester. Rumors were circulating which told of weird and alien creatures crossing the border into Linster and traveling across the countryside at night in small groups. Meanwhile, the King had at last arrived in Larchester, and his forces were now encamped there alongside those of Gurth. On the previous day, royal heralds had come to the gates of Elmstead, bearing with them the King's edict commanding the nobles either to disperse or else renounce their cause and join with him and hand over the person of Robin Goodfellow for judgement. The heralds had been promptly sent back to their sovereign bearing a categorical dismissal of the King's command, and thus a confrontation was now inevitable and imminent. Reports indicated that the King's forces were sizable, and that morning Hae-jin had dispatched the Bird to fly to Larchester to carry out a proper reconnaissance.

Throughout all of this, however, there was yet one factor which hitherto had remained in doubt: The Bishop of Larchester. The Bishop was a powerful landowner in his own right, and likewise the forces at his command were commensurate with his status. Moreover, the city of Larcherster now lay directly between the army of Robin Goodfellow and the combined forces of Gurth and the King. With the spectre of battle now inexorable, the sway of the Bishop could well prove the deciding factor. Yet up to now, the Bishop had given no clear indication as to which side he would take. Since their arrival the earls had dispatched multiple envoys to the Bishop's palace, but thus far these overtures had only been met with ambiguous responses. Yet equally, neither did it appear that the King or any of his followers had yet entered the city themselves. Perhaps the Bishop was stalling for time, waiting to see which way the tides of fortune fell. Or perhaps he was attempting to conceal a die which had already been cast.

Either way, Hae-jin needed more information, and quickly. The Bird was due back now, and should at this moment be awaiting Hae-jin's own arrival. As the column passed into the gates Hae-jin succinctly issued his orders to their captains and then made his way to a particular pavilion in the tent city. The Earls of Swinstoke and Wickhowe were already there, waiting outside. The moment Hae-jin appeared, Swinstoke became animated. "There you are, Greyflower", Swinstoke barked. "That wretched Bird has refused to speak to us; he insisted we wait until you were here as well. Damn cheeky I call it."

"Is the Bird inside then?", Hae-jin inquired.

"Aye, to be sure. He's been there almost an hour, fidgeting."

Hae-jin pulled aside the flap and stepped inside the tent, followed by the two earls. Inside, the Bird was perched on a table, looking about as dejected as Hae-jin had ever seen him. When he caught sight of Hae-jin, the Bird began flapping his wings agitatedly as he spoke. "Terrible, terrible news, Hae-jin!"

"What news? Have you inspected the King's encampment?"

"Yes, and Gurth's too."

"And what is your report?"

"The king has a lot of soldiers, Hae-jin. An awful lot. Five, maybe six thousand."

Wickhowe drew a sharp breath. "Surely not?", Wickhowe said. "The King doesn't have that kind of support; he shouldn't have been able to muster even half that many troops."

Hae-jin cocked an eye at the Earl. "Perhaps the remaining nobles are more loyal to the King than you had supposed", he said.

Swinstoke snorted. "That, or else the Bishop's already joined forces with him."

Hae-jin turned again to The Bird. "What about Gurth's encampment?"

"Worse still, Hae-jin. Hundreds of his men are there, and there are Drixi there!"

Hae-jin felt a wave of shock hit him. Drixi? Hae-jin had thought he was through with those bedratted eye-ball clad elfkin. Apparently not. "Drixi?", he demanded. "What are Drixi doing here in Linster?"

"Helping Gurth, that's what! With flying cavalry, no less. They've got a funny sort of corral-thingy setup in his camp holding two or three hundred of those winged lizard things they like to ride. And there are also Zard, Hae-jin. Hundreds and hundreds of Zard."

Hae-jin felt a deadening sense inside. Gurth, the King, the Drixi, and the Zard, all encamped only a few short miles away, just waiting to destroy them all. "How many all told then?", he asked.

The Bird squinted a bit. "Between both camps? I reckon eight or nine thousand. Hae-jin, what are we going to do? We're outnumbered almost two to one!"

Hae-jin turned to the two earls. There was a defiant gleam in

Swinstoke's eye even as he looked slightly more deflated than usual, while Wickhowe had already recovered his composure, and met Hae-jin's eye evenly. "It is absolutely critical now that we persuade the Bishop of Larchester to take our side", Wickhowe said. "Perhaps if the Bishop joins us, more will be inclined to forsake the king or even join our side."

"Perhaps", Hae-jin said. "But how do you propose that we convince him? Thus far our entreaties have borne little fruit."

"I will compose a letter to the Bishop myself immediately, explaining to him again the merits of our cause and beg him for an audience in person. I am convinced that I can persuade the Bishop, if only I have an opportunity to talk to him myself."

Suddenly the flap to the tent was pulled aside again, and the orange face of Alwog poked through. "Aha! There you are, Hae-jin. We've got a problem. Joan wants to see you right away. And tell the Bird to come also. I want to talk to him about that ninety silver marks per day he now owes us."

"Ninety-one!" came a voice from outside.

"Shut up!"

Taking his leave of the earls, Hae-jin followed the Wog out of the tent and made his way to the town proper. Hae-jin already guessed for himself what the problem might be. Ever since the alliance with the nobles, the serfs had demonstrated a complete disinterest in fighting, being quite content to leave all that up to someone else. This complacency might not in itself have been so bad were it not counterbalanced by the fact that there was also now no opportunity for pillaging, and the peasants would instead simply demand whatever they desired or needed from the merchants and tavern keepers. What few duties were left to them they performed only grudgingly, and with much dithering.

The reverse then happened whenever they were left idle, at which point the peasants were frequently unruly and rowdy and prone to heavy drinking. The yeomen and other freemen were far more manageable, but even they were at times inclined to falter and lose heart.

Through all this, Joan was proving to be the crucial link between Robin Goodfellow and his own army. She spent most of her days at a table outside the hall of Elmstead, hearing out the people's grievances and entreating them to do the work which was asked of them. In this respect she was a consummate diplomat, and her long held position of respect among the people enabled her to maintain cordial relations with them. Indeed, among the common folk she was even beginning to usurp Hae-jin in popularity, as bit by bit Robin Goodfellow the champion of the people disappeared and Robin Greyflower the lackey of the nobility replaced him. Even so, it was still all Joan could do to contain the peasants, and the matter grew worse with each passing day.

Hae-jin approached the hall from a back street, knowing that if he came by way of the front entrance the long line of people there would immediately beset him with both their adulation and their increasingly capricious demands. As Hae-jin approached the rear door, he nearly ran into a harried looking Hugh Mortimer. The old miller had been serving as Joan's adjutant, and by his appearance it seemed that it was a busy day as usual. "Ah, Hae-jin", the old man said. "There you are. Joan's looking for you."

"What's the matter?"

"Oh, the usual thing. The serfs, you know. Can't ever keep 'em happy."

"Can you tell her that I'm here? If I go out front there will surely be a commotion."

"Eh? Oh, well, I suppose you're right. Hang on a moment."

The old miller trudged sourly back into the building, grumbling to himself. Hae-jin stepped over the threshold likewise and followed Mortimer into the dim interior of the hall. He waited while Mortimer fetched his erstwhile mistress, and a few moments later Joan entered the room and sped quickly to Hae-jin's side, grasping both his hands in hers. "Hae-jin, thank you for coming so quickly", she said.

"What is wrong?"

"It's the tavern keepers again. They're refusing to issue any more credit until they've been paid a portion of what is owed them."

"But we only just increased the ale ration. Are the people still buying more drink?"

"Yes."

Hae-jin sighed. "Very well. Inform the merchants that Robin Goodfellow will cover their outstanding expenses, and that we'll release the money to them tomorrow."

"But we can't just keep paying for everything the people devour! We'll run out of money."

"I know. But it will have to do for now. We need to keep the people happy right now. Things will soon be changing and at that point it likely won't matter how much money we've got." Hae-jin then briefly related his most recent intelligence from The Bird.

Joan wrung her hands. "I'm worried, Hae-jin. I don't like the Earl of Wickhowe. How can you be sure that we can trust him?"

"I'm afraid I cannot be sure of anything, Joan. But we will never succeed without the aid of the nobles. You see yourself how the peasants are. There was never a possibility that we would succeed with them alone."

"That was your plan all along then? To join the nobles?", the woman said in a taut voice.

"It has always been necessary", Hae-jin replied firmly. "Whether it was the nobles, the clergy or the king himself, it was always going to be imperative for us to ally ourselves with the established powers at some point if we were ever to have any hope of succeeding."

"And what about me, Hae-jin? Was I merely another necessity?"

There was a sort of pleading looking in Joan's eye as she spoke, and Hae-jin felt taken aback. Her fear and dismay under their present circumstances Hae-jin readily understood, for he felt it no less himself. But there was something more to Joan's anxiety, something which reflected a far more personal dimension to her emotions which Hae-jin hadn't quite seen before. Or rather, Hae-jin hadn't wanted to see it. He had already experienced one loss, the pain of which was still far too recent for him to dare yield to another attachment. But now, circumstances demanded otherwise. Before all else, Hae-jin was after all a soldier. In his relationship with Joan there had always been both a practical and a personal dimension, which in the end were perhaps much the same thing to him. His sole devotion was to his duty, and his personal attachments were simply a part of his duty, to the point that they became more or less inseparable in his mind. He now folded both Joan's hands gently in his own and looked her in the eye.

"There is no one else whom I need now more than you, Joan. I could not have done any of this without you, and without you all of this would fall apart in an instant. There will never come a time in all this when I will not need you more than all others." Joan looked away, but there was a softening in her body language even as her hands tightened inside his.

Wickhowe's letter to the Bishop was dispatched with several heralds early in the afternoon, and it was not until well after nightfall that they returned. The Bishop sent his acknowledgement of the earl's letter, and pledged that after taking the matter under due consideration he would dispatch heralds himself on the morrow bearing his reply. The nobles were divided as to whether this should be construed as good news or bad, and for his own part Hae-jin could make no guess either way. For the moment there was simply nothing to be done but to continue to make preparations for the looming conflict, and pray that they might yet prevail upon the Bishop to support their side.

The wind sliced through the streets of Elmstead as the evening waned into night, stirring up little whirlwinds of dead leaves and forlorn detritus in its wake. Along the gutters and slimy crevices, small terrible creatures lurked and skulked. Rats, roaches, and other sorts of vermin, foraging among the garbage as they kept wicked and wary eyes out for both predator and prey alike. Hiding behind a pile of assorted rubbish at the end of an alley, Tom Oates was keeping an eye on the outer wall of the village, waiting. At this very moment there was a bit of hempen cord looped over one of the wooden timbers at a certain place on the palisade. It was so small as to go unnoticed by any casual inspection, but someone outside the wall who knew where to look would be able to affix a much stouter rope to one end of the cord, which could then be pulled through up around the palisade and back down to the ground so that it was secure enough for someone to climb it.

That bloody Fox thought he was clever, but he wasn't clever enough. More than once now Tom had managed to give the filthy animal the slip, and having at last contacted his master Tom had received his instructions. Now everything was about to change, and soon, very soon, Tom would be able to take his revenge on the Fox. And Mortimer. And Joan. And everyone else he hated. Tom was beginning to grow impatient. He was sure he had put the string at the correct location, and his allies shouldn't have had much difficulty finding it. They should already have been over the wall by now. Suddenly, Tom had the sense that he was no longer alone. He whirled around to see four tall, robed figures towering silently behind him, with hoods pulled low over their faces. Tom felt a thrill go through him as he looked up into the terrible visages beneath the hooded cowls of the beings before him. After a few murmured words he then led them out into the streets, passing discreetly through shadows and alleys towards a particular house within the village.

While elsewhere the rest of the village was largely asleep, Hae-jin was still awake. He and the Bird were engrossed at work in the main room of the house in which Hae-jin resided. Hae-jin sat on a stool before a large table set against one wall and was covered with scrolls and sheets of parchment. Beside him the Bird was perched on another stool, and the pair of them were reviewing lists and schedules under the light of two candles set on the table in tall holders, while a dying fire filled the rest of the room with a dim amber light. A point of contention had come up, and Hae-jin and the Bird were on the verge of an argument when suddenly Hae-jin raised his hand to his lips, and both fell silent.

Hae-jin listened for a moment. All was quiet now. But a moment ago, just at the limit of his senses, he had definitely heard a sound. Hae-jin turned around to look behind him. On the other end of the room were four robed figures, their hoods cast back to reveal the scaly countenances of Zard. The last of them was just filing in through the door, and all of them carried short, curved blades in their hands. Hae-jin leaped to his feet, seizing the stool he had been sitting on as he did so and holding it before him as a shield as he grabbed instinctively with his other hand for a sword which he wasn't wearing. As this was happening Hae-jin saw one of the Zard raise a clenched fist which held what appeared to be a thin, brittle piece of clay moulded in the shape of a human ear, which the Zard then cast violently to the ground. Upon hitting the ground the object shattered with a crack like faraway thunder.

Suddenly, Hae-jin felt a deadening sensation, as if his ears were being bombarded by a loud noise which didn't exist. He opened his mouth and shouted for help, but he could not hear his own voice. It was as though every sound was being drowned out by a deafening silence which filled the entire room.

The Zard lunged forward, dividing into two groups as three of them converged on Hae-jin while the fourth chased the Bird into a corner, who squawked and crowed inaudibly as he frantically tried to beat the Zard back with his wings in the freakish silence. Hae-jin grabbed one of the heavy candlesticks from the table and threw it at the first Zard, who ducked just in time and began assailing the stool with which Hae-jin was shielding himself as he frantically drew his dagger. The Zard's blade bit mutely into the wood with one chop after another, keeping his victim occupied as his comrades moved to flank Hae-jin from either side and finish him.

Meanwhile, outside in the town of Elmstead, the Fox was running furiously along the streets with his nose barely grazing the surface of the cobbles, following a scent. Keeping up with Tom had been troublesome of late, and there were a few times when the lad had managed to give Bartholomew the slip. Even now, Bartholomew was still one step behind the boy, but the scent of Zard was strong, and already Bartholomew was pretty sure he knew where the trail would lead. Sure enough, the trail led straight to the house where Hae-jin was staying. Bartholomew was racing for the door when suddenly there was a noise like distant thunder, followed by total silence as the scent of foul magic filled the Fox's nostrils. The door to the house was open, and Bartholomew leaped over the threshold in one bound and galloped into the main room. There before him he saw four Zard, three of whom were now closing in on Hae-jin, who was pinned in a corner.

There was no time now for subtlety. On a sudden inspiration the Fox took a deep breath, and inflated his lungs to an unnatural capacity. As he did so he suddenly began to grow, his fur, whiskers and paws disappearing as they were replaced by human limbs and hands. In an instant Bartholomew had completely transformed his shape into that of a human, an exact duplicate of Hae-jin in fact. The transformation was barely complete as Bartholomew charged forward, grabbing a broomstick as he did so, which itself transformed into a slender two handed saber of distinctly Zhongish appearance. In the weird silence of the room the Zard heard not a sound as they were charged from behind, and in an instant Bartholomew had hacked down one of the Zard who had been attempting to flank Hae-jin. He then struck down a second Zard, who died with his blade still buried in the wood of Hae-jin's stool, hardly having time to realize what was happening before the conjured blade stole his life. The last remaining Zard had been trying to flank Hae-jin from the other side, but now hesitated for a fatal moment of confusion as he stared at the duplicate humans in front of him. In an instant Hae-jin cast the last shambles of his stool into the Zard and rushed in with his dagger, stabbing the creature until it was dead.

Suddenly there was a pop and a rush of air in Hae-jin's ears, and Hae-jin wheeled around, finally able to hear again. On one end of the room, the Bird was standing on the body of another dead Zard, one claw still buried in the reptile's throat. Two more dead Zard lay on the floor in the middle of the room. And sitting primly beside the bodies was the Fox, with two tails swishing idly just above the floor, trying to avoid being soiled by the pools of blood which were now pooling here and there.

Ever since their first meeting the Fox's behavior had always been extraordinary, exhibiting an unparalleled degree of resourcefulness. Yet up to now, Hae-jin had never once suspected anything near the truth. Now everything fell into place, as he gazed at the two-tailed Fox before him. From the time in the Drixi castle, when the Drixi officers had been thrown into confusion by the preposterous lies of the Fox, to his ability to sniff out magic, and everything else that had happened up to the present moment, it all added up.

Of course, the first person to speak was the Bird. "Good heavens!", the Bird said. "What on earth is all of this!"

The Fox licked himself casually. "An assassination, that's what", the Fox replied cooly. "Or rather, an attempted assassination. One which I have foiled."

"That's not what I mean! For goodness sake, you've got two tails!"

Hae-jin now spoke. "The Fox is a Kumiho", he said.

"A what?", asked the Bird incredulously.

"Bartholomew is a fox-imp. In Hancheon we call such creatures Kumiho."

"I prefer the term Kitsune, if you please", Bartholomew demurred, "that is the name which my family has always employed privately."

"But why didn't you tell us this before!" The Bird exclaimed.

"You never asked", replied the Fox. "Besides, I hardly think it's any of your business anyway."

Hae-jin nodded. "Of course", he said. "You were under no obligation to reveal this to us. However, now that we know, I think we will do well to respect Bartholomew's privacy and keep this information in confidence."

"Indeed", murmured the Bird, "this will prove very useful indeed. I've seen Bartholomew's talents before, especially in dealing with crowds. Now that I understand their true nature I can see all sorts of possibilities."

"We are deeply indebted to the Fox already", Hae-jin said. "Indeed, the very fact that we are alive right now is due to Bartholomew. You came at a most opportune moment."

The Fox tilted his head nonchalantly. "Zard smell terrible, and as soon as I smelled one I knew there was trouble."

"I wonder how they got into the village?", Hae-jin mused. The Fox met Hae-jin's eye. Bartholomew was pretty sure that he knew exactly how the Zard had gotten into the village. Young Tom Oates was proving to be a most disobedient servant. Later on, he would definitely be having a serious chat with the boy. A very serious chat indeed. However, that was something Bartholomew would deal with later. The Fox cocked a suitably oblivious eye at Hae-jin.

"I cannot fathom how it could have possibly happened", the Fox said.

There was no further incident that night. Gurth's assassins had come, and they did not return to their master. Word of the attempted murder spread quickly through the town the following morning, and the atmosphere in Robin Goodfellow's army was tense as Hae-jin and the earls awaited the arrival of the Bishop's heralds from Larchester, bringing word of his decision. And when at long last the heralds arrived, the communication they brought was met with no small amount of consternation. The Bishop had agreed to an audience, but not with the earls. Rather, the Bishop insisted upon meeting with Robin Goodfellow, and him only.

"Damned insulting I call it", Swinstoke blustered. "Who does the Bishop think he is, anyway?"

Wickhowe was more circumspect in his response, although the look on his face betrayed his annoyance. "The Bishop's acquiescence is progress, at least", he said. "It is imperative that we accept immediately."

"Not so hasty, Wickhowe. What if it's a trap or something?"

The leading earls were gathered in the town hall with Hae-jin and his officers to discuss the Bishop's response. Now a disquieted murmur fell over the assembly at these words of Swinstoke.

"The fellow's right, you know", reflected Alwog. "This Bishop chap has proven to be a slippery customer thus far. I wouldn't trust him as far as I could throw his earlship here. Not for a thousand silver marks!"

"A thousand and one silver marks!"

"The point is well taken", said Wickhowe, attempting to regain control of the discussion, "It may well be unwise for our friend Greyflower to accept the Bishop's offer at present. I will concede that. But it is imperative that we give the Bishop some sort of response right away. Perhaps the Bishop would agree to an audience with a proxy?"

The young Earl of Donnock now arose. "If it would please the assembly, I volunteer myself to go in Robin Greyflower's stead."

"I don't believe that will be necessary", said Wickhowe, throwing a wary eye at the young earl. "The Bishop has already declined to meet with us many times. If he would meet with Robin Greyflower rather than ourselves, then perhaps someone from among Robin Greyflower's own officers would be an acceptable substitute?"

"What!" blurted Swinstoke, "are you suggesting we send a load of ugly hobgoblins to the Bishop's palace?"

"Hoy! Hae-jin, if my brothers and I have to put up with this sort of abuse then I'm raising our fee to a hundred silver marks a day!"

"A hundred and one!"

"Shut up!...no, come to think of it, I think you may be right this time...almost."

From the area around everybody's waistlines there came a scoff and a disgusted growl, and the sonorous voice of Ursilda broke the air. "Brambles and balderdash!", the Bear barked, "Enough with this drivel. Send the woman instead. She's one of the Bishop's own, after all."

All eyes now turned to Joan. "It is true", said Joan, "I do indeed belong to the village of Tresham, which is a possession of the Bishop. I met him once, many years ago when he was touring the estate, at which time I was presented to him with the village elders in my capacity as midwife."

Wickhowe mused thoughtfully. "You know, I think it might work", he said. "Yes, the Bishop may indeed be willing to meet with the woman. It's worth asking, at any rate. We should dispatch heralds to Larchester immediately with our response, and beg the Bishop to accept."

There was a bit more arguing and hand wringing, but in the end opinion overwhelmingly favored dispatching Joan as the emissary of Robin Goodfellow. Hae-jin alone objected strongly to the decision, but Joan herself was adamant in her acceptance, and finally even Hae-jin was forced to relent. Heralds were again hastily dispatched to the city, and by noon they had returned. The Bishop had agreed, and would grant an audience to Joan Greyflower.

It was now long past sunset, and Hae-jin was anxiously pacing the main room of his residence, which had since been cleared away of deceased Zard. Joan had departed shortly after noon in the company of three heralds, one from each of the earls. How long it might be before he received any word from Larchester he couldn't possibly guess. But being forced to wait was maddening.

Suddenly, there was a hammering at the door. From outside, Hae-jin could hear the frightened squawks of a very agitated Bird. Hae-jin ran to the front door and flung it open. A wicked breeze cut through his clothing as he beheld the Bird. "Hae-jin! You must come quickly! There is dreadful, dreadful news!"

"What happened! Tell me, what happened!"

"It's Joan, Hae-jin! The heralds just came back from Larchester. Hae-jin, the Bishop has arrested Joan!"

25

"The Bishop of Larchester"

It was getting late in the afternoon by the time Joan arrived at the gates of the city of Larchester. Just as the village of Tresham was dwarfed by the town of Elmstead, so too did the great city of Larchester vastly eclipse the township. A tall, heavily fortified stone wall surrounded the city, which was densely packed with many houses, shops and avenues, among which several thousand Linstermen made their homes and lived their lives. Joan's arrival had been expected, and her party was met at the gates by the Bishop's own heralds, who then escorted them to the Bishop's residence.

The whole skyline of the city was dominated by just two structures. One was the castle, a square block of towers and battlements sitting on a natural rise surrounded by fortified walls which enveloped the keep and grounds. The other (and far greater) of the two was the cathedral, which was situated nearby and was itself easily twice as large as the castle keep, its size further magnified by its close proximity to the castle. Everything else in the city was dwarfed in the shadow of these architectural titans, and indeed among the winding streets of shops and houses there was hardly a place to be found where the castle's stoic battlements or the cathedral's glimmering spires were not visible. Joan's party made their way through rambling streets lined with half timbered buildings which closed around her like a wild forest, each successive story piled on top of another, spilling over the heads of passersby like a tree-tunnel. At length they reached a broad avenue, created by the curtain wall of the castle on one side and the cathedral grounds on the other, wherein the Bishop's palace was located.

The Bishop's palace was a well built stone edifice located midway between the cathedral and Larchester Castle, though perhaps slightly more near the castle. It was by far the grandest house Joan had ever seen, and as she was led through its halls she found herself marveling at all the beauty which now surrounded her. Everywhere there were doors, lintels and trusses carved with elaborate relief and painted in bright colors, while brilliant tapestries covered many of the walls, and even some of the windows were filled with glittering glass. Here was a place where artistry thrived and flourished beneath the serene and immutable majesty of the pulpit, a garden of craftsmanship carefully tended and watered by indulgent patrons. Joan had been met at the door by a canon dressed in black priestly robes, who bade the heralds to remain and that Joan follow him to the Bishop's chambers. The priest escorted her through the many elegant passages of the palace to a lavishly appointed room which seemed to be some sort of antechamber for persons awaiting their turn for an audience. Joan was given a seat on a finely carved bench, and then the canon departed to inform the Bishop of her arrival.

For a while Joan had naught to do but wait tensely where she sat. All around the room there was much of beauty and interest to look at, but Joan's attention remained fixed on the fortified wooden door on the opposite side of the room, beyond which she could only assume the Bishop would be awaiting her. Her anticipation was at last broken when, with a great clack and creak, the heavy wooden door opened, and another canon emerged. "Joan Greyflower. His Lordship the Bishop of Larchester will see you now." Joan arose, trying hard not to tremble as she did so. Steeling herself, she followed the canon through the door.

Before her now was a room which appeared to be the Bishop's principal place of business. By the look of things, the Bishop was a busy man. Everywhere were various articles of administration, most prominent of all being a great table piled high with parchments and managerial bric-a-brac, with a few neglected looking plates containing portions of a half eaten meal sitting to one side of it. Directly behind this table was a high backed chair with a vaulted canopy draped with costly silks, and affixed with a colorful badge bearing the motto *Pax et Ordo*. And beneath this sat the Bishop himself. Robert Graves, the fifty-third Bishop of Larchester, was a stouish sort of man of medium height, dressed in a dark purple gown with a mantle and high collar trimmed with white ermine. A large golden cross rested on his breast, and on his head was a squarish cap of black velvet which sat low around his head almost like a helmet. His features were rounded and placid, and there was an inquisitive, almost contemplative sort of look in eyes as he regarded Joan. The Bishop dismissed the canon with a gesture, who departed and closed the door behind him. The Bishop leaned back in his chair, cradling his fingers together thoughtfully. "So you are the one Wickhowe sent as his representative", he said in a soft, cultured voice.

"I come in the name of Robin Goodfellow", Joan replied, as stoutly as she could.

"Who comes in the name of the Earl of Wickhowe, it would seem", the Bishop replied. "Joan Greyflower, is that not your name?"

"It is, my lord."

"And I am given to understand that you belong to my estate."

"I am midwife to the village of Tresham, and I was educated at the

Abbey of St. Etheltrude in accordance with the law regarding persons of cunning."

At this the Bishop's expression appeared to brighten a bit. "St. Etheltrude's you say? A fine place. The late abbot was a good friend of mine. You ought to have received excellent instruction there."

"Thank you my lord. I'm sure the monks did their very best."

The Bishop remained silent for another moment before speaking again. "Tell me then, Joan Greyflower. What do you want from me? I have received and read all of Wickhowe's many missives. What then do you have to say to me that has not already been said?"

Joan hesitated. She had been thoroughly coached by Wickhowe on precisely what to say, and had been rehearsing it in her mind ever since. But the Bishop's wording had caught her off-guard, and for a moment she felt at a loss to respond. She thought fast. The Bishop would likely have no interest in hearing words which were the invention of Wickhowe. She could only speak for herself now. "If you please, my lord, you can't know how desperately we need you on our side", she blurted. "This land will swiftly fall and remain forever enslaved to Gurth if we do not fight now, and without your aid all will surely be lost! You must help us if we are to have any hope of resisting both Gurth and the king!"

"And pray, on what justification should I so repudiate the king's lawful and God-given authority?"

Joan suddenly had a sense that she was back in her days at the abbey, being quizzed on some obscure article of philosophy. This was a different kind of diplomacy to that which she had been engaged in when dealing with the peasants, and her mind raced as she sought to adapt her strategy accordingly, attempting to cast her mind back to a past version of herself which she had long since forgotten. "I justify my plea on the higher authority which is incumbent upon all who strive to embrace justice", she said.

"Authority comes from the practical necessities of human existence", the Bishop said didactically, "Which is why God has gifted it to us. It is subordination to lawful authority which brings order out of chaos, and distinguishes men from simple beasts."

"But when that lawful authority becomes itself unlawful, it must be repudiated."

"Then you define for yourself what is good and what is evil, what is lawful and what is unlawful? If such were the way of the world, there would be naught but anarchy. By submitting to the legitimate institutions established by God, we gain the blessings of law so that there may be both order and justice. The path which you are presently following may come veiled with the laurels of virtue, but it shall bear only the fruits of evil."

"But is not Gurth the very fruit of evil? How can you say that those who now oppose him are the ones which have begotten evil?"

"And what makes you believe that Wickhowe is at all preoccupied with opposing Gurth, or cares at all about his excesses?", the Bishop said, his tone now taking a harder edge. "You do not know the kind of men you are dealing with, and you do not know the Earl of Wickhowe. I do. Now this man Goodfellow, I know nothing of him. I am told he is an alien, but I know nothing else of him, save that he has caused all manner of disruption and discord, provoking the people to lawlessness and undermining the King's authority during this time of crisis. You may say that the deeds of this adventurer are good, but I for one have not seen this."

"But his deeds are good, my lord! He has driven Gurth from his strongholds and fed the people and freed them from slavery!"

"So it is said. Yet elsewhere there are those who have robbed and murdered in the name of Robin Goodfellow, and all the while Gurth has been driven to ever greater extremes. Previously the king had a chance to assuage Gurth and bring some relief to the people, but under Goodfellow's provocation Gurth has been emboldened, and the king cannot at present resist his demands."

"Gurth would have made those demands nonetheless. Eventually the king would have succumbed, whether Robin Goodfellow had come or not."

"Perhaps, perhaps not. But it is not your station to make that determination."

"It must be my station! We, the common folk, are Gurth's prey. While the king sees to his own security, it is we who starve and we who are enslaved! Have you no pity in your heart for our state?"

"You misjudge me, woman. I pray daily for the deliverance of my people, and it is my most fervent wish that their penance shall soon come to an end."

"That end comes now, my lord, if only you would do something to bring it about."

"I assure you, I do what I can. I am aware that the people of my own estates are suffering. But there is much which I must attend to, and there are many duties which are incumbent upon me which go beyond the situation of any one man or one village. The people brought this curse on themselves, and there is only so much I can do to help them at any one time."

"But this is one time where you can do a single deed which will help them more than any other."

"Perhaps, perhaps not. You assume that by my acceding to your wishes you shall be assured the outcome you desire. That may not be the case, and it would be a grave sin for me to embark on so lawless and cancerous a venture with so little assurance of success."

"But my lord! The risks may be great, but we cannot forsake this chance for freedom!"

"What is chance but the idolatry of the reckless?"

"What is order, my lord, if not the idolatry of the complacent?"

"What is action, if not the idolatry of the covetous?"

"I do believe you are enjoying this, my lord."

The Bishop chuckled. "I see you have caught me out then. I am a very simple man really. My sole pleasure is argument. As a young student, debate was the only hobby I could afford, and today it is the only luxury I have left, one even for which I can rarely spare the time. I indulge my fancy when I can, while reaping the wisdom which it bequeaths. I have truly enjoyed our conversation, I found it most enlightening. However, I do regret that the matter has already been decided. I must now do what is commanded of me." The Bishop leaned forward, and picked up a small bell out from under a haphazard pile of papers, which tinkled almost absurdly as he gave it a brisk ring.

Behind her, Joan heard the door open again, accompanied by a particular sort of clicking and clattering noise which had become very familiar to Joan in recent days. She whirled around to see four fully armored men at arms file into the room, dressed in the livery of William of Bradlaw, the King. The Bishop now addressed the soldiers. "In obedience to the King's command, I am placing Joan Greyflower under arrest. Escort this woman to the keep."

There were not, of course, any dungeons beneath Larchester Castle. Cellars yes, but dungeons there were not. The city had its own gaols for confining common criminals. But within the upper stories of the keep there were a few secure apartments with which to house political prisoners, who in turbulent times might indeed be hostages of exalted status. Thus it was that upon being taken from the Bishop's palace Joan was marched only a short distance to the castle, where she was imprisoned in the keep in relative luxury. The fact that her surroundings were not particularly unpleasant were of small comfort to her though, for in the moment of her arrest Joan's spirits had sunk into an abyss of dismay and hopelessness.

Joan was hardly alone in her chagrin, though. The heralds which had accompanied her were sent away, and news of her arrest had reached Elmstead by evening. Shock and consternation then swept through the army of Robin Goodfellow. By morning, the great hall of Elmstead was surrounded by an angry mob, as the soldier-peasants shouted and wailed their demands for revenge. Their lethargy of previous days had evaporated in their fury at Joan's capture, and they were now possessed of a wild recklessness. Calls were made to storm the city immediately, curses were hurled against the king and the Bishop, and some even cursed the name of Robin Goodfellow himself. But Hae-jin was not present at the hall. Instead, he was in the camp of the nobles, where Robin Greyflower was embroiled in a stew of only a slightly different flavor. Word had arrived that the King's army had now entered the city of Larchester and joined with the forces of the Bishop, and the nobles were hardly in any less of an uproar than were the peasants. There was even whispered speculation among some as to whether it was yet too late to change sides and perhaps secure the King's pardon. A general conference of the nobles and captains of Robin Goodfellow's army had been called in the largest tent of the nobles' camp. Virtually everyone of importance was there; the earls, the Wogs, Rob Sykes, Ursilda. Only one individual was missing, for yet again at a critical moment the Bird was absent. No one had seen the avian all day, and in the grip of their present desperation Hae-jin felt a forlorn sense of hopelessness welling up in him as he reflected bitterly on the faithlessness of the Bird.

"Bloody disgraceful, I call it!", Swinstoke complained, "Damned shifty of the Bishop to have strung us along this far. I say it's time we got in there and thrashed the lot of 'em!"

"For once I agree with His Nibs here," chimed in Alwog, "We've danced around with these blighters for long enough. It's time we stomped on their toes!"

"We're outnumbered two to one, Wog," Ursilda growled, "not even I can sway those odds for you."

Suddenly there was a disturbance from the entrance of the tent, and in a moment the crowd gave way as Will Little pushed his way through them towards where Hae-jin stood. "Master Goodfellow! The King's heralds arrived from Larchester a few moments ago. Mortimer met them at the gate, and he sent me to bring you this."

Here Little produced a scroll, which he handed to Hae-jin. Hae-jin read its contents gravely, and then handed it to Wickhowe, and a shadow fell upon the earl's countenance as he likewise read it.

"Well?" Swinstoke exploded, "what in blazes does it say!"

"The King has received the Bishop of Larchester's pledge of loyalty and has joined forces with him."

"Damn it, Wickhowe, we already knew that!"

"Furthermore, the King commands that those who have allied themselves with Robin Goodfellow shall renounce their past treason and disperse immediately."

"That's nothing new either."

Here another voice called out from somewhere towards the rear of the assembly. "Does the king say anything about a pardon?", the voice said.

Wickhowe hesitated for a moment before replying. "Yes", he said cautiously. :The King's letter does state that anyone who joins forces with him and renews their oaths of loyalty shall receive a pardon. However, I would like to point out that the details are rather vague on any further specifics."

Swinstoke snorted. "I'll bet they're vague! Bradlaw is as slippery as the Bishop. As damnable a pair of eels as ever wriggled. I shouldn't wonder that they'd string us up the moment we set foot in the city, just like they did with the woman."

"Indeed", Wickhowe concurred quickly, "I have grave misgivings about the veracity of the King's offer. We cannot rely on him to deal fairly with any of us. We all know him, we have all known his duplicity. This is what has forged us together in the first place. Shall we abandon everything merely for the sake of another of Bradlaw's lies?"

An aggrieved murmur of accord swept through the crowd. Suddenly, from about the level of everyone's hips the sonorous voice of Ursilda again barked through the voices.

"And what about the woman? Does the letter say anything about her?"

Hae-jin exchanged a look with Wickhowe, and then took back the scroll and read from it aloud. "His Majesty further commands that the outlaw and renegade called Robin Goodfellow shall immediately be handed over for judgement. Otherwise, the woman Joan Greyflower shall be punished for her treason in his stead."

"You mustn't accept", Wikchowe insisted, "Without Robin Goodfellow, everything will fall apart in an instant. The peasants will surely mutiny, and they may even turn on us."

"But what about Joan!" blurted one of the Wogs.

"I doubt the King will be quick to act on his threats. The woman is far too valuable a hostage…"

"How can you be sure about that?"

"…besides, if he harms the woman then he risks inflaming the peasants even further. Perhaps even the citizens of Larchester could revolt."

Swinstoke scoffed. "Wishful thinking, Wickhowe. The woman's as good as hung. If we catch these eels off-guard we may yet have a chance. We should attack now while the King still thinks he has a chance at dividing us. Otherwise we might as well all go home and wait for the King to come and behead us."

Wickhowe turned to Hae-jin. "I implore you, Greyflower", Wickhowe said. "The situation is not yet lost. We may have to forsake the maid Joan for now, but there are still yet other paths to victory for us. We could withdraw from Elmstead for the present and fall back to our own respective fortresses. From there we can marshall again and prepare for an extended war against the King and his allies, harrying his minions elsewhere in the country and laying siege to their strongholds."

Hae-jin felt a sense of numbness. Outnumbered as they were and with their adversaries fortified behind the walls of Larchester, the outlook of a direct confrontation looked grim indeed. Yet, to fall back now was little better. Wickhowe's optimism notwithstanding, to flee Elmstead and take shelter among the castles of the nobles was to forsake everything which Robin Goodfellow had already achieved. The common folk would surely disperse once it appeared that Robin Goodfellow had given up, and it would then be only a matter of time before the King had besieged and subdued each earl in turn. And then there was Joan. Hae-jin felt an overwhelming sense of guilt and loss, as if everything he had suffered before he had brought again upon himself and those he had grown to love. Hae-jin pulled himself together. Before all else, he was still a soldier. He turned to the faces looking expectantly at him, and addressed the assembly. "I must take time to consider the matter. We shall reconvene in the evening, at which time we shall revise our strategy and formulate our response to the King."

It was a short while later that Hae-jin, Ursilda, the Wogs and Sykes were trudging their way through the streets of Elmstead, headed by circuitous routes towards Hae-jin's residence so as to avoid the crowds. It had already been announced that Robin Goodfellow would address the army in the evening (at which time Hae-jin hoped he would already have some kind of a plan in hand), but nonetheless it was better that they didn't attract much attention. The lot of them were in a sorry mood. None spoke and few dared even look at Hae-jin. At length they came to their destination. And there, hopping about agitatedly on the threshold, was the Bird. "Hae-jin!", the Bird cried upon seeing the others approach. "Thank goodness you're here!"

Hae-jin felt a wave of wrath sweep over him. "Of course I'm here!", he snapped. "I haven't left the town all day. Where in blazes have *you* been?"

"Here and there. Hae-jin, I must speak to you in private, it is of the utmost importance!"

"Then speak. You can start by explaining yourself and accounting for your absence again."

"No, I must speak to you in private!"

"Fine! Have it your way, then."

The others remained outside as Hae-jin and the Bird stepped inside the house and closed the door behind them. From within, they could hear what sounded like a heated argument in progress. Bit by bit, they began drifting about and settling as comfortably as possible here and there as Hae-jin remained closeted with the Bird. On and on the argument between man and Bird raged as their fellows waited under the baleful rays of the afternoon sun. Finally, after well over an hour the door of the house opened and Hae-jin emerged.

"Well?", demanded the Bear, "Now that we've all spent half the day loafing out here, can you kindly tell us what all that was about?"

There was a peculiar sort of look on Hae-jin's face as he spoke.

"The Bird and I have had a long talk", he said softly. "I have come to a decision."

"A decision?"

"Yes. I have looked at our options and assessed our situation, and I have concluded that there is no other viable course of action available to me that would not inevitably bring ruin to our mission and needlessly endanger my friends."

"And?"

Hae-jin took a deep breath, and looked outwards into the streets of Elmstead. The sunlight was glinting off the tiled roofs of the houses and bathing the otherwise dingy alleys with a soft golden glow. The air seemed to be filled with a kind of tranquility now, rather like the sense of peace that one gets when coming to the end of a long and arduous journey. Soon, very soon, it would all be over, one way or another. Whatever the outcome, Hae-jin could only hope that he will have somehow managed to do something good along the way.

"Hae-jin?"

Hae-jin recollected himself, and returned his attention to his comrades. It was time they were told. "I am going to surrender to the King", he said.

26

"The Moment of Truth"

Inside the keep of Larchester Castle, just beneath one of the turrets, there was a small chamber. It wasn't a bad sort of place, really. Cramped, yes, but hardly miserable. The stone walls were covered over with white plaster, and in one corner there was a very small fireplace which was more than adequate to heat a room of such diminutive size. There was also a small but comfortable bed, a table with a candle, and even a proper chair rather than a simple stool. Yet despite these modest comforts there was little which could alleviate the oppressiveness of the place. For it was, after all, a prison. For two days Joan had been confined to this place, never seeing or speaking to anyone except when she was brought her meals. No one ever harmed or mistreated her, yet solitude and despair were tortures enough by themselves. And worst of all was the boredom. The room possessed a single, tiny window which was bigger than a mere arrow slit, but still hardly enough for an interesting view. Nevertheless, Joan had spent most of her time with her chair drawn up beside it, watching what little she could see of the courtyard below while always keeping one desperate eye on the sky, hoping vainly that at any moment she might catch sight of the Bird, or perhaps a flying carpet, or anything which she might imagine that could save her from her misery and restore her to her friends.

Suddenly, from behind her there was a grinding of keys within the door. Save for the changing shadows outside, Joan had little sense of time in her prison, yet she was fairly sure that it was not the usual hour for someone to be bringing her her meal. The door opened to reveal the usual turnkey, a rather musty man who was ordinarily tasked with attending to Joan's sustenance. He gave way without speaking though, and through the door there now stepped a finely dressed canon of the cathedral, who addressed Joan curtly. "His Lordship the Bishop of Larchester has commanded that you be brought to his personal chambers."

Joan felt her breast heave as her breath quickened. At last she was saved from the monotonous agony which had been slowly killing her for two days. Yet there was little relief, for anguish had been replaced by fear, and she trembled a bit as she arose and compliantly followed the canon out the door. Outside were two men at arms dressed in the Bishop's personal livery, and with the canon in the lead Joan was marched down through the winding passages of the keep and out of the castle to the Bishop's palace. This time, the canon bypassed the anteroom Joan had visited before, instead leading Joan deeper into the more intimate recesses of the great house. At last, the canon came upon an isolated room with a heavy door, and upon opening it ushered Joan into the room as he softly announced her arrival to his master.

To one side of the room there was a narrow sort of daybed set along the wall, partially hidden from view by a heavy curtain of a dark green cloth. Most of the room's perimeter was lined with similar curtains of identical fabric, which was pulled aside and left open in many places to reveal shelves and cabinets piled high with books and scrolls. In the center of the room was a great writing table placed beneath the light from a row of narrow arched windows near the ceiling, filled with opaque glass, and beside this was another table, set with a scant meal which was largely uneaten. In marked contrast to the rest of the palace that Joan had seen so far, this room was starkly austere and utilitarian, the only decoration being a single wooden crucifix which hung on the wall above the curtains. It was not actually a bedroom, nor was it a proper study or even a dining room, but sort of a blend of all three. It was a place where one might go to work and somehow never leave, and Joan was left with the impression that the Bishop probably spent more of his time here than in any of the other (and much grander) apartments of his residence. The Bishop himself was seated at the writing table, a pair of hinged wooden spectacles resting precariously on the bridge of his nose as he read. Looking at the man now in the privacy of his spartan sanctuary, Joan suddenly had the sense that she at last understood the Bishop for what he was; neither a particularly saintly nor wicked man, but rather a preoccupied one. Across the broad spectrum of human virtue, there are those who are good, those who are evil, and those who are simply busy. The Bishop now looked up at his visitors. "Ah, Joan Greyflower. Do come in." The Bishop then nodded to the canon. "That will be all."

The canon bowed respectfully, and then stepped out of the room and closed the door behind him. Joan was now alone in the Bishop's private chamber. The Bishop had removed his eyeglasses now and was twiddling them in his hands, folding and unfolding them at the hinge as he gazed curiously at Joan. Joan decided that it might be best to start the conversation in a diplomatic tone. "How may I serve you, my lord?", she asked. Immediately thereafter, she had a sudden sensation that she ought to have chosen a rather different expression, under the circumstances. However, the Bishop seemed wholly unmoved, and continued to regard her thoughtfully.

"My lord?"

Finally the Bishop stirred. "I have summoned you, Joan Greyflower, to inform you of such tidings which are significant to your situation. Your ally, the outlaw Robin Goodfellow, has surrendered to His Majesty the King."

Joan felt a wave of shock and horror hit her, and as her mind reeled under the assault her heart sank as if it had been crushed beneath her breast. "No!", she breathed. "That can't possibly be! Hae-jin would never have done that!"

"I'm afraid he already has. I must confess, I was rather surprised myself. Even with you as a hostage I did not believe he would yield."

Tears of desperation were now beginning to fill Joan's eyes, and she fought to hold them back as she spoke. "Hae-jin would never have surrendered, not for my sake, not for anyone's."

"Perhaps your confidence is misplaced. Or perhaps not. As it is, Robin Goodfellow has sworn to present himself at the city gates at noon tomorrow and hand himself over to the king."

"I can't believe that!"

"Indeed, but it is true. The terms were quite specific. Robin Goodfellow agreed to capitulate on the condition that he shall surrender personally to the king before the high altar of Larchester Cathedral, in the presence of myself, the king's officers, Gurth and his allies, as well as the councilmen and officers of the city. And also yourself."

Joan swallowed hard. "I couldn't bear to witness that."

"Yet these were the terms. And I have prevailed upon the king to accept them in the interests of peace."

"You will never gain peace in this way."

"Perhaps, perhaps not."

The Bishop set down his eyeglasses now and leaned back in his chair. "Tell me, Joan Greyflower. Why do you suppose Robin Goodfellow surrendered under these terms?"

Joan shook her head mournfully. "My lord, I truly do not know."

"Neither do I." The Bishop regarded Joan silently for another moment, a quizzical, puzzled expression still on his face. Then he dismissed her, and Joan was led back to the tower and restored to her cell to await the coming day.

The following morning the streets of Larchester were abuzz with anticipation. The name of Robin Goodfellow was both feared and acclaimed, and news of his surrender had torn through the city like a ravenous blaze fueled with fairy fire. Now the streets were choked with people as the citizens of Larchester gathered to see the spectacle unfold. Indeed, many were simply curious to see what the notorious man looked like. As noon approached there was a cry from the city gates. Murmurs rippled back and forth across the crowd as the crisp commands of the guardsmen could be heard faintly on the wind. At last, the anticipated moment had arrived: Robin Goodfellow stood now before the gates of Larchester.

Hae-jin dismounted his horse where he had halted. He stood now on a wide stone bridge, an avenue in its own right which passed through the base of a great fortified tower built into the walls of the city. Before him was a triple column of the city guard, and behind these Hae-jin could already see other men at arms gathering. Nearby, the Earl of Donnock had also dismounted, and stood beside Hae-jin. Likewise too were the three Wogs and the great Bear Ursilda. Hae-jin had insisted that not only should he surrender, but so too should the nobles and his select captains. The Bird and the Fox Hae-jin had sent away, while Sykes had been instructed to remain with the other yeomen and keep order in Elmstead, but the remainder were to accompany Robin Goodfellow on his final ride. Of the nobles only Donnock had agreed to join him. Wickhowe, Swinstoke, and all the others had flatly refused and remained fortified in Elmstead. Now, men at arms wearing the livery of William of Bradlaw approached and Robin Goodfellow and his party were put into lowly shackles, the young earl included. Even the Bear was fettered as men at arms approached her with trepidation before casting a great chain about her neck and binding her jaws with a muzzle. Yet none offered any resistance, and in short order Robin Goodfellow and his accomplices were duly marched before the fascinated crowds through the long winding streets of Larchester all the way to the cathedral in fulfillment of the king's agreement. As Hae-jin at last mounted the steps of the cathedral he took a deep breath and gazed up at the vaulted portico above him carved everywhere with the images of heaven. Absolutely everything now depended on the success of the forthcoming encounter. Inside, the cathedral nave soared above like a stately forest of amber stone with its fanning vaults spreading wide overhead like a canopy of leafless branches. Far below, the aisles were packed with the gentility of the city, the wealthier merchants and householders as well as the lesser officers of the district. And there too were also the king's supporters. Gentlemen, squires and knights, all daughty men at arms who had pledged their allegiance to their monarch and gazed now upon the rebel with hardened eyes. Hard, yet curious, for the queer party of rebels elicited no small amount of wonder as they passed through the nave to the chancel. Now they approached the foot of the high altar where, at long last, the career of the renegade Robin Goodfellow was about to end.

The high altar was a large stone sarcophagus beneath which the first bishop of Larchester was buried, covered in gilded sculpture and capped with a great slab of fine imported marble intricately engraved with sacred inscriptions. The altar itself rested atop a wide raised dias, before which was assembled a host of the most exalted persons of the land; scores of nobles comprising the staunchest of the kingdom's peerage who had heeded the King's call. Likewise the council and elders of the city were there, and the Bishop of Lachester himself stood to one side on the steps of the dias surrounded by priests and deacons. And there also, standing just off the steps of the altar, as if the sanctity of the place were somehow hazardous, was Gurth arrayed in fine attire. With him were several officers, men dressed in dark velvet and tall robed captains whose cowls only partially concealed their hideous Zardish visages. And last of all were a group of Drixi officers dressed in silken robes of crimson banded vertically with black, cradling winged helms under their arms, and each man bearing an eye painted in the middle of his forehead. And in the center of it all, pacing too and fro like a caged animal, was William of Bradlaw, King of Linster. The king was a compact sort of man in his late twenties, athletic of build with a shock of red hair and a full beard to match. His features were handsome in their own way, and his eyes were sharp and wary, and bound close at his side was a great war sword on which he rested one hand with a determined grip. All in all, the king reminded Hae-jin of a captive leopard, a specific animal in fact which had once been a fixture in the court of Hae-jin's own former king in faraway Zhongyang, and had spent its days bound to a pillar beside the throne with a golden chain about its ankle.

There was a slight commotion to one side of the altar, accompanied by the clatter of armor. A portion of the crowd gave way now to a detachment of men at arms. In their midst was Joan, tearful but composed, her hands shackled together with irons. For a moment Hae-jin looked at her, his heart overwhelmed with grief as he met her haggard eyes which cried out silent in anguish and reproach. But each said nothing. Having come to the cathedral as agreed, the king now wasted no time with further pleasantries. "So this is Robin Goodfellow, the bandit imp and servant of my enemy?"

Hae-jin looked briefly towards the place where Gurth stood a safe distance from the altar, and then returned his gaze to the king. "I was under the impression that your true enemy is presently standing a short distance behind you. I am no servant of his."

"Treason and disloyalty are my greatest enemies, Robin Goodfellow, and so are you."

"I am none of these things to you. I am a foreigner and a betrayer to none in this land, and my quarrel is with Gurth alone."

"Then you are an invader, and an accomplice of traitors. Where indeed is the coward Wickhowe, who sends you in his stead?"

"I do not come in the name of the earl, nor do I come in the name of any save Linster itself. I myself, a foreigner, am come to deliver the people of this land from a foreign oppressor, who stands here now in our midst. And I entreat you as king of these very people to do the same, and drive out Gurth the Witch!."

From the assembly Gurth now stirred and spoke, appearing to Hae-jin visibly perturbed. "Your majesty! Why do you tolerate such insolence from this beggar? Slay this thief now, and put an end to his lawlessness!"

"It is you, Gurth", Hae-jin said calmly, "who has usurped the King's authority and imposed your own law upon this land, and it is I who seek to end it and restore the King's law."

"Fairy fiend, consort of goblins! You defile this land with your presence."

"Your Majesty, are you going to allow this witch to speak for you?"

"Villain! Elf-screed!"

"Enough!", the King bellowed. The King's voice reverberated through the soaring vaults and echoed through the halls of the cathedral as silence followed in its wake. The King now looked Hae-jin squarely in the eye. "I am the defender of this land", the King said. "I alone stand between Linster and all her enemies. It is not mine to choose between law and liberty, but to safeguard one with the other. And by my sword I shall preserve the liberty of this land and strike down the lawless each in their turn."

"Then break the chains of lawlessness, my king, and destroy your greatest enemy now while you still can!", Hae-jin replied. The King hesitated a moment. Then, he raised his fist, and from the surrounding galleries men at arms now stepped forward and converged on the place where Robin Goodfellow stood.

Suddenly, there was a commotion in the cathedral. Far down near the upper nave several persons had been hurled into the aisle. Two men had rammed their way through to the front row of the assembly and were now roughly shoving distinguished looking burghers about, causing all eyes to turn in their direction. Then abruptly the people gathered in the chancel were thrown into confusion, as a young boy pushed his way through their midst and began running helter skelter through the crowd, dodging dignitaries and soldiers and making a mad dash straight for the altar as above the tumult of voices Gurth could be heard screaming out in an unnatural voice. "Stop her, STOP HER!!!!"

But the boy was already mounting the steps of the altar, and as priests, soldiers and Zard scrambled and grabbed, he reached the top and slammed his hand down on the altar's stone surface. A blast of thunder tore through the aisles, hurling everyone in the vicinity flat to the ground as a blinding flash of golden light emanated from the altar and momentarily filled the cathedral before plunging it again into darkness. As the darkness lifted Hae-jin pulled himself up on his side and looked around. Everywhere people were scattered on the polished floors, a few unconscious but most already recovering and blinking bewilderedly. Gurth was nowhere to be seen, and headed away through the galleries Hae-jin saw several Zard and Drixi making a speedy exit. The altar itself was smoldering slightly, and a large chunk of marble had broken off the corner where it had been struck. And standing beside the battered altar was Lindsey, massaging her right hand while still panting with adrenaline.

"Well, there's your stinking curse taken care of!", Lindsey said tersely. "Now what are you going to do about it?"

27

"On Hostile Roads"

Two thousand years ago, the Reman Empire had been at the height of its power. From the western shores of Ursiland in the north, to the heart of Meridiana in the south, the Empire in its glory had spanned two continents, far larger than its twin on ancient Earth, and comparable only to the Mongol Empire which existed fleetingly on that world a millennium later. In Reme, the arts of magic had been set to order and subordinated to the service of the imperial state to a greater degree than had any other kingdom of men in the history of the Fairworld. Scryers, augurs and magicians were trained in state run academies to augment every aspect of the imperial system. Wightbeasts were legally integrated into society and regimented alongside men as citizens and defenders of the empire. From one end of the empire to the other the Imperial Eagle soared through the skies as a literal manifestation of the eyes, ears and lips of the Empire. With such resources at their command, the Reman Empire had expanded to unparalleled size and remained under stable and effective rule for generations under the tolerant scrutiny of the fairy-folk, who had permitted them to flourish unchecked. Yet despite all this, the Empire could not avert its own demise.

The great intractable deserts of the east had long thwarted even the vaunted might of the Remans, while to the west a new desert of unnatural character had appeared, and from it the Empire of Witches emerged to rival the empire of the Remans. While the Remans were the builders of kingdoms, the Witches were the devourers of them. The Remans had forged an empire through the ordered application of magic, while the Witches in turn built theirs on the ruthless and unfettered exploitation of the same, and bit by bit the Spreaders of the Desert consumed the lifeblood of the very land beneath them as their dark enchantments grew and swallowed up whole kingdoms, slaying or enslaving the inhabitants and leaving behind naught but naked rock and sand. Buffeted by hostile nations in the east and a bleak wasteland of expanding black magic in the west, the Reman Empire became pinched in the middle like the shadow of an hourglass on the map, its time steadily running out. At long last Reme itself fell, its avenues and houses emptied and the marble pillars of its vacant palaces haunted by the ghosts of the fallen as the darkness of the witches reigned supreme over a lifeless land. Yet in that hour new forces were awakened, mustered against the darkness by fairy whispers from all parts of the former Reman Empire and beyond. For three hundred years war raged over the land, until at long last the witches were at last crushed and their once great and terrible empire was reduced to little more than an unpleasant memory. Until now.

Far to the south of the Kingdom of Linster, beyond the last verges of the Hinterlands, there lie the Marklands. Once a backwater of the former Reman Empire, these eastern marches became the last remaining stronghold in the heart of the crumbling empire. In the centuries that followed, the fragments which survived the tumult slowly grew from a few scattered forts and motley prefectures into a collection of small independent states ruled by dukes and counts who were descended from the old Reman military elite. Situated between the Hinterlands in the north, the continent of Meridiana in the south and the trackless deserts of the east, the Marklands were a place where the peoples of two continents mingled and mixed, traded and bickered, lived their best and died their best. A true cultural crossroads, either for good or for ill.

Along a dusty road winding amidst a dry and rocky landscape dotted with patches of scrubby cypress and cedars, a column of Zard marched in cadence to the harsh rap of leather drums. Their hoods and robes were cast back as the light of the afternoon sun warmed the cool, scaley surfaces of their semi-warm blooded bodies, for the Zard were originally created from common reptiles long ago. Keen witchcraft had transformed them from simple, mindless creatures into fearless, intelligent warriors, and though bred by their creators to be capable soldiers in all sorts of weather they nonetheless remained far more dependent on their surroundings than any proper warm blooded creature.

Just ahead of the Zard were the gates of the Duchy of Skora, one of the more prominent city states of the Marklands. For many years now the Marklands had lived under the shadow of the witches, and in recent months that shadow had at last materialized into an iron shod boot. Virtually every state had been reduced to a tributary, and those who resisted were repressed with cold blooded brutality. The Duchy of Skora had been one of the last holdouts, and two weeks ago it too had fallen, buckling under the irresistible engine of witchcraft with hardly a single arrow shot. Having spurned the degradation of subservience to the witches, Skora had instead been reduced to a puppet, saved from total annihilation only by swift acquiescence in the face of imminent occupation. And even so, the cost had been high.

From the battlements of the Reman portico at the city gates there hung a sorrowful collection of tattered and bloody surcoats bearing the livery of the Knights Invictus, sworn protectors of the Marklands and enemies of all witches. Beside these were more gruesome trophies, the severed heads of the knights themselves, displayed together with their livery as a warning to all who would resist the might of the witches. Down below a number of Zard were loafing in the sunlight, languidly curating a long line of merchants and travelers who were gathered doggedly before the city gates beneath the mournful exhibition. Even under the yoke of oppression the economy carried on as best it could, and the roads which passed through Skora reached long and far. Hinterlanders, Marklanders and easterners mingled together with their wagons and goods, trying not to grumble as they stood aside and awaited their turn to enter the city, while through the gates a wretched procession of shackled slaves were being led out of the city on their way to the dark lands of the witches. Tucked in discreetly among the line of itinerants there was a small ox-drawn cart filled with a consignment of quartz, tended by two nondescript looking men and what appeared to be a teenage boy.

Lindsey stood next to the cart full of crystals, trying not to look nervous as she waited alongside Dackery and Falknir at the gates of Skora in plain sight of their enemies. She was still disguised in boy's clothes, though her ensemble was somewhat the worse for wear, bearing the marks of many long miles on unforgiving roads. For several weeks now, Lindsey and Dackery had been traveling in the company of Falknir, posing as gem merchants (complete with a cart full of good quality quartz provided by their outlaw allies). In doing so they had been able to follow some of the established routes which the outlaws regularly employed to mask their comings and goings, and thus far their journey had been tolerably smooth and uneventful, though not without its hardships. They usually managed to eat and sleep well enough, yet it was tough going all the same and they pressed an aggressive march, knowing that with each passing day their route would become ever more dangerous. And it didn't help matters that her company was at times less than harmonious. The man Falknir had proven to be a capable and resourceful individual, with a good knowledge of the local geography. But equally so, he proved also to be a man of an independent and assertive disposition, and an outspoken turn of mind. In many ways he was very much like Dackery himself, with just enough similarities between them to make a potentially volatile combination, and the two men frequently clashed with one another. At times it had left Lindsey feeling as though she were being treated like a child, left out of the decisions upon which her own fate rested as two men quarrelled with one another. And it had finally gotten under her skin. She was angry and frustrated with both of them, but also with herself for putting up with it all. She kept reminding herself that both men were risking their lives for her and her mission, but it was hard to keep focused on her own goal when her comrades could be such perfect asses at times. And things were starting to get serious. Day by day the iron fist of the witches closed ever more tightly on the Marklands, and it was becoming increasingly difficult for Lindsey and her fellows to avoid passing through areas which were under their direct occupation. The tide of war had beaten them to Skora, and now they were forced to creep through the city under the very noses of the witches and their reptilian servants.

The wretched procession of slaves had finally passed through the gates, and the sluggish Zard now lurched into action to try and process some of the line of merchants before the approaching column of Zard soldiery arrived from the opposite direction. Lindsey was getting nervous. The Zard were questioning everyone who came through. Their inquiries were rather cursory and they didn't seem particularly aggressive about the matter, but just one stroke of misfortune could prove utterly disastrous. Lindsey's group was only second from the front now. Ahead of them was a group of itinerant miners, Dwarves with extravagant bristling beards and dispositions to match. Their spokesman had paused to take great pleasure in explaining to the Zard their reasons for passing through (that being that the witches were a load of worthless gits who were ruining everything, and that he and his brothers were returning to their homeland to take up arms in order to give the witches and their Zardish thralls a proper thrashing should they ever dare to turn up in Dwarven lands). Lindsey had no experience in reading Zard expressions, but she had the feeling that they were getting irritated, if not actually provoked by the puny braggarts. By the time the Zard had heard enough and shoved the still blustering Dwarves through the gates, the lizards were plainly in a foul mood.

At that point, Falknir stepped up. Lindsey was scared. The Zard glared menacingly at Falknir as he approached, and at any moment Lindsey felt that everything could fall apart. But Falknir walked straight up to the Zard without a tremor, and began to explain in excruciating detail his business in Skora as a dealer in fine quartz, bombarding the simmering Zard with a barrage of spurious and irrelevant information. He had just offered to empty their entire cart out on the ground so that the Zard could inspect the all gems at once when the captain barked that he had heard sufficient and ordered Falknir and his companions to get out of the way and pass through. Blathering a few needless apologies, Falknir quickly hustled his comrades through the gates. They had passed the first test, and Lindsey heaved a sigh of relief as they entered the city, even as she knew that further dangers awaited them ahead.

The great marketplace of Skora was a veritable arena of commerce, with people, carts, animals and stalls all jumbled together in a wide cobblestone square enclosed by rows of arched galleries beneath a skyline of tall houses and square towers of dun colored stone and stucco. Even under foreign occupation the character of the city could not be wholly erased, and life went on as best it could. People went about their business with as much autonomy and grace as circumstances would allow, with the spirit of rebellion mixing indistinguishably with the murk of collaboration.

The sea of humanity which surrounded Lindsey as she and her comrades made their way through the market was a sort of kaleidoscope of complexions and features. The Marklands were a unique melting pot of peoples, both transient and resident, drawn to cities like Skora and its neighbors by the singular opportunities afforded in this exceptional land. People from as far as Zhongyang itself lived side by side with dark skinned men from the plains of Mahali, blonde Hinterlanders from the far north, and many wanderers from the eastern deserts of

Al Hajiz and beyond. There was even a small population of dwarves. Indeed, the very landscape of the city was a reflection of this variety. Rising high above the clay tiled rooftops of the common boroughs were the minarets and spires of many churches, mosques, and temples of varied traditions, silhouetted on top of each other amidst the fortified towers and vaunted manors of the metropolis. As Lindsey and her companions progressed along the perimeter of the square they came upon one of these places of worship which was adjacent to the market itself. Smaller and less grand than the soaring edifices which loomed above the rooftops elsewhere in the city, it was a squarish, plain sort of building with a domed roof and a six pointed star painted in blue upon its facade. Yet despite its humility it seemed to be the recipient of an unusual degree of attention, which piqued Lindsey's curiosity. Falknir had paused briefly to make inquiries about lodgings for the night, and Lindsey took a moment to examine the building more closely. The area immediately around it was less crowded than the rest of the marketplace, and all the nearby stalls were filled with all manner of trinkets, charms, and votives of every description. Outside the building there was a long line of people, apparently waiting to gain entrance. Yet they were not gathered at the great double doors of the temple, but rather at a smaller side door which was set low into the ground at the base of a small stairway, which descended a little way into the earth. No one was either entering or leaving, for the way was barred by Zard soldiery, and as she watched Lindsey saw the visitors being turned back one by one.

Suddenly, Lindsey realized that Dackery was standing beside her. He too was watching the events at the temple with a rather keen expression on his face. Meanwhile, Falknir had apparently finished his inquiries, and now came up to where Lindsey and Dackery stood and addressed them in a discreetly muted tone. "Well, I think I've found a good option for us", he said. "The Bronze Camel is located on the far side of the city near the north gates, which is very convenient, as I would prefer that we left as soon as the gates open again in the morning."

Dackery nodded. "I agree", he replied. "Tell me Falknir, what is that temple over there?"

Falknir squinted a bit at the structure across from them, apparently taken aback slightly by the sudden change of subject. "That would be the Great Synagogue of Skora, I believe. It's rather a famous shrine actually."

"What's so important about it?"

"There's a natural cavern underneath the building, which contains The Rock of Skora. Supposedly the rock has all sorts of curative powers. People come here from all over the Marklands and beyond in search of healing."

"Does it really work?"

"For the local economy, it's positively miraculous. The traffic from all the pilgrims brings in a fortune every year. As for the people who come to it looking for actual healing, I couldn't say myself, I've never tried it. But the reputation seems to be well earned. I know a fellow who swears that his second cousin's nephew grew back a lost foot immediately after touching it, and grew three extra toes on his other foot as well in the bargain (although I may not be remembering the details quite correctly). Why do you ask?"

Dackery made no reply. He was instead looking intently at the door. "I don't suppose we could take a quick look inside? It would be interesting to see."

"Eh? Surely not! We don't have time for sightseeing, Dackery. I for one would much prefer to be out of the city as soon as possible. Besides, it looks like the Zard have closed the place."

As Falknir spoke Lindsey was looking keenly at Dackery. There was an inscrutable sort of expression on his face, and Lindsey's mind was cast back to Dackery's odd behavior in the past. She felt certain he had been hiding something from her, but up to now she had been willing to accept that it wasn't any of her business.

Abruptly Dackery snapped out of his reverie. "Of course, you're quite correct. Perhaps I shall have another opportunity to come this way again."

"So long as the Zard don't take the whole place apart and cart it off in pieces, that is. It wouldn't be the first time. Come, we should go to the inn."

The Bronze Camel was indeed close to the outer gates. It was a small place, since under normal circumstances most visitors preferred lodgings closer to the city center where they would be conducting their business. But today, business at the hostel was booming. Falknir's desire to depart with the opening of the city gates reflected popular sentiment, and the inn was overrun with transitory persons anxious to spend as little time in the occupied city as possible. This suited Falknir's plans well, as it meant that in the morning there would be a large crowd waiting at the gates to leave, and one more cart would hardly be noticed. The downside of course was that accomodations were rather lacking, and Falknir's party was obliged to spend the night in the stables. Lindsey collapsed gratefully onto a bed of fresh straw, laid out in suitable places away from the draftier parts of the stables for the convenience of the inn's surplus guests. She was tired. They had been marching since early morning to reach Skora, after many long weeks of making such daily marches. They were now on the very edge of the witches' expanding sphere of control. Once they left Skora, they would soon be ahead of their enemies and would be able to make the final push to Linster in relative security. Or so at least Falknir believed. And Lindsey could only hope that Falknir's wisdom could be trusted.

Outside, the last glimmers of twilight were fading into darkness. To one side of her was the great frame of Dackery lying with his back to her, motionless like a mountain. To the other, Falknir was stretched out serenely on his back, his hands folded over his chest like a funeral effigy which had taken to twiddling its thumbs. His eyes were open and he was staring blankly at the roof, mumbling softly to himself (most likely considering the routes they would be taking on the morrow). Lindsey had gotten used to bunking near these two characters, and the discomfort of such close association had long since worn off. At this point, she was happy to have allies around her. If something should happen during the night, at least they were all together. Lindsey's hand stole up to her chest, feeling for the medallion which lay there next to her skin. Soon she would be in Linster, and would be able to deliver the dratted thing and hopefully break the curse. What would happen after that she couldn't guess. At least she was still with Dackery. He at least could take her back to her own world, as for all she knew she might never lay eyes on Hae-jin, Joan, or that stupid Bird ever again. For all she knew they could all be dead. She gripped the medallion between the fabric of her tunic just a bit tighter. She'd spent weeks being strong and focused, but right now all she wanted to do was just have a good cry.

Lindsey's eyes snapped open. Had she fallen asleep? Apparently so. The room around her was completely dark, save for a few rays of moonlight which filtered in through the windows of the barn. Something had happened to wake her up. But what was it? Lindsey looked around herself. To one side, Falknir was sound asleep, snoring gently. To the other, there was an empty bed of straw. Dackery was gone.

Lindsey pulled herself up on her elbows. Maybe Dackery had just gone to relieve himself. But maybe he hadn't. Lindsey rolled onto her knees and quietly pulled herself to her feet. There was no need to wake Falknir too. Lindsey crept to the door of the stable. Outside, the moonlight was flooding the deserted street. Almost deserted that is, for as Lindsey looked out into the street she spotted a lone figure walking away from her. And the silhouette was unmistakable: It was Dackery. Apparently he wasn't headed to the loo after all. What the hell did he think he was doing? Dackery was just rounding the corner ahead, and would be out of sight in a moment. Lindsey darted out of the door after him, and began to follow discreetly in his wake. Dackery's path was taking him straight back to the city center. Everyone so often he would duck into cover somewhere as the cries of night watchmen echoed through the streets. At length he took a turn, and for a moment Lindsey lost sight of him. Lindsey ran to catch up. Rounding the corner, she found herself back at the great market of Skora.

There was a particular sort of eeriness about the empty marketplace in the dead of night. The crowded throng was long gone, and in its place was a dark maze of vacant stalls and covered carts. On the far side of the great avenue she could just make out the yellow glow of a lantern, probably that of a night watchman on the lookout for people like herself sneaking around among the closed shops. What the hell did Dackery think he was doing coming here? Lindsey could only think of one thing which might have brought Dackery back to the market at this time of night, but she couldn't fathom why. Wary of the lights from the watch, Lindsey kept her head low as she threaded her way between the deserted stalls, and headed for the Synagogue.

The area around the Synagogue was equally deserted. There were no guards present, but there was a wrought iron gate across the doorway which presumably led to the underground shrine. It looked like it was closed, but Lindsey felt sure that Dackery must have been headed this way. With a last look to make sure the coast was clear, Lindsey darted across the cobbles to the Synagogue and crept up to the side door. The door was closed alright. But looking closely at the lock, Lindsey could see that something was not right about it. It was a mess, in fact. All warped and covered with a green-ish white crust, as if it had been partially eaten through by some powerful corrosive. Lindsey reached out to the bars, and tried giving the door a gentle push. It swung open freely before her without a sound. Apparently Dackery had also taken the time to oil the hinges as well. The man was thorough, that was for sure. With a last look back behind her, Lindsey slipped through the doorway and closed the gate behind her.

The passage before her took a sharp turn to the left and began winding its way down into the heart of the earth. The steps were carved out of the living rock and were just a bit slippery. Every few feet a wooden post had been mounted in the center of a step, supporting a thick rope which divided the entire stairway into two lanes, apparently for the purposes of separating the incoming and outgoing flow of people. But now, the rope served as Lindsey's only guide, for the moonlight coming through the door did not illuminate far down the twisting passage, and soon enough Lindsey was making her way in total darkness. Or rather, nearly total darkness, for as she wound her way down underground Lindsey had the vague idea that there was a faint glow of light coming from further ahead.

Abruptly, the passage came to an end, and Lindsey found herself inside a sizable cave filled with red light from a single candelabra which was set into the wall nearby. The ceiling was like a firmament of tiny stalactites, which pierced the roof like stone roots of some monstrous tree, while along the walls were deposits of calcium stacked in rounded terraces like great stone fungi. The floor was rocky and uneven and piled high with all manner of bric-a-brac; votive offerings and cheap charms left behind by a myriad of visitors. But there was a decent path going through the center of it, worn into the rock over the centuries by the tread of countless pilgrims. And in the center of the chamber there was a great stone pillar. And standing at the base of the pillar, was Horatio Dackery.

The pillar was almost completely black, soiled and discolored from centuries of touch by the hands of pilgrims. Only the top of the pillar was left clean, and Lindsey had a vague idea that it was made of some kind of clear crystal, though in the scant light it was difficult to tell. Dackery appeared to be examining the stone closely. He stood with his back to the door, and apparently hadn't noticed that anyone had come in. And Lindsey wasn't about to let him know she was here. Not yet anyway. Dackery was up to something, and Lindsey wanted to know what it was.

Dackery continued to examine the stone for a while. Then, he reached out and pressed his palm against it, muttering some inaudible words as he did so. He then waited a moment, almost as if he were expecting something to happen. Then, he pressed his palm to the stone again, this time muttering something else. Again he waited, but nothing seemed to happen. Dackery appeared to be getting frustrated. Lindsey thought she heard him mutter something uncharacteristically indelicate, after which he pressed his palm to the stone for a third time, and muttered yet another incantation.

Suddenly, the air was filled with a subtle humming noise, just barely audible. At the same time, Lindsey noticed that some color was starting to appear on the clean portion of the stone, almost as if it were emanating from within the crystal itself. And while this was happening, a change seemed to come over the person of Horatio Dackery. It was subtle, but at the same time unmistakable. His posture straightened, and his bearing somehow became more animated. It was almost as if he suddenly looked younger. Much, much younger in fact. It was as though he had always been terribly old and frail by comparison, in a way which Lindsey had never really noticed before now.

Suddenly, Lindsey thought she heard a sound behind her. She whirled around to see a terrible reptilian visage towering above her in the gloom of the passage behind her. "What are you doing in here, human?", the Zard hissed, "The shrine is closed. No one is permitted to enter. How did you get in here?" Lindsey replied by ducking down under the Zard's arm and making a dive past him. But the Zard was too quick, and as she scrambled past she felt a pair of scaly arms envelop her body and crush her under an iron grip. And then, just as suddenly, the claws went slack, the arms fell away, and the Zard fell to the ground with Linsey tumbling down with it. Lindsey scrambled to her feet and looked around.

The Zard was lying in a crumpled heap on the floor, its throat split open with a great wide gash which was gushing forth blood, while to one side Horatio Dackery stood panting, a bloody dagger still clenched in his hand. Lindsey felt sick. Dackery looked at Lindsey. Lindsey looked at Dackery. For a moment neither of them spoke. Dackery then gestured to the Zard corpse before him. "I will do my best to conceal this. Hopefully no one will discover it until tomorrow. Go back to the inn, and wait for me there. We will leave tomorrow as planned as soon as the gates open."

"No, let me stay and help you."

"No, just go to the inn, and stay out of sight. There may be other Zard patrolling the streets."

Lindsey decided it wasn't worth arguing anymore. She wanted answers, but now wasn't the time. With a last look at the broken body of the Zard, she fled the shrine. She made it back to the inn without incident, managing to avoid the night watch on the way. There she lay breathless on the straw, hoping and praying that Dackery would make it back safely also. Finally, after what seemed like an eon a dark shape loomed up beside her, and Dackery returned to his own place on the straw. In the morning, a small crowd of travelers were gathered at the north gates of Skora, cooling their heels restlessly as they waited for the portcullis to open for the day. Among them was a group of gem merchants, who stood silently together without speaking. By now Falknir had realized that something must have gone terribly wrong during the night and was positively fuming. But he kept his peace, waiting until they were all safely out of the city before giving vent to his wrath. At long last the trumpets were sounded, the gates were opened, and one by one the travelers were passed through.

It wasn't until noon that the missing Zard's body was discovered, buried under a pile of votives in one corner of the shrine. Troops were then dispatched throughout the city streets, questioning all passersby and hauling anyone of interest before their captains for interrogation. The order was dispatched to secure the city, and guards were doubled at every gate. No one was to be allowed out, and all who came in were to be thoroughly questioned. The gates soon became clogged with people, those trying to leave were turned away while those coming in were being processed at a snail's pace.

At the southern gate, the line was far worse than it had been on the previous afternoon when Lindsey and her comrades had come the same way. Everyone was questioned thoroughly, and every cart was now inspected and searched. A scruffy looking man with close cropped hair had now come to the head of the line. For weeks now, Kren had been following the trail of Dackery and Lindsey. Long weary years of living in hiding had taken its toll. Kren had had enough, and Horatio Dackery had at last given him a chance to reverse his fortunes and redeem himself before his former masters. All would surely be forgotten and forgiven if Kren could deliver the girl Lindsey to them. He knew he was on the right trail. Indeed, Dackery was probably less than a day ahead of him at this point. But up to now he hadn't been prepared to take any chances. It wouldn't be enough just to inform his masters of Lindsey's whereabouts; he had to make sure the girl was delivered straight into their hands. Otherwise, it might instead be Kren himself who wound up at the wrong end of a witch's dagger.

But now, it looked like he was running out of options. The Zard at the gates were questioning everyone closely. And beside the Zard captain there now stood a man in dark robes with the hood pulled low over his eyes. Apparently the witches were taking direct oversight over the security of Skora. For all he knew, the face behind it could be a former acquaintance. It was now Kren's turn. He trembled a little as he approached the Zard, and glanced furtively to one side at the dark robed man. The Zard captain gazed at Kren with a cold, piercing eye. "Name?"

Kren hesitated. The man in the robe was looking straight at him now, and Kren could almost imagine a hint of familiarity to the visage which was just visible from beneath the hood. "Name?", the Zard demanded. Suddenly, Kren felt his spirit give way. He was sure he was going to be caught, if not now then soon enough. It was now or never. "My name is Kren."

"And what is your business in Skora?"

Kren took a deep breath and straightened. It was time to assume a role which he had long since forsaken. "I am on an errand of great importance to the Empire. I have vital information which must be dispatched to the Black Speakers immediately. Take me to your commanding officer."

28

"Manhunt"

"I still can't fathom what on earth could have gotten into your head, Dackery", Falknir said. "You are by far the most determined tourist I've ever met. You could have gotten yourself killed back there!"

"I have already apologized for my actions", Dackery replied. "I admit that I made a mistake."

"A mistake! I should say it was a mistake. Next time you decide to make a mistake, please let me know in advance and give me the address of your next of kin, so I can notify them of your demise."

The sun was lying low on the horizon, and an orange glow was filtering through the treetops and reflecting on the blacked walls of a burned out and partially collapsed tower, not far from where Dackery and Falknir stood arguing, while Lindsey loitered restlessly nearby. A few weeks ago this had been a commandery of the Knights Invictus, The Order of the Unconquered Sun. When Skora fell to the witches the knights had withdrawn to their commandery a few miles outside the city, and made their stand there. Now, all that remained was a blackened hulk surrounded by rubble. The knights themselves were routed and scattered, and the heads of the fallen were taken back to Skora to be displayed as grisly trophies and a warning to all who dared defy the majesty of the witches. The Zard had done a thorough job of demolishing the commandery, and only a few minor outbuildings had been neglected. It was in the shadow of one of these which Lindsey and her company had paused to take refuge for the night, having marched far beyond the last roadside inns along the road from the city. They had been marching doubletime since dawn, and even though there was yet a bit of daylight left they were all exhausted and in dire need of rest. The commandery had proven to be a convenient shelter at which to spend the night, being a bit removed from the main road and neglected by all and sundry since its destruction.

Falknir was still grumpy about the incident in Skora, though the complete details of the adventure had been withheld from him. For her own part, Lindsey had been waiting all day to talk to Dackery privately herself. Dackery's business was his own, but now his actions had put them all in danger. She felt he owed her an explanation, and she was determined to get it. Up to now they had been busying themselves in concealing their cart and making sure their animal was tied up in a place that wouldn't be easily observed. When this was done, Falknir left to take a brief look around the area before they settled in for the night. For the moment, Lindsey and Dackery were alone. Lindsey looked at Dackery, not sure how to broach the subject. Meanwhile, Dackery was taking stock of their surroundings. "There is certainly plenty of tinder hereabouts", he said distantly, "but I am wary of building a fire. I would prefer not to advertise our presence here, under the circumstances."

"Yeah, about that. Mr. Dackery, I think it's time you and I had a talk."

Dackery cocked an eye at Lindsey, his expression inscrutable. "Of course, Ms. Fluger." Dackery took a seat on the rubble, heaving his great form onto a stack of fallen stone and settling as comfortably as he could. Apparently he expected the talk to be a long one. "What do you wish to discuss?"

"I want to know what you were doing back at the shrine in Skora. I know you've been hiding something from me all this time, and up to now I've avoided asking questions because I know it's not any of my business. But now we're in trouble because of it, and I think you owe me an explanation."

"There was no need for you to follow me to the shrine."

"You snuck out to the shrine in the middle of the night, and a Zard got killed because of it. It could have been one of us who was killed instead."

"I went to the shrine of my own volition, and left you and Falknir out of it. If anything had happened, it would have been I alone who bore the consequences."

"You know that's not true. If something had happened to you, you know that Falknir and I would have done everything to help you, and even if you had gotten away then we'd still be on the run just like we are now. Why did you do it?"

Dackery was silent. Lindsey was pretty sure that he knew she was right, even though he didn't want to admit it. But Lindsey wasn't going to push it any further. She knew him well enough now that she was pretty sure she wouldn't have to. And indeed, after a few moments of silence, Dackery spoke. "The Rock of Skora is indeed a powerful artefact", he said. "The people who come to it for healing are not deluded in this respect. Whether or not any of them are actually capable of accessing that power is another matter, but it is indeed real. I know because I've seen such things before. The Rock of Skora is not unique. There are many objects like it scattered about the Fairworld. They are relics from the Age of Beginning. Essentially they are just fragments left over from the creation of the world, rather like discarded bits of scaffolding. So far as the Good Folk are concerned, objects like these are little more than dangerous rubbish. But for those of us with sufficient knowledge to make use of them, such things have the capacity to grant mortals the means to tap the power of creation itself. I've known for some time that there was such an artefact nearby. I have been drawn to its power for days now, and when Falknir told us of the shrine I knew I'd found the source. And I knew I could not afford to forsake the opportunity to draw upon its magic. You see Ms. Fluger, the fact is that I am dying.

"I am already well over one hundred and twenty. The only reason I've lived as long as I have is through my own efforts in that regard. I have learned how to channel the energies of objects like the one in Skora to rejuvenate myself. Through this and other means I have extended my life beyond that which nature would otherwise allow. But it is still not enough. When I was a young man, I realized that there was a hidden world beyond that which I could see around me. In searching for this world I suppose I had hoped to find the answers to all of life's questions, and in my mind my search for this hidden world became unified with the quest for Truth itself. This quest ultimately led me to The Fairworld and to the Good Folk. But I soon learned that the Good Folk were not the answer that I sought. They are flawed and imperfect, and unworthy of man's trust. And in learning this, I learned the hardest lesson of life: That there is no one you can rely upon but yourself. Not gods, not fairies, nor even men. And in learning this truth, I found a new purpose in life. The universe offers no salvation save that which men may seize for themselves. And so it became my mission to secure my own salvation by unlocking the greatest secret of all: The secret of immortality.

"There is an answer out there, of that I am sure. The Good Folk are immortal, and they are hardly so far above us. If beings as flawed as they can be immortal, then surely men can snatch the secret from them. Already I have succeeded enough that I have outlived five generations of my family. But the final key is still out there, somewhere. I have spent close to a century trying to track it down, and with each year I grow just a bit closer. But my time is running out. I will not be able to keep extending my life forever, and soon nothing will be enough to forestall the spectre of death. These days I must take every opportunity to strengthen myself that I can, which you must understand is why I could not neglect the Rock of Skora."

Lindsey swallowed. At last she finally felt like she understood the man's behavior, yet somehow, she still didn't know what to make of Horatio Dackery. She couldn't quite bring herself to judge him one way or another. She simply felt sorry for him. "So is that what you wanted me to get for you out of Harin's Vault? That book you took is part of all this, isn't it?"

"Yes. The book I took from the vault is a rare treatise on the subject of immortality, perhaps the most complete there is. I have long known of its existence, but hitherto I had believed it would be forever outside my grasp. Thanks to you, that is no longer the case."

Lindsey bit her lip. "So why are you helping me now? You got what you wanted. What if the Zard catch up with us and kill us all? If all you want is to be immortal, then why are you risking your life for me?"

Dackery shrugged. "If it weren't for you I would never have gotten into Harin's Vault."

"I didn't open the vault for you. You don't owe me anything."

"But perhaps I do."

"I don't want to hear it!"

"I suppose not. Perhaps it was just the decent thing to do nonetheless. Yours is a worthy endeavor. It would be a tragedy if it came to nothing. I would rather not see a young person throw away her life playing some pointless game of the fairies. You have a light of your own, Lindsey Fluger, and I will not stand by and watch that light be extinguished."

Lindsey didn't know what else to say. A part of her was still angry at Dackery, yet at the same time she felt grateful to him, not only for having told her the truth when she demanded it, but also for all his deeds up to now on her behalf, which seemed all the more profound to her now that she knew the truth. In all, she couldn't make up her mind whether she admired the man or pitied him. Lindsey shuffled awkwardly. "Well, I guess we better finish getting settled for the night. Do you think we should...."

Suddenly, Dackery held his finger to his lips. Lindsey looked around. At first, nothing seemed out of the ordinary. Then, she turned around. There, perched high up on the ledge of a burned out wall, was a shabby, soot colored bird. Lindsey's mind flashed back to Dackery's house in Connecticut. She had seen just such a bird there too. Its presence here could mean only one thing. The witches had at last caught up with her.

Out of the corner of her eye, Lindsey saw Dackery digging into the pouch on his belt. As he did so, the bird on the wall spread its wings, which suddenly began to grow as the bird transformed into a man in a dark hooded robe, still crouching on the top of the wall with his arms spread wide and a pair of small, fist sized silver shields gripped in each hand. All of a sudden there was a string of ear splitting pops like overcharged firecrackers as Dackery drew his pistol and began firing at the man on the wall. Almost simultaneously a string of fuzzy images like small shields flashed into existence in front of the man, and immediately winked out again as they absorbed the first barrage of bullets. As Dackery dug frantically into his pouch for a fresh magazine the man twitched one of the shields in his hand as another string of images appeared, this time hurtling straight at Dackery. The man was now twitching both his hands madly as Lindsey and Dackery were subjected to a hailstorm of small ghostly shields, which struck at their bodies like so many flailing fists. At the same time two more men in dark robes appeared from behind concealment and rushed at Dackery. In a moment Dackery was overwhelmed, as one of the men grabbed him from behind while the other was trying to pry the pistol out of his hand. Lindsey scrambled frantically over to where her axe lay on the ground and snatched it from its cloth covering, but was immediately knocked clear off her feet by another wave of ghostly shields pummelling her body.

Suddenly, there was an unearthly shout and for a moment the pummeling on Lindsey's body stopped. She looked up to see Falknir a few feet away, throwing rocks at the man on the wall while yelling all manner of weird curses. The man had twisted his body slightly to confront the new threat, and the ghostly shields were now appearing before him again and absorbing the rocks thrown by Falknir. Lindsey scrambled to her feet and ran over to Dackery, axe in hand. With a shriek, she raised her weapon and swung it into the body of the man holding Dackery from behind. Lindsey continued screaming as again and again she struck the man until at last he fell to the ground, hacked to death. With one arm now free, Dackery pulled a dagger from his belt and furiously stabbed the man in front of him over and over, until he too died.

As Dackery's assailant crumpled to the ground Lindsey heard a shriek of helpless rage come from somewhere behind her. She spun around to see the man perched on the wall suddenly transform back into a bird. With another wail, the bird shot into the air and soared off into the darkening sky. Falknir now jogged over to where Lindsey and Dackery stood. "Well, that wasn't any good at all. I came running as soon as I heard all the noise. Everyone alright? What the devil was that weapon you were using, Dackery?" Bending down, Falknir picked up Dackery's pistol and examined it. "Curious", he muttered. "A pistol of some sort? Breechloading, it would seem. Must use stacked charges or something, to have fired so many shots. No flint or frizzen though. What's this inscription here? *Savage Arms Co, Utica, NY, USA, CAL .32 something something something*....is that a spell of some sort? I shouldn't think so. No poetry to it at all. I say, are you alright?"

Lindsey hadn't been listening. She was speechless, standing frozen with her bloodied axe still clenched in her hands and tears streaming down her face as she stared fixedly at the bloody remains of the man she had just killed. Meanwhile, Dackery had been examining the other corpse. He had just pulled aside the dark hood, and drew in a sharp breath as he did so. "Falknir, come over and have a look at this."

"Eh? My God, that's Kren!"

Lindsey snapped out of her trance. Painfully she drew her eyes away from what she'd done and looked at the other body. Its features were features partially disfigured by a gaping stab wound, but even so she recognized the man's face instantly. It was indeed Kren. Lindsey felt sick. Falknir and Dackery looked at one another.

"This is very bad, Dackery."

"Indeed."

"The witches must know everything by now."

"Or very nearly."

"My God, just think what he could have told them! All of us are in danger now. Casimir, Ibrahim, the monastery. Our whole brotherhood is in dire peril. They must be warned!"

"Not possible, Falknir. They could all be dead by now, anyway. We have no time to lose if we are going to save ourselves."

"You're right. If Kren is here, then his masters can't be far behind. We'd better get moving, it's a race now. Forget the cart and the ox. They're no good to us now."

In a short while the three fugitives had gathered a few meagre belongings. They then fled into the woods as the night fell all around them, while far in the distance the faint sound of Zard trumpets pierced the air. Soon, the woods and highways north of Skora were teeming with the soldiery of witches. The ponderous engines of bureaucracy being what they are (even among witches), it had taken Kren some time to navigate the echelons of the occupied city before he could finally present his case to the dark captains of the witch army. Though Kren was a known traitor, they had believed just enough of his tale that he was dispatched along with two others in pursuit of the feigned gem merchants, who were reported to have left the city by the north gate early that morning. By the time the lone survivor of that expedition had returned with tidings of Kren's death, the captains of the witches had already been in contact with their far away masters and had confirmed his story for themselves. At that point, no efforts were spared. The legions of Zard poured forth from the city, and for days they scoured the land.

The sun was low on the horizon, casting its last rays like the desperate glimmers of a dying candle into the thorny depths of the woodland. Suddenly, the air was broken by the coarse thud of an axe burying itself into the living heart of a growing tree. A pair of Zard soldiers were taking turns chopping into the woody flesh of a stately cedar. A little further away there were more Zard foraging around in the brambles, gathering kindling. Everywhere, the woods were alive with Zard soldiery. Search parties were combing the woods in serried lines, while high above dark birds soared over the treetops, peering into the depths of the forest below. As night fell the search carried on, though at a noticeably slower pace. As the warmth of the sun faded so too did a bit of the Zard's vigour, and as a harsh cold began to settle in the Zard were building great fires. There they gathered, basking in the warmth of the dancing flames as they rested and fed upon the flesh of wild animals.

Elsewhere in the forest, not so very far from the roaring fires of the Zard, there was another encampment. In a miserable hollow beneath the sorrowful canopy of the trees, two men and a girl were huddled together in the cold, with no fire to warm them. For four days Lindsey, Falknir and Dackery had managed to elude the marauding patrols of the Zard. But their time was running out. With each passing day they became more and more hemmed in. Now, they were surrounded on all sides. Lindsey tried to curl up a bit more on the hard ground as she drew her cloak closer about her body against the biting cold. They hadn't dared light a fire for fear that it might be spotted by the relentless Zard hunters, or seen from the air by the shape shifting scouts of the witches. They had been running with almost no rest for days now, and they had only paused for another brief respite before making one final break for freedom past the Zard lines. Falknir and Dackery had tried to be optimistic about it, but they could hardly conceal their own despair. Deep down they knew it was hopeless just as well as she did. Lindsey felt her thoughts begin to wander and amble aimlessly as she drifted into a comfortless sleep. The cold was getting worse, and was starting to seep in through her clothes and bite into her skin.

Suddenly, Lindsey snapped awake. She was definitely a lot colder. And wet. Lindsey pulled herself up, and looked around. Dackery and Falknir were nowhere to be seen. Lindsey was alone. And all around her there was a soft blanket of fresh fallen snow. Lindsey pulled herself to her feet frantically, her breath freezing into mist on the chill wind as she did so. She was definitely not in the same place in which she had fallen asleep. The mournful, Zard infested woods were gone, and she stood now amidst a snow covered hillside. Before her was an enchanted vista, rolling away from her feet beneath the dome of an indigo sky filled with stars like a sea of glittering diadems. She was standing on a gentle ridge overlooking a great valley filled with craggy pinnacles and majestic hills clothed in shadowy evergreens, which plunged deep into hidden gorges obscured by the night. All around her were tall dark conifers, their silhouettes ornamented with a dusting of snow like silver gilding upon their inky limbs, while far in the distance the trees gave way to a sea of spindly white mountains, with great snowy flanks sweeping up to their summits and piercing the sky like a thousand spears. In the very center of the valley there was a lone peak, a single mountain which rose up from the heart of the earth like a giant spire. At the foot of the mountain were the glimmering lights of a great walled city, while perched about halfway up one face, only faintly visible in the night, was what appeared to be a small castle with two great towers, clinging precariously to the precipitous slope of the mountain. Far on the horizon there was a faint orange glow like the last glimmers of sunset, while to one side of the great solitary mountain the moon was just visible, hovering low in the sky in a waning crescent of lustrous gold. Lindsey had the strange feeling that she had seen this vista somewhere before. Or at least something very much like it. Her mind cast back to the last time she had been transported somewhere in her sleep. Yes, that was it! The last time something like this had happened she had come away in possession of a magic coin (which she had promptly lost), which had borne an image of a mountain together with the moon. That's where she'd seen this place before; it had been depicted on the coin which Elred had given her.

"Where are you going?"

The voice had come from behind. Lindsey turned around, half expecting what she would see. There, sitting cross-legged in the snow beside a merry fire, was Elred. Lindsey felt a wave of relief sweep over her. She still didn't know what was going on, but all of a sudden she now felt a surge of hope where once everything had been hopeless. "Elred!"

"Good evening Lindsey. Come, sit down by the fire and warm yourself."

Elred spread his hands and gestured towards the fire, the bells on his wide sleeves tinkling a bit as he did so. At the same time the fire seemed to get just slightly bigger, popping and sparking cheerfully. Lindsey walked over to the fire. Across from Elred she now saw a little rectangular brass stool covered with a blue velvet cushion and pierced with images of stars and crescents. She sat down, grateful to be spared a seat in the wet snow, and huddled close to the hot fire. Elred beamed inscrutably at Lindsey, a benevolent smile playing faintly across his otherwise enigmatic and alien features. "I've been looking for you", the elf said.

"Uh, thanks. That's good to hear. I was kind of hoping you were. How did you find me?"

"Horatio Dackery has an impressive network of contacts. We were confident that you had left Connecticut in Dackery's company, and as such we began looking up his associates for news of his possible whereabouts. As it turns out, they were seeking us out at the same time. This eventually led us back to Camilla Helwig, and from there we had to scour the Marklands in search of you. Dackery is very good at covering his tracks when he wishes to, which no doubt saved your lives even as it hindered us in the process. As it is, in the end it was the Zard themselves who ultimately led us to you. We were certain you were in the area, but had assumed that Dackery would have avoided Skora in the wake of the occupation. But the movement of so many troops over the last few days was impossible to overlook, and it didn't take long for us to learn what they were up to. From there we simply shadowed their search parties and worked ahead of them. And I'm happy to say we got to you first."

"Thanks. I'm grateful for that. Where am I now?"

"Here. Which happens to be quite far away from where you were."

"And what about Dackery and Falknir?"

"They are safe for now. In a short while you will be re-joining them, and then my associates will escort you to Linster. That is, if you still intend to go there."

"I do."

"Excellent!"

"What about Hae-jin and the others? Are they alright? What happened to them?"

"They are well. They are in Linster at present with the Bird."

Lindsey felt a lump appear in her throat. She hadn't thought about the Bird in days, but she was still angry at him about what happened at Harin's Vault. "Yeah. I think I'm going to have a talk with the Bird next time I see him. I don't suppose you ever found out why he abandoned me back there at Harin's Vault?"

"I think it would be best if you asked the Bird himself about that the next time you see him."

"I figured you'd say something like that. Are we done here?"

"If you wish. You have chosen a difficult path, Lindsey. A difficult path, and a dangerous one. My brethren and I are grateful for your deeds thus far, but there remains only so much I can do to protect you should you choose to proceed further. But for the moment, the immediate danger has passed."

Lindsey jerked, feeling suddenly off balance, as if she had taken a gentle fall. Elred was gone. The fire was gone. Lindsey was lying in the same dank hollow in which she had gone to sleep before. Dackery and Falknir were crouched tensely beside her, swords drawn as they peered out into the darkness of the woods. Lindsey rolled onto her knees, noting vacantly as she did so that her shoes and hose were still wet and cold, and as she squatted beside her fellows a few tiny bits of clinging snow fell away from her clothing. There were lights out in the woods. Five, maybe six of them. And as Linsey watched, she could just make out the shape of humanoid figures making their way towards them through the trees. Lindsey clamoured to her feet. As she did so Dackery and Falknir both started with surprise, and one of them hissed a vain warning to stay back, but Lindsey ignored them as she jogged over to the newcomers.

There were three of them, carrying lanterns bearing celestial designs wrought in elaborate piercework. They were dressed in loose fur lined tunics of dark blue velvet which were richly embroidered with images of stars, and buckled at their waists were cross-hilted swords bearing the image of the crescent moon set within their pommels. Their feet were shod in tall, fur lined boots, and about their shoulders were great cloaks of deep midnight blue. Of the three, two were men, one of whom was blonde and bearded while the other was dark haired and clean shaven. The third was a woman, slight of build and only a bit taller than Lindsey herself. And she was not precisely human. Her skin was the color of fine ivory, her ears were pointed and her eyes were a bright violet color. In some respects she resembled a Drixi, though being much shorter in height. Her features were likewise much softer and far more human, and her hair was jet black. And as Lindsey approached, she observed a silver badge affixed to the woman's cloak, which bore the image of a lone mountain arrayed beneath the crescent moon. From behind her there came a scrambling and puffing sound, and in a moment Falknir was standing beside her, panting slightly. "Oh my sainted aunt", he breathed, "Sauvlanders! What in the name of Arthur's Beard are the likes of them doing here?"

The woman cocked a black eyebrow in his direction. "My brethren and I are here to take you to Linster", she said simply.

"Ah? That's jolly considerate of you. Though I'll admit I'm a bit bewildered. The Sauvlands are thousands of leagues from here. You've come a dreadfully long way just to pick up a few vagrants. What on earth brought you here?"

"I think I know", Lindsey interjected, "Elred sent you, didn't he?"

The woman nodded. Falknir seemed to have run out of things to say for the moment, but that was alright, as it was plain that they needed to get going as soon as possible. The woods were still teeming with Zard, and Lindsey had no desire to put the Sauvlanders in any danger. She was about to ask how they planned to proceed when suddenly she caught her breath as three more blue-clad men stepped out of the woods, leading with them six extraordinary horses. They were great majestic creatures with coats of pure white or silvery grey, with tremendous wings of matching plumage folded against their sides. Without speaking further, the Sauvlanders mounted their steeds, taking their passengers with them in tandem.

Lindsey found herself horsed with the blonde haired bearded man. Of the six Sauvlanders, he was the only one who was unshaven and the only one with fair hair. And upon closer inspection, Lindsey realized that unlike the others this man was apparently human, with rounded ears and grey eyes. She felt a little giddy as he caught her up and gently eased her into the saddle before him, and there was an awkward but not entirely unpleasant moment when he wrapped his arm firmly around her waist and held her tightly against his body. It was going to be a cozy ride, that was for sure, but Lindsey was past caring and even laughed a little at herself as she decided that she could probably endure it. His clothes had a smoky, comfortable sort of smell to them, and his grip on her body was firm but not really any more personal than it needed to be. Besides, she had a feeling that under the circumstances she would prefer to have a very secure seat indeed. For abruptly, the Sauvlander spurred his horse, and the creature reared and spread its great wings. With a tremendous sweep of its wings it leapt into the air and soared into the starry night sky.

29

"The Lady Edith"

Not far from the borders of Linster, there was a tree. There was nothing at all interesting or important about it, save that on one of its branches there was perched a Hawk. There was wasn't anything especially important about the Hawk either, save that there weren't many of his kind in that particular land. Virtually all the wild things around the countryside were but simple creatures. The wightbeasts themselves made their abode in far more distant and lonely places forsaken by men, for they preferred to keep nothing in common with humans.

The sun was getting low in the sky now, and the Hawk was peering out into the meadows. He had been watching for signs of small, delectable creatures suitable for fine dining, when abruptly a flicker of movement from an entirely different direction caught his eye. With a snap he turned his gaze skyward, and there beheld the most extraordinary sight. Six winged horses, just visible as they sailed high in the sky, headed northward towards Linster. In a few moments they were out of sight, and the Hawk shook his head to himself as he returned his attention to his previous task. Peculiar things were afoot these days, that was for certain. It seemed that all manner of noisome wights were taking to the air these days, all apparently headed to either Linster or

Tollardy, or one of the other nearby kingdoms up north. A fortnight ago there had been practically a whole army of them mounted on great winged reptiles. And before that there had been those queer folk riding what looked for all the world like a rug. All very irregular. And disturbing. If things continued in this way, the solitary Hawk thought to himself, he might be well advised to move to a less crowded place. What's this? A mole? Rather small perhaps, but it would do. In a flash, the Hawk shot away from his perch and dived to the ground in pursuit of his supper.

Far away, the six winged horses soared onward under the golden light of the setting sun. For two days and a night Lindsey had been traveling in the company of her erstwhile rescuers, pausing only briefly to rest and refresh themselves and their winged horses. During that time, the Sauvlanders hardly ever spoke, and Lindsey never even learned any of their names. As night fell on the second day the Sauvlanders had made only a very short pause before pressing on into the night, for they were now nearly upon the marches of Linster, and they wished to reach their destination before dawn so as to enter the country under the cover of darkness. As the faint glimmers of orange light cut across the horizon, the Sauvlanders made an abrupt turn and began to spiral downwards towards the gloom of the earth below.

They alighted in a small yard adjacent to a darkened farmhouse. Those saddled with passengers remained aloft at first, while the three remaining horsemen landed ahead of the others to secure the farmyard. From above Lindsey watched as they made their descent. They circled the yard twice, making a measured inspection of the premises, and then landed, rolling off their horses lightly and drawing their swords as they did so. After taking another quick look around the yard on foot they knocked on the door. A ray of light appeared as the door was opened, and a moment later the men on the ground signaled to their comrades above, and in another moment Lindsey herself joined them on the ground, along with the others.

Silhouetted in the door of the farmhouse was a woman. She and the Sauvlandic woman were speaking together in hushed tones, and a moment later Lindsey was called over along with Dackery and Falknir. After a few more muted words, the Sauvlanders returned to their horses and Lindsey and Dackery were ushered into the house. As Lindsey stepped through the door she took a last look into the yard, just in time to see the last Sauvlandic horsemen spur his steed into the sky and disappear against the darkness.

The interior of the farmhouse was comfortable, if rather spartan. A large roaring fire on end filled the place with an orange light, and Lindsey now looked briefly to her comrades. Dackery appeared somewhat the worse for wear, which was understandable for a man of his size who has been obliged to share a saddle with another for many long hours. Falknir, however, was blithely glib as usual. "Taciturn folk, those Sauvlanders", he said. "Remarkable, really. Up to now I had never met one, and I wasn't even sure they existed."

"But who are they?"

"That's the sticky question, really. Stuff of legends, those folk. Legends and rumors. Supposedly they come from a mountainous country somewhere in the Hinterlands. It is believed that the Sauvlanders have some kind of peculiar relationship with the Good Folk, but the details are all terribly murky, and the stories about them are often contradictory."

"Apparently they're good enough friends that they gave us a ride when Elred asked them to."

Lindsey now turned her attention to their new host. The woman had taken a seat in a high backed chair. Behind her stood a grizzled looking man dressed in farmer's clothes, yet his bearing was oddly stiff and refined, more like that of a nobleman's servant or bodyguard than that of a peasant. The woman now beckoned silently, and Lindsey stepped over and took a seat on a stool beside the fire across from her hostess.

The woman was extraordinarily good looking, daintily built with large dark eyes and finely chiseled, almost exotic features, set off by dark, silky hair largely hidden beneath a twin lobed hat shaped vaguely like a pair of recurved horns. She wore a long gown of emerald green satin which was fitted tightly about her body, while leaving her neck and shoulders bare. Her skin fairly glowed under the light of the fire as she draped her delicate limbs languidly over the arms of the chair. Lindsey was left with a rather uncomfortable sensation that she had just been thrown into a new and rather exalted level of society. Linsey gulped. "Um…hi. My name is Lindsey Fluger", she said.

The woman gave a slight, almost indulgent nod in acknowledgement. "So I have been told", she replied. "Your arrival has been long expected."

"Uh huh? I guess that's nice to hear. And you are?"

"My name is Edith."

"Okay. Nice to meet you, Edith. Do you by any chance know a woman named Joan Greyflower?"

"I am aware that there is a peasant woman by that name, yes."

"Um..okay. Do you also know a guy named Moon Hae-jin?"

"If you are referring to the outlaw Robin Goodfellow, then yes I am aware of his exploits."

"*Robin Goodfellow*? That's a new one. Are you sure we're talking about the same person here? Do you know where he is?"

"At the moment, the Zhongling and his rebels are fortified in the town of Elmstead, which they occupied some days ago. Thus far His Majesty has been unable to mount a proper response to the insurrection, and Robin Goodfellow has remained unchecked. But your presence here changes everything. It is now time to escalate matters."

"Now just hang on a second here. I am friends with Joan and Hae-jin. I have no idea who you are, or how you fit into all of this. How do I even know we're on the same side?"

The woman Edith pursed her delicate lips. "Robin Goodfellow and the woman Joan each have a particular role to play in this little drama, just as do you. And so in turn do I. Your task right now is to break the Curse of Gurth. Joan Greyflower's task was to exploit her position among the peasants so that Robin Goodfellow's rebellion would ensure that Gurth is driven out of Linster after the curse is broken. My task is to exert my own particular influence elsewhere towards the same end, and to ensure that this enterprise will carry on nonetheless should Robin Goodfellow fail. Does that answer your questions?"

"Uh, maybe. Just one more question, does the Bird know about you?"

"Up to now my part in this matter has been withheld from the others involved, including the Bird. As they say, it doesn't pay to put all one's eggs in one basket. After the curse is broken that will again remain unchanged. Your discretion in this regard will be expected, of course."

"You mean you don't want me to tell the others about you?"

"Precisely."

"Great. The Good Folk sure do like secrets, don't they?"

"The situation is far from secure. Even now, things could still fall apart at any moment. You and your associates will remain here tonight under the protection of my people. In the morning, you will be taken to the city of Larchester. You will then be removed to a place which I have prepared for you, where you will remain in hiding until the appropriate time. There are developments underway inside that city which will serve our purposes ideally, if properly exploited. The political situation is now in crisis. It will only take a few more days before it comes to the boiling point. When that happens, I will send for you."

The woman Edith now arose, her skirts draping advantageously about her diminutive shape as she moved with a practiced grace. "I must now depart. No doubt we shall speak again in due course." With another perfunctory half-nod, the woman withdrew from the farmhouse with no further comment.

As the night wore on a thick blanket of clouds rolled across the sky, and the following day the sun was obscured beneath a dreary grey curtain. Small raindrops fell now and then, giving only a mockery of sustenance to thirsty fields, and splashing coldly on the faces of men and women hurrying about their business deep within the dense streets of the great city of Larchester. All around there was a tense sort of atmosphere. It had been many days since news had come that the Earl of Wickhowe had turned rebel and joined with the outlaw Robin Goodfellow, bringing with him a large coalition of the nobility which was now fortified in the town of Elmstead frighteningly nearby. And now the forces of the King himself had arrived, and made camp on the opposite side of the city and joined his forces with those of Gurth. While prevailing public opinion favored loyalty to the monarchy, many were afraid that the King was coming under the influence of Gurth, and in time all vestiges of liberty would be annihilated, whether it be consumed by the torch of rebel looters or crushed by the iron gauntlet of the witch.

Still, life went on as best it could. Much as it was far away in the Duchy of Skora, so too in Larchester did the indefatigable forces of commerce press ahead undaunted. At the gates of the city, the guards had just stopped a pair of men leading a ox drawn cart which sagged under the weight of several large barrels, great voluminous casks each large enough to carry a whole pig or two. "Ho there, fellow", one of the guards said. "What have we here today?"

"Beer", one of the wagonmen replied. "A gift to the cathedral cloister from the Lady Edith."

"Again?"

"Aye. The Lady Edith has taken a vow to bequeath the nuns five barrels of ale every week for a year, so that she may be blessed with a betrothal by next Pentecost."

"Ha! Fine shopkeepers, those nuns. From what I've heard, I doubt the Lady Edith needs any help snaring a husband. The nuns will hardly have to pray at all. Would that the rest of us could be so profitably employed. Pass on through!"

With a lurch the cart moved over the knobbly cobbles into the city, making its way awkwardly through the crowded streets to the cathedral, where it turned into a small side yard attached to the cloister. The men knocked on the door, and in a few moments a woman in clerical habit emerged. After a brief conversation the men began unloading the cart and ferrying the ponderous barrels one by one into the building. When they were finished, they took their payment and departed.

Inside the gloom of the convent, a group of nuns were now gathered around the barrels, whispering to one another. One of them then knocked sharply on the surface of one of the barrels. She paused and listened for a moment, and then knocked on another. And this time, something inside knocked back. The nuns burst out in another round of animated whispers and began flitting around the room, gathering all manner of superfluous tools, while the one who had done the knocking had already seized a stout iron bar and was assertively prying the lid of the barrel off. In a moment the lid was gone, and as the nuns gently tipped over the barrel Lindsey rolled out onto the convent floor.

Lindsey had seen plenty of movies in her time where people got packed into barrels in order to be smuggled in and out of various places. But until now she had never quite appreciated what a uniquely hideous experience the whole thing really was. She gasped for air as she lay on the stone floor, barely conscious after her ordeal and hardly aware of the gaggle of cooing nuns who were now fussing over her. In a few moments the other barrels were opened as well, and Dackery and

Falknir were deposited on the floor beside Lindsey in equally poor condition. As Lindsey's mind slowly came back into focus she found herself lying on a bench, her head propped up on a temporary cushion and her view of the room obscured by a round, jolly face surrounded by a wimple.

"Gah!", Lindsey blurted. "Where the hell..I mean where the heck am I?"

The nun patted her on the cheek with a soft, plump hand. "There there, dearie, you've had quite a time I'm sure. Just take a wee rest for now. Here, have some warm beer."

Bit by bit Lindsey felt life returning to her cramped limbs. Not long afterward she was taken to the officer of the mother superior. For the time being, Lindsey, Dackery and Falknir were to be housed in the convent. Separately, of course. In point of fact, in a spirit of strict propriety the two men were put up together in a tiny chamber about as far away from quarters of the women as possible, whereas Lindsey was lodged together with the nuns. And there the three of them remained, secreted within the veil of the cloister, quite literally at the backdoor of Larchester Cathedral itself.

The days passed wearily, with many long hours of tedium. Lindsey at least had the company of the nuns, and could occupy some of her time helping out with odd jobs around the convent. Dackery and Falknir were worse off, being largely restricted to a few rooms set apart from those frequented by the women. At least they had access to the nuns' copious supply of fine beer with which to console themselves. All the while they waited for word from the Lady Edith, or The Bird, or perhaps even Elred himself. But none came. Finally, one night as Lindsey lay quietly in her chamber, she was awakened by a soft, persistent knock at the door. Outside was one of the nuns, one with whom Lindsey had become friends with over the last few days. A few hushed words later, and Lindsey was ushered to the office of the mother superior. Then at last, Lindsey was informed that the time to act was upon them.

Hae-jin, who up to now had been leading a rebellion under the name of Robin Goodfellow, was about to surrender himself to the king. At noon the following day he would present himself at the city gates, after which he would be brought to the cathedral and handed over to the king in the presence of the city council, the Bishop, and as many of the prominent personages of the kingdom as could be gathered. This was to be Lindsey's moment to break the curse. The medallion which she had taken so many weeks ago from Harin's Vault was to be publically delivered to the cathedral and set upon the high altar, with the most august officers of the land as witnesses, including the king himself. Yet even at this juncture, they were taking no chances. With Gurth's agents spread throughout the city, Lindsey was to proceed in secret until the last possible moment. As high noon approached, Lindsey, Dackery and Falknir were taken together through the winding corridors of the cloister to the Cathedral itself. A small side door was the only access point, which led to a secluded portion of the building which was virtually an extension of the cloister itself, where the nuns were accustomed to attend high mass while still remaining sequestered from the rest of the outside world. Again, the only passage to the rest of the building was a small janitor's door, through which Lindsey and her comrades were ushered.

Lindsey's heart raced as she crept into the vaulted aisles. Packing the nave was a great multitude, their backs to her as they faced inward towards the transept, peering and whispering to one another, while from far within chancel the King was now speaking. Lindsey had spent the morning with Dackery and Falknir planning their next move, which they were now about to put into action. Dackery and Falknir began pushing their way forward into the crowd, preparing to create a suitable distraction while Lindsey made her way to the altar. Lindsey was on her own now, creeping through the aisles as sonorous voices echoed across the cold stone arches. Lindsey's hand quivered as she stole inside her clothes and retrieved the medallion from around her neck. This was it. Everything depended on her now.

There ahead of her now were the backs of a lot of dressed up people, nobles maybe, while over their heads Lindsey could just make out the great square block of the altar itself. She crept closer over the slates of the floor, every limb shaking now. Suddenly, there was a rustle of cloth, and Lindsey felt a soft hand grab her by the shoulder. Out of the corner of her eye she could just make out the shimmer of a green satin dress as a pair lips pressed close to her ear. "Go. Right now, go right now!"

Lindsey needed no further encouragement. She bolted forward, ducking below the elbows of the crowd and weaving between the nobles. Her heart was pumping now, the world around her whirled with confusion as she ran madly through the burgeoning pandemonium. There, there were the steps to the altar. She dodged back and forth as people tried to grab at her as she scrambled up the steps. Suddenly the visage of a Zard rose up unexpectedly before her as one of the terrible reptiles had broken off from the assembly to intercept her. She swerved aside and covered the last steps to the altar, clenching the medallion in her hand. There, she'd reached the top! With a yelp, she opened her hand and slammed the medallion onto the face of the altar beneath her palm.

With a flash, the world around her fell silent as it was filled with a golden light, the only noise being a faint sound like gentle thunder in the distance. In a moment the levels of light returned to normal. Lindsey was standing beside the altar, one corner of which had been shorn clear off and was now lying on the floor. Yet the medallion was still resting on the broken corner even as it lay cockeyed on the floor, apparently stuck to the surface. As she looked closer, it appeared that the medallion had been somehow fused with the marble. There was also a horrible stinging sensation in her hand, and as Lindsey looked at it she saw a bright red welt on her palm which was shaped like an outline of the medallion. The image was quickly fading away even as she looked at it, and in a moment it had disappeared completely, leaving behind only a nasty sting like a bad burn.

Lindsey took a deep breath, and looked around as she massaged her hand. Scattered absurdly across the floor were all manner of exalted persons in varying degrees of shock. It was over. After all this time, after coming all this way, she'd finally done it. "Well, there's your stinking curse taken care of", she said. "Now what are you going to do about it?" The comment was more or less rhetorical, but Lindsey felt a sense of satisfaction nonetheless as she addressed it to no one in particular.

Suddenly, there was a commotion far down in the nave of the cathedral. From her vantage point at the altar Lindsey could see clear down the center of the church, and hurtling through the great doors now was a great golden Bird. The resplendent creature soared over the heads of the assembled crowd, and as it did so the Bird cried out in an unnaturally amplified voice. "Men of Linster! People of Arthur and scions of Albion, hear these words! The Curse of Gurth is broken! The yoke of the oppressor is lifted, the shackles of black magic are sundered! Linster is free from the bonds of witchcraft! Rally now to the side of your king, and drive the witches from this land! Long live the king!"

The cry reverberated back and forth between the stately columns of the great cathedral. Down below, unseen among the feet of the people, a small Fox darted through the crowd, carrying the cry to every corner of the building. Bartholomew had been running discreetly around the city for days now, spreading word of the surrender of Robin Goodfellow, building excitement and anticipation for the coming events to ensure that as big a crowd as possible would be present to receive a special message when the time came. Up to now the exact nature of this message had been withheld from him; Hae-jin had simply promised that when the time came it would be obvious, and that Bartholomew was to spread it as far as possible. And so it proved to be, and the Fox now darted cheerfully and invisibly through the crowded cathedral and then out into the street, spreading the news throughout the city and rallying the people to the cause of the king and Robin Goodfellow.

Hae-jin had hauled himself to his feet, and with his hands still shackled he sprinted up the steps of the altar to Lindsey's side. He didn't actually hug her. His hands were still cuffed together, and besides, Hae-jin wasn't the hugging sort anyway. But the look on his face as he met Lindsey's eye was just as good. "We meet again, Lindsey Ann Fluger."

"Yep, sure thing, Moon Hae-jin. Or should I say Robin Goodfellow? I guess you've been kind of busy lately."

Hae-jin shrugged. "As have you. I am glad that we have both survived to see one another again."

"Yeah, me too."

Down in the crowd, Lindsey saw a bearded, red headed man who she could only guess was the king. Guards and courtiers were fussing all around him, and mingling in the king's party Lindsey spotted a woman in a green satin dress. It was Edith. She smiled slightly as she caught Lindsey's eye, but said not a word otherwise. As Lindsey watched, Edith had accosted one of the king's soldiers, and pointed to Hae-jin and the others as she spoke to him. With an obedient nod, the man at arms produced a set of keys and set about unshackling prisoners. Cocking an eye at Hae-jin, Lindsey nudged him by the elbow and the two of them descended the steps of the altar to rejoin their friends. No sooner was the muzzle removed from Ursilda's lips did the great Bear begin to speak. "Well, here you are at last, Evecub. You took long enough getting here. That silly Bird must have mislaid you quite badly indeed."

Joan wasn't so reserved as Hae-jin was. The moment her arms were free she flung them around Lindsey, blubbering tearfully in the process, while to one side the Wogs were already arguing over whether a hundred and twenty silver marks per day could be divided evenly by three.

The entire cathedral was now alive with voices. The Bird was still making the rounds over the heads of the people, but already everyone was babbling excitedly to one another. Dackery and Falknir had finally pushed their way through the crowd and made it to the chancel where Lindsey was still engaged. At the nearest opportunity, Falknir grabbed Lindsey by the elbow and took her aside for a moment. Even after all these weeks of traveling, Lindsey still didn't feel like she quite knew the man properly, and there was a peculiar gleam in his eyes as he spoke to her. "Well done, my friend!", he said. "You have achieved something truly great this day. What you've begun here today will have consequences, and one day we'll take those consequences right up to the witch's doorstep." Lindsey was about to ask Falknir what on earth he meant by all that, but all of a sudden there was a commotion in the crowd, and the two of them were sucked back into the action again.

It seemed that Gurth had disappeared. Up until now Lindsey had had no idea that her nemesis had been present in the cathedral at all, and was more than a little bit shaken by the revelation. As it was, no one had laid eyes on him since the moment the curse had been broken. His servants and officers had fled the building, but of Gurth himself nothing was known. It was as if he had disappeared into oblivion.

Meanwhile, in the city of Larchester things were moving quickly. Word of the marvel which had occurred inside the cathedral spread through the city like wildfire, carried in no small part by the deft efforts of Bartholomew Fox-Goodburrow. Vague, contradictory tales were told of how the mysterious amulet had appeared in the cathedral and how the altar had been broken. Some said the Bird had done it, while others said that an angel had appeared in a flash of light and vanished immediately after the miracle was complete, while still others who had been closer to the scene said that the angel had come in the guise of a young boy. Either way, the name of Lindsey Fluger remained unuttered and unknown. But all through the streets the people were celebrating and toasting the health of both Robin Goodfellow and the king. Never before had William of Bradlaw been so popular, and for the moment the only remaining demand of the people was a royal pardon for Robin Goodfellow and his comrades. This the king granted, and more. For despite the jubilation of the people, the king and his officers were wary. Gurth was still unaccounted for, and his army was still encamped not far from the city. In the choir of Larchester cathedral, the king had gathered with his captains. The Bishop likewise was there and so too were others, including a woman in a green satin dress who had somehow slipped in, whispering here and there to men of exalted status. In such council the king was prevailed upon to forge an alliance with Robin Goodfellow, and later that very afternoon Hae-jin was brought before the king at the door of the cathedral before a large crowd. There, on the steps of Larchester Cathedral, Hae-jin swore the appropriate oaths of fealty to William of Bradlaw, and as the crowd cheered Hae-jin was knighted as Sir Robin Greyflower.

As the sun was setting, a great feast had been proclaimed. All the city was breaking out in celebration, and in the great hall of Larchester Castle the king sat at banquet, with Sir Robin Greyflower seated at his right hand. The night was not far gone when a messenger arrived. A lone rider, coming from the city of Elmstead and begging an audience with Robin Goodfellow. Hae-jin was called away from the table, and was led to a small side room. Standing in the flicking candle light and looking as though he had seen a ghost, was Will Little. Something was wrong, and Hae-jin had a sudden feeling that he knew what it was. "Little!", Hae-jin cried. "What brings you to the city? What is wrong?"

"Sire, I bring terrible news", the yeoman said. "The Earl of Wickhowe has broken off his alliance with you, and has taken most of the other nobles with him. They've broken camp already, and are marching now towards Beckby. And sire, they're joining forces with Gurth!"

30

"A New Name"

It was nearing midnight. A dark, moonless night had swallowed the land like a choking miasma. Ploughing through the dreary murk of the darkness, three horsemen rode fast for Elmstead, heedless of whatever hazards might lurk invisibly in the darkness along their path. Up ahead, a few bright specks were just visible in the gloom. There were lights in the town of Elmstead. Apparently the three horsemen were not the only ones who were awake at this unwonted hour. The whole town, it seemed, was alive with revelry. In a short while the riders had approached the gates, and were passed through. They avoided the streets full of merrymakers, and instead made their way around the perimeter to the other side of town where Wickhowe's army had previously made camp.

Hae-jin now rode through the empty encampment of the nobles. Beside him were the Earl of Donnock and Will Little, who bore a lantern with him which cast a few amber rays upon an oppressive scene which was only faintly visible in the darkness. Where a day ago there had been a bustling tent city filled with redoubtable soldiery, there was now only detritus and bare ground, beaten and denuded with the passage of so many feet. The effect of the desolation was magnified in the obscurity of the darkness. For, despite the apparent emptiness of the place, of the nearly four thousand soldiers who had previously been quartered there, almost a fifth still remained. Here and there a few isolated shelters loomed into view in the darkness as Hae-jin passed by. And up ahead, there was a bright orange triangular glow from a fire within one of the great tents. As Hae-jin and Little approached they were met by a pair of deferential squires, who took change of their mounts and bade them enter. Inside, seated alone on a simple folding chair, was the Earl of Swinstoke. Of Wickhowe's followers, only Swinstoke had remained behind. Some eight hundred men from both his own retinue and that of Donnock's were all that remained of the once mighty host which had made their lot with Robin Goodfellow.

"Damndest bit of treachery as I ever saw", the earl grumbled loudly. "You should have heard the man! No sooner had you departed for Larchester did Wickhowe start spreading his poison. He said that you had given up, that you were a broken reed and had betrayed the cause (which, to be fair, seemed true enough at the time), that we had all made a mistake in joining forces with you and that we should leave you to your fate and carry on ourselves. No offense, mind you, but the old liar *was* right about that part, or so it appeared under the circumstances. I mean, we hadn't any notion you were going to break the curse and all. Damned silly of you not to have told anyone, look at all the trouble it caused! You could have at least trusted me, I wouldn't have uttered a word to anyone, not a word! Anyway, once we heard the news about the curse and all Wickhowe changed his tune. Or rather, he adjusted the lyrics slightly, if you know what I mean. He said that you had compounded your betrayal by joining forces with the king, and would soon be turning on us. I for one said he was being an ass and that we should seize this chance to drive out Gurth once and for all. But Wickhowe, he's a slippery one. Now that I think about it, I don't think he ever gave a damned fig about getting rid of Gurth. It was always about the king. Bradlaw is weak, and Wickhowe is ambitious. I shouldn't wonder that Wickhowe hopes to depose the king and replace him with one of Bradlaw's miserable relatives, so that Wickhowe himself can run the show from behind the scenes as Lord Protector of the realm, or some such. It's just the sort of thing he would do, the wretched blighter! Anyway, Wickhowe insisted that our only option left was to join forces with Gurth. Can you believe it! Wickhowe said that a temporary alliance with Gurth was the only way we could still hold out against Bradlaw's tyranny. Only by getting rid of Bradlaw could we finally put an end to all the corruption and the taxes and cast off the oppression of the Tollards, after which we would be free to deal with Gurth as we wished. Again, I told him he was an ass, but he didn't listen. And neither did any of the others."

From outside there was a rustle, and Hae-jin turned to see the flap of the tent be cast aside and Rob Sykes stepped in. "Hae-jin! Er, should I say M'lord?"

"No worries, my friend. How are things in the town?"

"Surprisingly good, actually. The peasants are in high spirits. The good news from Larchester was well received. You and the king couldn't be more popular. Nobody seems to realize the implications of Wickhowe's betrayal...not yet anyway. I warrant that'll change when it comes time to fight. With Wickhowe's and Gurth's forces combined, man for man I reckon we're almost evenly matched now."

"Except that a seventh of our side is made up of peasants, while Gurth's forces are all proper soldiers (including the flying cavalry of the Drixi, no less). And though the curse may be broken, Gurth is still a powerful sorcerer in his own right, with all manner of black magic at his command."

Sykes uttered a low whistle. "Lord, I hadn't thought of that."

"We'd both better start thinking hard, my friend. Gurth is against the wall now. The hyena is at bay, and at bay he will fight."

While Hae-jin and his captains conferred anxiously in the forlorn tents of Elmstead, in the great city of Larchester the celebration continued unabated. The usual nightly curfew had been suspended, and the revelries continued far into the night. Deep in the great hall of Larchester Castle, the king's feast carried on unabated, with much merriment and abandon. Lords and burghers toasted one another's good fortune, while heavily intoxicated Wogs told lewd jokes and sang ribald songs as they danced on tables alongside the jesters before the bemused (and equally intoxicated) nobles.

For her own part, Lindsey did not partake much in the revelries and feasting. She'd endured a fair bit of privation during her long journey through the Marklands, but over the last week she'd had plenty of opportunity to eat her fill under the gentle hospitality of the nuns. Rather, having spent weeks traveling alone with two men, what Lindsey craved most was conversation with a female confidant, and she'd spent long hours talking with Joan about everything that had happened since their separation at Harin's Vault so long ago. Even so, as the night waned on Lindsey grew weary even of talking, and at length she retired to the apartments which had been set aside for her. Her accomodations were extremely comfortable, if not particularly exalted. She had a whole room to herself, even if it was a tiny one, with its own fireplace and a deep, warm bed best of all. The mattress appeared to be stuffed with straw, but the linens were soft and the pillow itself was filled with downy feathers. It seemed that people in Linster didn't wear very much to bed during the warmer months of the year, but for her own part Lindsey was quite content to curl up in a somewhat baggy men's undertunic that was just long enough to do the job. She had just slipped her legs under the covers and was leaning over to blow out the candle at her bedside when suddenly she recoiled away with a squeak. There beneath the candle, shrunk down to the size of a large mouse and sitting nonchalantly on the ring of the candlestick, was Elred. "Good evening, Lindsey. Just going to bed?"

Lindsey gathered the bedclothes around herself a bit as she recovered from the surprise. Now she leaned back against the pillows and looked bemusedly at the diminutive intruder. "Hello Elred. You've gotten smaller since I last saw you. What the heck are you doing in my bedroom?" Elred just sat there with his arms folded, that perpetual smile still plastered on his face. "I thought it would be nice if we had a chat, especially after this morning. You broke the Curse of Gurth most admirably."

"Thanks. Seen the Bird lately? I haven't had a chance to talk to him yet. I don't suppose he's been avoiding me or something?"

"Oh, I'll make sure he speaks to you before you leave. As it is, you have my most sincere thanks. You have done a great and worthy deed in the service of the people of Linster. I apologize that this little excursion got so far out of hand, but now that it's all been sorted out I'm very glad to inform you that your part in this matter is at last finished. Tomorrow I will be taking you home to your own world."

Lindsey felt taken aback. She hadn't thought about going home for weeks. "Um, yeah. Thanks. About that, though. I think I want to stay here for a while longer. There's a lot still going on, and Hae-jin and Joan are still going to need help."

Suddenly, the look on Elred's tiny face became more serious. "There is no need for you to remain here. Your part in this is fulfilled, there is no reason for you to be involved in the coming conflict."

Lindsey bit her lip. "I don't know what you people think you're doing screwing around with other people's lives, but if Hae-jin and the others are staying, then so am I."

"Your role in Linster is completed. Hae-jin's role in Linster is not, and will continue for some while yet. This is what he agreed to in the beginning. Hae-jin knew what he was getting into (more or less), and he knew the risks he would be facing. He is a soldier. You are not."

"I don't care. I'm going to see this through, Elred."

The elf was silent for a moment. "Well", the elf said at length. "I suppose I could keep harangueing you, but I perceive that your mind is already made up."

Elred glanced over to a darkened corner of the room, and beckoned with his hand. From its resting place in the corner, Lindsey's axe now shot lightly through the air. With a start Lindsey jerked out of the way even as the weapon abruptly slowed and fluttered down weightlessly onto the bed beside her. Elred now hopped off his perch on the candlestick and leaping onto the bed he began to walk along the length of the axe's handle, peering deep down into the grain of the dark bone until he reached the violet steel of the axehead. "Vorpal is a curious thing, Lindsey. It has a certain memory to it. This particular weapon dates from the age of the great witch wars almost two thousand years ago. The original owner was probably one the great warriors of that time. Given that it wound up with the Drixi, I suspect he had seen many great and terrible things before having come to a rather unfortunate end. No doubt those experiences have left their impression upon this weapon, and remain within it still. There are indeed some vorpal objects which are specifically designed to impart the experiences and instincts of their past owners on to their present possessors. This axe does not appear to be one of them. However, I think I can perhaps force the matter. I'm sure what we require is already there, it only needs drawing out." Elred sat down cross legged on the metal, and pressed his hands into the cold steel as he concentrated. "Yes. Yes, there it is. Are you quite sure you want to go through with this, Lindsey?"

"Um, I'm not sure what you mean."

"If you are going to remain now in Linster alongside your friends, then you will be exposed to great danger. You will see things which no eye should ever need to see, and you must do things which no hand should ever need to do. You do not yet have what it takes to endure such things. Without my help, you will surely be struck down. I can protect you from all of that simply by taking you home now. But if you truly wish to remain, then this is the next best thing I can do for you. But you must choose now."

Lindsey took a deep breath. She couldn't say she entirely trusted the Good Folk's shenanigans, or approved of the way they went about things. But thus far Elred had been faithful to her. If he said she was going to be in danger, she had no reason to suppose he was wrong. Linsey unfolded herself from the bedsheets and knelt on the mattress beside the axe. "I've already made up my mind, Elred", she said. "Just show me what I'm supposed to do."

Elred sighed. "Very well", he said. "Place your right hand...you are right handed?...right, place your right hand on the steel."

Lindsey laid her hand on the icy metal. The room seemed terribly quiet now. The axe was beginning to feel slightly warmer, even as Lindsey herself felt an unpleasant chill creeping up her spine. Forming in her mind now was the impression of a man. Not an image, but rather an idea of a person, a specific human being. There was a strange sort of intimacy to it, almost as if she were physically touching him. Then abruptly, Lindsey had a feeling like that of a sudden realization, as though a puzzle she didn't know existed had just come together before her eyes. The axe resting against the skin of her palm was more than just an exotic object to her now. It was a familiar tool. She felt as though she knew exactly how it should be handled, how it should move, and how with just the right incantations in mind she could make it do all manner of things beyond that of any ordinary weapon. As she pressed her palm harder into the metal she felt years of one man's experience and instincts filling her mind and spreading out through her body into her limbs and muscles. Then suddenly, with a jolt through her stomach, Lindsey came to a horrible, nightmarish realization. She was now a killer.

Wave upon wave of misery swept over her, as the shadowy memories of another person's battles burned into her mind. Pain, suffering, and death, as though she had seen it all herself, and done it all with her own hands. Worst of all, amidst the flood of memories she realized that she herself had already become a killer long ago. Far away in the lands of the Drixi, now sealed within Harin's vault, was the withered body of a Zard which she had struck down with this very axe. And nearer still in the woods of Skora there perhaps still lay the body of a witch, hacked to pieces by Lindsey herself with that same axe as she tried to save Dackery's life. It was too much to bear. With a violent sob she tore herself away from the awful weapon and flung herself into the pillow, crying. How long she lay there crying she never knew. At length, her mind slowly drifted back from the dark and terrible places, as bit by bit the nightmare cries were drowned out by the quiet refrain of a soft flute.

Lindsey pulled her head from the pillow, curling up slightly to draw her rumpled shirt back over her legs a bit. Elred was back on the nightstand, reclining with his back against the candlestick and his skinny legs stretched out as he played pensively on a wooden fipple flute. The elf looked up as he observed Lindsey stir, plucking the flute away from his lips as he did so. "Are you feeling better?", he asked cordially.

Lindsey sniffed. "Kind of. Maybe. Mostly not."

"I'm sorry. It will get better with time, but I'm afraid that the things which are in your mind now will never go away, not completely. But now at least you are prepared for what is to come." Elred turned now to face Lindsey fully as he sat cross-legged on the nightstand beside her.

"You have come through much since leaving your world. You are no longer the same person you were a month ago. Hae-jin has become a new person also, and has taken on a new name. It is now time for you to do so as well. I now name you Linnian, which means Transcendent Heart."

Lindsey sniffed again, choking down a weak laugh as she did so. "Uh huh? Linnian? That sounds a lot like my real name, Lindsey Ann."

"Quite right. It's a portmanteau of your first and middle name which I made up just now, and ascribed to it a meaning which I think suits you. After all, who you really are is what always determines the real meaning of your name."

Elred stood up. "Sleep now, Linnian. The coming days will be difficult. But for the moment, you shall have rest. We shall speak again." And with that, Elred stepped behind the candlestick and vanished.

Lindsey hugged her pillow a bit closer. She felt like she was going to cry again. Bit by bit her thoughts faded into silence, as exhaustion slowly overtook her. Soon, she lay still, her breast heaving gently as she passed into a dreamless sleep filled with only the gentle melody of elven flutes.

By morning word of Wickhowe's new alliance had spread throughout the city of Larchester. The festive spirit of the previous night had dampened a bit, as the people slowly realized that the conflict was not yet over and that war was still very likely. At Larchester Castle the king accepted the renewed allegiances of Swinstoke and Donnock, while Wickhowe and his fellow conspirators were officially attainted.

Gurth's army had broken camp late on the previous afternoon, and according to the latest reports, it was headed northeast towards Ardgar Castle, which had been a possession of Gurth's for some time and was the nearest stronghold which remained under his control. And also according to those reports, Gurth himself had been seen among his men. Wickhowe's army had likewise broken camp early the previous evening, and was likewise headed northwards, towards the village of

Beckby, which stood now between them and Ardgar Castle. It was apparent to all that Wickhowe was intending to link up with Gurth at Ardgar, at which point their combined strength would be very nearly equal to that of the king.

Early in the morning, the king met with his officers in the great hall of Larchester Castle, which was still strewn with the leftovers of the previous night's festivities. The spirit of rejoicing had vanished as abruptly as it had come, and was now replaced with the deadly sobriety of the king's war council. With his own forces now combined with those of the Bishop of Larchester and the army of Robin Goodfellow, William of Bradlaw had nearly sixty-seven hundred men at his command. The most recent reports suggested that Wickhowe still possessed three thousand men, while Gurth commanded twenty five hundred or more from the combined forces of the Zard, Drixi, and his own men. If engaged separately, the king's forces would likely overwhelm either Gurth or Wickhowe's. But were the enemy to successfully marshal together, the king's army would be scarcely a fifth larger. The outcome of such a contest would be far from certain. For his own part, Hae-jin feared greatly that the flying mounts of the Drixi and untold powers of Gurth's wizardry could easily negate any slight numerical superiority the king might have. Therefore, Hae-jin and the king were in agreement: Wickhowe had to be stopped at Beckby, and destroyed there before he could reach Gurth. From there, the king would be positioned to lay siege to Gurth at Ardgar Castle, and destroy him in turn. By late morning, the king's combined army was on the march, still slightly groggy from the night before. Wickhowe already had a significant head start. The king's plan was ambitious, and his forces marched double time to quickly close the gap between them and their quarry. Yet Wickhowe continued to maintain his lead. By the next morning, it was clear that Wickhowe would beat them to Beckby.

It was with some surprise then, that in the early afternoon outriders returned to the King's army bearing encouraging news. Wickhowe had reached Beckby at noon, and after crossing the River Beck had promptly halted and made camp just north of the village. If the king pressed his march, his army would reach the southern fringes of Ashbeck Wood by the early evening, and would be positioned directly between Beckby and Ardgar, cutting off Wickhowe while still almost a day's march away from Gurth. Hae-jin was concerned by this development. It made no sense to him that Wickhowe should have given up his lead so needlessly. The king however was elated, and ordered his army forward. By nightfall his forces were in position, and they made camp in the fields south of Ashbeck wood. In the morning, the king would at last do battle with the Earl of Wickhowe.

31

"The Battle of Beckby"

A cold, unpleasant sort of night passed. The faint glimmers of starlight had been banished by a dense, sickly fog which oozed across the downs, spreading a damp, chilling vapour everywhere, which suffocated the very land beneath it. By morning, the fog had largely lifted, leaving behind only a dank mist which filled the lowlands that lay between the king's encampment and the distant towers of Ardgar Castle to the west.

Lindsey sat beside a tent in the king's encampment, gazing out across the vista as the rising sun greeted the morning with blood red rays. She was arrayed for war, or at least as well as could be managed under the circumstances. With so little time before the army's departure she had been obliged to make do with whatever gear could be quickly procured for her. Just about everything available was too big, and there was no time to make any substantive adjustments. It was a blessing that a boy's chain shirt and gambeson had been found which were at least close enough in size to be functional, but Lindsey's body still swam uncomfortably within the oppressive volume of thickly quilted linen. On her head was an impeccably crafted helmet which was by far the best piece of her equipment. It was a small rounded bascinet fitted with an aventail (being one half of a matched set of great helm and cervelliere belonging to the young Earl of Donnock, who was employing a different helmet that day). Tied around her helmet was a thick strip of scarlet cloth, which she wore in lieu of any proper livery. Despite the strenuous protestations of Hae-jin, Joan, and just about everyone else, Lindsey had stubbornly insisted on coming along with the army alongside her friends. Only Ursilda had stood up for her at first, but in the end the others acquiesced, though reluctantly. Lindsey was subsequently placed under the command of Rob Sykes as a member of Hae-jin's bodyguard. Also in the bodyguard were Ursilda and the Wogs, and likewise Falknir, who had volunteered straight away and had subsequently talked Dackery himself into joining the battle as well. All of them wore broad scarlet ribbons as their uniform. The old banner of Robin Goodfellow had been cast aside for fear it should be confused in the heat of combat with the livery of Gurth, and in its place Joan had procured several substantial bolts of scarlet cloth, which had been cut up the night before and hastily distributed among the company. Hae-jin himself now wore a crude scarlet jupon over his armor, which was sewn with several of the Bird's golden feathers, while his standard was a great ten foot long pennant of the same material, rounded on the fly and sewn with still more of the Bird's feathers. Even Ursilda had been coaxed under protest into donning a thin ribbon of scarlet. For their own parts, Joan, Hugh Mortimer and Will Little did not join the bodyguard, but rather took prominent places among the peasant soldiers of Robin Goodfellow's army, where the need for capable leadership was keenly felt. Of the Bird Lindsey had seen very little, for he had been constantly engaged in scouting for Hae-jin. So far Lindsey hadn't any opportunity at all to speak to him, and as she sat there cradling her axe she wondered grimly whether she would ever get another chance now.

All around her the camp was bustling with activity as men and horses were made ready for battle. Across the encampment, Lindsey caught sight of three figures mounted on pure white steeds. It was the lady Edith, still attired in a green gown and horned headdress. She was accompanied now by two knights in green armor, their faces obscured by lowered visors. Their harnesses were of a noticeably foreign looking appearance compared to that of the Linsterish soldiery, being wrought in distinctively swept lines and possessing an almost iridescent finish which was heavily embossed with elaborate floral patterns. No one seemed to be paying any attention to them, and as Lindsey watched, the party trotted through the perimeter of the camp headed in the direction of Ashbeck Wood. Suddenly, Lindsey's attention was drawn away by a rude shout from one of the Wogs, and Lindsey scrambled to her feet and jogged over to where her friends were now gathering around Hae-jin.

The king's army was divided into three battles arrayed abreast. The middle was personally commanded by William of Bradlaw himself alongside the Count of Gillnock, an elderly veteran who had served faithfully alongside Simon the Second during the Tollard wars. To the king's right was the vanguard, under the command of the Bishop of Larchester along with the Earl of Duncarden, a man of fervent loyalty to the king. To the king's left was the rearguard, which was commanded by Sir Robin Greyflower alongside the Earls of Swinstoke and Donnock. Hae-jin had placed Swinstoke in command of his heavy cavalry, while the infantry he split between himself and Donnock. Hae-jin wanted to ensure his formation could adapt quickly to an unexpected change of fortune, for the situation before him filled his heart with misgivings.

Before them now, just to the other side of the River Beck, was the Earl of Wickhowe, holding the field defiantly while outnumbered almost two to one. The earl too had split his army into three division;, the middle under his own command, the van under the Baron Gatehurst and the rear under the Baron Kirkweld, two men who had replaced Swinstoke and Donnock as Wickhowe's chief captains. It seemed to Hae-jin that Wickhowe ought to have at least fortified inside the town of Beckby just south of him rather than face the king in the open. Yet Wickhowe appeared weirdly determined to compound one poor decision with yet another. As the king's army advanced a few trumpets could be heard from within the ranks of the enemy, but Wickhowe's men remained otherwise motionless.

All that separated the two armies now was the river itself. The King's army was situated on a gentle rise with the river before him and the downs to his back, while Wickhowe's army stood firm on the other side of the river, just beyond bowshot of the opposing bank. A single bridge near the village of Beckby was the only crossing, and Hae-jin marveled that Wickhowe had been so careless as to leave it intact and unguarded. The leaden air of the dreary morning was filled with the deadened sound of drums as the king's army advanced purposefully upon the bridge. As they reached the crossing the army ground to a halt, abruptly bottlenecked as the men began to tramp across in a jumbled press, while still others attempted to ford the water.

All of a sudden, from within the ranks of the enemy ahead, the sound of trumpets again filled the air. This time, the front rank of the enemy sprang forward, as Wickhowe's longbowmen advanced into bowshot and unleashed a storm of arrows on the forces of the king. At the same instant, a shout went up in the village of Beckby, and yet more archers appeared from concealment in the town and loosed their arrows upon the king's flank.

From his position in the rearguard, Hae-jin craned his neck from his saddle to observe the looming debacle which was threatening to unfold. The king's front rank was faltering under the brutal assault, the men on the bridge halted and cowering while the men in the river were falling as they fled from whence they came, or else scrambled to the other side and threw themselves behind the scant protection of the opposite bank. But as yet the rear ranks were holding fast as the king's captains rallied the men.

Suddenly, Hae-jin's ear's were filled with a deafening thunk followed by a hideous scraping noise, as he felt a metallic object of some sort glance off the arched crown of his helmet. A moment later, a soldier standing near Hae-jin uttered an agonized cry, and dropped to the ground clutching his shoulder, from which a small bundle of feathers were protruding from a deep wound. His cries were soon joined by others, as abruptly the ground around them was struck with a downpour of small, wicked iron darts fletched with thin quills, falling from the sky like hail.

Hae-jin looked skywards, shielding his face as best he could with a gauntleted hand. Up above, cruising at a height beyond bowshot, were the Drixi on their great leathery mounts. Hundreds of them were arrayed in groups of wedge-shaped skeins well out of reach of enemy archers on the ground as they poured out their lethal consignment over the hapless enemy below. Now every part of the king's army was in tumult as men and horses fell on all sides.

The Drixi had passed beyond Hae-jin's position now, and the lead fliers were already starting to circle back to make another pass. Sykes now rode up alongside Hae-jin. "Sire!", the Yeoman said. "We are taking hard losses. If we remain out in the open the Drixi will continue to thin out our ranks. The men will surely rout if we don't do something now! We cannot retreat to shelter at Beckby, Wickhowe's men are fortified there."

Hae-jin's mind was racing. "There's Ashbeck Wood", he replied. "That's probably where the Drixi were hiding all night, and it's our only shelter left. Take my bodyguard, and go to Donnock. Tell him to take half his men and seize control of the woods."

"But Hae-jin, the Drixi will surely try to stop us!"

"That's exactly what I want them to do. Get into those woods and slay every Drixi you find there!"

Sykes argued no more. With a shout he rallied his followers as ordered and made his way to Donnock, leaving Hae-jin without his bodyguard.

As some four hundred of Donnock's men detached from the rest of the army and drove for the woods, Hae-jin saw the Drixi abruptly change course. It was clear to him now that he and Bradlaw had walked straight into a cunning trap. But even the best strategy has a flaw, and Hae-jin hoped he had found it. For the Drixi could not control the air and occupy the woods at the same time, and as Hae-jin watched the majority of the Drixi riders began to descend and one by one dove beneath the treetops.

There was still one part of the enemy's plan which Hae-jin didn't yet understand. Even with the threat of the Drixi above them, the king could still retreat into the downs westward. Unless there were something there to prevent it. A dark shadow suddenly passed over Hae-jin's head, and with a sudden flash of gold plumage the Bird landed on the ground beside him. "Hae-jin! Terrible news, terrible terrible news!"

"Stop blathering and give me your report!"

"Hae-jin, I've been scouting out Gurth's castle as you instructed. I can see no sign of his troops, but the downs are still full of mist. And Hae-jin, the mist is moving!"

Hae-jin gulped. Too late, he understood what Gurth's plan had been all along, as the rest of it now fell into place. "Which way is it headed?", he demanded.

"Straight for us, coming uphill from the downs."

"How fast?"

"About a marching pace."

So that was it. The wizardry of Gurth was subtle and insidious as always. With Wickhowe as bait, Bradlaw had been lured into the open, caught in a killing field between Beckby and Ashbeck Wood while Gurth closed in from the rear under cover of a bewitched fog. There was no time to lose. Spurring his horse, Hae-jin cried out to his trumpeters, and slowly the rearguard began to shift position as Hae-jin frantically turned his division around to face the new threat behind them.

Meanwhile, Donnock's forces had now passed under the canopy of Ashbeck Wood, with Hae-jin's bodyguard in the lead. Further in, nearly three hundred Drixi had dismounted, and drawing bows and short spears they spread out into the woods to engage Donnock's men. Like most of the woodlands in Linster, Ashbeck was well tended and largely clear of bramble, and beneath the shadowy canopy a brutal contest ensued among the stark timbers, which were dispersed over the forest floor like asture wooden columns supporting the leafy roof of some enchanted woodland hall.

Lindsey ran through the maze of trees, trying to keep up with Syke's advancing spearhead. An arrow shot past, grazing the side of her helmet, followed quickly by a second, which Lindsey deflected with her axe, her hands plying her weapon instinctively as protective incantations passed unbidden through her mind. She'd caught up with the rest of the bodyguard now. Just a few feet ahead of her, Sykes and several other men were engaged in close quarters with black and scarlet clad Drixi. Ursilda roared with fury as she barreled through the trees, scattering Drixi before her as the Wogs followed in her wake, skewering all they came upon. Nearby, his boyish frame enclosed in a brilliant plate harness, the young earl of Donnock strode through the fray wielding a mighty poleaxe with deadly effect. Falknir, armed with his sword and a borrowed shield, was fanatically laying waste to Drixi all around, while behind him Dackery advanced doggedly, his own sword sheathed as he rested his pistol on the rim a particularly large shield, emptying magazine after magazine into the bewildered foe. Through it all, the Fox threaded his way imperceptibly through the Drixi ranks, dodging back and forth between trees and legs as he cried out in feigned voices and sounds, sowing further discord wherever he went.

A man at arms fell down beside Lindsey, clutching his face where an arrow had lodged beneath the brim of his helmet. The Drixi had fallen back into a defensive position, forming into two ranks encircling the place where their mounts had been tethered. Now the archers were shooting in earnest from behind a bristling wall of speartips and swords. Another man near Lindsey was struck down, and with a yell Lindsey charged forward straight into the wall of steel ahead. She had hardly covered a few yards before she ground to a halt under a hail of arrows. Even with strings of enchantments fresh on her lips she could hardly move her weapon fast enough to intercept them all, and she found herself pinned behind a tree.

Suddenly, from behind the Drixi ranks there came a terrible, inhuman cry. The woods ahead became filled with unearthly shrieks, primeval and terrified. A great beating noise filtered through the trees, and through the branches above Lindsey caught sight of a host of massive, leathery creatures leaping into the air. The Drixi saw it too, and abruptly their assault faltered as they observed that their mounts were disappearing through the treetops into the sky. Then, with a roar a vast shape barreled through the trees behind them. An enormous humanoid, twelve feet tall and armored in a peculiar suit of mail consisting of a score of chain shirts cut open and sewn together over a thick gown of sheepskin. The creature strode through the ranks of Drixi carrying a crude wooden shield taller than the height of a man and swinging a great ironshod club which was sharply bent on one end rather like a hockey stick, with which he battered and swept aside the confounded soldiers in his path. Even before she could see his face, Lindsey was sure she knew what it was. One doesn't see a creature like that and forget him easily. She had no notion how or why he came to be there, she only knew that Barri the giant had turned the tide for them. The Drixi were in full retreat now. With their mounts bolted they were stranded on the ground in a hostile land, fighting a war none of them really cared much about. As trumpets sounded the withdrawal they fell back in as much order as they could manage, while some of their number sped to the few beasts which remained on the ground and mounted up in pursuit of their runaway animals.

Only a few Drixi remained now in the sky over the fields of Beckby, and even these had ceased their harassment of the king's forces and had broken off in pursuit of the flying stampede. In the vanguard, the Bishop of Larchester had forded the river and positioned his division between Wickhowe's main army and the village, cutting off any retreat for Wickhowe in that direction, while a detachment under the Earl of Duncarden broke off from the van to assault Beckby itself. The king's forces now surged ahead across the bridge, and Wickhowe's men closed distance to engage in close quarters while the king's men were still bottlenecked, but were driven back again as the rest of the Bishop's battle closed into bowshot of Wickhowe and unleashed their arrows.

To the rear, Hae-jin's battle had wheeled fully and his men were stumbling into position as a great wall of mist was creeping up from the downs before them. The sound of tramping feet and the harsh rhythm of Zardish drums filtered steadily through the fog, and as the foul cloud engulfed Hae-jin's front ranks the terrible outline of ranks upon ranks of both men and Zard loomed through the gloom as the two armies closed on one another. Soon, the mist was filled with stricken cries and the clash of steel, as the two sides fought desperately in the dim claustrophobia of the accursed mist. Without Donnock, Hae-jin's men were outnumbered nearly two to one. Hae-jin himself fought in the midst of it all, with no bodyguard, and his scant vantage point from horseback his sole means of retaining any command of the situation.

Ahead of him now, Hae-jin noticed that his front line was beginning to disintegrate. It was hardly perceptible in the mist, but Hae-jin could see that men were starting to break and run, and only the obscurity of the fog was preventing the panic from spreading into a full on rout. Backing his horse slightly away from the action, Hae-jin peered into the mist. Just visible in the gloom he could see flashes of light emanating near the place where the line was breaking. Hae-jin spurred his horse forward in that direction, trampling a few Zard and black clad soldiers as he pushed for the lights. It seemed that the magic fog wasn't the only bit of sorcery Gurth had prepared for the occasion. As Hae-jin approached, he could now see a shape resolving in the mist.

There, hovering above the heads of the embattled soldiers, was the outline of a man encased in armor, floating over the battlefield with his arms outstretched. Hae-jin could not see his face, but he was sure the man suspended in the air was Gurth himself. On his head was a great helm fitted with fantastic horns which gave him the appearance of a demon, and hurtling from the open palms of his hands were scintillating balls of purple lightning which whirled around the heads of the men, diving and whipping between their legs and arms and darting up again to explode in their faces. Some men were thrown to the ground stunned, but many more were simply scattering in terror.

Gurth had to be stopped now, before the panic spread any further. Hae-jin spurred his horse again and charged straight for Gurth. With a snap, the helmeted head of the witch jerked up to look at him, and with a jab of his right hand he threw a ball of lightning straight at Hae-jin's mount. With a terrible cry the horse bucked and shied from the freakish missile, and Hae-jin was cast to the ground as the horse bolted off into the mist. Hae-jin clamoured to his feet, but was instantly knocked back down again as a barrage of ball lightning burst in his face. Now, Gurth was hovering quite close, and as he bore down on Hae-jin the witch's hands began to glow with a swirling mass of purple arcs.

Suddenly, from behind Hae-jin came a ray of amber light, and as Gurth looked up a bright golden ball hurled through the air and struck the armored man square in the center of his chest, knocking him clear out of the air and sending him tumbling backwards to smash into his own rear rank.

Immediately, the ground around Hae-jin exploded with thrown dirt and hooves, as a pair of green armored knights on white horses charged past him and smashed through the ranks of Zard ahead, scattering them in all directions. A third horse followed and reared to a halt just beside Hae-jin. A woman in a green gown rolled out of the saddle and thrust the reins into Hae-jin's hand. The woman then stepped forward, spreading her arms wide as a gust of wind gently whisked up her dress around her ankles. Quickly the wind grew, whipping around her skirts and whirling up her body as it surged with force, until with a boom it burst into a full on whirlwind, blasting her headdress clear off and blowing up her hair into the mad windstorm above her. To all sides of the woman's body the diabolical fog was being blown away, until it was completely dispersed.

As the light of day flooded the battlefield Hae-jin turned as he heard the blast of a trumpet from behind. On the crest of the downs was the Earl of Swinstoke at the head a hundred mounted men at arms, their armor gleaming under the light of the sun, while over their heads there circled The Bird, still gathering up a few stragglers and ushering them into the ranks. With another trumpet blast, the cavalry couched their lances and charged down the hillside straight into Gurth's exposed flank. The flank collapsed completely under the assault, as Zard and man were broken and scattered under the devastating impact of Swinstoke's charge. With the enchanted mist banished and their sorcerous commander nowhere insight, the army of Gurth began to rout.

Hae-jin leaped into the saddle of the horse beside him, even as the woman now turned to face him and wordlessly pointed in the direction of the enemy. Hae-jin spurred the horse forward and called upon those around him to charge. The army of Robin Goodfellow now surged forward, hard on the heels of the fleeing servants of Gurth as they stumbled through the sloughs and defiles of the downs and fell under the onslaught of arrows and the vengeful blades of the enemy.

To the east, the king's forces had at last crossed the River Beck and were now savagely engaged with Wickhowe's front rank. William of Bradlaw fought valiantly from his steed, his lance discarded as he lay waste to all around him with a horseman's warhammer. Up ahead, the king espied the standard of Wickhowe. He began to turn his horse in that direction when another rider pulled up alongside him and the Count of Gillnock laid his hand gently on the king's reins. "Sire, Larchester is drawing up on Kirkweld's flank. The enemy's rearguard will soon collapse, we should keep them occupied while Larchester routs them."

The king cast the venerable man's hand aside. "Wickhowe is nearly before me now", the king bellowed. "I cannot allow him to escape me!"

"Sire, leave Wickhowe! It will not be long before he is driven from the field."

"Which is why I must face him now!"

Over a final protest from the aged count, the King pressed forward with his bodyguard towards the standard of his nemesis. There, pitched in combat alongside the remnant of his own bodyguard was the Earl of Wickhowe, fighting on foot with his sword in both hands, his horse cut from under him.

The king cast his warhammer to the ground, and dismounting he drew his sword to face his enemy on even terms as he shouted a challenge to Wickhowe. The earl turned, and upon seeing the king he now advanced. As they closed distance on one another both men grasped their swords like short spears, with one hand on the hilt and the other on the blade. A brutal contest ensued, as both men jabbed at one another at terrifyingly close range, attempting to drive the point of their weapons into the vulnerable recesses of the other's harness. In short order they were grappling with one another, breastplate to breastplate, leveraging their swords like crowbars. Wickhowe suddenly got the upper hand, and hooking the pommel of his sword under the king's knee he threw the man to the ground. Wickhowe now couched his sword under his arm like a lance and began to drive the point into the king's mail clad armpit, when abruptly his head jerked to one side as he recoiled under the impact of a mace, which came crashing down on one side of his helmet. Wickhowe staggered under the conconcussion and his sword arm fell slack for a moment as a horseman dismounted beside him and cast aside his mace. Drawing a dagger, the horseman seized the earl and pried his dagger under the man's visor, driving it home. As the defeated man collapsed lifeless into the field, the horseman stepped to the side of the king, and Bradlaw arose to meet the eyes of the Count of Gillnock. "You faced your enemy with gallantry, sire", the old nobleman said. "But the Earl of Wickhowe is now no more."

All around the two men, the army of the late earl was now in full retreat. Kirkweld had withdrawn under the Bishop of Larchester's assault, and Gatehurst had soon followed, while the troops under Duncarden had at last taken Beckby after a brutal house to house struggle. With Kirkweld and Gatehurst in flight, the last vestiges of Wickhowe's army were routed. The Battle of Beckby was over.

32

"The Storming of Ardgar"

It was well past midday. Now and then, the sun would peek through the rolling banks of clouds which sailed through the sky like the shrouds of so many ghosts. Down below, the fields of Beckby were still. The clamour of battle had faded, leaving behind only the silence of the tomb.

Hae-jin rode at a canter through the field, still mounted on his borrowed steed. The creature seemed to have a mind of its own, heeding directions dutifully in a detached sort of manner that seemed more in the way of professional courtesy than inbred domestication. But if it were a wight, Hae-jin could not guess, for the creature remained mute as it carried Hae-jin to and fro as he roamed the field to marshal the king's army in pursuit of the enemy. The armies of Gurth had been driven from the field. Those of Wickhowe's alliance who remained were now in full retreat, falling back to their respective strongholds. Zard and Drixi alike were broken and scattered, and the tattered fragments of Gurth's regular men were fleeing across the heathland towards Ardgar Castle. Hae-jin was proud of the performance of his troops, particularly the peasants. Many long days of training and drilling under his command had paid off, and the Army of Robin Goodfellow had held firm at the critical moment and carried the day. The king's victory had been costly though. Hae-jin reflected bitterly that he ought to have foreseen the trap Gurth had laid for them, and he cursed himself for not having heeded his own misgivings prior to the battle. Nevertheless, he was not the only one who had made errors. The king and his captains had likewise fallen into the trap just as he had. Meanwhile, Gurth himself had spread his forces too thin, and relied too heavily on the effects of his magic and the terror of the flying Drixi mounts. The latter, in particular, had proven a sorry miscalculation on Gurth's part. They had been spread thinnest of all, being obliged to hold Ashbeck Wood and assault the king's army from the air at the same time, and the price paid in Drixi losses had been high. Higher, perhaps, than their precarious alliance could tolerate.

Abruptly, Hae-jin was interrupted in his gloomy reverie by a flash of golden feathers, and Hae-jin pulled his mount to a stop as the Bird fluttered to the ground beside him. "Excellent news!", the Bird said. "The Drixi are on the run. I think it's safe to say that they've wholly abandoned Gurth by now. As far as we can tell they are simply preoccupied with regrouping and recovering as many of their mounts as possible. Most of them are still stranded on the ground, and we've taken many prisoners."

"That is indeed good news. Is there any news on Gurth?"

"Yes, I have seen him! I spotted him in the downs with a company of his men, headed for Ardgar Castle. There's no chance of us catching him before he gets there. We will just have to lay siege to him straight away before he can flee the country entirely."

Hae-jin gritted his teeth. "We won't be able to lay siege to him in time. The king is already on the march in pursuit of Gatehurst and Kirkweld, and my men are spread all across the downs hunting down the Zard. I doubt we could lay siege to Ardgar before late tomorrow, by which time Gurth could be gone. Go find Swinstoke, and tell him to assume command of the hunt. Have him dispatch the heavy cavalry back to my encampment and wait for me there. Then go round up the Wogs, Ursilda and the others, and send them back to the camp as well. And then, go to the Drixi prisoners, and tell them that Sir Robin Greyflower wishes to parely."

"Eh? What do you want to talk to the Drixi for?"

"I'll explain later, just get going! I'll have much more for you to do when you get back."

Without further protest the Bird shot into the sky and sailed off on his errands.

The wind was starting to pick up, and the sun was soon overwhelmed by the mounting procession of mournful grey clouds. Hae-jin's encampment was largely deserted. The king's baggage train had already departed to catch up with the rest of the king's army, while most of those who remained were roaming the countryside in search of Drixi and Zard. A few banners still flew here and there above the tents, the fabric flapping loudly in the breeze against the surrounding silence.

Lindsey was sitting on a stool near where the Bird had told her to meet the others, her back slumped and her eyes downcast as she idly turned her axe in her hands. The weapon had served her well that day. The instincts Elred had drawn out from it had kept her alive, and even now she was still depending on the strength it had given her. She gripped the shaft more tightly as her mind filled with the terrible memories of the battle, the horrifying sights and sounds of the day flooding unbidden into her thoughts and piercing her soul like an endless rain of ice shards. She could still see their faces, ghostly Drixi visages floating up before her exactly as they were before she slew them. Waves of guilt and remorse swept over her, even in the knowledge that the people she'd recently killed had been trying to kill her in turn. The bit of fortitude imprinted in her mind by the ancient weapon was just about the only thing that was keeping her sane at that moment. So many people had died that day. And many more still would not live to see the next day. Even now, the young Earl of Donnock was lying in his tent under Joan's care, fighting for his life after having taken a thrust to the upper thigh from the spear of a dying Drixi. A shadow fell across Lindsey, and she snapped out of her plaintive revery as a vast shape loomed above her. She looked up to see the towering form of Barri, and in a slightly terrifying moment his mammoth frame descended as he lurched and sat down beside her with a resounding grunt. "Ullo, girlie. Noice axe."

"Um, hi. I didn't expect to see you again. How did you get here anyway?"

"Walked."

"Uh, yeah. Me too. Mostly. I thought you wanted to stay and work on your rock pile....I mean, your monument, that is."

"Well, that'll be another longish story. That Bird just don't give up. He came round again, said the noice girlie was in trouble and all. I told him he were a silly git to go and get the noice girlie in trouble like that. But then I got me to thinkin' about wotcha said, about puttin' somethin' properly heroic and all on me monument. I figured it were a shame if anything bad happened to the noice girlie just because the Bird were a silly git. So I fetched me club, and me shield, and me metal suit and I went. It were a long walk, it were, but I saw a lot o' different country and all manner o' queer folk along the way. Got it all up here in me head, and I'll put it all in me monument when I get back."

There was a small ruckus coming through the camp now, and rounding the corner of the tent were the three Wogs, laden down with piles of Drixi loot and quarrelling loudly with one another. They stopped speechless in their tracks when they saw Barri, but his presence on the battlefield had been impossible to miss and it didn't take Lindsey much more than to explain he was a friend of the Bird's for the

Wogs to dismiss him and go back to quarrelling. Bit by bit the others started arriving, first Ursilda and then Dackery, Falknir, and Sykes. Finally, Hae-jin himself arrived. As he drew up his horse near where the others were gathered he dismounted and took hold of the reins to secure them. But the horse gently turned its head and deftly pulled the reins out of Hae-jin's hands, turned around and began ambling off on its own into the camp. Hae-jin had a feeling that it would be best to leave the animal to its own devices; it had only been tolerant of him for as long as it had intended. As he watched, the horse trotted over to where a woman in a green dress was standing apart from the rest of the encampment, presenting its bridle submissively to her as she took possession of the reins once more, and led the animal out of sight. "I don't suppose any of you know who that woman is?", Hae-jin asked, turning to the others.

"I can't imagine!", the Bird mused, "Her appearance was certainly most propitious. Uncannily so. We must interview her straight away!" For her own part, Lindsey remained silent on the matter. She kept her promises.

"All that will have to wait for now", Hae-jin said. "At the moment we have more urgent matters to attend to. You all fought valiantly today, and we have achieved a great victory. But it is not over yet. Gurth has fallen back to Ardgar Castle. His forces are scattered and dispersed, but even now they are surely attempting to regroup. The Earl of Wickhowe is dead, but many of his followers have survived and are making an orderly retreat. Even without the earl, their fear of the king's wrath may be sufficient to keep their alliance intact for a time, and the situation will remain unstable so long as Wickhowe's coalition persists. It is my hope that the king will be prevailed upon to issue a general pardon to anyone who defects, which may go a long way in thinning out the ranks of the rebels and driving them to capitulation. But so long as Gurth remains unchecked the rebels may still be inclined to fight rather than take a chance on the king's clemency. It is imperative that we deal with Gurth once and for all now, while the rebels are still in retreat. Therefore, tonight we are going to take Ardgar Castle."

"Tonight!", blurted Alwog, ever the spokesman for his brothers. "You can't be serious! Why should we take the castle now? Let's just lay siege to the place and starve the lot of them out."

"Foolish goblin!"

The shrill voice cut over the words of the Wog, as the woman in the green dress stepped unexpectedly into their midst. Her hat was long gone, and her dark hair was draped elegantly over her supple shoulders even as it remained in tangled disarray. Vacantly, Lindsey found herself mildly annoyed that the Lady Edith still managed to look stunning even when she was a mess. Hae-jin looked at the woman quizzically, though likewise with a certain measure of satisfaction. At least he was going to find out who this interloper was, and might perhaps even benefit from her obvious powers. "And who might you be, good lady?"

Edith returned Hae-jin's gaze austerely. "Who I am is unimportant. Suffice to say that I am called Edith, and like yourselves I too am a servant of the Good Folk. You will require my assistance if you want to be assured of taking Gurth this night."

Hae-jin recollected her action during the battle that morning, and saw no reason to disagree with her statement. He was still not satisfied with her account of herself, but for the moment he would not press the matter further. "Your assistance is most gratefully accepted."

"But Hae-jin!" blurted Alwog again, "How do you expect us to manage all this? The whole army is scattered like rabbits in a rainstorm."

"I still have a hundred mounted men at arms at the ready", Hae-jin replied, "which I will take to Ardgar very soon. Gurth has only a small garrison left. At this moment our good Fox is already within the walls, learning the ways of the castle. At the appointed hour a small detachment will infiltrate the castle, and the Fox will guide them to the gatehouse. With the gates in our possession, my men shall enter the castle and take it by storm."

"You've lost your wits, Hae-jin. How are we going to get inside Gurth's castle? I assume it's us lot who'll be doing the dirty work."

"I have been negotiating with our Drixi prisoners. In exchange for their help, I have promised the Drixi that we will cease hunting their fellows down and will grant them all safe passage out of the country."

"Ha! That's a good one. And what makes you think the king will honor your promise?"

"I believe that the king will act sensibly on the matter. His attention is focused on Wickhowe's remaining allies, and this is by far the easiest way to be rid of the Drixi."

"Pish-tush! I'm glad *I'm* not depending on any of your promises. Except for that hundred and fifty silver marks a day, that is."

"A hundred and fifty-one!"

"Oh do shut up, you idiot!"

"I have presently at my disposal eight Drixi riders", Hae-jin explained, ignoring the squabbling Wogs, "who will assist us in infiltrating Gurth's castle from the air. Sykes will lead the assault, and the three Wogs will accompany him, along with four others."

"I must be one of those four", Edith interjected.

Hae-jin nodded in assent. "I therefore require three more volunteers."

Now Falknir stood up. "I volunteer myself and Dackery, of course."

Lindsey bit her lip. She wasn't going to sit this one out. "I'm going too, Hae-jin."

Hae-jin turned to Lindsey, a troubled look on his face. "I think you should stay here. Joan is overwhelmed caring for the wounded. She will need your help."

"Don't kid me, Hae-jin. I'm not a doctor, Joan doesn't need me. I'm going along with the others, and that's that." Hae-jin looked at Lindsey, a certain look of pain and concern on his face. But again he nodded, and said nothing more.

As night closed in on the Kingdom of Linster the cloud cover became nearly complete, plunging the land into an almost stygian darkness relieved by only a few faint stars which barely reflected on the dark towers of Ardgar Castle. A noble old Linsterish fortress, the castle had sunk into darkness and disrepute, for Gurth had occupied it long ago as a suitable seat from which to exert his dominance over the region. Inside, lights had been lit and through the gloom of the courtyard Tom Oates was running across the cobbles. Tom had fled to Gurth's encampment outside Larchester after the failed assassination of Hae-jin many days ago, and had accompanied Gurth's retinue all the way to Ardgar Castle. He was now on his way back from the gatehouse, bringing news from a party of scouts which had just returned. Tom scampered up the steps of the castle's square, monolithic keep and slid nervously past a pair of towering, wolflike creatures flanking the doorway on either side, witch-beasts in the service of Gurth, with inky black fur and red eyes that glowed faintly with an inner fire. Scrambling through the dank passages of the tower he now made his way to Gurth's chambers. He found Gunth at his table, hunched over his scrying stone. He was still encased in his armor, though its surface was marred and scratched, and his horned great helm was nowhere to be seen. As Tom entered the room the witch looked up angrily. "What are you doing here? Get out!"

Tom quivered. "My lord, a patrol has just returned!"

"And?"

"My lord, they've spotted the enemy outside the castle."

"Where?"

"I'm not sure, I think they were just in the village."

"How many of them?"

"I...I don't know exactly. I think perhaps a hundred, maybe more. I don't know!"

"Worthless child!" Gurth heaved his frame out of his chair and lunged at Tom. The boy cringed and fell aside as Gurth shoved past him and trudged through the door. "Get out of my way, I'll see to the matter myself."

Tom stood alone in the doorway, his fists clenching and unclenching with a helpless passion.

"You've been very naughty, Tom. A good servant doesn't run away without leave. Why should you forsake a good master for a bad one?"

Tom spun around. He could have sworn he heard the words just as clear as day. But he saw no one. Stumbling slightly, he stepped through the door and ran away down the hall, leaving the empty room behind him. Then, as if from nowhere, a small red Fox crept out into the middle of Gurth's chamber, his nose twitching madly. The scent of magic was overwhelming, filling the room and washing over Bartholomew's senses like a tidal wave of intoxication. Everywhere there were treasures of all manner and description. Here in the heart of the witch's stronghold were all the possessions and secrets of Gurth, which Bartholomew had so long coveted. But it was not yet time. Gurth himself still needed to be put out of the way. Summoning all his force of will Bartholomew darted out of the room and scampered out through the hall, headed for the rooftop.

High in the sky above Linster, lost in sea of darkness, Lindsey was clinging to the mail-clad body of a Drixi rider, the wind whipping terrifyingly all around her. Eight Drixi Windhelms had been cruising in circles for some time now, each carrying with him a dubious passenger. As she clung to the Drixi, Lindsey felt a bizarre sort of horror in the knowledge that only a few short hours ago she had been engaged in mortal combat with the man's comrades, and was personally responsible for the deaths of more than one of them. It was terrifying now to think that her life was completely in his hands as they soared through the darkness. But thus far the Drixi had kept up their part of Hae-jin's bargain.

The Drixi were flying almost tail to tail, still barely visible to each other in the darkness as they sliced through the chill night air. Lindsey could only hope that the Bird's vision held up to its reputation and that they had been brought to the right place. All of a sudden, there was a faint glint of gold fluttering beside the lead Drixi. Was it the Bird, come to tell them it was time to descend? Abruptly, the lead Drixi pitched down, the ghostly shape of his mount dropping out of sight. With expert precision, each Drixi guided his own mount down in turn, falling into line with hardly any need to see one another. Down and down they spiraled, tightening their circles as they descended, while the well-trained pterosaurs instinctively trimmed their wings to kill their speed.

Suddenly, the huge dark shape of the castle's roof loomed up in front of Lindsey's mount, and the Drixi rider swerved abruptly to correct his course at the last instant. Then, with a muffled thud the pterosaur hit the roof of Gurth's keep, crawling softly to a halt on its legs and wingtip claws. One by one, the Drixi deposited the rest of their passengers, and then departed again into the sky.

Creeping carefully across the steeply raked rooftop, the intruders gathered together in the gloom; five humans, three wogs, and the Bird, whose iridescent plumage was only faintly visible in the sparse starlight. In a moment they were also joined by a small red Fox, who was almost completely invisible in the darkness. After a short consultation they gingerly felt their way slowly across the roof to where the Fox had located a suitable point of descent, while the Bird disappeared alone into the air and made for the outer walls. Theirs was a tightly woven plan, and each had a part to play in precise sequence.

Along the castle walls, Gurth's men had mounted a sparse guard. There were barely enough of them to fully man the walls at once, and most of these were garrisoned for the night, reposing as best they could. In the inky darkness, a meaty claw soaked and reeking with moat water gripped the edge of the parapet which ran along the castle's southern face. Just as she had done at the Drixi fortress so many weeks ago, Ursilda was now scaling the walls of Ardgar. And just as before, she was there to create mayhem, trusting that the others would execute their parts as competently (nearly) as she. A few moments ago the Bird had touched down beside her and given the word to attack. Now as she heaved her great form over the battlements she loosed a mighty bellow which echoed through the night, announcing to the inhabitants of Ardgar Castle that their doom was upon them. For Ursilda had come! A cry went up from the southern wall. Soon, Gurth's men were pouring out of the barracks, stumbling through the darkness as they converged on the south wall. Faintly through the gloom, the form of the great wightbeast could be seen silhouetted on the battlements, hurling men in all directions.

As the pandemonium continued to spread along the southern end of the courtyard, on the opposite side of the castle Lindsey stole along in single file with the others, with Bartholomew leading them stealthily to the gatehouse. The attention of the garrison was now entirely focused on the opposite side of the castle, and for the moment the way was clear as the sounds of tumult and discord echoed across the courtyard. It was as if the great Bear was doing battle with the entire fortress at once. Lindsey could only hope Ursilda would make it through somehow. Or for that matter, than any of that any of them would make it through.

There was a shimmer of green satin in the dark, and Edith stole up beside Sykes. "Continue to the gatehouse as planned, I will remain behind and make sure that Gurth is kept occupied."

"Woman, are you mad?", Sykes hissed, "You cannot face him alone! M'lady, stop!"

Syke's protests were in vain, for Edith had already slipped away in the darkness. From down at their feet, the voice of the Fox whispered in the darkness. "Let the woman go. I'm sure she will manage. We have no time to waste!"

Reluctantly, Sykes resumed following the Fox, creeping along at the base of the wall while chaos reigned in the darkness all around. There, just ahead was the gatehouse. With the Fox as their guide they made for the most discreet entrance they could manage and threaded their way through the passages to the great winches. Ardgar castle was protected by a drawbridge, behind which there was a double set of doors, each with its own portcullis, and the ponderous engines which controlled these defenses were nestled within the upper stories of the gatehouse directly above the gates themselves. Bartholomew already knew what guards would be posted along their path, most of whom would be keeping watch from the battlements, or may otherwise have dispersed to join the fracas in the courtyard. What few unfortunates they came upon were dealt with swiftly at the point of a dagger, and in short order they had captured the first winch room.

On the first level above the gates there were two great windlasses, one for the drawbridge and the other for the inner portcullis. The windlass for the outer portcullis was located on the next floor up. As soon as they had taken the room, Sykes and Falknir threw themselves onto one of the winches while the Wogs took the other. Only Dackery remained with Lindsey now, and the two of them ran upstairs to the upper level. A single windlass was there, a great cylindrical timber bound up with oily chains and pulleys and pierced with square holes to accept a set of removable levers, which were stacked against the wall nearby. From down below Lindsey could hear the ominous creaking of the engines working in the lower room. It wouldn't be long now before the guards above them realized what was happening and descended on them with force. Lindsey and Dackery quickly siezed the levers and ramming them into the windlass began straining themselves against the torpid machine, while the Fox kept watch at the door.

A shout went up from the battlements, as down below the drawbridge came crashing down to the ground. A moment after it came to earth, an enormous, humanoid hand slithered out of the murky waters below and grasped onto the ledge of the bridge. With a heave and a splash, Bari the giant pulled himself out of the moat where he had been hiding under the shadow of the drawbridge, and rolled to his feet atop the bridge. The outer portcullis was nearly lifted now, and with a bellow the giant shoved it up the rest of the way and barrelled on through the gates, prepared to hold them against all comers. Meanwhile, high above in the gloom the Bird had been keeping watch. With the drawbridge down he now flew madly to the village where Hae-jin's horsemen were waiting.

Lindsey and Dackery were now securing the portcullis in place. From the room down below, Lindsey could hear the terrible clamour of heavy combat. The guards were attempting to storm the lower room, and from the sound of it Sykes, Falknir and the Wogs were giving them a terrific fight. Lindsey met Dackery's eye as he dug into his belt pouch and retrieved his pistol, racking the action to load the first round from his last remaining magazine. Distantly, Lindsey thought she could hear the sound of a trumpet coming from outside the castle. If Gurth's men captured the winch rooms now, they would be able to drop either portcullis down straight on top of Hae-jin's men. It was all up to them now to make sure that didn't happen. Suddenly, there was a cry from the door, and with a great blast of purple lighting Bartholomew was hurled from the threshold and cast senseless against the far wall.

With a howl, two great wolf-like creatures then galloped through the door, their jaws slavering and their eyes burning with a red fire. With a deafening barrage Dackery emptied his last magazine into both creatures, and the foul animals tumbled over one another into a heap on the floor. And then, Gurth himself strode into the room.

Lindsey had no doubt who the man was. Gurth was arrayed in a luxurious, taupe colored suit of armor, expertly crafted, with an evil looking aesthetic. His left hand was empty, and in his right he carried a weapon with a curved, pick-like blade on one end and a small hammer head on the other, mounted atop an iron shaft about two feet long with a writhen handguard shaped like a coiled serpent. He wore no helmet, and his face was disfigured with a massive, sooty burn, which ran from the top of his head clear down the entire left side of his body, leaving his fine armor charred and partially deformed. The valor of the Lady Edith had clearly been spectacular, yet clearly too it had been in vain.

Gurth glared at Lindsey with a look of blind rage, followed by dawning recognition. "You!", he snarled.

Suddenly, Dackery drew his sword and placing himself between Lindsey and Gurth he fell upon the enemy. As Dackery lunged forward Gurth threw up his empty hand, and from his armored palm a blast of violet ball lightning burst in front of Dackery's face. Immediately, Gurth followed up with a strike from his war pick, and with a mighty blow Gurth plunged the beak of his weapon deep into Dackery's body. Lindsey screamed in agonized horror as Dackery's form fell limply to the ground. With a shriek of rage she seized her axe in both hands and hurled herself at the witch. With an incantation on her lips she torqued her weapon in a tight arc and brought the enchanted blade down on

Gurth's left arm just below the elbow, cleaving through the hardened steel plate as though it were only thin metal foil and shearing his arm clear off.

Gurth recoiled and cried out in agony as his severed arm fell to the ground, its dead fingers still twitching with a few sparks of purple lightning. Yet even as blood gushed forth from his maimed body Gurth's strength seemed to intensify rather than dissipate. His eyes blazed with violet fire as his body surged with unnatural forces. With another shriek, Lindsey pressed the attack. Down through the corridors of the gatehouse they fought, as Lindsey drove the witch away from the winches. Weapon clashed against weapon as Lindsey expended every last bit of skill the weapon had given her. Yet even so, Gurth was slowly gaining strength. They fought all the way out onto the castle walls, and the walk beneath their feet was beginning to pool with the witch's blood as Gurth now fought with a diabolical fury, as if every shred of power he had left was being channeled and consumed all at once. With a final, mighty curse on his lips, Gurth's weapon blazed with lighting as he brought it down on Lindsey, shattering the shaft of her battle axe with a great blast and hurling the girl away from him to slam hard into the doorframe of the gatehouse.

Gurth now stood triumphant on the walk, his foe lying broken and helpless a half dozen yards away. Yet as the witch gazed out into the courtyard, he realized that all was at last lost. During his battle with Lindsey, Hae-jin's horsemen had made it across the drawbridge and poured into the castle. The noble men at arms were now fighting in the courtyard alongside the giant, while under the shadow of the walls the great Bear had slain many men and was driving the survivors to their deaths beneath the swords of Hae-jin's mounted sergeants and knights. The violet light faded from the witches eyes, and as his shoulders sagged and slumped he cast his weapon aside and lurched back along the walk in the direction of the keep, defeated.

Deep within the keep, Tom Oates was hiding beneath a table in Gurth's personal chambers, a spanned crossbow clutched in one hand and a quiver of bolts and loading lever in the other. From the door there suddenly came a crash, and as Tom was scrambling to lay a bolt on his weapon he saw Gurth stagger in through the door. Tom stared with shock at his master's appearance. His frame was slouched and broken, his armor battered and blasted, and his left arm was no more.

"You, boy", the witch commanded, "Help me." Tom scrambled out from under the table and ran over to his master's side. As the sounds of fighting in the courtyard were slowly diminishing he assisted Gurth in fitting a crude dressing to the stump of his arm. The clamour of battle outside had all but faded away now, and the call of a trumpet now sounded in the courtyard. Tom helped Gurth gather up a few precious belongings, and then taking up his crossbow he followed as the witch heaved his way through the passages to the rear of the keep. In the back of the building, very nearly on the top story, there was a large balcony. Adjacent to this was a bizarre architectural feature: A tiny stable, high above ground among the topmost floors of the keep. A lone horse was quartered there, a sinister looking animal with long shaggy hair of an unnatural blue-grey color. Gurth commanded Tom to help him saddle the horse up. In a few moments the animal was ready, and with his one good arm Gurth swung himself awkwardly into the saddle, while Tom fetched his crossbow and quiver.

"Take me with you, my lord", the boy said. "I shall serve you faithfully wherever you go." Without a word, Gurth spat in Tom's direction and spurred his horse. The animal leaped clear over the guardrail of the balcony and climbed skyward, galloping on thin air. A wave of cold fury swept over Tom Oates, and as the horse was disappearing into the gloom the boy knocked a bolt in his crossbow and loosed a shot at the retreating shape of his master. An inhuman shriek cut through the night, the death cry of an animal. Faintly in the shadows, Tom saw Gurth's horse buck and tumble in the air as it fell with its rider into the abyssal darkness below.

From behind Tom, there now came a gentle cough. Tom whirled around. There, sitting primly in the doorway, his fur just a bit singed and bedraggled, was that cursed Fox. The Fox gazed at Tom with a pair of wild amber eyes, and he licked his jowls languidly. "Well done, my lad. You have proven to be a good servant after all. Gurth was never a fitting master for you. You deserve to serve one who is far wiser, and far mightier than he. Come, we have a great deal of work to do." Tom lowered his weapon as his arms fell slack. The rage inside him faded away, leaving behind only weakness and pliance. Setting down his crossbow, he obediently followed the Fox back inside the keep, running to keep up as the Fox darted through the halls in the direction of Gurth's chambers.

Inside the gatehouse, the upper winch room was still, save for the desperate sobs of Lindsey as she cradled Dackery's body in her lap. She had crawled back inside to find Dackery lying alone on the floor, with no sign of the Fox. She had torn off a portion of her under turnic and was pressing the bunched up linen as tightly as her shaking hands could against the gaping wound in Dackery's body as she cried uncontrollably. From the door, there was a stumble of footsteps, and Falknir stepped in. He looked a mess, but healthy and in good spirits. "Aha, there you are! Good news, the castle is ours! I say, is everything alright?"

Lindsey could only blubber a sob in reply as Falknir stepped authoritatively over to Dackery's side and took the cloth from her hands. "Let me attend to Dackery. Go out to the courtyard and find Hae-jin. Joan had the good sense to make Hae-jin bring her along after all. She's attending to the wounded now. She'll see to it that our friend makes it through." With a final sob and sniff, Lindsey tore herself away from Dackery's side and ran away to the courtyard. As she wound her way among the victorious soldiers, the word was going around that a broken body had been discovered lying outside the castle walls. At long last, Gurth was dead.

33

"A Late Return"

The clouds had departed. The sky was radiant with a spotless blue, and the stately walls of Larchester Castle fairly glowed in the sunlight. Yet beneath the lofty towers, where dark passages wound their way into the subdued serenity of the earth, the cellars of Larchester Castle remained in quiet obscurity. Deep within one of the stygian passages, a soft yellow light now appeared in the darkness, illuminating the walls like the faint glow of a wisp. Rounding a corner there now came a small, pallid child bearing with her a lantern. And following cautiously in her wake were Lindsey and Hae-jin.

It had been nearly a week since the storming of Ardgar Castle. In the aftermath of the battle, the Lady Edith had been discovered deep within the the keep. The entire room in which she had been found was a complete shambles, the walls blackened with soot and every scrap of furniture reduced to kindling. Edith herself had been found in the middle of it all lying senseless across the floor, her body covered in small, sooty burns. As it turned out, her two green clad knights had followed in the wake of Hae-jin's men, and had promptly spirited Edith's body away as soon as it was discovered, and no word had been heard of the woman since. Until now, that is.

That morning, Lindsey and Hae-jin had been summoned in the name of the Lady Edith to her chambers, which apparently were located deep within the bowels of the castle. It seemed an odd residence for a lady of quality, to be sure. All around them stone lined arches created a claustrophobic tube of masonry as they followed their diminutive guide ever deeper into the darkness. At last they came upon a door set within a recess of the passage. As the child opened the door the passage was flooded with a muted orange light which seemed painfully bright in the gloom, and Lindsey and Hae-jin were ushered inside. As they crossed into the room the pair abruptly froze in their tracks at the sight before them. There, reclining on a sort of divan, was the Lady Edith. Her eyes were closed, and she was stretched out on her back, nude save for a folded silken sheet which covered most of her torso. Her immaculate skin was now covered everywhere with swollen pink welts where the burn marks had been. Yet what had so jolted Lindsey had not been Edith herself, but rather her attendants. In one corner of the room, two sets of iridescent green armor were stacked up neatly, and stooping over the woman were two human skeletons, unsupported and erect as they sat on stools beside Edith. Each held a small bronze bowl in one fleshless hand, and they appeared to have been rubbing some mixture of oil and herbs into the welts on Edith's body. As the door opened the ghastly figures stopped and turned sharply to glare at the intruders. For a moment they stared at Lindsey and Hae-jin, regarding them balefully with deep, empty sockets, before returning again to their task. As they did so, Edith's large eyes fluttered open. She twisted her head to one side to look at her guests, and nodded to them in acknowledgement with a particular stiffness that seemed wrought more from lingering pain than any amount of hauteur. "Sir Robin Greyflower, Lindsey Fluger. Thank you for heeding my summons. I apologize for exposing you to these graceless circumstances. I do hope my Sandernacks did not alarm you." Here she gestured off handedly to the two skeletons who were again busying themselves massaging her skin with fingers of bare bone, seemingly oblivious now to their mistress's guests. "They are simple automatons, harmless and obedient. Mineralized remains such as these form an ideal substrate with which to fabricate arcanic automata, particularly when one has an intact and complete structure to work with. Pay them no mind."

The woman went on. "Obviously, what you have seen here must remain confidential. Likewise, my involvement in this whole affair should pass without further comment or discussion. My work here is finished. You shall not hear from me or be summoned to my presence again, at least not for the present. Sir Robin, it is your duty to maintain vigilance here in Linster. Gurth is dead and his curse is dispelled, yet the shadow of the desert persists. Linster was not the only place where Gurth had wrought his wicked machinations. His villainous spellcraft has ensnared many a land, and has secured many sources of slaves for his masters. Breaking the curse of Linster was the key to unravelling the entire fabric of this witchcraft, not just here but everywhere that has been touched by the plagued hand of Gurth. This is a hard blow to his masters, and they will soon be enduring shortages of labour, which will greatly impede their ambitions. This is why the liberation of Linster was so critical, and why the Good Folk chose to involve themselves at this time by engaging the likes of us. But it is only a delay. The witches have been slowly gaining momentum for centuries, and the deeds we have wrought here in Linster will not alone be sufficient to stop them. This is why you must remain vigilant, Sir Robin. The freedom of Linster is in your charge for safekeeping."

Lindsey had been listening carefully all this time. Now, she spoke up. "That's great. I just hope the Good Folk will have Hae-jin's back when the time comes. But what do you want from me? Did you bring me all the way down here just to tell me to keep my mouth shut?"

Edith met Lindsey's eye reservedly. "I expect you to maintain proper discretion regarding everything which has transpired between us. The rest is not mine to decide."

As predicted, Lindsey did not see Edith again after that. Nor did she even see much of Hae-jin, for that matter. Hae-jin remained heavily involved in the king's ongoing campaign, while Lindsey had been spending most of her time with Falknir caring for Dackery, who was making a slow and painful convalescence. Somehow, over the course of their fractious adventures together, Falknir and Dackery had become loyal friends, and for her own part Lindsey had grown to care deeply for Dackery. Here was a man who had made it his sole ambition in life to secure his own immortality. Yet in a characteristically weird twist of the human spirit, Dackery had repeatedly risked his life nonetheless for the sake of others, not the least of which was herself. Indeed, in that terrible moment in the gatehouse of Ardgar, Dackery had very nearly thrown his life away on Lindsey's behalf. And Lindsey held him in the highest regard for it. In fact, one could even say that she loved him. She loved him in a polite, hands-off and asexual sort of way, the kind of love that is reserved for the most sacred of friendships..

Joan had been assisting Lindsey and Falknir in caring for Dackery, applying her keen arts as she rotated between him and the many other wounded who were under her care. The young Earl of Donnock was recuperating quickly (though retaining something of a limp), and by now even Dackery's recovery was certain. Which was timely, for Lindsey herself was soon to depart Linster. With both Gurth and the Earl of Wickhowe dead, the war was winding down quickly. The king had been persuaded to issue a pardon to the remaining rebels, with the sole exception of the barons Gatehurst and Kirkweald. All those who defected and renewed their oaths of fealty to the king were to receive clemency, and as their allies deserted them one by one the two barons at last fled to Tollardy with only a handful of steadfast supporters. Likewise, the king had grudgingly honored Hae-jin's promise to the Drixi, albeit with a certain exasperation which was due more to the autonomy with which Hae-jin had brought the matter about than anything else. Having gathered up the last of their stragglers, the Drixi had departed in good order and flown southwards back to their homeland, where the news of the debacle and terrible losses which had occurred in Linster was not at all well received. The Arbiters responded to the outpouring of wrath from the people by laying the blame for the entire forlorn enterprise squarely on the shoulders of Gurth and his imperious masters, and vowed to reject any future overtures from the witches. In Linster, the scattered remnants of Gurth's forces were doggedly hunted down by the soldiers of the king. Over the following months most were either killed or else fled Linster's borders, though rumors continued to persist of small bands of men and Zard lurking the woods and prowling the fields at night, or else hiding in the wilderness near the southern marches.

In the great cathedral of Larchester, the high altar had been left as it was, its shorn face preserved and the broken corner placed in a gilded crystal reliquary at the foot of the altar, with the infused medallion from Harin's Vault displayed for all the world to see. All should remember the deeds which were done on that day, lest in forgetting the Curse of Gurth should one day return. But as the months passed it became more and more apparent that the curse was gone for good. Bountiful harvests passed into mild winters with little sickness, and near the village of Tresham the wheels of Mortimer's Mill turned faithfully once more. Hugh Mortimer himself spent the rest of his days in prosperity and comfort. The Army of Robin Goodfellow had gradually dispersed, and for his part Hae-jin was granted an estate by the king and named Earl of Tresham. And not long afterwards, Hae-jin was wedded to Joan Greyflower.

After long and arduous haggling with the Bird (and each other), the Wogs had at last settled upon a final sum of four thousand, five hundred and one silver marks. They made their new home in Linster, having also been gifted a large house not far from the town of Elmstead, which quickly fell into disrepair, with the gold of the Wogs reportedly buried in the dirt beneath it. Will Little and Rob Sykes were each granted enough land to raise them to the status of gentlemen, and likewise Sykes eventually moved to Hae-jin's estate as his chief retainer.

Not long after the battle of Beckby, Barri the giant began his long journey home, shepherding with him a large flock of sheep gifted by the king. He had been offered many other rewards as well, and had briefly considered accepting some sort of large, shiny object to put on top of his monument. But in the end he had decided against it, feeling that someone was sure to pinch it eventually, and what good is a monument if folks are always nicking bits of it away? As for the great Bear, Ursilda had steadfastly refused to accept any reward at all, and instead simply disappeared into the wilderness, grumbling to herself about how much difficulty she would have with her cubs after they'd been spoiled for so long by load of silly dryads.

No one had seen or heard anything at all of Bartholomew Fox-Goodburrow since the storming of Ardgar Castle. To all appearances he had completely disappeared. Yet somewhere in Linster, secreted away in some dank, forgotten hollow, a small Fox was perched over a dark tome, pouring studiously over its pages. Behind him, a third tail gently swished the ground in a room full of evil treasures, while Tom Oates sat sullenly in a corner, waiting on the Fox's whim as the world outside went on without him.

And so it was that on a fine day, nearly two weeks after the death of Gurth, Lindsey herself at last made her goodbyes. Now she stood alone on a parapet of Larchester Castle, wearing a simple dress of an ordinary Linsterish woman, with the remainder of her meagre possessions tucked in a travelling bag. The wind whipped her hair as she gazed across the green fields and rolling meadows of a kingdom at peace, glowing like a sea of emeralds in the golden light of the sun. Beside her there was a sudden beating of wings, and with a flurry of golden plumage the Bird now alighted beside her. "Well well well well well! Here we are at long last! Are you ready to leave?"

"Um…yeah. About that. What with everything that's happened recently we've never really had a chance to talk. I think now's a good time."

"Eh? What's there to talk about?"

"I think you know. You've been avoiding me for almost two weeks now. It's time we had it out. What happened back there at Harin's Vault, when you disappeared just as the Zard were coming for me? Where were you when I needed you?"

The Bird squirmed slightly. "Well, er, there were a few issues that cropped up…"

"Don't play any more games with me. I've kept faith with you this whole time. I want the truth."

The Bird appeared almost to shrivel before her. Then at last he spoke. "Well, er, if you must know….you see, it so happened…..well, in point of fact….oh dash it all! I was asleep, alright? If you really must know, I was asleep. I slept through the whole bally thing! It had been a terribly long day and I had made so many doors and I was so terribly exhausted….. by the time I realized anything was wrong Dackery had come and you were already gone. It's all completely my fault, and I can't tell you how sorry I am for it."

For a moment, Lindsey was speechless. That all her adventures over the last month and a half had been the result of something so simple, so stupid, and so venial was more than she could quite comprehend for a moment. She didn't know whether to laugh or cry. Then, with a sigh she put down her bag and gingerly put her arms around the astonished avian. Somehow she had managed to live through everything, and making a fuss about anything else was pointless now. There was simply nothing left for it but to forgive the Bird.

A short while later the Bird traced a square in the flagstone walk, his beak scraping lightly across the stones. With a resounding crack a few stones fell away through space and landed somewhere else with a thud, and shortly thereafter Lindsey herself slipped through with the Bird.

Lindsey now found herself in a forest of giant ferns. As she looked around herself she realized that she recognized the place. Great blades of verdant grass towered into the sky above, and just across from her was a familiar grove of scarlet toadstools. And seated cross-legged beneath one of the toadstools, was Elred. The Bird hopped over to where the elf sat, chatting merrily as he did so. "I apologize for yet another detour, but Elred wished to speak to you once more."

Lindsey walked over to the others, and curled up on the moss with them. "Hello again, Elred. It's been a while."

The elf smiled benevolently, yet enigmatically as always. Without a word, he reached over into the moss beside him and plucked up a long axe with a bright blade of violet metal. Lindsey recognized it instantly. It was her own battle axe. Her mind flashed back to the terrible memories of her combat with Gurth, and she fought quickly to bury the thoughts. The black narwhal handle had been shattered during the battle, and Lindsey had thought the pieces had been lost in the aftermath of the fighting. As Elred handed the weapon to her now she could see that the axe had been fitted with a new shaft of warm, dun colored wood, which fit smoothly and far more comfortably in her hand than had the spiral twist of the old one. "I do believe this is yours, Linnian", Elred said, "I took the liberty of collecting it after the storming of Ardgar. I gave it to a friend of mine to repair, and while he was at it I asked him to make a few slight alterations."

As Lindsey looked more closely, she could see that something was indeed different. Near the rear of the axe head, safely removed from the functional portions of the edge, there was a small pearl weirdly embedded in the metal, as though it had been pressed into soft clay rather than steel. Carved into the wooden shaft was a phrase written in tiny characters of some forgotten script, which Lindsey could only just make out (even with the gift of tongues). As she spelled out the words in her head, the axe suddenly faded out of existence, contracting into a tiny, lavender tinged pearl in her hand, complete with a suitably placed hole bored through it. "Well, that's a neat trick", Lindsey said. "Pretty convenient too, come to think of it."

"I thought so as well", Elred replied. The elf now pinned her with a keen gaze. "You have proven yourself far beyond what was ever asked you. The Bird read your heart very well indeed. You have achieved great goodness, and there is much good which you could yet do. We never forget those who have helped us, and we shall not forget you. In point of fact, I would like to have your permission to call upon you again some time."

Lindsey bit her lip. She was pretty sure she knew what Elred was asking. He mind shot back to Camilla Helwig, far away in her solitary house in the south. She too had served Elred's kind. Lindsey already knew what it was like to work with these folks, and it wasn't exactly pretty. But it was tempting. Terribly tempting. "Sure. Why not? Look me up whenever you want, and I'll decide for myself if I want to come along next time you have something going."

"Capital! I wouldn't wish for any more than that. Give me your right hand, Linnian."

Lindsey hesitated for a moment. Then, she put out her hand, in what was quite possibly the second most reckless act of her entire life. The elf now laid his own hand over Lindsey's. It felt soft, almost like a child's. As Elred gripped Lindsey's hand she felt a queer, electrifying tingle penetrating into her palm and spreading out into the tissue of her hand with growing intensity. It had almost become painful when abruptly Elred slacked his grip and released her hand. Lindsey now looked at her palm. There, outlined with a faintly luminous sheen of deep violet, was the image of a great mountain with a crescent moon hovering just beside it. And to one side just beneath it, was a small image which looked an awful lot like an outline of the medallion from Harin's Vault which was now embedded in a reliquary in Larchester Cathedral. As she watched, the image quickly faded away, until there was nothing left except a small red welt where the image of the medallion had been.

Elred smiled. "You are now a bearer of The Feymark. You can recall this image whenever you wish, and anyone you show it to will know you are a friend of the Good Folk. Needless to say, be very careful whom you show it to. We shall speak again." With that, the elf arose and stepping behind the stalk of the mushroom he vanished.

The Bird now hopped over to a bare patch of loose dirt. "Well, I think it's high time I actually got you home." The Bird then drove his beak into the dirt and traced another outline into the ground, which fell away with a dull patter of pebbles. The Bird darted through, and once more Lindsey sat down on the ledge and swinging her legs over the edge she dropped through behind him to land on a carpeted floor with a disturbingly loud thud.

Lidnsey picked herself up and looked around. Her dorm room was pretty much exactly as she had left it. The lights were turned off and the room was lit through the window with the pale light of a clear afternoon sky. The carpet showed no sign that anyone had ever been cutting holes in it to make magic doorways. However there was an annoying distribution of dirt and small pebbles scattered across it which had fallen through the door which she and the Bird had just passed through. Lindsey sighed. "Well, I guess it's now time to call the police and tell them I've found myself. Someone's got to have filed a missing persons report for me by now."

"Oh, that's all been taken care of", the Bird said cheerfully, "I'm afraid we didn't have time to fabricate a proper doppelganger or anything fancy like that, but I think we came up with the next best thing. So far as the world is concerned you have been sequestered all this time in your room with an acute case of infectious mononucleosis. It seemed the simplest solution at the time. We fabricated the necessary medical documents and distributed them to the appropriate individuals. There's a stack of letters from your professors excusing your absence. We also took the liberty of commandeering your phone and social media accounts, and have judiciously employed them to maintain the illusion that you were safely convalescing here, in your dorm room. To top it off, we had a brownie or two move in and occupy your room to complete the illusion that someone was living there. It looks like they cleared up nicely before vacating this morning, which is a good sign. You can't ever be sure with brownies, you know." The Bird now hesitated a moment. "Well, I suppose it's time for me to be going."

With that, he hopped over to the window and pried it open with his beak. As he leapt up onto the sill, Lindsey spoke. "Hey, wait a minute! Are you going to leave just like that? Aren't you at least going to leave me your address or something? Come to think of it, though all this I never did find out what your name was. Do you even have a name?"

The Bird puffed his feathers a bit, seeming slightly flattered. "Why, yes in point of fact I do. My name is Lahetti." And with that, he took off out of the window and disappeared into the sky.

Epilogue

It was a warm, sunny day in the very twilight of spring. The university was abuzz with activity, as the students struggled frantically to survive their examinations as they looked forward to the blessed dawn of summer.

Lindsey was pressing her way through the crowded corridor of the girl's dormitory, a backpack swung casually over one shoulder as she made her way back to her room. She had stuck it out through the remainder of the spring semester, and was planning to continue in the fall. She was determined to finish her degree, no matter where life took her thereafter. Despite a battery of excused absences in consideration of her purported ailment, it had nonetheless been hard going to recover after having missed a third of the term. However, she had proven up to the challenge, and among those who knew her there were not a few who commented that she had come through her illness a much stronger and more energetic person. The cheap black dye in her hair was long gone, and in its place was a tousle of deep walnut, which was her own natural color. Gone too was the heavy eyeliner, and indeed even her entire silhouette was subtly altered, for she had gained a healthy amount of weight. And yet, for the first time in her adult life she felt good about how she looked.

Indeed, having spent her adolescence hating her own body, Lindsey was quite confident and content with her own self, and took a certain relish in showing off just a little bit, almost as a sort of rebellion against her former self. On her feet were a pair of practical, no nonsense hiking boots, which were curiously mismatched with a fashionable pair of tight, high cut summer shorts and black camisole top. And ever present around her neck was a small choker necklace consisting of a single lavender tinged pearl strung on an elastic band. This she wore at all times, quite literally day in and day out, whether in bed or in the shower, in street clothes or dressed up. Never for the slightest instant was she without the pearl around her neck.

Lindsey had just turned down her own corridor when up ahead she saw a man at the other end of the hall. He was a grizzled sort of gentleman, lean of build with a closely trimmed salt and pepper beard, and dressed in heavy grey slacks and an old brown blazer. And he was standing right in front of Lindsey's own door.

How the heck he'd gotten into the girl's dormitory and what in blazes he thought he was doing hanging around her room Lindsey couldn't guess. Her hand darted anxiously up to the choker around her neck as she broke into a jog down the hall. Yet even as she closed distance the man stepped away from the door, and with his back turned he headed around the opposite corner and down the stairs.

"Hey!"

Even as she called out, the man was already long gone. As Lindsey came panting to a halt beside her door, she noticed that there was a small card stuck to it, tucked in the tiny gap behind the doorknob. Lindsey snatched up the card and read the legend.

LAURENCE MEDINA
CERTIFIED SPECIALIST

Below this was a third line containing a phone number. And beside this, drawn on the card with a blue pen, the ink still bleeding into the paper, was a small image. The image of the moon and the mountain.

The End

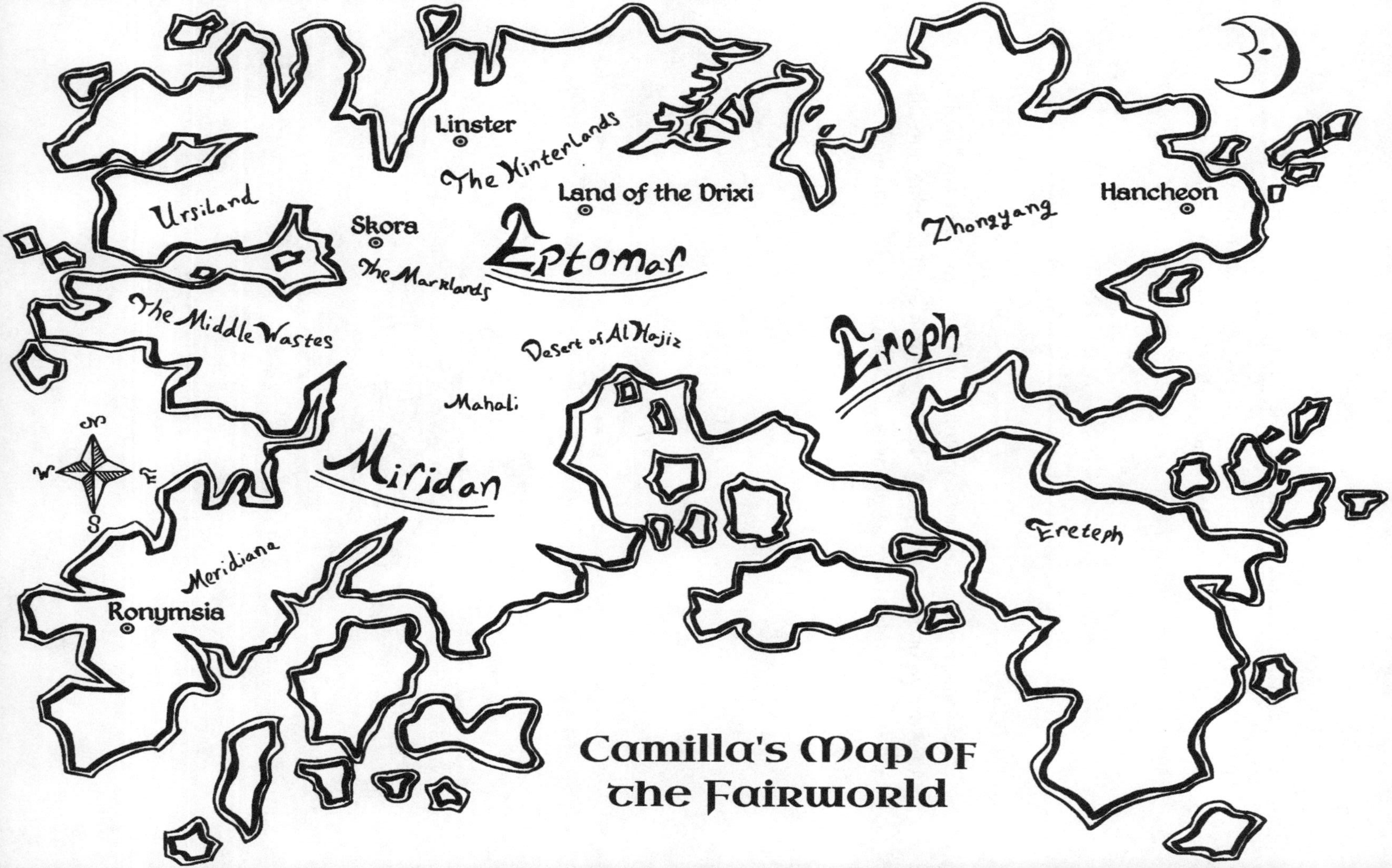

Camilla's Map of the Fairworld

Jack Twohey has a tendency to write novels. When one is done, it gets tossed onto the ever growing mountain of other novels which Jack has written previously, at which point Jack shambles off to go write another one. It is with some difficulty that we (we like to call ourselves "The Management") try to collect said novels and distill them into a form suitable for public consumption. When not preoccupied writing more novels, Jack likes going on long, rambling walks, learning nerdy things, crafting nerdy things with his own hands, collecting nerdy things which other people have crafted with their own hands, making music from time to time, and going dancing in the evening.

CPSIA information can be obtained
at www.ICGtesting.com
Printed in the USA
BVHW040936161222
654321BV00003B/169